CITYSCAPE AFFAIR
BOOK THREE

Together

JESSICA HAWKINS

***USA TODAY* BESTSELLING AUTHOR**

With a single decision, Olivia Germaine's fantasy has become a reality. Now, she's faced with two commitments —one she must make, and one she must break. But in order to accept a love she never thought possible, Olivia will have to let go of the broken past that defines her...and of deeply rooted fears that could ruin everything.

Everything is what David Dylan wants to give her, and it's what he demands in return. He'll do anything to prove to Olivia that despite his playboy ways, he's worth leaving behind the stable future her husband can offer her.

But even though he's a man who always gets what he wants...this time, David may be fighting for something unattainable.

Come Together is also available in:
Audiobook
Ebook

2nd edition © 2020 Jessica Hawkins

1st edition © 2013 Jessica Hawkins

Beta by Underline This Editing

Proofreading by Paige Maroney Smith

Cover Designed by Najla Qamber Designs

Chapter One

The sizzling was almost enough to make me scream. Plumes of smoke spiraled up from the fajitas platter that'd just been delivered to our table. Neither Gretchen, Lucy, nor I had even touched the chunky guacamole or done anything beyond salt a full basket of tortilla chips.

A mariachi band played in one corner of the Mexican restaurant. Tension grew as silence stretched between my two best friends and me.

Finally, Lucy blinked. "Wait. *What?*" she asked, horror clear on her face. "What did you just say?"

"I'm leaving Bill," I repeated.

Lucy shook her head in disbelief. "And you're telling us this over fajitas?"

I shrugged, not casually, but because the question had no appropriate response. I glanced from Lucy to Gretchen, who reached out to clasp my hand. I was drowning, and she could tell.

"Is this why you've been distant since I returned from Paris?" Lucy asked me. Her eyes cut to Gretchen. "And why don't you look surprised?"

1

"I'm not," Gretchen said evenly.

"Did something happen while I was on my honey-moon?" Lucy continued, touching her new wedding band.

"Something happened," I confirmed. "And that some-thing is that I'm in love."

Up until that moment, Gretchen had looked almost relieved. Now she gasped as a breathtaking smile broke out across her face. "You are?"

"Well, I'd have to be to go through with this, wouldn't I?" I asked.

She nodded, her mass of blonde curls bouncing joyfully.

"You're in love with your husband," Lucy stated, straightening her shoulders. "Bill."

"Luce." I took a deep breath and addressed her with unwavering focus. "You and Gretchen have been my best friends for a long time. When something this big happens in my life, I want to share it with you. I'm in love with someone else, and I'm leaving Bill for him."

She braced herself against the table and hissed, "What the fuck?"

I winced. Lucy was sweet, doe-eyed, and polite. She didn't hiss, she squealed—and she rarely cursed. "I know it's shocking," I said. "I wanted you to hear it from me before I talk to Bill."

Her mouth fell open. "You haven't told Bill?"

I shook my head.

"Who is this guy?" she asked.

For "this guy," I'd taken the leap—literally and figura-tively. And he'd caught me in his arms, taking my weight with ease. Last night, rain had drenched us, our lips had joined, and relief had melted the muscular arms around me. Our foreheads had met. He'd told me he loved me.

I'd told him he was my home.

A small smile dissolved the tension in my face. "I'm leaving my husband for David Dylan."

Lucy's brown eyes doubled in size, and her knuckles whitened. "Ex-*cuse* me?"

My smile faltered as reality slashed through the sweet memory. Lucy didn't find this sweet at all.

"What are you talking about?" Lucy asked. "Do you hear what you just said?"

"You're in shock, Lucy," Gretchen said. "Just listen."

"You knew about this?" Lucy shot back, redirecting her glare at Gretchen.

"Some of it."

"David Dylan," Lucy echoed. "As in, my client, Andrew's friend, Dani's—" Her eyes darted frantically over the table as she tried to find the word.

"Yes," I said softly. "Your client, your husband's friend, and the man your sister was seeing."

Lucy's eyebrows met in the middle of her forehead. "How did this happen?"

"I'm sorry to spring it on you both, but like I said, you're my best friends." I looked between them. "I need you now. I need you there after I tell Bill."

Lucy ignored what I'd said and quietly repeated, "*How?*"

"David and I have a . . . connection. I wish I could show you how I'm feeling, Luce, because it's impossible to describe. Bill has always been good to me, and I love him, I do. I don't want to hurt him. But with David, it's different, it's—"

"Of course it's different," Lucy interrupted. She held up her fingers to tick off each point. "David is gorgeous. Wealthy. Charming. *Experienced*." Her hands flew up in exasperation. "He knows exactly what you want to hear."

"You set him up with your sister," I pointed out.

3

"That's something else entirely. He knows she's not the type you just fool around with."

"And I am?"

"No, but that's irrelevant because you're married. You're *married*," she repeated. "What are you doing?"

I just stared at her, my mouth hanging open slightly.

"He is a total player," Lucy continued, her face contorting with disgust. "I set him up with Dani so he could see that there are women out there worth settling down for. But he's not the type of guy you leave your husband for. Jesus Christ. I mean, does he think of you as some sort of challenge?"

She had pinpointed my greatest insecurity and shoved it in my face. David was a player. He had women falling all over him, and I knew he'd taken advantage of that. What made me different? Was it because he'd had to chase me? Without evidence to deny Lucy's claims, I remained quiet and wrung my hands in my lap.

"I've talked to him." We both turned to Gretchen. "I've talked to David," she said, "and this isn't a game for him. He is crazy about her. He *loves* her. He told me."

My skin prickled as I thought of my David—sexy, tall, and strong, with an enormous and loving heart. It gave me the strength to beat back the doubt creeping in.

"That's utterly ridiculous." Lucy's hard-edged voice cut into my thoughts. "He'd say anything to get what he wants," she told Gretchen. "What makes her different from the hordes of women he sleeps with?"

"It's different because every time we're in the same room," I said, "I can barely stand not to touch him, to feel him, to look into his eyes. In his arms I feel safe. I feel loved. Not the way Bill loves me, but in a way that I could almost open up my chest and give him my heart."

They both gaped at me, not bothering to hide their

4

surprise. Lucy visibly grasped at words. "I . . . wow," she said softly. "I never thought I would hear something like that come out of your mouth. It's so . . . not you. It's romantic and—and emotional."

I sighed my relief and nodded.

"But I don't think you've thought this through," she said slowly, shaking her head. "You met David—how long ago? When I announced my engagement . . . oh, God, I'm going to be sick." She put her head in her hands. "This is my fault."

"Technically, I met him the night we went to the ballet. Remember?" I said. "Andrew's firm had tickets. David was there, and we had this . . . this *moment*. I never thought I'd say this, but it was like we were meant to meet that night."

Gretchen smiled. "It's really romantic, Luce, if you think about it."

Lucy looked up finally and pinned me with a glare. "Have you slept with him?"

My eyebrows joined with confusion. It was true, what I was doing to Bill was awful, but this was *Lucy*, the idealist. Couldn't she see the romance of David and me? "I mean, yes, we—"

"Oh my God," Lucy said.

"I couldn't *not*," I said, pleading with her to understand.

"That's bullshit," Lucy said. "You're stronger than that. You've always been strong."

I frowned. "Which just goes to show how hard I fell for him."

"Stop. Just stop. You've been lying to all of us, including my sister, for what? Seven fucking months?" She scoffed. "Is seven months even long enough to know that you're ready to give everything up?"

I hesitated. "How long did it take you to fall in love with Andrew?"

The way her face morphed had me shrinking in my seat. "If you think messing around with someone like David is anything *close* to what Andrew and I have, then you know nothing about love. That's ridiculous."

"Come on, that's not fair," Gretchen said defensively. "Have you ever seen Liv this passionate? About anything, even Bill? You know this is the right thing, you just don't want to say it."

Lucy averted her eyes as I looked from her to Gretchen. Had she just said I was doing the right thing?

"This is *not* right," Lucy mumbled, crossing her arms. "Bill loves you, he trusts you, and this is how you repay him?" She paled, her face almost green. "You made a vow to him. Doesn't that mean anything?"

My chest grew heavy, and a lump formed in my throat. "Of course, it does," I said, just above a whisper. "I love Bill, but things just aren't right with him."

"So you go to counseling," she cried. "You don't fuck someone else."

I tried picturing David's face from the night before, the way he'd looked right after I'd told him he was my home. But I couldn't remember in that moment, and I began to waver. Had I thought this through? Did I owe my marriage another chance? What was I thinking, agreeing to leave my husband of five years for someone I barely knew? Tears pooled in my eyes, and I bit my lip to hold them back. Gretchen scooted her chair closer to mine and hugged me from the side.

Lucy cocked her head, peered at me, and sighed. "Look," she started gently, "you don't have to do this. You said you haven't told Bill?"

"He only knows David and I slept together. He's

known for weeks, but he never even asked if I had feelings for David. I do—"

"Then it's not too late to call this off," Lucy said. "I can see that you're really wrapped up in David, but we'll help you through it. Couples survive affairs all the time. We'll get you through this with Bill." She took a deep, bracing breath. "And it will be *so* hard for me, but I promise not to say anything to Andrew about you wanting to leave. Bill doesn't have to know."

"But," I said. "David . . ."

"Forget him," Lucy urged. "Is he worth losing everything?"

With a stuttering breath, I nodded slowly.

Her face fell. "Everything?" she asked blankly. "*Everything?*"

I didn't know what she wanted me to say. *Everything* was what David had promised me the night before. Believing him was a leap of faith. For the first time in years, my heart and my instinct overruled my sense. This risk could leave me with nothing. But it could also gain me everything.

I just stared at Lucy until she rose from the table.

"I can't," she said, snatching her purse from the back of her chair. "I can't watch you do this."

"Lucy, wait, please," I begged as she turned to leave.

She looked back and fixed steady eyes on me. "Don't tell Bill. If you decide to do the right thing, call me—I'll be there. But I won't sit back and watch you throw everything away."

After she stormed away, I turned to Gretchen. "What am I doing? Am I making a mistake?" I never let myself get swept up in the moment—because there were consequences. Last night, I had. Had I truly considered the fallout I was facing? I fought back tears. "Oh, God, Gretchen. What if I can't go through with it?"

She put her arms back around me and held me close. As we sat in silence, the doubt Lucy had planted began to take hold inside me, feeding off the guilt and shame I'd been harboring for months. Gretchen separated from me finally and brushed a piece of my hair from my forehead. "I want to say something, but I'm afraid it will come back to bite me in the ass."

I swallowed and nodded that I understood. Before I could respond, she continued.

"I'm going to tell you anyway," she said, "because I love you, and I think you need to hear it." She sighed and picked at her nail polish, obviously deep in thought. Seconds ticked by until she eventually spoke again. "You're not making a mistake," she said softly.

"What?" I asked.

"Bill's not right for you. I never thought so. You're my best friend in the world, and all I ever wanted for you is to find happiness again, for someone to open your eyes to all the love out there." She sat back in her seat. "When you said 'yes' to Bill's proposal, I couldn't believe it. I could *not* believe that he was the one you chose when you could have anyone." I started to laugh, but she snapped her fingers at me. "*Anyone*, Olivia. I mean it. And not only that, but you deserve more than what Bill gives you."

"But Bill has given me so much," I said. "And all he asked for in return was the same—security, love, and eventually, a family."

"He loves you." She nodded. "He'd never intentionally hurt you. But that's not a reason to commit the rest of your life to him. Sweetie, you picked him because he was safe, like I said before, and because he couldn't hurt you. How could he, when you never let him close enough to?"

"But maybe I should've. Maybe I owe him a real

chance," I said. "And maybe Lucy's right about counseling."

"And *maybe*," Gretchen said, "he never gave you a reason to let him in. The last few weeks that you and David weren't speaking, you thought it was over between you two. If Bill had left you when you told him you cheated, do you think it would have hurt as much as losing David did?"

Shame descended as my gut told me it wouldn't have hurt nearly as much.

"I want to see you with someone you love so much, you can't bear it," she said.

"How do you know David's that person?" I asked.

"I've only seen a fraction of what you've been through this last month. Only what you've let me see. And just that little bit was heartbreaking. But it also gave me faith that you were within reach again."

"Within reach?"

"You've been so closed off since your parents' divorce, honey. You have to let go of that. You have to take this chance on love. I know I had no right to call David and tell him to go to you last night. I know that Bill will hate me forever if he finds out." She bit her bottom lip and glanced at her plate. "But I needed to see for myself if David was going through the same thing as you. And I could hear in his voice that he was. I mean, I don't know if he threw *cereal* against the wall," she said with a small smile, "but it wouldn't surprise me if he had."

I laughed lightly, even though the pain was fresh. Two nights earlier, I'd thought I'd die on my couch of heartbreak, shame, and grief. I knew if *I'd* seen Gretchen the way she'd seen *me*, I would've done the same thing. Now, like she'd promised me months ago, she was helping me move the heavy couch and all its baggage in my head and put garbage by the curb where it belonged.

She rubbed my arm. "Like I said, I might regret saying this, but I think you're making the right choice."

"Breaking Bill's heart, leaving my apartment, telling my parents I'm a cheater, divorce . . . you think it's right?" I asked.

"My gut tells me yes."

I sighed, and though it weighed my heart with shame, I said, "Mine, too."

Her smile broke. "So what happens now?"

My heart began to pound. Bill was on his way home a day early from his work trip to St. Louis. He'd be back tonight. At eight o'clock. I'd been avoiding his calls, so all this I knew from an e-mail. I swallowed dryly and glanced at the clock on the wall over Gretchen's head: six forty-five.

"Bill gets home in an hour."

"Will David be there when you tell him?" she asked.

I shook my head. "I told him he couldn't be."

Gretchen took my hand. "Are you sure about that? I'll bet David's freaking the fuck out."

"He is." David had made it very clear he didn't want me to feel alone in this, but I couldn't think of anything worse than Bill having to face me *and* the man I was leaving him for at the same time. "But I'm sure," I said. "This is something I need to do on my own."

Chapter Two

My nerves had been humming steadily since leaving the restaurant. With a wave of nausea, I jumped up from my kitchen table, ready to run to the bathroom. As the urge to vomit passed, I sat down again and flattened both hands in front of me.

Though dark and chilly out, the rain had finally let up earlier in the day. Gretchen had agreed to come home with me and had just left my apartment to wait downstairs until Bill and I had finished talking. I looked over at the door—and my small duffel bag beside it—for the hundredth time.

I knew I should focus on what I'd say to Bill, but David's presence in my mind was, as usual, too big. It almost felt as though life hadn't quite begun until I'd found myself wrapped in his big arms. Last night, I'd jumped —*launched*—myself into them, securing my body to his as though losing him meant death.

Then we'd fought in the rain. He'd wanted me *that* moment. He'd wanted me to get my things and come home with him. Then he'd demanded to be there when I told Bill.

To all of those things, I'd said no.

Now that I'd made the decision, Bill needed to know the truth before anything further happened. David hadn't been happy when I'd told him I'd be going home with Gretchen tonight because I didn't feel right going straight to his place.

In the end, I'd won the argument, but I could see it had cost David to give in. He'd made it clear that he'd be eagerly awaiting my call with an update.

I jolted from my thoughts with the jingle of keys outside the door. In slow motion, one slid into its slot as my heart slid into my stomach. I saw, but barely registered, my husband enter the apartment and set down his stuff. He said something, but a dull buzzing in my head drowned it out. That, and the deafening pounding of my heart.

Bill came closer, his face drawn with . . . something. Concern? My hands began to shake and white spots pierced my vision. Air no longer entered my body, but I had no way of controlling that. I blinked . . . I blinked . . .

Darkness. My world moved, slowly at first and then faster. I was being shaken, and that didn't help my nausea.

"Liv, wake up," Bill said, his voice frantic. "Are you okay?"

I opened my eyes and took in my surroundings. I was in Bill's arms, on the kitchen floor as he stared at me, his eyebrows furrowed with anxiety.

I just looked back at him, studying his features, inches from my face, for what might be the last time. His soft brown hair. Crooked nose. Light and mild eyes. I wanted to tell him I loved him, that everything would be okay, and that I'd never meant to hurt him. I wanted to tell him I was leaving because he deserved to be loved in a way I wasn't capable of. I wanted to tell him I was leaving because we *both* deserved better. But I didn't know how to say all of that, so I just said, "I'm leaving."

"You fell off the chair," he replied. "You might've hit your head."

My eyes remained on him. "I'm sorry," I whispered. "For everything. But I'm leaving . . . you."

I hit the floor with a *thud*, wincing when my elbows connected with the linoleum. Bill stood and looked down at me, blinking with obvious disbelief. "You're what?" he asked. "*Leaving* me? What does that mean?"

I eased off my back and onto one elbow. Everything I'd planned to say vanished from my thoughts, and now I just searched for anything.

"I'm done with the games," Bill said quietly. "Just say it. *You* are leaving *me* . . . even after *I* gave you a second chance."

"I'm so sorry," I said as I got to my feet. "The last few months, the terrible way I've treated you . . . I tried to forget him, to make things work between you and me."

"You have a hell of a way of making things work."

"I didn't want this," I said.

"The affair has been an adjustment," Bill said, rolling his neck. "Maybe I'm doing it wrong. There are probably better ways of handling it. I've done a lot of thinking since you told me, though. I see there are things we could work on." He seemed to pause to collect himself, then cleared his throat. "I want to try, Livs. I don't know if I'll ever get over this, but I want to try."

"Bill," I whispered, fidgeting in the middle of the kitchen. "I love him."

Bill's jaw flexed, and I read the shock in his eyes. "You *love* him?"

"Yes."

His entire body jerked. "You never told me things had gotten that far."

"You didn't ask," I stated.

"I didn't ask? Oh, excuse-fucking-me." He began to pace the kitchen. "It didn't occur to me that a logical person like you could fall in love with someone like that."

Someone like that didn't fall in love—only lust. Gretchen had reacted the same way at first, and Lucy believed that, too. I crossed my arms. "I think it *did* occur to you," I said, "but you didn't care enough to ask."

Bill stopped and rubbed his fingers over his forehead. "Of course I care," he muttered.

"I know you do," I said with a sigh. "I didn't mean it that way."

"And what about me?" Bill asked, looking directly at me. "Don't you love me?"

I swallowed the rising lump in my throat. "It's not that simple."

His hair flopped over his forehead, and he pushed his hands through it. "What's more simple than that?"

I drew in halting breaths. "Bill, I love you, I always will. But this isn't working—"

"It's not working? I don't understand how that's *my* fault. It *was* working, then you slept with another man, and now it's *not* working. How am I the one who gets screwed?"

"There are things," I said slowly, "that I didn't know I wanted. And now I see that you and I have never been right together."

"*Right?* You wield that word like it has magical powers. Like saying it gets you out of all sorts of shit. The houses we've seen weren't 'right.' Having a kid now isn't 'right.' Nothing is ever 'right' for you." He resumed his tread around the kitchen, his dress shoes slapping the tile. "Did it ever occur to you that maybe your version of right is wrong? Is it *right* slumming around with a slick jerk like David Dylan and ending a perfectly good marriage for a fling? You really need to look at the facts here, Liv. You've always been able to do that because you're sensible."

"I'm not sensible," I said. "I'm scared."

"The Liv I know is smart, practical—she doesn't act on emotion like this."

"I know, but maybe that's not me," I said. "That's who took over when my parents divorced. I needed to protect myself then, but when it was time to move past that, I couldn't." I watched him pace back and forth. "I'm sorry you got that version of me, the one who couldn't love you like you deserved."

"I feel more confused now than I did all last month," he said. "I don't know what's happening."

"I think one day you'll look back, and you'll thank me for this."

He whirled to face me. "*Thank* you? Thank you for the fuck what?"

That'd sounded right in my head, but hearing it aloud, it'd been the wrong thing to say. I didn't respond.

"Look, maybe we need to take a break," Bill said. "Cool off for a couple weeks or something, I don't know. Didn't you say that Davena and Mack did that once? You idolized Davena before she passed away, even more than your own mother. Look how in love they were, more than anyone we know, yet even *they* needed a break."

I nodded. "Yes, but—"

"I can get on board with a break, all right?" he said. "They're busting my ass at work right now. I can focus on that while you sort everything out."

David's face flashed across my mind—I wanted to get back to him. But Bill's willingness to try to change forced me to admit the truth. I wasn't just leaving this marriage for David—I was doing it for myself. To get back to the girl I'd been before I'd had my heart broken by my parents' split. "No."

"No?" Bill asked. "What then?"

"Nothing," I said.

"There can't be *nothing* I can do," he said. "There has to be a solution here."

I glanced at my duffel bag by the doorway. "I'm leaving you, Bill. Tonight."

He stopped and looked at me. "There's no way this can be it. It just doesn't make sense."

"I know it doesn't to you, and I doubt it ever will," I said. "But I'm leaving."

"Leaving, huh?" He let out a sinister laugh. "You keep saying that. Why can't you just call it what it is?"

"Meaning?" I asked.

"I want you to tell me what *you* are doing to this marriage."

I shifted from one foot to the other as his intention became clear. "I *did* tell you."

"No—you know what I'm asking," he said.

My heart jumped. My nails bit into my palms as I made two fists. He wanted me to recognize that in the end, I was the reason we were facing the one thing I'd spent my life hiding from. "Divorce," I said.

"This is a joke," he said. "David Dylan? Really? You're living in a fantasy, Liv."

"I don't really know how this works," I said with a deep breath, ignoring his baiting and trying to move the conversation forward. "But we can talk more when you've had time to process this."

His chin quivered, and at even the threat of his tears, my heart broke a little. I pressed my lips together to collect myself.

"Look at you," Bill said. "You can't even cry over *this*, the end of your marriage."

I was all cried out. But my tears had been for David when I'd thought I'd never have him or the kind of life where I'd be able to love freely—and even the night before, when he'd almost left me on this very kitchen floor. Bill was right. For some reason, I was rarely able to cry for him, in his presence, like he wanted. I couldn't explain that, so I only blinked at him, scared that *he* might actually cry.

"Where are you going now?" he asked.

"Gretchen's."

He gave a terse laugh. "Figures."

"She cares about you, too, but she's my oldest friend."

He rolled his eyes. "So you're just going to stay on her couch? Then what?"

"I don't know," I said, furrowing my brows. The last twenty-four hours had been a whirlwind, and I'd only planned as far as staying with Gretchen for the night.

He sighed heavily. "Stay here tonight. Let's work this out."

I thought of David, awaiting my call, pissed that he couldn't be here. And of Gretchen, likely freezing downstairs on a cold November night. And then I thought of staying the night here with Bill and how, actually, no part of me wanted to. "I should go," I said gently. "We can talk more later."

He shook his head at the floor. "Maybe by then you'll realize." He paused and swallowed audibly. "Get this . . . thing out of your system. We'll talk in a few days."

I flinched at the word *thing* but nodded, then lifted my left hand up to my face and studied it. Bill's grandma's ring was beautiful, but I'd never quite felt a connection to it. I looked on it with appreciation and respect, but it didn't make my heart spill over. It'd always felt strange, not forming an emotional attachment to my wedding ring. I touched it reverently before I twisted it off my finger and held it out to him.

Bill looked between the ring and my face so quickly that my heart dropped. "You're giving me back your ring?" His voice dropped, eerily low and calm. His face reddened, and he stalked toward me. "You're giving me back your goddamn ring?"

I backed away, tripping over a dining chair and dropping the ring. "It—it's your grandmother's—"

In one quick motion, he overturned the kitchen table so it crashed against the floor. I yelped as he punched a hole in the wall.

"Get out," he snapped.

Unable to make my feet move, I said, "I thought you'd—"

"I said . . ." He stormed over to the door, grabbed my duffel bag and tossed it out into the hallway. "Get. *Out.*"

Without a word, I watched his hands twitch and flex as I slunk by him. The door slammed after me. I bent down gingerly and picked up the bag while locks bolted on the other side of the door.

I looked around at the place that was suddenly, somehow, no longer my home. I focused on circulating cold air through my lungs as I made my way downstairs and to the street, rattled by the way calm, easygoing Bill had suddenly exploded.

I glanced down at my hand, different without the ring that had barely left my finger in five years. Not right or wrong, just different. Final.

I found Gretchen pacing on the sidewalk. "Hey," I croaked, my voice catching.

"Shit," she said, whirling around and hurrying over to me. "I almost came up there to make sure you were okay."

"I'm fine," I said. "I'm fine."

"Oh, honey, you're not fine," she said, pulling me close.

"No," I stated. "I'm not. But maybe I will be." Hurting Bill was gut-wrenchingly awful. Something had given me the strength to do it, though. That something was David's confidence in us, his bolstering love for me, and the promise of moving into new territory with him. I found strength in the idea that now, David would show me what his version of home meant.

Gretchen put an arm around me, and we began to walk toward the train. "How'd it go?" she asked.

"I don't know," I said. "How are these things supposed to go?"

She shrugged. "No clue. Did he cry?"

"Almost. I gave him back the ring."

I caught her grimace.

"I don't feel right keeping it," I said defensively.

"Yes, but . . . maybe it's a little soon for that."

"Soon?" I asked. "What do you mean? Soon, like, David might change his mind?"

"Uh, no. I mean soon, like, Bill is probably really upset right now and giving back the ring might've been a little insensitive."

"Oh." My face flushed, but I nodded. "I should warn you," I said, "Bill isn't really happy with you, which is completely unfair. He might think you're involved somehow."

Her eyebrows knit, but her arm tightened around me as we walked. "I don't care," she said finally. "Maybe one day, we can all be friends again, but for now, I just want to be there for you."

"Thanks," I said but frowned. Our threesome was incomplete without Lucy, and remembering her disappointment in me stung anew. "I wish Lucy was here."

"I know," Gretchen said, squeezing me to her. "She'll come around, don't worry."

I wasn't sure how, but Gretchen had arranged for us to have her apartment to ourselves for the night. Her two roommates, Bethany and Ava, were gone, and I was thankful for some peace and quiet.

"I have champagne and leftover cake if we're celebrating," Gretchen announced, "or ice cream pints and beer in case you feel like wallowing. Movie choices are *The Break-Up*, *The Notebook*, or *Kill Bill*."

My mouth fell open as I stifled a laugh. "*Kill Bill?*" I asked. "Gretch. That's awful."

"I know." Her eyes twinkled. "I couldn't resist."

"I think I might like to do a little of both," I said. "Celebrating and wallowing."

"I can make that work," she decided, disappearing into the kitchen.

I curled onto her couch, pulled a throw over myself, and rubbed my sore eyes. I needed to call David. Gretchen's company was nice, but I couldn't help wanting to see him now that it was allowed. I'd told him I'd need some space after my talk with Bill—after *all* of this, even—but now I wasn't so sure. I wanted to be held by him, to let him comfort me, to finally kiss him without nagging, ever-present guilt. I wondered if it would automatically be gone and what that would feel like.

But it was logical to take a night and process my feelings over what had just happened. I shot David a quick text to tell him it was done and that I'd arrived safely at Gretchen's. I promised I'd call him in the morning before work, then shut down my phone for the night.

Gretchen floated into the room with a plateful of cake and chocolate chip cookies. On her next round, she juggled two pints and a large bowl of popcorn.

"Oh my God," I said with widened eyes. "This is heaven." I hadn't eaten the fajitas after all, and I'd expelled anything in my stomach while waiting for Bill. I realized that anxiety had kept me from eating much the past twenty-four hours, and I was suddenly starving. Lastly, she brought out two beers and two glasses of champagne.

"Your feast, m'lady," she said, tossing a piece of popcorn in the air and catching it in her mouth. "Have at it."

We vetoed all chick flicks in favor of *Caddyshack*, one of our childhood favorites. The days to come would be hard, and I didn't think I had any right to be laughing, but for the rest of the night, I only wanted to get lost in distraction. As soon as Rodney Dangerfield had been declared a menace, a knock came on Gretchen's front door.

"Are you expecting someone?" I asked.

She shot me an uncomfortable look and shook her head. "Could it be Bill?"

I sat up as Gretchen left to get the door. But as soon as she reappeared with a smile, my heart lifted knowing what she'd say.

"It's David," she said, confirming my suspicion. "And he's being rather persistent about seeing you."

"He has a habit of persistence," I said, trying to suppress a smile. Giddiness worked its way through me at the thought of seeing him. I stood immediately and walked toward the door before pausing. "Wait. Is this okay with you? I don't want to ruin our night."

"It won't ruin our night," she said, tilting her head. "But are you ready to see him?"

21

"I am," I said and surprised her with a big hug. "I love you."

"I think I like this version of Olivia with David," she teased, smacking me on the behind.

I opened the front door and met David's wall of a body as he leaned on the doorjamb with outstretched arms. Even the sight of him in a hoodie and jeans stole my breath, but it was the intensity in his light brown eyes that swirled desire in my lower tummy. His black hair was wild in a non-purposeful way, as though he'd been running his hands through it. "I tried to call," he said.

Unable to gauge his mood, I bit my bottom lip. "I . . . I turned off my phone."

"Tell me it's over."

"I did," I said. "I texted you—"

"I want to hear you *say* it."

It wasn't the first time I'd encountered this determined, edgy version of David with features as sharp as a knife. The one who took what he wanted, and by the way he wet his lips—*I* was the *what.*

"It's over," I said breathlessly.

David dropped his arms and scooped me up by my waist, hugging me against his long body. Underneath me, his chest heaved with relief. One hand slid up my back and grasped the nape of my neck. "I've been so worried," he murmured before his lips landed on mine. His warm, mint-flavored mouth invited me in, our heads tilting in opposite directions to get even closer.

I melted into him as my arms found their way around his neck, and I claimed my reward for everything I'd been through—not just that day, but for months and months. I kissed David freely, joyfully, and with less of the guilt I'd grown accustomed to.

When we parted, I smiled at him and sifted his silky

dark hair through my hands. "It's over, David," I whispered. "Over."

His forehead rested against mine. "You have no idea what it does to me to hear you say that."

I giggled softly and wrapped my legs around him, aligning my crotch with his erection. "Actually, I do."

"You can't expect me not to get a hard-on the second I see you," he said. "I've been thinking about taking you again since I left your apartment last night."

I blushed. "Well, can you wait a little longer?"

He inhaled through his nose and squeezed me tightly. "No," he said but patted my ass to get me to unhook my legs before setting me on my feet. "How did it go with Bill? What happened?"

"It was hard. Very, very hard." I rubbed my forehead. "I was nervous."

David crossed his arms over his chest, back in serious mode. "How'd he react?"

"He was confused. I don't know if he believes it's really over."

"Confused," David muttered, looking away. After a moment, his eyes returned to mine and narrowed. "Angry?"

"More sad, I think. He got upset when I gave him the ring back."

"Upset how? Did he touch you?" The words rushed out as though he'd been holding in the question all day. He took my wrist and pushed up my sleeve, running his hands over my skin while keeping his eyes on me.

"No," I said. "He flipped over a table and put a pretty decent hole in the wall, but other than that, no damage done."

"Jesus Christ, Olivia." David frowned. "That's why I

wanted to be there. The thought of you alone with him in that state makes me crazy."

"We were together a long time," I reassured David. "I know he'd never hurt me."

"You can't know how anyone will react in a situation like this. You just ripped the carpet out from under him."

"I'm aware." Why was David bringing this up again? The deed was done. I took my arm back. "We had this conversation last night."

"Bill could fly off the handle," David explained. "He could've hurt you, and there would've been nobody there. In the future, don't expect to get away with that."

I gaped at him. "Get away with *what*?"

"With telling me how to protect you. How to love you. How to keep you safe."

I teetered between frustration and swooning over his overprotectiveness, but before I could respond, he took my left hand and ran his thumb over the tender place where my wedding ring had been. "I have to say, though—this makes me very happy." David bent his head, kissed the empty spot, and raised his eyes to mine as he rumbled, "*Very* happy."

My insides quickened as my heart melted. With his lips still on my hand, I warned, "It's going to take a while for me to be okay."

"I know, baby." He dropped my hand and pulled me back into his all-encompassing embrace. "But I'm not going anywhere. We're in this together."

I didn't know how to feel. The only other person who made me feel that secure was my dad, and I didn't see much of him anymore. Bill was there for me the best he knew how, but it didn't always feel as if he was on my side.

David, on the other hand, stood next to me, in front of me, *and* behind me. "Thank you," I whispered up at him.

"Sure I can't convince you to come home with me right now?"

Tempting though it was, it didn't feel right to jump from Bill's place to David's. And I needed a break to regroup. I placed my hands on his chest. "I'm sure. Let's start with breakfast Saturday morning."

"Today is *Thursday*," he said, his eyebrows low. "I thought the deal was you stay here tonight only."

"I don't think we had a deal." My heart fluttered with more anxiety than excitement as I added, "In fact, we have absolutely no plan."

"You might not, but, baby, I have plans for you." His gaze dropped to my mouth. "And I'd like to get started on those plans *immediately*."

Oh, God. I couldn't begin to imagine what a night with David would look like now that nothing stood in our way. I bit my bottom lip so hard, I almost whimpered. Despite the fact that I loved the sound of finding out his plans *immediately*, I needed to hold on to *some* sense. "I just need a day or two to sort through everything," I said.

He moved his hips against me in a leisurely thrust, and the hard-on I'd felt before was considerably . . . *harder*. "I can't wait that long," he said.

"David," I said, laughing in disbelief, "we're obviously not very good at restraint, but I think you can wait an additional night."

"If that's what you think, then you don't know me," he stated.

I laughed again, this time at the fact that he thought a couple nights was a long time to go without sex. At that realization, the smile immediately slid off my face. *Was* that a long time for him? At this point, if I weren't in the picture, would he have called up Maria? Dani? Amber?

Some other Brittany whose name popped up on his caller ID?

"What?" he asked.

"Nothing."

"It's not nothing. What was that?"

I let it go, not wanting to ruin these moments we'd fought so hard for. I ran my hands up his chest and replaced my arm around his neck. "I just think it's funny that after all these months, you can't wait another day."

"A day? I've been waiting way longer. A really long fucking time, in fact," he declared. "Sue me if I want nothing more than to lock you in my apartment, throw you on my bed, and have you until you beg me to stop."

His words, aside from knotting my insides with excitement, rang familiar. He'd said something similar to me once before. The last time, I couldn't respond the way I'd wanted, so this time I did. "I'll never beg you to stop," I told him.

His chest vibrated against me when he growled. He still looked slightly angry, but now his eyes bordered on hungry. "Then we're in trouble if we expect to have a life outside the bedroom."

I couldn't suppress my grin. He was so adorable when he didn't get what he wanted.

"I'll give you your space," he said with obvious reluctance, "but in exchange, I want the whole weekend."

Just me and him, alone. Saturday morning to Sunday night. As much as the idea elated me, it also scared me. What if we weren't as compatible as we'd thought? What if a whole weekend with one woman was too much for him?

But he looked positively giddy about it, so I moved my hands back against his hard pecs and nodded. "You got it. This weekend belongs to us."

He bent his head and kissed me softly on the lips. "You're amazing. Thank you for today."

I blew out a breath as my body warmed. I was just getting to see this sweet, romantic side of him, and I liked it a little too much.

"Go back inside," he said, "or I will kidnap you and take you home now."

"Okay." I tried to pull away, but his arms remained locked around me.

"And turn your phone back on," he added. "I *hate* being out of touch."

"Yes, sir." I smiled. "Talk to you tomorrow."

He leaned over, gave me another kiss, and left.

Chapter Three

My name echoed in the distance—faintly at first and then again, louder . . .

"Olivia! Wake up."

With a hand on my arm, my eyes flew open to darkness. I vaulted into a sitting position. "Bill?" I wheezed.

"Shh, sweetie," I heard. "It's me. Gretchen. Were you having a nightmare?"

I closed my eyes and reclined back onto Gretchen's bed. "Mhm."

"What about?"

"I don't remember." I rubbed my eyes. "I have them sometimes. About the attack in my office."

"Mark Alvarez?" she asked. "I didn't know that."

"Alvarez restrains me as he threatens payback for Bill. But this nightmare was different. Bill was in it, too."

She stroked my shoulder. "Is there any news about Alvarez?"

"He's behind bars, and he's not going anywhere. But it's hard to forget what his hands felt like on me."

I woke up several times after that, half-expecting Bill, other times David, but confused when I found Gretchen.

Was Bill confused, too, tossing and turning in an empty bed? He'd be angry. Sad. Embarrassed. But for some reason, picturing him waking up confused made my throat thicken. I lay staring at the ceiling as the room brightened with the rising sun until Gretchen stirred eventually.

"I'm worried about Bill," I said.

She yawned and rubbed her eyes before flipping on her side to face me. "Should I ask Andrew to check on him?"

"Would you?" I didn't mind asking for a favor since Bill and Andrew, Lucy's husband, were close. "I don't think Lucy wants to talk to me."

"Sure. I'll call on our way to work."

We got ready together and headed to a café down the street. After putting in an order at the counter, Gretchen called Lucy, who told her that Andrew would go by my— *Bill's*—apartment. Lucy didn't want to speak to me however. And considering Gretchen stopped mid-sentence during her update on how I was doing, it appeared that Lucy didn't care to hear about me.

Gretchen hung up and assured me again that Lucy would come around, but I wasn't so sure. I'd stomped on her values, everything she believed in, and the vows she and Andrew had just taken. It hurt to think that I'd tainted the meaning of love and commitment for Lucy in a similar way my parents had for me. And to realize that I might lose friends in addition to a husband. But even though I was still laden with grief, doubt, fear . . . remembering why I'd done it—to actively pursue happiness, love, and passion —brought a certain lightness, too.

"So what're you going to do about a living situation?" Gretchen asked as we waited for our coffee drinks.

"Trying to get rid of me?" I teased.

"You know you can stay at our apartment as long as you want," she said. "Between work and our social lives, my roommates and I are hardly there anyway."

"I don't know if Bill would appreciate my breaking up our marriage for one long sleepover at your place."

"Touché. So?" she asked. "What are you going to do?"

I sighed as a barista passed us our drinks. We left the café and started toward the train. "David and I made plans to spend the weekend together," I said, cupping a hand around my latte's comforting heat. "So we're starting with breakfast tomorrow. I haven't really thought beyond Sunday."

Ugh. Apartment hunting. Something I never thought I'd have to do again. I grimaced. "I guess I should start looking for my own place."

"Like, your own apartment?" Gretchen asked. "What about David?"

"What about him?"

She nudged me with her elbow. "Don't tell me you haven't thought about moving in with him."

I widened my eyes. I truly had *not* thought about that—there'd been no time. "Already?" I asked. "David and I haven't even been on an official date yet. We should probably start there. Shacking up is serious."

"Hel-*lo*?" she said. "Did you not just end your marriage for him? I'd say that's pretty serious."

"No, I know. But really, Gretch, David helped me see the cracks in my marriage. I'm doing this for myself, not just for him. And I don't want to put too much pressure on us."

"Pressure?" she asked.

"Well, yeah. Ending my marriage for him?" I scratched the tip of my nose. "I mean, I don't want David to feel like he owes me anything."

She sipped her coffee. "Don't do that."

I glanced over at her. "Do what?"

"Don't prep yourself for disaster before things even get started."

"I'm not," I said defensively. "I'm just trying to be realistic. David and I have time now. I don't want to push him. Or myself." I paused, chewing on my bottom lip. "I mean, I don't even know if he's ever lived with a woman."

It occurred to me, not for the first time, that I was essentially leaving my life behind for a man I didn't know much about.

Gretchen twisted her lips as she thought. "I don't know. Dude seems pretty intent on taking things to the next level with you."

I laughed at how accurate that was. If it were up to David, we'd be much further along already. "Yeah, but, don't forget—*you* were the one who kept reminding me he's a bachelor who's spent his life doing what he wants . . . and who he wants. This may take some getting used to for him." I massaged the back of my neck as we slowed down on the sidewalk. "Like I said, we've got something we didn't have before—time."

"True. All right, girl," Gretchen said, breaking off toward her train. "See you tonight?"

"Yup."

She started to leave but turned and came back to me. "I'm serious, Liv. Don't start this relationship with one foot out the door. Believe David when he tells you what he wants."

I *did* believe him. I'd had to in order to take the leap of faith I had. But trusting in a relationship built on passion and lust that had seemingly become love overnight? I wasn't so sure. Relinquishing control in favor of blind faith would be a process—with an outcome I wasn't sure I'd ever be able to fully achieve.

———

Saturday morning, I re-packed the small duffel bag I'd taken from my apartment to Gretchen's. My nerves frayed with anticipation, excitement, and unfortunately, guilt. Spending a weekend with another man felt wrong, but spending it wrapped up in David could only be all kinds of right.

It was only when I realized David had never responded to the last text I'd sent him that some anxiety crept into my thoughts. Since he'd left Gretchen's apartment, we'd been in constant contact, planning to meet up for breakfast today. But when I'd written him last night to triple check our plans, he hadn't responded.

Gretchen invited herself to breakfast, I figured because she had a habit of being nosy, so we walked arm in arm to the café David and I had decided on.

Once seated inside the bustling brunch spot, I unfolded a napkin onto my lap. "I started researching apartments yesterday," I told Gretchen. "God, it's been a while since I looked. I can't *believe* how expensive rent will be on my own."

"That's why I have roommates," she said and shrugged. "Honestly, having people around isn't so bad. Remember how much fun we had when we were roomies?"

"I'm going to be a *divorcée*," I pointed out. "I can't have roommates."

"No? Not even David?" She smirked. "Maybe you should see if he wants to split rent?"

I rolled my eyes. "It's definitely too soon for us to move in together."

Gretchen nodded, looking over her menu. "I really envy what you're doing, you know," she said.

"Which part?" I asked. "Cheating on my husband, blowing up my marriage, or falling for someone who could have literally any woman in Chicago?"

Gretchen closed her menu and leaned on the table. "He chose *you*, Liv. Trust in that." She tilted her head. "What you're doing is risking everything for love. To know so strongly based on a feeling alone that you want to be with David? That's amazing."

I let that new perspective sink in as the waiter poured three glasses of water. Could I try viewing my situation through that lens instead of just thinking of myself as terribly selfish? "I think I knew David was 'the one' the moment we locked eyes," I said thoughtfully. "I just couldn't see it through everything else."

"So that would make it love at first sight," Gretchen pointed out and smiled mischievously. "And you went on and on at Lucy's bachelorette about how you believed soul-mates were bullshit."

"I still do," I said, waving her off. "I don't believe in all that." Despite my brush-off, I couldn't help but smile to myself. It *was* bullshit . . . wasn't it?

"I believe in it—and Lucy does, too. Once she sees you and David together, she'll understand."

"Gretch, *you* haven't even seen us together," I said.

"Well," she said, drawing out the word and burying her nose back in the menu. "I may have spied on you guys a little when he came to my apartment Thursday night."

"*Gretchen*," I scolded but laughed.

She smiled. "Heard anything from Bill?"

"Not a peep." I sipped my water and browsed the list

of brunch items. "Maybe you could find out how Andrew's visit went?"

"I'll call Luce later," she said, flipping the menu closed. "I'm going to order a club sandwich. Man, I still can't believe you're head-over-heels in love."

At her abruptness, I grinned. "I'm head over heels in *something*. I mean, what happens to all my stuff? Our joint bank account? I have some savings, but it's pitiful in comparison. I mean, what happens to that money?"

Gretchen looked sympathetic. "Divorce. That's what happens."

"It's going to be hell," I said, raking my fingers over my scalp and resting my head in my hands. "My parents' divorce took almost a year. Your parents' was even more contentious."

"But it was worth it in the end," she said. "And yours will be, too."

"I don't even have a lawyer. Bill *is* a lawyer, so of course I've never needed one before. I guess I should ask my . . ." *Shit.* I hadn't even encountered for all of the difficult conversations ahead of me. I groaned. "I'm so not looking forward to telling my dad about this."

Gretchen grimaced. "Will he be upset?"

"How can he be?" I asked. "He gets divorced all the time."

She giggled. "He's only been divorced *twice*. But maybe he'll know a good lawyer."

We both looked up when David walked into the restaurant. Something always shifted when he entered a room. I didn't call him over as he scanned the restaurant but took the opportunity to appreciate my new . . . *what, boyfriend?* . . . from afar. I couldn't decide who was sexier—businessman David in his tailored suits or this weekend David I laid eyes on now in jeans, a hoodie over a t-shirt, and aviators.

When he spotted us, he stalked in our direction. "What'd I say about your phone?" he asked, no regard for the other diners looking at him.

He sounded angry, but I barely noticed. I could only admire the sexy way David moved, surprisingly graceful for someone as tall and sturdily built as him.

His hand found the back of my chair and the other planted on the table, boxing me in. He focused in on me like he was waiting for a response, but I'd been too busy appreciating him to remember the question.

"What?" I asked. "Did you say something?"

He whipped off his sunglasses and cocked his head at me. "I've been trying to get ahold of you since yesterday. You haven't returned any of my texts or e-mails, and my phone calls won't go through. Hell, I almost drove over last night just to make sure you hadn't skipped town on me."

"Huh." I took out my phone and showed him the screen. "I don't have any missed calls."

He took the phone from me and straightened up. After a moment of swiping and tapping with a furrowed brow— a sexy look I doubted I'd ever grow tired of seeing—he cursed under his breath.

"What?" I asked.

"It's disconnected."

Reality sent a tremor through the moment. "Bill must've canceled my plan," I said.

"Sounds like something he'd do," Gretchen volunteered.

I sighed, took the phone back, and mentally added a new phone plan to my growing list of expenses. I bit my bottom lip, looking up at David. "Sorry. I didn't even think to check my e-mail last night."

He closed the space between us to kiss me. "Hi, beautiful."

I smiled. "Hi."

He inhaled and gave me a harder kiss before taking the seat next to mine at the small, square table. I darted my eyes around the restaurant just to make sure I didn't know anyone there. It was definitely weird, kissing in public.

David signaled for a waiter. "What have you guys been doing?"

"Just watching TV, hanging out," Gretchen said. "We haven't been feeling very motivated."

"Understandable," he said and swung his head to me. He reached over to grasp my thigh. "How are you feeling, baby? Honestly?"

"All right," I responded, squirming slightly under the endearment.

He squeezed my leg. "One step at a time," he said so only I could hear. "Together."

I nodded and covered his hand with mine.

When the waiter returned, David ordered coffee for the table, four different breakfast items, and closed the menu. "What do you want?" he asked me.

My mouth fell open. "All that food is for you?"

He patted his stomach. "Haven't eaten since dinner last night. But you can have whatever you want off my plate."

I shrugged at the waiter. "I'll just have the oatmeal with fruit."

As Gretchen placed her order, David leaned back in his seat and nodded at the duffel bag by my feet—the one that currently fit my entire life. "That your stuff?" he asked.

"Yep."

"Everything?"

I nodded. "For now."

"Work clothes?"

"Some of it." Well, two outfits I'd have to get creative

about stretching into four. I scratched above my eyebrow. "I'll manage."

David glanced skeptically at the bag and then back at me with his eyebrows drawn.

"Okay, I *might* need to get more things from the apartment," I conceded. "Bill didn't take my key, so I can go next week while he's at work."

"No need." David grinned. "We'll go shopping."

"Oh, no, it's fine," I said. It was beginning to hit me that between a lawyer, rent, a new life and limited funds, things were going to become very tight for me.

"I'll take you. My treat." He glanced at Gretchen, who made no secret that she was listening to every word. "We'll sit down and talk logistics later," he added, "but let me get you some things for work."

"Logistics?" I asked.

"Yeah, money, apartment stuff, all that shit. We'll figure it out, but for now . . ." He winked. "I want to take my girl shopping."

"I couldn't possibly accept—"

"I'll go," Gretchen volunteered, and I gave her a look.

The waiter carried over a tray of three coffees, setting one in front of each of us.

"Olivia, don't argue with me," David said, ignoring Gretchen as he picked up his mug. "Let me do this for you."

Gretchen kicked me under the table, and I yelped. She raised her eyebrows at me and nodded furiously. Turning down free clothes? A foreign concept to her.

David laughed silently, even as I narrowed my eyes on him.

"You're a little persistent, aren't you?" I asked as I stirred sugar into my coffee.

"You have no idea, stubborn lady." He opened his

hand on the table, gesturing for mine. "You and I are going to be an interesting couple."

A couple. With David Dylan.

I tapped the sugar spoon on the edge of my glass, set it down, and put my hand in his. I studied the way his large one engulfed mine. Protective. Gentle. Dominant. I cocked my head.

I was David Dylan's . . . girlfriend?

"What's wrong?" David asked.

"Nothing. This is all just so . . . weird," I said, glancing at Gretchen. "I have a new life."

"So, you're like her boyfriend—right, David?" Gretchen chimed in.

"I don't know if that's quite the right word," he replied.

I blinked at him. *What?*

"Roommate?" Gretchen suggested.

I jumped at David's burst of laughter.

"Gretchen," I squealed, staring daggers at her.

David squeezed my hand. "*Boyfriend* isn't strong enough, but if we need something to call me, then it works for now."

Gretchen sipped her coffee and hummed thoughtfully, alerting us that there was something on her mind.

"Yes?" I asked her.

"It's Saturday."

"So?" I asked just as I noticed David shake his head at Gretchen.

"Isn't tonight—"

"Nothing," David cut her off. "Tonight, Olivia and I will finally get some much-needed alone time."

I looked between the two of them. "What's tonight?"

"It's The Revelin's official grand opening soiree," David said, "but I'm not going."

"Wait. What?" I asked. I'd seen The Revelin hotel, David's big project on the Riverfront, when it had just been a half-finished construction site. We'd spent a night in the finished hotel, and it had opened to the public already, but still. This was David's moment to take the credit. "That's a huge deal. You have to go."

"It's not important," he said, tearing his glare from Gretchen to look at me. "I'm taking care of you right now."

"No." I shook my head with determination. "Absolutely not. If you don't want me to come, I understand, but you are definitely going. How can you say it's not important? It *is* important, you've dedicated—"

"Whoa there," he interrupted, smiling. "I don't even want to go. I already did all my schmoozing bullshit at the soft opening. Although, can't say I regret that night one bit," he added. I blushed, remembering the oh-so-wrong, but oh-so-right night of life-altering sex in his hotel room . . . and then in the hotel room's *pool*. "Really, I don't care about it," David continued. "The hotel's been open long enough for us to know everything's going smoothly. I would much rather spend a quiet night with you."

No way. I took my hand back, sitting up straight in my seat. "You worked hard on that project, and you deserve to be honored," I declared. "You're going to that party, David Dylan, with or without me. I'm a big girl, I can take care of myself for a night—"

"*All right*." He cut me off with his palms in the air. "I'll go. But I'm sure as hell not going without you. That is, if you're up for it."

"I'm up for it," I stated firmly.

"Then unless you have a gown rolled up in that bag, we definitely need to go shopping," he said.

My shoulders relaxed somewhat, and Gretchen

bounced in her chair. "Fine," I relented, and he gave me his amazing, boyish grin that I just about lived for.

"Since my firm handles Revelin's PR, I'll be there too," Gretchen said. "I'm bringing Greg."

I looked back at her. "I thought you guys broke things off because you went home with another guy at the *last* Revelin party. Are things back on?"

"Yes," she said with a shy smile. "He didn't care about the other guy since nothing happened. It took a while, but he finally convinced me that this time is for good."

"For good?" I asked, my eyes big.

"Yup. I'm tired of playing it safe." She looked at David and explained, "College boyfriend who dumped me two days before graduation. I've been butt-hurt about it ever since, but I think I'm ready to move on now." She turned back to me. "He says he's changed, and I could either go on not believing him or take a chance. We decided a couple weeks ago to give it a real try."

"I'm so happy for you," I said sincerely. "I'm sorry I haven't been around to talk to."

"You were around," she said. "You just weren't reachable."

"You can thank David for that," I said, nodding at him.

"We weren't even speaking a couple weeks ago," he said.

"Exactly."

David squeezed my leg under the table again, higher this time. It sent a thrill up the inside of my thigh. I couldn't wait to be back in his arms, just us, exploring each other . . .

David raised his eyebrows at me, jerking his head toward Gretchen.

"Right," I said, forcing myself out of the fantasy and

back to the table. "So we'll make a night of it then? We can all meet up at Revelin."

As the waiter returned with our food, David sat forward and picked up a fork. "Should I see if Andrew wants to come? I can put him and Lucy on the list."

I shoveled some oatmeal into my mouth.

Gretchen looked down into her coffee cup.

"Hmm," David said with the ensuing silence. "What'd I miss?"

I swallowed my food, shifting in my seat. "Lucy isn't . . ."

"Ah." He lifted his chin. "Not too thrilled with us, I take it."

"That's putting it mildly," Gretchen muttered.

David reached out to touch my cheek. "I'm sorry. You need her right now."

I shrugged helplessly. "She doesn't agree with what we're doing."

He dropped his hand and drummed his fingers on the table. "I'll talk to Andrew," he decided. "Don't worry about a thing. Just eat your breakfast."

I smiled inwardly at his confidence. Unfortunately, I wasn't so sure he could fix this. I doubted he'd endured the wrath that came with threatening the values of someone as steadfastly good as Lucy.

By the time I'd finished my oatmeal, David still had a side of bacon and a stack of pancakes to get through.

Gretchen dabbed her mouth with her napkin. "I have to run soon. Revelin isn't my client, but I offered to help with set-up this afternoon. Should I get the bill?"

"I'll take care of it," David said absentmindedly.

"Actually, there's something I need to do," I said to Gretchen, "and I'd really like you here with me."

"Anything," she said, setting her elbows on the table. "What is it?"

"I have to call my dad."

"Ah. Papa Germaine." Gretchen moved to the seat next to me, across from David. "Dad's a little tough," Gretchen explained to him. "He doesn't suffer quitters well. Er, not that you're a quitter, Liv. But you know what I mean."

David cleared his throat. "If you need me to talk to him—"

"I've got this one," I said and smiled at him. I turned to Gretchen. "Can I borrow your cell?"

She took out her phone, and after a moment of playing with it, she handed it to me with *Mr. Germaine* pulled up on the screen.

"You have my dad's number?" I asked.

"Of course, silly. In case of emergency."

My father picked up on the first ring. "Hello?" he said, robust even through the phone.

"Dad?"

"Hello?" he repeated, even louder.

"Dad! It's me, Olivia."

"Liv, kiddo. What's up?" he asked, his tone softening. "Whose phone is this?"

"It's Gretchen's."

"Everything all right?" he asked.

"Well, yes and no." I scratched under my nose. "Do you have a minute?"

"Hang on, I'm on the course."

David arched an eyebrow at me.

"*Golfing*," I mouthed.

He nodded.

Muffled voices sounded in the background until my dad returned. "Go on, Olivia."

"Dad," I addressed him slowly, suddenly self-conscious with two pairs of eyes glued to me. "I don't really know how to tell you this."

"Out with it, Olivia," he said. "Come on."

I sighed. There was really no use in beating around the bush with my dad. "Well, I've ended things with Bill."

"Excuse me?"

"Bill. It's over," I said and repeated, "I ended things."

"What did that son of a bitch do?" Dad asked.

David pushed his empty plates out of the way and set his forearms on the table, watching intently.

"No, he didn't do anything, it was me," I said quickly, then paused as the words settled over the table. "All me. I did this."

"I see." Dad paused, and I could imagine the wrinkles between his eyebrows deepening. "Why?"

"I—well, it's just that . . . I wasn't happy," I said.

"No?" he asked. "You two seemed all right last time we all had dinner. Not that I'd describe Bill as a particularly joyous person."

I inhaled a deep breath. Harvey Germaine, a Texan businessman who didn't bullshit, appreciated the blunt truth above all. "I cheated on him, Dad."

With David's eyes glued to me, I waited through a tense silence for my dad's reaction. "Are you there?" I asked.

My dad grunted. "Did Bill kick you out?"

"No, I . . . I left. For someone else. I am leaving him for someone else. The man I was unfaithful with," I explained, completely aware of my awkwardness but unable to help it. "He is who I'm leaving Bill for."

"Who is?" Dad asked.

"Um, well, David's an architect—"

"Who the hell is David?" Dad asked. "And what kind of man steals another man's wife?"

"He's a *good* man," I promised my father as David took my hand. "He's smart, accomplished, respected—but I made this decision on my own. If you're going to blame anyone, blame me."

"I want you to come home," Dad said. "We need to talk about this."

"I can't right now," I said. "I have work. That promotion keeps me really busy."

"Come next weekend then." He cleared his throat. "Put the ticket on my card and whatever else you need. Where are you staying? Do you need a hotel?"

"I'm at Gretchen's until I find a place," I said.

David's hand tightened around mine, and I met his quizzical look.

"Get a hotel until you can get here," Dad said. "I'll pay for it. And bring this guy. I want to meet him."

"I'd like you to meet him, too." I cocked my head at David, who jutted his chin in agreement. "I'll find a time for us to come out," I said. "I do need to talk to you about the divorce and all that. I have no idea what I'm doing, Dad."

"I'm sure you don't, kid. It won't be pretty." He sighed. "What am I saying? It's a fucking mess. Are you absolutely sure this is what you want?"

David nodded. I nodded with him. "Yes. Yes, it's what I want."

"Then we'll handle it. Use my card to get a ticket. Come as soon as you can. And Olivia?"

"Yes?"

"Bring him."

I wasn't sure if David could hear every word, but I didn't think so judging by the fact that he didn't look scared.

"Thank you for being supportive," I said.

David swiveled in his seat as the waiter approached. Before he could set down the bill, David handed him his credit card.

"I love you, sugar. Say hi to Gretchen for me," Dad said. "And don't make one goddamn move until I meet this guy, all right?" He exhaled a sigh. "I want to know this David isn't screwing around."

I smiled at my overprotective father. "Yes, Dad. Bye." I hit *End*, glancing between David and Gretchen. "He didn't seem that upset, but he wants to meet you, David. Frankly, I don't think he can wait. He also wants me to get a hotel for the week."

"I'll move some things around," David said. "We'll go to Dallas next weekend."

I smiled at him appreciatively. "Thanks."

"But you're not getting a hotel," he added.

"I'm not?"

"No," he said firmly. "In fact, what was that about looking for an apartment?"

"She's getting her own place," Gretchen answered for me, elbows on the table, chin in hand, watching us like we'd been hired as her entertainment.

David gave a short laugh just as I slow-blinked my irritation at Gretchen. "Thanks," I told her. "I think we can take it from here."

She shrugged. "Just trying to help."

David signed the bill, pocketed his credit card, and stood, looking between the two of us. "We'll finish this discussion in the car, Olivia." It sounded like a threat, but he held out his hand to me.

Gretchen's eyes widened, and she mouthed, "*Sorry.*"

David and I walked out of the restaurant hand in hand. "Look at us," he noted, "engaging in a public display of affection."

I laced my fingers through his. Bill and I had held hands plenty of times, but I didn't realize until this moment how erotic it could be. "I love your hands," I said softly, because I did. They were big, they overtook mine, and they were capable of making me feel things. *So* many things. Protected. Loved. Aroused.

"Okay, this is getting weird," Gretchen said behind us. "Go bang it out, and I'll see you two tonight, okay?"

We hugged good-bye on the sidewalk. Once Gretchen had left, David carried my duffel bag to his Porsche. "I'm *definitely* sending her a fruit basket for all her trouble," I said.

He chuckled. "You and your fruit."

Before I could open the car door, David turned and maneuvered me up against the side of the Porsche. He placed his arms on either side of me, trapping me. "You're not getting your own place."

"I can't live out of a duffel bag at Gretchen's forever."

"Move in with me," he said. "Today."

My mouth fell open. The last forty-eight hours had been a whirlwind. Weren't we moving fast enough? Wasn't David even the *slightest* bit scared or apprehensive about what lay ahead for us? "*Move in?*" I exclaimed. "Today? That is absurd. And wildly inappropriate. And just . . . *no*. We can't do that."

His jaw set and his eyes hardened not inches from mine, but he took one hand off the car to gently thread his fingers through my hair. "*Today*," he repeated, tilting my head back. "I'm not wasting any more time. I want you in my place," he paused to kiss my neck, "watching TV in my den," he added, brushing his lips along my jaw, "cooking in my kitchen," a peck on my cheek, "fucking in my bed," a kiss on the lips, "sleeping in my bed, and," another kiss on the lips, "waking up in my bed. Every day."

"David," I said, utterly breathless from his simultaneously generous and greedy mouth. I didn't know whether to swoon, protest, or rip off his clothing right there. "It's so soon. Everyone will talk."

"I don't give a fuck. Like I promised, I'll always be your shield." He gave me a hard peck on the mouth. "You and I are going to have fun, honeybee."

"Tonight?"

"Tonight. This weekend. Forever," he said. He tried to open the door, but I stayed planted in front of it, struck dumb, still trying to decide how to react. He picked me up by my waist and turned to set me on the curb so he could get to the car. I practically fainted myself into the seat and watched him round the hood with casual confidence. Completely unaffected, even though I was hot and bothered and unsure as to whether or not I had just agreed to move in with a boyfriend I'd officially had less than an hour.

Once we were pulling away, David said, "So let's see . . . where should we start? Burberry, Versace, Gucci . . ."

I suppressed a smile. "It concerns me that you're so familiar with women's designers."

"Ralph Lauren, Chanel, Prada—*aha*," he said when I perked up. "Prada it is. We'll go there first."

I half-laughed, half-gaped. He read me like a book. Was that good or bad?

"Come on," David goaded. "The Olivia I know is not this shy. She once told me I was a player who only wanted what I couldn't have, but look at us now."

I rolled my eyes. "Don't get too cocky. It's only been a couple days."

"There she is," he said, laughing as he shifted gears and sped up.

Chapter Four

David had it in his head that he didn't want to be disconnected from me for any reason. Therefore, the first stop we
made after breakfast was to get me a new cell phone.
Ignoring my protests, he added me to his plan and
demanded the most capable phone available.

We parked the car at his apartment and walked the
short distance to Magnificent Mile. I was no stranger to
nice things—despite Bill's aversion to spending money, I'd
spent my own money on quality over quantity—but for
some reason, I felt nervous and out of place. It was a lot to
take in, this new life. I learned quickly that if I didn't
follow David into a store that seemed far too expensive,
he'd leave me out on the sidewalk. It wasn't that I didn't
love to shop, but I was uncomfortable spending someone
else's money. He insisted on it, though, threatening to give
the salesgirls free rein if I didn't participate.

By the third store, a medium-sized boutique with
collections by various high-end designers, I'd begun to
loosen up and picked out a few things on my own.

Despite the fact that David wore jeans and a zip-up

hoodie that didn't exactly fit in at these high-end stores, salesgirls flocked to him like flies to honey.

"We're looking for a new wardrobe," David said to one as she approached.

"*David*," I scolded. "We're only supposed to be getting a few things for work."

"Oh, right . . ." He gave the woman a conspiratorial look. "Bring the wardrobe, though."

She smiled at him brightly, no doubt thrilled to be in the presence of such an extremely handsome man who'd basically just handed over his credit card.

"Size zero?" she asked me.

"Probably—"

"We're aiming for higher," he said, rubbing my back. "But we can come back when that happens."

I agreed that I'd lost too much weight recently and needed to put some back on—but then buying new clothes seemed a bit pointless. "Maybe we should wait to shop until—"

"Here, put these in a fitting room," David interrupted, handing the salesgirl what I'd already chosen, "and pull whatever else you think she'll like."

"Yes, sir," the woman said. "Champagne while you shop?"

"Of course," he said.

I smiled. "Now we really are Edward and Vivian, but that puts me on the verge of prostitute territory."

"We haven't even slept together yet," he pointed out. "As a couple, anyway."

"So you're not doing this to get in my pants?"

"Hmm." His arms found their way around my waist. He ran his hands down my back and over the seat of my jeans before pulling my hips against him. He kissed me chastely on the cheek and then a little less so along my jaw. "That would certainly be a perk," he whispered in my ear. "I want to take you in my bed tonight like the first time."

"Why wait?" I asked, aroused just by his breath on my skin.

The salesgirl's voice cut into our moment. "You're all set up, if you want to follow me," she said, directing me into a full dressing room and David to a chair just outside of it.

Locked in the small but immaculate room, I stripped down quickly.

"Come out," David instructed.

"Okay, but I'm not dressed yet."

"Olivia, there are other men in this store," he admonished. "Come out *when you're ready*."

"Do you really want to see? It's boring work stuff." It wasn't at all—the pieces she'd picked were so beautiful, they could pass as art. Fine wool, silk, lace, chiffon—to me it was heaven, but to a guy, I knew—it was boring work stuff.

"I want to see everything," he called.

"If you say so." I dressed myself in a red, long-sleeved silk blouse with delicate gold buttons and two hanging fabric strips that I tied into a bow. A fitted, navy wool skirt stopped just above the tops of my knees.

When I exited, David leaned forward in his chair and set his elbows on his knees. His eyes scanned me head to toe. "Damn." He blew out a breath. "That looks sexy as fuck."

I laughed. "I'm all covered up. You act as if it's lingerie."

"Come here," he said. I sat in his lap, and he leaned me back against one arm. He skidded his other hand down the fabric of the skirt, stopping at the hem. "You just reminded me. There's something I've been wanting to tell you for months."

"What's that, handsome?" I asked, shifting suggestively against his crotch.

He groaned softly. "Remember the night you were attacked, I brought you to my apartment and you stayed in my guest room. I said you looked exquisite in my t-shirt and sweatpants, and you laughed because you didn't believe me. I promised that one day I'd tell you *exactly* how exquisite you looked."

I bit my lip and nodded, remembering the moment perfectly. I'd wanted nothing more than for him to leap across the bed and devour me whole.

"Up until then, I'd never seen anything sexier," he said, running his nose along mine. He slid his palm down to my knee and partway up the skirt. "You, bare-faced in my clothing, nothing underneath. I should get a medal for my restraint. I wanted to fuck you so bad, I would've moved Heaven and Earth right then to make it happen."

My breathing sped as I became instantly aware of the ache between my legs. David's noticeable excitement underneath my thigh wasn't helping.

"That's all. Go on," he said, urging me up. "Try something else."

I stood slowly, letting the blood recirculate through my body. Back behind the door, I stripped down to my undergarments and then, when an idea occurred to me, stripped all the way down. I took out my new phone, located the only number I had stored, tousled my hair a bit, pinched my cheeks, and snapped a photo in the mirror.

I hit *Send* and turned my attention back to what I'd try next. It wasn't long before David's phone *pinged*, and he rustled in his seat. The dressing room door opened a sliver and he slipped in, raking his eyes over my naked body. He held a finger over his mouth and took two large strides toward me.

"Hands behind your back," he said quietly, and I complied. He took my chin in his hand. My heart raced, and arousal pulled deep inside me as his stare burned. "Open," he whispered, squeezing my jaw. I did, and he stuck his index finger in my mouth. "Suck."

I ran my tongue over him, looking up from under my lashes. I sucked tentatively at first and then harder. He moaned loudly, so I reached out to touch his erection through his pants.

"No." He placed my hand back behind me, removed his finger from my mouth, and reached between my legs. With agonizing slowness, he slid the wet finger inside me. I rolled my lips together and breathed heavily through my nose. One finger turned into two. He explored me gently from the inside, massaging me with an expert touch. His other hand found my breast, rolling and pinching my nipple so that I moaned into the sting. When his palm pressed against my clit, I writhed into it.

He slipped a hand under my hair and held my neck. "Don't squirm," he warned softly.

His gaze grew darker, more penetrating as he finger-fucked me faster. His complete, undivided attention was unnerving, and I wanted to look away, but he held me in place. The overly bright fluorescent lights flooded the room, sharpening my vision as things began to feel surreal. My mouth fell open, and I gasped for air as my orgasm threatened.

"Fuck me," I implored, wringing my hands behind my back.

He shook his head as he pushed his fingers deeper. My head jerked back, but he continued to hold me upright, seeking out my eyes with his.

"*Come*," he mouthed at me.

"How are the sizes working out?" I heard from somewhere far away.

David's eyes bored into me with his palm still firmly against me. "Answer her," he demanded in a whisper.

I reached out to grab his arms as the orgasm crested. "Fine," I called.

She said something else, but my ears rang as waves of pleasure hit me. The world spun around me, and I could only cling to David to keep me centered. "Fine," I repeated, squeezing David's biceps and thrashing against his hand.

As I came down, I wilted against him, and he held my weight, trailing quick kisses along my jawline until he reached my neck. He removed his fingers from me and wiped them on his jeans, laughing silently.

"*What?*" I mouthed as I tried to control my breathing, still gripping one of his arms for fear that my legs would give out.

"She asked if she could get you a different size in anything. You said 'Fine.'"

"Oh," I breathed, managing a small laugh. "Oops."

He smiled widely and shook his head before swiping my panties from the floor. "Here."

I glanced down at his tented pants and then back up. "What about you?"

"I can wait," he said. "I don't want our first time as a couple to be in a dressing room."

I nodded, even though I wouldn't have minded at all. I took my undergarments from his outstretched hand. As soon as I'd clasped my bra, he was crouched at my feet holding open a dress. I placed my hands on his shoulders and stepped into it. He drew it up my body and zipped me into it from behind.

It was simple and black, conservative enough for work but still trim over my slight curves.

"You have a dress like this, don't you? With the thingie?" he asked, motioning to the shoulder.

I smiled, amused that he was at all familiar with my wardrobe, although I couldn't remember wearing that particular dress around him. "I have one with a rosette, yes. Different designer but similar."

"It suits you."

Something about the dress tugged at my memory, but I quickly forgot when he perched his chin on the top of my head and looked at us in the mirror. "If you look like this every morning on the way out the door, then I'm fucked. We'll never make it to work."

I turned in his arms and smiled up at him, running my hands over his t-shirt and under his hoodie. It was our first moment truly alone to appreciate each other since everything had happened. Things were beginning to feel right. David dipped his head for a leisurely kiss. It was nice not to feel guilty or as if I'd been simmering with need for months.

"We're going shoe shopping next," he said. "If I have to bend this far down every time I kiss you, I'll throw my back out before I hit forty."

I laughed and rose onto the balls of my feet for a last peck. "Get out of here so I can change."

David had given the staff his credit card long before we ended up at the register, so I never even saw the transaction. Suddenly the salesgirl was handing me several large bags, which David chivalrously intercepted, and we left the store.

After he'd put them in the trunk, we stood on the sidewalk. "Listen, I have some work to do back at the apartment," he said. "Give me your wallet."

I cocked my head but dug it out of my purse and handed it to him. He stuck it in his back pocket, pulled out *his* wallet, and handed me a credit card. "Go find a dress for tonight, anything you want, anywhere you want." I started to object, but he stopped me. "Surprise me. If it feels too weird to spend my money on yourself, then do it for me. Pick out something you think I'd like."

I took the card and opened my mouth but didn't know what to say. "Thank you."

"Don't thank me," he said. "It makes me feel like I'm doing you a favor. I'm not. Like I said, we'll talk money, logistics, all that shit later. Just take this for now. Oh, and this . . ." He burrowed his hand into his hoodie pocket and produced a bundle of items. "Keycards and keys to the Gryphon—come in the back entrance. You remember which apartment it is, right?"

"Penthouse," I said with a defeated shrug.

"I know it's a lot," he said softly, "but we're in it now. Might as well get comfortable."

"Where'd you get all this?" I asked, palming my foreseeable future.

"I've had it for a while. I told you," he said, touching me under the chin, "I've been waiting for you."

Chapter Five

As I walked to David's apartment, evening gown in hand, the last forty-eight hours played through my mind like a movie. Things had never felt as simultaneously terrifying and clear as they did now. I wondered how Bill was and decided to call Gretchen with my new phone number when I got back.

David lived in a *hotel*—one of a few residences comprising the top floors of the Gryphon Hotel. That fact was abundantly clear as I skipped the back entrance as he'd suggested and crossed the lobby instead. Not to be outdone, David was at the top—the penthouse—just under the rooftop venue that'd hosted *Chicago Metropolitan Magazine*'s Meet and Greet. It was intimidating to say the least, but it also thrilled me. It meant views of my beloved Chicago from almost every angle.

I swiped the card in the elevator as I'd seen David do. When I reached his floor, I stepped into the foyer and looked around. Various emotions rushed through me as I remembered fleeing his apartment months ago. Desperate to escape, I'd run out in just the sheet from his bed and changed here in the foyer as I'd waited for the elevator. I blushed when I noticed a camera in one corner, wondering if it belonged to David or the hotel. Neither possibility lessened my embarrassment.

I walked to the front door and halted there, unsure of how to proceed. I dug out the single key and flipped it over and over in my fingers, thinking, immobilized. My phone pinged.

David: *Coming in?*

I smiled at David's text and unlocked the door. Apparently, the cameras belonged to him. As I entered, another message came through.

David: *Last door on the right before my bedroom.*

I took in the semi-familiar space and automatically walked the path to the bedroom I'd once run from. When I reached an open door just before it, I stopped and peeked into an office I'd never seen. In a leather swivel chair, David nodded into the desk phone at his ear. Behind him spread a jaw-dropping view of Chicago's skyline. He motioned at me to come in, so I draped the garment bag that held my new dress on an empty chair and walked toward his waving hands.

"Sketches are almost finished, but I still need to meet with Greer about preliminary estimates," he said into the receiver as I settled on his lap. He kissed me quickly on the cheek as he listened.

Judging by the two oversized computer screens, piles of paperwork, and a drafting table, I sat in his home office. A display of flat screen security televisions made up one corner, and I blushed when I noticed that one of them watched the foyer. Thankfully, nothing beyond the entryway was included. He winked when he noticed my gaze. I didn't see much to indicate a personal presence— no pictures, no framed awards or articles, nothing distinctly special about the office's inhabitant.

"Let's set that up then." He paused, covering the mouthpiece to ask me, "When should we go see your father? Can you get Friday off so we can make a weekend of it?"

I bit my lip. My boss frowned upon taking time off, but I had plenty of vacation days because of it. I gave him a half-shrug. "I'll try."

He removed his hand and placed it on my lower back. "Monday," he said into the phone. "I probably won't be in on Friday. No, it won't be resolved by then. Make it Monday." After a moment he hung up and ran his hand up and down my back. "How was shopping? Is that your dress?"

"It was great," I said and pecked his cheek. "Thank you."

He sighed. "I've had a serious boner since the boutique."

"Well, there are ways of fixing that," I teased.

"I'm well aware, Miss Germaine, but not until tonight. I want to take my time with you. Good things come to those who wait."

"And those who don't?" I asked, brushing my lips against the corner of his mouth. He turned his head and caught my mouth for a heated kiss, pulling me closer so his erection pushed into my hip.

"You taste so good," he murmured when he released me. "Tell me you're moving in, and I get to do this when-ever I please."

"David," I protested, placing a hand on his chest. "It's too soon—"

"We have a house together, for God's sake," he said.

Oh, yes, the Oak Park house. I'd purposely been avoiding the topic. David had bought my dream home on a whim because he couldn't stand the thought of someone else buying it for me. Not two days into our relationship and there was a house involved.

"*You* have a house," I corrected.

"*We* do, Olivia." His eyebrows furrowed. "Great as it is, that house means nothing to me without you in it."

That, I already knew, since he'd practically given it to me days earlier when he'd almost walked out of my life. "That's way in the future anyway," I said. "I still have a whole divorce to get through."

"Again, *we*," he corrected. "I'm going through it with you, no matter how hard you try to do it alone."

"Right, okay," I said slowly, "but it's ridiculous for me to go from being married to someone else right to moving in with you."

"What's ridiculous is you paying rent on some shithole when you'll be here with me every night anyway."

Butterflies filled my tummy at the enticing thought of falling asleep and waking up next to this god on a regular basis. "*Every* night?" I repeated.

"If you think I'm willing to spend even one night away from you, after every night we've already spent apart, after everything I did to get you . . ." He shook his head. "Then you have no clue what's been going on in my head the past few months, honeybee. You're my girl," he said softly, "and I want you here."

I smiled and touched his hair, because I thought it was cute when he called me *honeybee*. But it was downright sexy to be his girl, and I showed him so by shifting on his lap in a way I hoped would entice him to break his rule about waiting until tonight.

"Don't try to distract me," he said. "We're having this talk now."

I blew out a sigh and stilled. "You're a cock block."

He grinned. "Don't worry. I won't let you off so easy tonight."

My insides clenched, and I wished we were already home from the party. I stood. "Okay. You're right. Let's talk."

He frowned. "Where are you going?"

"I can't think straight being that close to you."

"If thinking straight is a requirement, then might I suggest we do this over the phone?"

"Very funny," I said, moving to a dove-gray, heathered tweed couch on the other side of his office. I removed my shoes and sat against one cushioned arm with my knees bent. He followed my lead, and after toeing off his own shoes, sat opposite and extended his long legs on both sides of me.

"I could get used to this," he said, letting his eyes drift over me. "I look forward to spending my days learning what you love, what you don't, and all the little details in between."

I put my hand on his shin. "Me, too."

"I want our relationship to be completely and totally open," he continued. "Honesty—and the irony of this is not lost on me, but it's the most important thing to me when it comes to us. No lies. No fibs. No telling me you're goddamn fine when you're not. Nothing."

I took a deep breath. It would be hard. Not that I wanted to lie, but I'd spent my life beating back the things I didn't want to feel. Telling Bill I was "fine" and having him accept that made things easy. Telling David how I really felt, whether it was mad, sad, happy, jealous—that would be a challenge.

"Hey," David called, and I realized I'd been staring off into space. "You hear me? No 'fine' bullshit."

"I'll try," I promised.

He eyed me another moment and continued. "If Bill calls and tries to get you back, I want to know. I'll be fucking pissed, but I'll do my best to control it. Because I need you to come to me."

I narrowed my eyes. "This is a two-way street, isn't it?"

He raised his chin at me. "What does that mean?" he asked.

"You haven't exactly been a saint through all of this. Dani, Maria, Amber, all the other girls—I think there was a Brittany in there . . ." My nose twitched. "They're gone, right?"

The angles of his face sharpened, and he looked almost angry. "Gone. I have nothing to hide from you, and I never have."

"What about Oak Park?"

I had him there, and he knew it. Even though the Oak Park house had been my dream home, it had also symbolized the beginning of a new future with Bill. And David hadn't hesitated to snatch it out from under us.

David looked away and didn't speak until his gaze found me again. "I'm sorry about Oak Park. The thing is, when I had you there in front of me, and we were in that house, run-down as it was—I saw us there, together, as a couple."

I sucked in a breath. He'd seen it, too. We belonged in that house—everything about it had been right. I remembered how awful I'd felt having that thought when I was supposed to be building a life with someone else.

"I knew one day it would be real," he said. "By the

time we were leaving, I'd already done some initial sketches in my head. We'd work on it together, move in, raise a family, be fucking happy. When you told me Bill had made an offer, well . . . it hit me like a ton of bricks, Olivia. I was shocked. I wasn't going to give up that dream."

He was so beautiful when passionate, and I loved listening to him as much as watching him. I thought back to the day we'd seen the house together, how suddenly quiet and stiff he'd gotten when I'd told him about our offer.

"I guess I had this idea that you and I would eventually end up together," David said, "and that news sort of shattered it."

"You thought that?" I asked.

"Finding out Bill might get you that house was one moment where I worried I really was living in a fantasy— that I might never have you. Instead of waiting to find out, I acted. I'm sorry I didn't tell you sooner, but I'm sure as hell not sorry that I did it."

"I saw it, too," I blurted.

"Saw what?" He asked.

"Us. There. Together. It scared me. I realized my problems with Bill ran deeper than I thought, and that . . . my feelings for you did, too."

David's expression softened. "I always follow my gut, Olivia. It's how I've done most of my business. It's how this happened." He motioned between us, and I nodded in agreement. "It's why I bought the house," he concluded.

I extended a leg and rubbed the inside of his thigh with my foot. "Thank you for the home," I said. Maybe I should've stayed angry, but David's belief in us awed me. "I don't think I ever said *thank you*."

He caught my ankle and massaged it gently. "Do you accept the terms of the honesty agreement?"

I nodded, simply because I couldn't fathom David would let me get away with anything else. "I do."

"Next, what birth control do you use?"

My thoughts screeched to a halt with the change in topic. I blinked at him. "What?" I asked. "I'm on the pill."

He touched his thumb to the corner of his mouth. "We need it to be the Fort Knox of birth control, considering my plans for you."

Oh, my. That was a good thing, wasn't it? I nodded slowly.

"I just made a joke," he said. "Why do you look scared?"

I shifted against the back of the couch. Although eager to find out David's plans for me, the pill brought up memories I'd rather forget. Like when I'd accused Bill of hiding my pack. "Toward the end, Bill and I fought a lot about birth control," I said. "He pressured me to go off it."

"Pressured you?" he repeated. "How?"

"He wanted kids," I said frankly. "And he didn't believe me when I said I wasn't ready."

Anger flashed in David's eyes. "You think he loves you —if he did, he'd never push you into something like that. He's a coward."

David couldn't know what it meant to hear him say that after all the fighting Bill and I had done over the topic. I momentarily wondered if I should elaborate, but Bill had exhausted the subject of children for me. It was the last thing I felt like discussing, so instead, I said, "It was definitely a sore spot in our relationship."

David went uncharacteristically quiet, watching me. Finally, he asked, "When was the last time?"

"Last time what?"

He swallowed. "You and Bill."

I bit my lip, flashing back to Bill's constant interrogations the past month. What good would it do, giving David that information? "Why do you want to know?"

"I just do. I want to know."

"Are you going to hold it against me?"

"No." He squeezed my ankle. "I'm sorry if that's what you've been dealing with."

I sighed and looked out the window at the city. "Bill and I haven't been intimate much lately. He was respectful because I was grieving over Davena, but he didn't know, couldn't know, that my feelings for him . . . changed. After you. Or rather, I began to notice how they were different."

David waited for me to continue.

I let my gaze drift back to him. "We only did it once since . . . isn't this weird?"

Though he appeared to be clenching his teeth, he slackened his jaw and said, "Go on."

"Only once since you and I were together at your apartment. And it was, I don't know, a couple months ago maybe."

"I'll tell you right now," he said, "that will never happen around here. If anything, I'll need you to tell me if I'm being overbearing in the bedroom."

I couldn't imagine I'd ever ask David to stop. I pulled my knees to my chest, hugging them. "It's been difficult these last several months. He tried, but I was cruel."

"Because of Davena?"

"She was a rock in my life. My mom and I have never known how to be there for each other emotionally, but it wasn't that way with Davena. She and her husband have been family friends since I was born. We became much closer once I moved to Chicago, though."

"It was hard, wasn't it? Her death?"

I blinked up at him. "Incredibly, but walking away from you was debilitating, and I spent the next three months trying to forget our night together, wishing things were different, wishing I could see you, talk to you, be with you."

He rolled off the arm of the couch, leaned forward, and put his hands on my knees. "Things couldn't be different because they had to happen this way. I had a rough time, too, but it's going to get better now. Trust me." He reclined back, tugging my legs free, sliding his hands down until he held my ankles.

I nodded breathlessly at his sincere words and at his skin on mine. "Next order of business?" I asked, afraid I might melt into a puddle of desire just from our proximity.

"Finances," he said tentatively. "If I were Bill, I'd have an axe to grind right now."

I'd thought the same thing. I'd left almost everything behind, and after the way Bill had shut off my cell service, I had a bad feeling he might not stop there. "We share a joint account, but he controls it," I said. "I paid the bills—phones, rent, utilities, et cetera—but it's all in his name. I have my own savings. It's not much," I offered, "but maybe I can get some money in the divorce. Although, if I've learned anything from TV courtroom dramas, I know infidelity isn't exactly encouraged." I looked around the office and over at the view. The rent for this place had to be more than I even made in a month, maybe two. After a few moments of silence, my eyes returned to David's.

"I'll take care of you, Olivia," he said carefully.

What exactly did he mean by that? I blinked rapidly but didn't respond.

"Did you hear me?" he asked. "Money isn't an issue. I've seen to it that I'm one of the top architects in the country. I own property and a business. My sister and I each received a hefty inheritance from our grandfather. Between that and work, I have more than enough to take care of us both. And," he added with a crooked smile, "a family, when it comes to that."

I looked down. It was the second time he'd mentioned family, and it made me uneasy. If I let my mind dive into the specifics of what that could mean, though, on top of everything else—I might blow a fuse. I pushed the feeling aside for later.

I should've felt excitement about being taken care of, but it only made me anxious. Remembering the honesty policy, I said, "I feel weird about it."

"If you didn't, I'd be a little concerned," he said, his smile still hooked at the corner. "It'll take time to get used to, but just know that you don't have to worry. I don't care what you do with your paychecks from the magazine. Rip them up for all I care. You'll never have to pay rent or a mortgage again. I'll get you a credit card, which you'll use going forward."

"David, living off my paychecks alone will be sufficient."

"Use that money for whatever you want," he said. "I'll get you a card Monday."

"We'll see," I decided, as if we were just making weekend plans.

"So can I buy us tickets for Friday then?" he asked. "To Dallas to see your dad?"

"I have to double-check with Beman, but let me get the tickets. My dad offered."

"I'd prefer to buy them."

"But—"

"Didn't Bill spoil you?" he asked.

I blanched, then shook my head. "He hated spending money. You should've seen his face when we got the bill for Lucy's bridesmaid dress," I said. "He was almost purple."

"Mmm, I did love that dress," David mused. "It was

worth every penny. Those days are over. Prepare to be spoiled."

"Let my dad buy the tickets," I said. "He's a little controlling, and he won't want to seem cheap." I narrowed my eyes as a realization hit me. "Come to think of it, you guys have a lot of similarities."

David nodded, but his eyes were fixated on my mouth.

"Should I be weirded out about that?" I asked.

He grunted.

"David, are you listening?"

"What? No. I'm still thinking about that bridesmaid dress," he admitted, tugging on my ankles. "Come here."

I scooted forward onto his lap. "Let's skip tonight," he said huskily.

"No way. It's your big event," I whispered. "I wouldn't miss it for the world. In fact, I should start getting ready."

He wrapped his arms around my lower back, pinning me to him. His lips came gently to mine, and he slid his tongue along my bottom lip. I opened instinctively for him, relishing how he felt in my mouth. Before I realized it, we were enmeshed in a quickly escalating kiss. I rocked against his hardness, groaning as our groins connected. He bent me back over his arm, and I let my head fall back.

"I want you," he said, kissing his way down my chest.

"You have me."

Slowly, he straightened me up and sighed. "Not yet. Tonight."

I climbed off the sofa and let him give me a tour of the apartment. In his bedroom, my evening gown in hand, he opened the French doors of his closet to reveal an expansive walk-in closet. I nearly jumped up and down at the sight. It'd been years since I'd had a closet that could fit more than the bare minimum.

But David looked nervous. I didn't understand why

until I stepped in further and saw that the entire left side was vacant.

"I couldn't sleep last night so . . ." David cleared his throat and nodded at the empty space. "This is your side."

I took the dress from him, walked over, and hung it on the empty bar. I spotted my shopping bags from earlier in the day neatly lined up underneath.

"Oh, David," I said, tears pricking my eyes. His long arms wrapped around me from behind. "Are we really doing this?" I asked. "Is this going to work?"

"It is, I promise. I promise you, Olivia, you are home."

A few tears fell, and I turned in his arms to face him. I reached up and felt his face, still in awe that I could touch him without feeling anything but . . .

I love you.

I wanted to tell him, to make him feel as adored and comforted as he'd made me feel these last couple days. To give him the same thrill I'd gotten when he'd confessed his love for me.

But the words caught in my throat.

Chapter Six

An enormous rock shower, big enough for several people, took up one corner of David's bathroom. It gave the space a spa-like vibe, elemental and unrefined with rough edges but extremely relaxing.

Knowing it would take me much longer than David to get ready for his hotel grand opening tonight, I wasted no time getting started.

While I showered, David would be working out. He'd informed me of that by pulling open the steamy glass door just as I'd stepped under the stream of water. His eyes had run over my naked body. I'd been not just comfortable but confident hours earlier in the dressing room, but suddenly, dripping wet, I'd felt exposed.

"Don't cover yourself," David had said, and I'd realized I'd crossed my arms over my breasts. "Let me enjoy the fact that you get better every time I see you."

I'd reddened at his compliment but had dropped my hands to my sides and let him look as water had soaked me.

"Jesus," he'd grumbled finally, adjusting his pants. "I'll be downstairs at the gym."

That had been more than an hour ago. Post-workout, it was David's turn to shower as I blow-dried my hair wearing the one thing David had thrown onto the pile of clothing during our shopping trip without having me model it first—a white silk robe that barely covered my ass.

Aside from the shower, David's bathroom also had a large, built-in bathtub wrapped in matching slate-colored rock. After I'd styled my hair, I sat on the edge of the tub and dialed Gretchen.

"Hello?" she answered.

"It's me," I said. "This is my new number."

"I was about to write you off as spam," she informed me before telling me to wait as she updated my contact card. When she returned on the line, I asked, "Did you speak to Lucy?"

"Yep," she said and hesitated.

"And?"

"And . . . I guess Bill is pretty fucked up. He doesn't know what to do with himself and keeps telling Andrew he knows you'll return once you realize your mistake."

My heart sank. It wasn't surprising—it'd only been a few days—but some small part of me had hoped once the shock had worn off, that Bill would start coming to terms with the reality that I was gone.

"Should I go see him?" I wondered aloud.

"Better let it be for now. At least until he cools off." Gretchen sighed. "Andrew said Bill's most pissed off that you gave the ring back since he thinks you're just getting this out of your system."

I nodded. "Yeah. That was the reason he punched the wall."

The shower stopped, and David appeared in my

peripheral vision, scrubbing his hair with one towel, another slung low on his hips. I couldn't resist letting my eyes wander over him, and he gave me a wolfish grin.

"*Gretchen*," I mouthed, pointing at the phone, and he nodded.

"I invited Andrew and Lucy to come tonight," Gretchen told me, "but they declined. I guess Bill is going over to their place to hang out."

"Well, I'm glad he has Andrew," I said, "even if it means I don't have Lucy right now."

Gretchen hummed her agreement. "Hey—Lucy said Bill told her you fainted?"

"Oh. Yeah," I said. "Did I not mention that?"

"No. You're not pregnant, are you?"

Please, God—no. The air left the room as my mouth hung open. The thought was too terrifying. Too permanent. I didn't want that. It hadn't even occurred to me that I might be pregnant. The odds were slim to none. I was still on birth control, and aside from a few nights earlier with David, neither he nor Bill had come inside me without a condom in several months.

"No, definitely not," I said. "It was pure anxiety."

"Let's hope so," she said. "Are you okay?"

"My elbows are a little bruised," I said, inspecting my arm. "But that's it."

I looked up because I sensed David glowering down at me. He took my arm in his hand and turned it over.

"I'll see you tonight," I said distractedly to Gretchen and hung up.

"You said he didn't touch you," David said.

"He didn't. I fainted."

"You *fainted*?" he repeated.

"Just for a second. I was nervous."

David frowned. "What if it's something serious? Could you be—"

"No, I'm not pregnant," I said. "I did the math. I simply didn't eat enough on Thursday, and I forgot to breathe," I said.

David and I stared at each other until I rose from the edge to fix my makeup.

"The diet or whatever you're doing stops here," he said. "I don't like the idea of you not eating."

"It's not a diet," I said irritably. "I don't eat when I'm depressed or nervous. Things should even out soon enough."

He eyed me skeptically but dropped the subject when his phone chimed with a text message. He picked it up from the bathroom counter and cursed.

"What?" I asked, sweeping powder over my nose.

"It's Maria."

I dropped the powder brush into my makeup bag and glared at his reflection. "*What?*" I repeated loudly.

His fingers flew over the screen as he typed. "I forgot to cancel on her tonight."

To *cancel?* But why would Maria even think they were going together in the first place if he'd ended things with her? "You're kidding, right?" I asked.

"I invited her ages ago, and with everything going on, I just forgot." David looked up, caught my expression in the mirror, and waved the screen in my direction. "Don't be upset. I'm telling her now."

"Telling her what?" I asked.

"That I don't need her to come."

I whirled from the counter and gaped at him. "You haven't broken things off with her?"

"There's nothing to really break off," he said as he typed. "I just call her when I need her."

Disgust roiled through me at the insinuation. "*Need* her?"

David slowly raised his eyes, as if realizing how that had sounded. At least he had the decency to look sheepish. "For, uh, events and stuff."

"Tell her that you will not be needing her for *anything, ever* again."

He set down his phone. "I will, Olivia. Trust me, this is a non-issue. I'll tell her next time——"

"Tell her *now*."

"I'm not saying that over a text message."

I was leaving my *husband* for David. How could he not have even thought to reach out to Maria yet? "You need to . . . to . . ." I blanched, turning back to the counter. "Why do I even have to tell you to do this?"

"Hey. I'm sorry," he said, coming up behind me and encircling my waist. "Maria and I have been friends for years, so I'd rather say something like that in person. But I'll call her tonight. She won't care. It's not like she was my girlfriend."

"Tonight?" I asked. "Promise?"

"Promise." He inhaled and with a moan, said, "God-damn, you smell amazing."

I studied his eyes in the reflection. They'd always told me the truth, and they conveyed nothing but sincerity now. I relaxed in his grip.

He picked up my eye shadow palette and examined the rainbow of nudes, pinks, and purples. "Why bother with this shit anyway? You look perfect right now. Just go to the party as you are."

"In my robe and no makeup?" I laughed. "I think I might get a few looks."

"Jealous looks. This robe was the best purchase of the day." He slid his palm over the front of it. His hands felt so fucking good on me, but I shook my head at him. He'd had his chance at sex earlier. Now that I was almost done getting ready, I wanted to wait until we got home.

Besides, each time we touched and reignited a spark, the harder it was to resist giving in to the burn. The tension building between us would make for an explosive first time as a couple.

"All right," he said, releasing me. "You can put on your dress—only so I can take it off later."

He stepped aside and pulled aftershave from a mirrored cabinet. The irresistible smell instantly transported me back to Lucy's office, to the first time David and I had kissed after I'd done up his bowtie.

When he'd left the bathroom, I finished applying my makeup, then slipped into my dress. I stepped back to study my reflection.

I hadn't realized how long my golden-brown hair had become. It now sat a few inches below my shoulders. I'd parted it off to the side and curled it into a soft wave. I turned to the side in a Versace column dress nearly the color of my skin—tight and long-sleeved, a slinky fabric that shimmered in the light. With a high back and a deep "V" that plunged down the front, I couldn't wear a bra, but my small breasts didn't need one. I opted for dark pink lipstick and rosy cheeks since I was otherwise colorless. Plum eye shadow and carefully applied mascara in *Noir* darkened my green eyes. Despite my four-inch heels, the dress still grazed the floor.

David entered the bathroom, one hand fumbling with his cufflink until he looked up and paused in the doorway. In the mirror, I watched his eyes skim over me, and his hands dropped to his sides. "You're beautiful," he said. "Give me a spin, gorgeous."

I smiled and turned against the counter. He whistled

low and came to me, pinning my hips against the counter and taking my face in his hands.

"A nude dress?" he whispered. "Do you want me walking around with a hard-on all night?"

"That's the idea," I said between breaths.

He ran one hand down my neck and spread it over my right breast. As he slowly closed it, he squeezed my nipple in the curve between his index and middle fingers. "Not sure how I feel about this," he said, as it hardened.

"You don't like what you see?" I asked.

He raised his eyes. "I don't like what *other men* see."

"What other men?" I asked. "You'll be the only man there as far as I'll know."

"*Mmm.*" He wet his lips. "As long as you and your perfect tits don't leave my sight."

I swallowed as arousal crested in me. "I don't plan to."

He brushed some hair from my face, and his forehead creased. "There will be photographers there tonight. They'll take your picture."

"I figured." I sighed. "I don't think I'm ready for that, David. It would be tasteless considering everything that's happening."

He frowned and brushed the pad of his thumb along the hollow of my cheek. "I was looking forward to showing you off."

"Showing *me* off? Maria's a hard act to follow."

David released me suddenly and stepped back, a frown firmly on his face. "Don't say that."

"I'm *teasing*," I said, half-rolling my eyes. "But, come on, David. Maria is like Gisele Bündchen 2.0 . . . she's stunning."

"Are you *kidding*?" Genuine shock crossed his face. "Olivia, you are the most beautiful woman I've ever laid eyes on. After everything we've been through, you must know that. Don't you?"

My tummy fluttered with butterflies. Though I appreciated his conviction, objectively, I couldn't compare to a supermodel. "You're sweet," I said with a shy smile.

He took my shoulders and turned me to the mirror. Wrapping his arms around my waist, he kissed the top of my head. His fingers trailed my neck as he pulled my hair into a loose ponytail. "Nobody even compares. I'm not blind. I know Maria is beautiful, but she's nowhere near you, honeybee." His hands complemented his words as he slid them down and over my backside, inspiring a burning need within me. "I had to know you the moment I saw you. That's never happened to me. Any man would be lucky to have you, Olivia."

I stared at his reflection. "I only care that you want me."

"I want you, all of you, any way I can have you," he murmured, kissing my neck. "And any*where*."

Words failed me. David's model good looks—his sharp, defined features, jet-black hair, and heavy, serious eyebrows —put him in another league. The cleft of his chin and the fullness of his bottom lip softened an otherwise razorblade jawline. He could've been a movie star, and he was telling *me* I was beautiful? I searched his chestnut-brown eyes, finding only honesty.

"Now, tie me up, would you?" he asked.

With my quizzical look, he raised his chin in the air to expose an undone bowtie.

I turned, fixed him up, and patted his chest once he was ready.

He grabbed my wrists and kissed one of my palms. "One of the best and worst nights of my life," he murmured, resting his forehead against mine.

"Tonight?" I asked, alarmed.

"No—the night of the bowtie. You don't know how badly I wanted you while I was also scared to death of driving you away."

I melted into him as I remembered how I'd done up his bowtie right before an electric, sinful, and terrifying first kiss—after which I'd immediately had to face my husband.

"I love knowing that my bowtie is the only one you'll be tying from now on," he said.

I loved knowing that, too, and I showed him with a kiss to rival our very first one.

David and I fought again in the car. He insisted on sneaking us through the back entrance, but I ordered him to walk the red carpet and receive the praise he deserved for his work—even if I couldn't allow myself to stand by his side. He'd been grumbling when I'd slipped onto the sidewalk a few car lengths before we were due to hit the entrance and its mess of photographers.

Since Gretchen hadn't arrived, and I didn't know anybody at the party, I checked my coat and headed straight for a temporary bar that'd been set up in the lobby, then ordered drinks for David and me.

While I waited, I pulled out my new phone and checked my e-mail.

From: Bill Wilson
Sent: Sat, November 10 05:48 PM CST
To: Olivia Germaine
Subject: Hey

Tomorrow will be hard. I guess I feel like Sunday's our day. *Was* our day. This has been a lot to process. I still feel a little like I'm in a nightmare. Andrew caught me up on some details. I'm worried about you & don't trust this David guy AT ALL. He has no relationship history to speak of according to Andrew but many many flings. I worry he thinks this is some sort of game?

I get that we have things to work on, Liv. I feel like I've been a good husband, but I'm willing to listen to whatever it is you think went wrong. You've always been hard to get through to, though, so I hope you realize this will take two.

You know how I feel about therapy, but I'll do it for us. Forget this guy, Liv. He's a womanizer. Come home so we can work this out. It'll take time, but I know I can forgive everything one day.

Love, Bill

Jesus. I'd wanted Bill to put aside his anger and face reality, but although he seemed to be coming at things from a calmer perspective, he still couldn't wrap his head around the fact that we were through.

I thanked the bartender for two tumblers of scotch—a

rich and flavorful ode to David's and my first meeting—and took a long sip of mine.

Did Bill's words have merit? The logical, sensible person I'd been throughout our entire marriage said yes. I could see Bill's point. Looking in from the outside, my relationship with David had all kinds of red flags. But I was trying to break free of that mold and learn to find—and trust in—my instinct again.

Bill couldn't possibly understand any of that, so I couldn't let his possibly valid points get under my skin.

I looked into my nearly empty scotch glass. I was a nervous drinker, and Bill's e-mail had definitely put me on edge. After a beat, I finished it off and started in on David's. He'd probably have mingling to do anyway, and I wasn't sure when he'd get around to finding me.

"Thirsty much?" asked a familiar male voice.

I turned and smiled. "Mr. Brian Ayers."

My new friend always looked handsome, and tonight was no exception. Brian wore a trim, deep purple velour tuxedo, a silver button-down shirt, and a matching striped bowtie. I couldn't help but smile at his quirky style. As if it wasn't Brian enough, he'd topped off his outfit with pristine white tennis shoes.

"How are you?" he asked, leaning in to kiss my cheek.

"No date tonight?"

"Nah."

I raised my eyebrows at him. "And why not?"

He shrugged. "Not feeling anyone lately," he explained. Brian's blue eyes and long blond hair were even brighter against his tan. It didn't take a genius to know by his looks or the muscular arms hiding under his blazer that most girls would find him a catch. So why was he still single?

Since Brian and David were friends, I wondered if he knew about us yet. If he did, he didn't give anything away.

As I considered mentioning it, Gretchen and Greg walk into the event, heading to the bar before they even spotted us.

When Gretchen saw me, she practically ran over. "Hello," she called, then tossed over her shoulder, "Greg, honey. Get me a drink?"

Gretchen sent him off with a kissy sound.

"Nice to have someone to order around, eh?" Brian asked her.

She glanced at Brian, and her face soured. "Oh. Didn't see you there. Can you excuse us?"

"Certainly," he said, rolling his eyes once she'd turned her back. The two weren't particularly friendly—something to do with Brian turning down Gretchen's advances —but it surprised me that they still weren't over it.

"How's it going so far?" Gretchen whispered once she had me alone.

Despite having Bill's e-mail fresh in my thoughts, I easily refocused on my dreamy day with David. "Sort of amazing," I gushed with a big smile.

"You *look* fucking amazing. You're *glowing* in this dress. Tell me everything."

"You might flip out," I warned.

"Tell me."

"Well," I said, "after breakfast, David took me shopping. And basically bought me an entire boutique's worth of stuff."

"Shut *up*," she said, nearly jumping up and down. Her eyes scanned my dress. "Who?"

"Versace," I said, waving a hand over myself. "But there was Prada, Chloé, McQueen—just come over, and I'll show you everything."

She made a noise from the back of her throat and closed one eye as if to brace herself. "Shoes, too?"

"Yep."

"Please tell me the sex wasn't as good as you remember so I'm not raging jealous."

"We haven't done it yet as a 'couple.' He wants to wait until we get back tonight so it's special or something."

"Oh, God," Gretchen said as her eyes rolled up into her head. "He's perfect."

"What's that?" Greg asked, handing her a drink.

"You," Gretchen said, pecking him on the lips. "You're perfect, sweetie."

"Where's David?" Greg asked.

"We came in separately because of the photographers," I explained. "I'm sure he's circulating the party."

"Speaking of which," Gretchen said, rising onto the balls of her feet and waving at a woman I presumed to be a colleague from her PR firm, "I'm going to check in with work."

Once she'd left us alone, Greg rubbed my back. "How're you holding up? Gretchen told me everything."

"All things considered, I could be a lot worse," I said. "How about you? Work it all out with Gretchen?"

"Hope so, Livvy. I told her that once we're more settled, I want us to get a place together."

I raised my eyebrows. I couldn't imagine Gretchen wanting to move that quickly—or Greg, either, for that matter. I'd hardly gotten to know the person he was now, but the guy I'd been close with back in college had clearly been easily scared off by commitment.

"How does that make you feel?" I asked cautiously.

He exhaled forcefully. "Great."

"It's okay to be nervous about that, Greg."

He winked. "I'm not."

"All right, just don't make promises you can't keep," I warned.

"Greg." David's deep voice came from behind me just as his arm rested across my shoulders. He stuck out his other hand to shake Greg's hand.

"Hey, man," Greg said, grinning. "Welcome to the family."

David also grinned, but it was directed down at me. "Right," he said. He slid a hand along the nape of my neck, lifted my hair, and let it fall onto my back. "I missed you out there. Next time I want you by my side."

His hand in my hair and against my skin felt so nice, so reassuring, that I closed my eyes and nodded. "Next time, yes."

He whispered his next words near my ear. "You have any idea how incredible you look in that dress? Every man in here is drooling over you."

I opened my eyes and smiled slyly. "They are not."

"They are. And I don't love it, but it'll be fine as long as they keep their distance."

I gave him a teasing smile, but he didn't seem to think it was funny. Greg disappeared. David continued playing with my hair, murmuring about how good I looked, until a client from his New York project interrupted us. David kept me close with an arm around my shoulders as they chatted.

I looked around for Gretchen or Greg. When I didn't see either of them, I turned my attention back and joined the conversation David was now having with multiple people. The wives in the group couldn't tear their eyes from him, but neither could I. As he relayed details about the development of the hotel, most of which flew over my head, I admired his easy confidence. It took a great deal of effort not to stop him for an impromptu make-out session, or at least press a kiss to his square jaw, the only place I could reach without him bending to meet me.

While we made our way around the party, I was no longer walking by his side; I was floating. He never lost contact with me, either holding my hand, my shoulders, or touching my hair. When women inevitably flirted with him, I linked my arm around his waist, and he answered by squeezing me closer.

As one woman ignored her husband to gush about the hotel, I decided I couldn't take any more flirting without a stronger drink. I tried to tug my hand out of his, and he looked down at me immediately. "What, baby?"

I glanced at the woman apologetically, because she'd had to pause mid-sentence. "I'm just going to refresh our drinks," I told him. "Excuse me."

"Wait," David said, dragging me back by my hand.

"What?"

He wrapped his arm around my waist and drew me close for a kiss. Embarrassed by the display, I tried to pull away, but he tightened his grip. "Don't be long," he murmured before releasing me.

I crossed the lobby completely flushed and on cloud nine. Since a mass of people crowded around the makeshift bar, I opted for the dark and sexy lounge instead, where David and I had gotten drinks during Revelin's soft opening.

I set down my purse and had just put in my drink order when I turned and saw a man coming toward me. Even in the dim lighting, I recognized his gait, as familiar to me as anything. A fuming, disheveled-looking Bill marched in my direction.

Chapter Seven

I was imagining things. I *had* to be. Except that I wasn't. Bill was disheveled. He was fuming. And he was marching in my direction, as real as the ground under my high heels.

"What are you doing here?" I asked as he approached.

"Are you trying to make me look like an idiot?" he accused.

"What—"

On his last stride, he thrust a finger in my face, and I stumbled backward. "How dare you ask me to buy you that house when you *knew* that son of a bitch was going to make an offer?"

My heart dropped to my feet. He'd found out that David had made an offer on the Oak Park house. But how? It didn't matter. Any way he'd heard would be a shitty way, especially because it hadn't come from me. "I know how this looks," I said, trying to keep my voice calm, "but I had no idea David planned to buy it."

"Bull*shit*. I've tried to be patient, but this is too far." He gritted his teeth. "Did you guys meet there to screw or what?"

I covered my mouth at the horrible accusation. David and I *had* made plenty of mistakes, but none of it had been premeditated or intended to hurt. "*No*," I said, choking back a sob, but the look in Bill's eyes told me he wouldn't believe anything I said.

"Playtime is over, Olivia. I tried making this easy. I tried giving you space. Now we're doing this my way." Bill seized my arm and dragged me out of the lounge.

I tried to wrench my arm away, but he held it in an iron grip. "Let go," I said.

As we crossed the lobby, conversations stalled when people began to look at us.

"Olivia!" Gretchen called from somewhere behind me.

"Bill, stop," I said, trying to stop but handicapped by my high stilettos. "My purse—"

"We'll get it later. You're coming home with me right now," Bill said, "and we're going to forget this ridiculous shit ever happened."

"Bill, calm down, and let go of me," I implored. "*Please*."

He halted abruptly and whirled to face me. "Why?" he asked. "Afraid I'll make a scene at your little party?"

I stared at a face as familiar to me as anything, but I barely recognized Bill through his ugly sneer.

Over my shoulder, Bill barked at a partygoer, "What the fuck are you looking at?"

"I know you're angry," I said to him, "but this isn't you. Please, you're hurting me."

His grip loosened. "Why'd he buy that house?"

My throat dried. I didn't know how to explain it like this, with people staring, with Bill only able to hear what he wanted to believe. "I—I don't . . ."

"Jesus," Bill said, drawing back to look me over. "Did

he buy you this dress, too? Is that what you want, to be treated like a spoiled brat? You're looking for someone like Daddy?"

"Why are you doing this?" I asked through a haze of tears.

"*You're* the one doing this." He gripped my arm again and yanked me forward. "And I had to hear it from our goddamn realtor—"

"Liv!" Gretchen screamed behind me.

"Stay out of this, you nosy bitch," Bill called over his shoulder just as Brian Ayers hopped into our path.

"Hey, now. You don't speak to a lady like that," he said as Gretchen caught up. Brian's eyes shot to my elbow. "Olivia, who's this?"

"I'm her husband," Bill said. "Who the hell are you?"

"Just let go, man," Brian said, pursing his lips, "and we can have a rational discussion about this."

"Great," Bill said, twisting to look at me. "Are you doing this guy, too?"

"I beg your pardon," Brian said, grabbing Bill's arm. "I said fucking let go." Bill tried to shrug him off, but Brian pried his hand away just as heavy, determined footsteps bore down on us from behind.

"What the fuck?" I heard David ask. As soon as the question was out of his mouth, he'd shoved Bill out of the way before positioning himself between us. "Don't fucking touch her."

"*You*," Bill snarled at him. "Don't tell me that I can't touch *my* wife."

"She's not yours anymore," David said.

"Oh, yeah?" Bill strode up to him. "And what happens when you get tired of her? Then she'll just be a washed-up divorcée nobody wants."

"Bill, please—I know you don't mean that," I said, trying to get between them, worried someone would go too far.

"Get back," David said softly and ushered me behind him with obvious restraint.

"You're just a phase," Bill said to David, "and that phase is over. Move. I'm taking her home."

"Just try me," David said evenly.

"You think you're a real big shot, don't you?" Bill asked. "You bought her a *house* so you could get in her pants? Do you think she's some sort of whore?"

David lunged forward and grabbed Bill by the shirt. "Watch your mouth, motherfucker. All I need is an excuse to level you," he said.

It wouldn't be a fair match, and I'd never known Bill to get in a physical fight. I didn't want to find out how that would go. "David, let go of him," I said, and David pushed Bill off.

"Come home with me, Liv," Bill said, unruffled. "Let's fix this. He can't make you happy." His tone softened. "You know he can't."

David's body tensed, and I refrained from touching his back to show comfort. "I'm sorry, Bill," I said. "But leave David out of this. It's not his fault."

"Not his *fault*?" Bill's breathing deepened, and his lips curled back as he looked at David with disgust. "Does he have you brainwashed?"

My eyes jumped between them as they stared each other down. I tried a few tentative steps forward, but David's arm shot out to catch my shoulder. I walked as far forward as he'd let me. "We can talk next week once everyone has had a chance to cool down," I said to Bill. "I'll explain everything about the house."

"Come home now, Olivia." Bill's eyes pleaded with me. "I'm not messing around."

I bit the inside of my cheek as David's hand tightened on my shoulder. It tugged at my heart to say the words, but I knew David needed to hear them just as much as Bill. "I'm sorry, but that's not my home anymore."

Bill's eyes locked on David behind me. "You son of a bitch," Bill said, his voice cracking. "You stole my wife. You *stole* my wife!" He lunged past me to throw his palms into David's rigid body. I jumped back, tripped over my dress, and grasped at air as I fell.

David whirled to catch me as Bill raised his fist.

"Watch out," I screamed as Bill landed a punch in David's side.

David threw up his arm to block Bill's next blow, then threw a right hook into Bill's nose. With great effort, Bill pummeled him to the ground, where David flipped him over and gained the upper hand within moments.

David jumped up and pulled Bill's torso off the ground by his shirt. "Stay away from her," he said with a hard shake. "This is your only warning."

"Yeah, you can have her, the trashy slut," Bill responded, grimacing when he sniffed. Blood streamed from his nose as he looked over to where I still lay on the ground, too shocked to move. "On your back where you belong."

"Get up," David said, his face darkening.

"David, don't." He looked beyond control, and I was terrified of what he might do. "He doesn't mean it."

David ignored me as he hauled Bill to his feet. "I should fucking destroy you for that comment."

Bill flinched as David drew back his fist and went to hit him but stopped short. "Ever speak to her like that again, and I will. And if you *ever* touch her like that again, you're good as dead, motherfucker." David released him with a forceful push. Bill launched himself toward us, but Brian and Greg pushed between both of them. Greg held Bill back a few feet, restraining him while he cursed at us.

Gretchen squatted and extended her hand to me, but not before David swooped down to help me onto my feet.

Bill wiped blood from his nose. "I'm done with this shit, Olivia," he said. I felt the need to run and comfort him, but David's powerful hands grasped my shoulders. "Divorce is on, and you aren't getting shit, do you hear me? Screw you. *All* of you."

He turned and stalked off, leaving the five of us to look after him.

"Oh my God," I stammered. I turned in David's arms and touched his face and then his side lightly. "Are you okay?"

When I looked up, I stopped as his eyes turned black with rage. "You are never—I mean *never*—allowed to be alone with him," he said. "Am I clear?"

"He has a right to be upset, but he let his temper get the best of him," I said. "As did you."

"*Am I clear?*" David boomed into the quiet lobby. I shivered, acutely aware that everyone's eyes were on us. He stared at me. I stared back. He couldn't keep me from seeing my own husband. But after a moment, I gave in and nodded. We'd discuss this later, when we could have a rational conversation away from here.

"What happened?" David demanded, looking between all of our startled faces. "What happened before I got here?"

"I don't know, man," Brian said. "I ran over here when I saw him dragging Olivia away, and he was calling Gretchen names."

David's gaze whipped back to me. My entire body flinched when he reached for me. "I'm not going to hurt you," he said incredulously.

"I know." I offered my arm. "I'm sorry. I'm just shaken up."

"Does it hurt?" he asked, touching my elbow.

It smarted a bit from being gripped and twisted, but it was nothing compared to what David had been through. "I'm fine," I said, my hand hovering where Bill's punch had landed. "I'm more worried about you."

"Don't be," he said, grasping my face in his hands. "I'm so sorry. That must have been hard to watch, but he had it coming."

I shifted in my heels and held David's gaze. "I know you want him to be the bad guy, but he's not. He's going through a lot, too."

"There's no excuse for coming at you like that."

"Are you okay, really?" I asked.

He leaned in and pecked me on the lips, then rested his forehead on mine and sighed.

"David?" I asked. "Are you hurt? What about your hand?"

"It's good."

"What if you broke something? Should we get an x-ray?"

"No," he said with a small smile. "I know how to properly throw a punch."

"*Ahem*. Um . . ." Brian tapped David on the shoulder. "Excuse me?"

David pulled back and looked me in the eye. "Next time come get me. Scream at the top of your lungs if you have to," he whispered. "Don't try to do this on your own."

"Can someone please inform me what the devil is going on?" Brian asked.

We all looked at his confused expression.

"Oh, God, you are so out of it," Gretchen said.

Brian frowned. "You're welcome for sticking up for you, princess. I didn't exactly see your boyfriend helping out."

"I was in the bathroom," Greg said defensively.

"Jesus Christ," David muttered, looking over at Greg and Brian. "What would've happened if I hadn't been there?"

"I would have defended her honor," Brian said, puffing up.

There was a moment of crackling silence before everyone except David burst into laughter.

"What?" Brian asked.

"You're such a kook," Gretchen said.

David stroked my hair. "*Now* can we go home?"

"I'm sorry, home?" Brian interrupted, leaning between us. "Am I to understand that you two are . . .?"

"Dude," David said. "Yes, *we are*. Get lost."

"I didn't realize you were looking, Olivia," Brian said. "I would've thrown my name in the pot." I laughed, but with David's menacing snarl, Brian covered his nose. "Don't punch me out," he said. "I'm only ribbing you, Dylan. Anyone with two eyes could see you've been smitten with her for a long time."

Sneaky Brian. He'd known all along? No wonder he'd teased David months ago at the Meet and Greet when he'd tried shooing him away to meet one of the female attendees.

Brian sighed loftily and kissed me on the cheek as David fumed. "I'll leave you to it then. Good evening," he said as he pivoted and walked away.

As my adrenaline wore off, and reality sank in, I

grimaced. "I'm so embarrassed," I said. "I ruined your night—and in front of all your colleagues."

"I could give two shits right now. I just want to take you home," he purred into my ear, and I shuddered at his breath on my neck.

I needed no more convincing than that. "We have to go," I announced to Gretchen and Greg.

Gretchen knowingly rolled her eyes and handed me my purse. "I thought you might need this."

"Thank you," I said, clutching the handbag to my breast. "I mean it."

"Yeah, yeah, we'll talk later. *Bye*," she sang and turned to Greg. "Come on. Let's get another drink."

"Or we could go home and do what they're going to do," he suggested, glancing back at us. I laughed as they walked off.

David already had his phone to his ear. "We're ready to leave," he said into it. "Bring the car, and make it quick." He hung up and tucked his phone into his tuxedo jacket. "Brian's such an asshole."

"He's only picking on you because you react," I said.

"I react because he's a good guy, and that makes him a worthy opponent."

"Opponent?" I asked.

David took my hand and walked us to the coat check. "Every man is an opponent for your attention, but very few of them are worthy."

"I'm not a gold medal, you know."

"Oh, but you are, my gilded honeybee," he said gruffly, taking my coat from the attendant and helping me into it.

Once bundled up, he led me to the front of the hotel. As we stopped at the curb to wait, his eyes softened. "Are you sure you're all right? You fell hard."

"Nothing is that bad as long as you're here," I said honestly.

He wrapped me close to his side and kissed my temple. "I feel the same."

"I really am sorry to have embarrassed you," I said.

"Don't say that again," David said. "It wasn't your fault."

"Bill's just . . . he's mad about the house." I scratched under my nose. "I knew it would hurt his feelings. I was too chicken shit to tell him sooner."

"Thank fuck you didn't, if that's how he was going to react."

"I'm sorry," I said a last time.

He glanced down at me. "I'm thanking my lucky stars every time I'm with you, even if it's messy."

"Yes," I murmured to myself. "And it's going to get very messy."

"Anything else you want to tell me?" he asked.

Remembering our honesty pact, I pulled up Bill's earlier e-mail on my phone and handed it to David. As we waited for the car, he read the screen, still holding me close with his other hand. His grip tightened on my shoulder, and he gave the phone back to me. "I'm a *womanizer*?" David grumbled. "Bill doesn't believe it's over between you and him—at least, he didn't when he wrote this. Do I need to worry about that?"

"No. Let it go," I said. "I just want to forget all of this for a little bit."

"For now," he agreed.

A black town car arrived, and we walked to meet it. David opened the door and motioned for me to get in. He folded his large frame in after me, and the driver pulled away from the curb.

"Come here," David said.

With the heater on, I slipped off my coat and scooted to his side of the car.

"Closer," he said in a lowered voice. I inched toward him until our legs touched. "Closer."

"I'll be on your lap."

"You read my mind."

He urged me up, and I sat across him, hugging his neck, my thighs on his. He sighed into my hair. "Did I tell you how amazing you look in this dress?"

I smiled to myself. "Yes."

"Did I tell you that all night, I couldn't stop thinking about the look on your face in the dressing room earlier? You, coming all over my fingers . . ."

I moaned softly and writhed in his lap. One hand dug into my hip as the other slipped inside the deep "V" neckline of my dress to grasp my breast. My mouth parted with a sharp inhale when he pinched my nipple between his fingers.

"I can't believe I get you all to myself tonight," he said, his thumb and index finger tightening around the small bud. His voice sank into a low, gritty rumble. "Finally, nowhere for you to run."

"I won't run," I uttered, arousal whirring through me and clouding my thoughts. I bent my head to speak in his ear. "I'm all yours, all night."

His answering groan echoed through the car. Embarrassed that the driver had probably heard, I giggled softly and buried my nose into the crook of David's neck.

"Sorry," he whispered. "Can't help it." He released my nipple but his big hand slid up and ran leisurely over my collarbone.

"What are your plans tomorrow?" I asked.

"My plans are your plans, baby. Reminds me, though. How often do you walk the dogs from the animal shelter?"

"Oh. Twice a month or so," I said. "I know it's not very much. I used to be more involved."

"You're incredible, you know that?" he asked. "I love you a little more every minute. But this minute is a big one."

My breath caught. Nobody had ever said anything like that to me. David's love was new, but I had a feeling it'd existed in secret for a while. I needed to tell him I felt the same, but at the thought of laying so much on the line, my heart seized up.

"Did Bill ever go with you?" David asked, completely unaware of the battle within me.

"Ah . . ." I cleared my throat and ushered away the scary thoughts. "He came with me a few times over the years. You know how it is because you work as much as Bill does—if he wasn't swamped with paperwork on the weekends, he just wanted to relax."

"Sure. Tomorrow's supposed to be warm," David said, brushing hair from my face. "My family is barbequing again. We could pick up a couple dogs and go see them. If you're not ready for that, we can just walk the dogs."

"Really?" I asked with surprise. "Are you sure?"

"Sure? I can't think of anything better to do on a Sunday. Well, that's not true—but we'll have the whole day to fill."

In the dark, I searched his eyes with mine. The shelter, his family, taking a day off when I suspected he had work —it was so thoughtful. "This minute is a big one," I echoed his words from earlier. For now, that would have to be my way of saying I loved him, too.

I pecked him quickly on the lips, but he held me to him, melding our mouths into a heated kiss. His hands roamed over my dress, lingering on the curves of my breasts. He traced a fingertip along the deep neckline of my dress but didn't go further than that. I moved closer to him, and he broke away, inhaling sharply as if in pain.

"What?" I asked softly. "What's wrong?"

"Nothing," he said, and I realized the car had stopped. "Come on. We're here."

As we traversed the hotel lobby, passing by others dressed up for a Saturday night, David asked, "So do all these people in your new home bother you?"

I laughed. It was the first question I'd asked him about living in a hotel. I snaked my arm around his waist, turned on by the fact that he already considered his home mine, too. "That's yet to be determined."

He grinned and at the elevator bank, punched the *Up* button.

"What a beautiful couple," an elderly woman said as she boarded behind us.

"Thank you," I said. "My architect boyfriend here designed a gorgeous hotel on the Riverfront, and tonight was the grand opening."

"That's quite an accomplishment," she said. "Congratulations."

David's eyes crinkled with his smile. "Thanks."

"Oh, my. You shouldn't smile like that at a woman my age," she said, fanning herself with exaggeration. We laughed and bid her goodnight as she exited the elevator.

"I might have to keep you on a tighter leash," I teased.

His smiled faded. "I think I should like it if you did," he said, his eyes narrowing. As the elevator ascended, his body seemed to grow bigger, his bearing predatory, as if I were cornered prey, and he was about to strike. "Go on," he said.

"Go on?" I repeated breathlessly.

After a charged moment, he nodded at the elevator's

open doors. I hadn't even noticed our arrival at the penthouse. "We're late for a very important date," he said.

"And what date is that?" I asked as we stepped off.

"You, me, and literally nothing else. Leave everything else here." He unlocked the door and held it open so I could pass through before him. As I did, though, he snatched my elbow. "I said *everything*."

Over my shoulder, my gaze met his brown eyes, dark and lusty. With only one thing on my mind, I dropped my coat and purse on the ground.

He let the door slam to merge his body against my backside, gripping my shoulders roughly in his hands. "I've been crazy for you all day," he rasped in my ear. "And although I love this dress, I want it off. Now." He dragged the zipper down and dropped to his knees. I gasped when his lips touched the base of my spine. His hands skated up my exposed back and slid over my shoulders, releasing the dress so it slumped at my feet. He reached around to my front and spread his fingers across my stomach. His moan vibrated against the small of my back, sending a shiver up my spine.

He stood and wrapped an arm around my chest, his hardness pressing against my back. His other hand dropped to pull open my inner thigh and touch me through my underwear. Panting, I swayed when he released me suddenly. "*Christ*," he muttered. "Two steps in the door, and I'm a goner. I really can't control myself around you."

Through oversized windows, the city lent the only light to the room as he circled around to stop in front of me. I put my hand in his and stepped out of the dress, following as he led me down the stairs into the sunken living room.

"Leave those on," he instructed, motioning to my black stilettos. He removed his blazer and turned on the fireplace as my lingerie-clad body, alive with desire, wavered unsteadily in the four-inch heels. "Don't move," David said. "I want to memorize everything about this moment." He emptied his pockets onto a side table and unclasped his Rolex. He leisurely undid his bowtie next while his hooded eyes remained fixed on me. His limbs, strong and brawny, moved fluidly as he shed clothing. I wanted to learn the contours of his body with my eyes, my fingers, my tongue. And when he looked at me that way, like it was the first time, I could barely help from melting at his feet.

He sauntered over and grasped me to him by my lower back. His hand spread there as his lips captured mine in a rough kiss. I drew him into me with my arms around his neck, wanting him closer, deeper, our bodies merging the way our mouths were. His hands explored my skin—impatient and tender all at once, as though he'd studied every inch of me but was only just now touching me.

He guided me backward until I hit the couch and sat. I didn't remove my eyes from him as he stepped out of his underwear. I licked my lips—he was big. Thick. Hard. So hard that I believed him when he'd said he'd been that way since the dressing room. As I'd done in the past, I squirmed at just the sight of him, suddenly unable to think of anything but how he'd feel inside of me.

With his big body, David crawled over me, and I eased lengthwise onto my back. "My patience is gone," he said, his eyes fixed on mine. "I can't decide whether to devour you quickly or slowly."

"We have all night," I whispered.

"All night," he repeated with a nod. "I'm going to kiss you everywhere. Here," he ran his thumb across my bottom lip, "and here," he added, touching a fingertip over my heart. His hand moved between my legs as his voice deepened. "Here."

My pulse quickened, anticipating his mouth on me. He gave me his weight as his hands steadied my face. His kiss started as a breath, a promise of what was to come, but it quickly became harder as we crossed from want to need.

He pulled away to rain kisses down my neck, over my chest, breasts, and stomach. He kneeled to kiss me through my panties, and I sighed. His hands ran up my thighs and spread me open. I fisted the leather couch while he kissed me through the sheer fabric of my underwear.

"David," I groaned.

"I love it when you say my name," he responded through gritted teeth.

"David," I repeated. He yanked my panties aside and licked the length of me. "Oh, David," I said again. Holding me wide open, he inserted his tongue and ate me like a man starving. He'd gone down on me before, but not like this. I bucked into the couch, throwing my head back and moaning as he fucked me with his tongue. He thrust his fingers inside, withdrawing every few seconds to rub my wetness over me. When I was burning with a need for release, and so close to grasping it, he spoke against me.

"Ready for me?" he rumbled, even though I clearly was.

"Yes," I cried.

"Tell me."

"I'm so wet for you, David," I said, writhing as his fingers worked inside of me. "Stop. Please. I'm going to come."

"Why should I stop?" he taunted.

"Because I want you to fuck me."

He chuckled. "You love getting fucked, don't you?"

"Yes," I breathed. "Only by you."

He withdrew in an instant and dragged my panties off.

"I'll fuck you, and you'll come on my cock like you want, baby. Grab your heels."

I grabbed the spiky stilettos in both hands and spread my legs. His massive body moved over mine. He propped himself up with one arm and took his shaft in his other hand to rub his crown through my wetness.

"I've missed you," I cried, the words falling passionately from my mouth. "Please."

He drove into me, forcing the breath from my lungs. "I missed you, too," he said, looking down between us. His jaw clenched as he withdrew slowly. His hands on both sides of my body gripped the couch as I whimpered, pulling on my shoes.

"Christ, Olivia." He rolled his hips again, leisurely this time, until he was rooted deeply inside me. "Tell me how it feels."

"Heaven," I breathed, jutting my hips upward. "More."

He grunted, and my body shook with the next plunge.

"Harder," I demanded. "Give it to me, David."

He reared back and drove into me again and again, giving it to me the way I'd asked for—hard, without mercy.

"God, you can fuck me," I cried. "Just you, baby, you know how to fuck me and—" I gasped as his one hand moved to my clit and began to move in small circles.

He leaned closer without slowing his rhythm so our faces were almost touching. "And?"

"You're the only one who's ever made me come."

He growled. "The *only* one," he repeated. "And the only one who ever will."

"Yes," I cried. "Just you. Please," I begged. "Don't stop."

"Hold on to those fucking heels." He gave me a hard

thrust and pinned me to the couch, harnessing our sexual tension and driving into me until I vibrated with it.

My insides tightened and coiled into a pulsating knot of pressure. I clenched my teeth and yelped when a heel broke off in my hand.

He exhaled heavily and, without disconnecting, picked me up in one quick motion. I kicked off my shoes as he tossed a few pillows on the floor by the fire. He sat carefully with me in his lap and lay back so I was astride him.

I settled my knees on either side of him and lifted up to sink down slowly. "Oh, my, God," I said, closing my eyes. I drew up and released myself onto him again, this time all the way. I began to rock over him, moaning as we aligned. I blindly gripped his shoulders as if I'd fall into oblivion if I let go. He broke my rocking motion by thrusting up to meet me, taking over, even from underneath, bouncing me forward with each surge of his hips.

The room filled with the sinuous sounds of our satisfaction. His hands found my hips and maneuvered me against his steel cock harder, forcing me to bear down on him until I couldn't contain my cries. He braced me as he hit me as deep as he could, my fingers digging deeper into his skin as I whimpered.

"You can take it," he grated.

A high-pitched noise escaped me as he pushed me to the brink and then drove into me even harder.

"Lean back, all the way," he instructed as his hands captured mine. I obeyed, gasping at the new angle. My back arched, and my head fell back as he gripped my wrists, using them as a lever to buck into me. My orgasm was completely in his control, just as he wanted, just as I wanted, and when he decided it was time, he hit the spot.

"I can feel you coming," he said. "Break for me, baby."

"Oh, David, *yes*," I cried up to the ceiling as my blood simmered throughout me.

Stars pierced my vision as he grabbed the base of my neck. His visceral cry sent me flying, my orgasm exploding just from the sound of his pleasure. I grabbed his hand at my neck, and my other hand clamped on his shoulder to ride him through the bliss.

I dropped my gaze to watch as he gave me one grueling last thrust and came apart under me, groaning while his fingers bit into my skin. I fell forward and clutched him as he gushed inside of me, his grip tight until he'd finished.

I lay on his chest, quivering against him, the left side of my body burning from the suddenly hot fire. His hands found their way over my back and up to my hair, clasping me close. "I love you," he whispered into my hair. His coarse and perfect palms spanned back and forth over my hypersensitive skin.

"That feels amazing," I said with a soft moan.

He kissed the side of my head. When I slid off his wet cock, I was once again devoid of the other half of my puzzle.

"Where are you going?" he asked, reaching out to hold me in place.

"Bathroom. Architect's orders."

He laughed lazily at his own rule of peeing after sex, as though he lacked the energy for anything more. He let me go and said, "Use the guest room, it's closer."

I couldn't help but grin giddily as I passed through the room. I remembered our chaste night after my encounter with Mark Alvarez and how badly I'd wanted David to touch me through the t-shirt he'd given me.

As I fixed my hair, I froze when voices floated in from the other room. I grabbed a towel from a linen cabinet, tucked it under my arms to secure it, and snuck out into the hallway. Peering around the corner, I almost dropped the towel at what I saw.

Looking as stunning as she did every time I'd been in her presence, David's *supposed* ex stood in the doorway. What the *hell* was Maria doing here?

Chapter Eight

Dressed in a body-skimming black dress that displayed ample cleavage and dark, muscular legs, Maria oozed sexuality from where she stood on the doorstep of David's apartment.

She batted her lashes up at him as he towered in the doorway. "But, *Dah-veed*," she was saying, drawing out his name in her buttery Latin accent, "I've been here for *years*, waiting. I don't deserve this. I deserve a real chance."

I clutched my towel closed, trying to catch up with the conversation as Maria scanned his naked torso and boxer briefs. Jealousy reared in me as her eyes landed on his bare feet, which somehow felt more intimate.

David leaned on the doorjamb. "Come on, Maria," he said. "You know what we are."

She arched an eyebrow. "After three years you feel absolutely *nothing*? You cannot turn it off just like that," she said and snapped her fingers.

"Don't play games," he said. "Things have always been casual."

"Not casual, David. I'm not clingy like the other girls,

but I'm here when you need me, when you don't want them anymore." She flattened a hand on his chest. "But now, you dump me like nothing? I've put in the time, *cariño*. I deserve more."

A flush made its way up my neck. She touched him freely and called him *darling*—and she'd been doing those things for *three years*? That was more than half the time I'd been married.

David calmly removed her palm from him his chest. Instead of letting go, he held her hand in his and covered the back of it with his other. "Maria, I love you, but—"

"Then let me make you happy." She bit her lip. "I want a ring."

I inhaled sharply. *A ring? Love?*

There was nothing "casual" about any of this. Either David had lied or he'd downplayed their relationship. I had reason to question him after the way he'd bought the Oak Park house, then planned to omit that fact until *after* I'd agreed to leave Bill.

And I *had* left Bill. For David. For David, I'd upended my life—while he held another woman's hand? I backed away and into an end table that knocked against the wall.

David's gaze shot over his shoulder. "Olivia."

Maria's eyes darted to me and her mouth dropped open.

I looked at their hands, and David released Maria's immediately. My face flamed with embarrassment. Why hadn't I pushed harder for the truth about his past? Why hadn't I insisted on taking things more slowly? Now, I was stuck in this apartment with nowhere to go.

I spun around and returned to the guest bedroom where I'd just washed up, where I'd spent my first night in this apartment—the only space I could think of to call my own in a foreign place.

Moments later, David banged once on the locked door. "Open up, Olivia."

I paced the bedroom. Feeling suddenly exposed, I re-wrapped my towel, securing it as tightly as possible under my arms. "You didn't tell her about us?" I cried.

"I did."

I whipped open the door. David reached for me, but I put up a hand to stop him. "Don't touch me. When did you end things with her?"

"Just now," he said like it was obvious, "when she came to the door."

"Earlier, you said you'd call her."

He sighed. "I've been with you the entire night. I haven't had a chance to call her—and furthermore, it's not necessary. There's nothing to end."

"Really? According to her, you can't turn it off just like *that*," I said, snapping my fingers in his face.

He took my wrist and said on a growl, "I'll say this one last time. You have no reason to worry. It's *done*."

"You were holding her hand!"

His eyebrows furrowed. "To comfort her. Regardless of anything, she's still a good friend."

I ripped my hand away. "I must've misunderstood the definition of *friendship*. Do you let all your friends touch you when you're naked? What if our roles were reversed, and it had been Bill on your doorstep, his hand on my bare chest?"

David's expression dimmed. "Careful."

"Or what?" I challenged him. "How could you not have ended *everything* with *everyone* after everything I gave up for you?"

I'd changed so much for him. My entire *life*. Shame I'd been harboring rose in me for ending my marriage to start something completely unpredictable. I'd fallen for David in the blink of an eye. Maria was just another reminder of how fast David and I were moving, and how unsteady our foundation was.

David braced both hands against the doorjamb. "Come to bed with me, and we'll talk through this."

"I'm sleeping in here tonight," I said.

"Not a chance in hell."

"*Excuse me?*" I gritted my teeth. "What are you going to do, put me over your shoulder and haul me to your bedroom?"

"If that's what it takes."

I shouldn't have been so shocked when my pussy fluttered. I'd dreamed of, fantasized about, and fallen in love with David *because* he knew what he wanted—and he took it.

That included me. But now that he had me, how far would he go to keep me? My breathing labored, desire coiling my insides at the thought of holding hostage the one thing David wanted more than anything else tonight.

"Go find your friend Maria if you need it so bad," I said.

His jaw locked. "Olivia—"

"I'll see you in the morning," I said before I slammed the door, locked it, and flung myself onto the bed. Confusion, anger, and lust mingled in me. I wanted to punish him as badly as I wanted him to throw me on the bed and fuck me until there was no question I was the only woman for him.

David tried the door handle again. "So help me God, Olivia. Unlock the door."

"Leave me alone," I said, partly because I knew he wouldn't. And that kind of power over him had the spot between my legs nearly dripping with desire.

"If I want to come in, a locked door isn't going to stop me," he warned.

My heart skipped. David had broken down many emotional barriers to get to me—could he, *would* he, take down the physical ones, too?

I knew the answer. He would. Nothing could keep him away, and the thought thrilled me. *Dared* me.

"Go away," I said.

The door thumped with his weight once and then burst open with the second hit.

His dark beauty overshadowed anything else in the room as he stalked toward the bed. My insides quivered at his delicious determination to have me no matter what, even as I scrambled to the headboard, cornering myself.

"Get back here," he said.

"Make me," I said.

"*Make* you?" he growled. With lightning speed, he grabbed my ankles and dragged me to the edge. Leaping onto the bed, he secured my hands on either side of my head. "Are you going to listen now?"

"Let go," I demanded, wriggling under him as my towel slipped, then fell open.

"Stop squirming," he said sharply.

"*Make me*," I repeated.

His eyes darkened. He spread my thighs with his knees. When his grip loosened, I freed my hands to shove his unyielding chest, relishing the fact that he wouldn't budge. That since day *one*, he hadn't ever budged.

"Think you can fight me off?" he asked coolly. He caught my wrists again, trapping them easily in one large hand above my head. Taking my jaw in his other hand, his knees pushed my legs open wider before he dropped his pelvis. "How about now?"

I bucked against him, suppressing a moan when my clit

connected with his hardness. He released my face to reach beneath us and pull his underwear down. His erection fell heavy against my pubic bone.

"Take what you want," I dared. "I can't stop you."

He thrust his crown against my stomach, trailing pre-cum over my skin. Reaching between my legs to find me slick, he groaned and squeezed my wrists together. "Your cunt's so fucking wet," he grated out, his fingers slipping and sliding over me.

"It's your semen from earlier," I shot back.

He buried his face into my neck. "*Christ.*"

At just the thought of penetration, I writhed beneath him. I bucked my hips into him again, this time doing it over and over to chase my orgasm, moaning each time we connected.

"You don't even need me to fuck you," he said as I closed my eyes to the blissful feeling of being utterly dominated. "You're going to come anyway."

I was close, just rubbing against him, but I wanted him inside me badly. "I need it," I said with gritted teeth.

He pinned one of my thighs down against the mattress and pressed his head between my folds. "Open your eyes and tell me what you need," he demanded.

"You," I breathed, my lashes fluttering open. "I want to come with you inside me."

"You got it," he said and impaled me with one single, long drive. I cried out, squirming to adjust to the way he filled me, but he kept my hands firmly locked above me.

I held his hungry gaze as he sucked in a sharp breath, reared back, and surged into me again. Within a few fast, hard thrusts, I came in a vicious orgasm, calling out for him.

He pulled out suddenly and flipped me over onto my stomach. His fingers opened me seconds before he rammed into me from behind, eliciting a guttural noise from my throat. I bit into a pillow and clutched the edge of the mattress as he began to fuck my already raw opening. His mouth dropped to my shoulder blade, sucking hard and pulling my skin between his teeth. I gasped and crossed my ankles to make it tighter for him. He responded with a muffled curse and bit down harder.

"You're so goddamn tight," he said into my hair, and I clenched around him. "*Fuck.*" He ripped at the bedding around me with two fists as he came, draining himself into me.

I didn't even have time to catch my breath before he withdrew and hauled my hips into the air. "Not finished with you yet," he said. His fingers played in my overflowing slit, spreading his semen up and between my buttocks. I tensed and bit the inside of my cheek as he circled my anus. "You ever been fucked in the ass?"

I only had the wherewithal to shake my head into the mattress and submit to whatever fate David had planned.

He made a noise of pure lust. I braced myself, but his hand fell away and he fed his cock into my pussy again with a loud groan. "God*damn*," he rasped and powered into me. He filled his need, showing me how much my body could take. His balls-deep thrusts leveled me onto the bed and ground me against the mattress until another orgasm threatened.

"I can't, it's too much," I whimpered.

"You can," he said, unrelenting.

I gripped the bed with white knuckles, and despite my protests, my body sang for him. With one hand clasped over my shoulder, he continued fucking me, through my orgasm and after it, until he came vigorously again, filling me with his heat.

He crumpled onto my back, heaving, and buried his

mouth into my neck. "It's all for you," he whispered hoarsely, his breath tickling my ear. He slid his hands up my arms and settled them over mine at the edge of the mattress. "You're everything," he said, repeating it as he unhooked my fingers and laced them with his. "Don't shut me out, baby. I need you. I need this."

The sheer need and hints of sadness in his voice brought tears to my eyes that I didn't have the energy to fight. With my body limp on the mattress, I shuddered underneath him, hiding my face in the pillow.

"Shh," he said, stroking my hair with one hand. "I'm so sorry she came here. Forgive me."

He lifted off me and kissed my shoulders tenderly. Once I could move again, I took my time turning onto my back. David sat against the headboard, breathing heavily, watching me with steepled knees. "It's over with Maria. I swear, Olivia. I didn't know she'd come here. I didn't know that all these years, she thought *she* would be the one. I told her it's over. I took her keys away. Please. Don't leave."

The pained expression on his face killed me. I only wanted to kiss it away. I climbed onto his lap and straddled him. Being sore and swollen made it uncomfortable to sit on him, but I didn't care. I wanted us as close as possible. He answered with an all-consuming hug, clinging to me like I was a buoy in stormy waters.

"I know it's complicated," I said softly. "Everything is so complicated. But I need to know. Do you still love her?"

He drew back to look me in the face and exhaled a short laugh. "Love? What makes you think I love her?"

"After three years, David? You just told me she has keys to your place, and . . ." I forced the depressing words out, barely managing a whisper. "I heard you out there. You told her you love her."

"Just now?" he asked. "Olivia, I love her as a person, I

won't deny that. But I've never been *in* love with her. I didn't love her or any of them, my sweet, sweet girl," he said, squeezing me. "It never occurred to me . . . if I'd known you thought that, I would've told you from the start that I didn't love her."

I believed him. But I could also understand if Maria had thought she was getting more than David had to give. Wasn't I the same, falling blindly in love with a man who could change course at any moment?

"I'm sorry I locked you out," I said.

"I'm sorry I was so rough with you," he said, sliding his palm up my back. "I've never been that out of control. You reduce me to a fucking animal."

"I like it," I said with a small smile. "I like that you need me like I need you."

He nudged my chin up with his nose and kissed the underside of my jaw.

"And I actually *liked* being restrained," I added softly, eyes up to the ceiling. I'd never entertained the idea, thinking I'd hate being at another person's mercy.

"I knew you would," he murmured.

"How?" I asked.

"You want me to take control."

"But . . ." I'd gone through great measures to ensure I was in charge of my emotions. "I always like being in control."

"Not wanting to give up control is not the same as wanting to be in control."

I nodded, awed by his ability to pinpoint how I felt better than I could.

"You'd tell me to stop if it was too much?" he asked.

"Yes," I promised. "But it's not."

"Sometimes, you have to let go, and let me take over, Olivia. I want it, and I'm not just talking about sex."

I shuddered involuntarily. To agree would be so easy, but I forced myself to see the reality of what he was saying. Letting him take the reins and giving myself over to him was too tempting. It edged me closer to the brink of completely drowning in him. "I know you want to be gentle with Maria," I said. "And I'm sorry if I've cost you a friend. But I'm terrified you'll suddenly change your mind and this will all go away. *Terrified*."

He rubbed a thumb between my eyebrows to ease my frown lines. "You have nothing to be afraid of."

"You two have so much history—"

"And what about Bill?" he asked. "Are you going to run back to him?"

I didn't see how I possibly could after the past few days. Even if David and I didn't work out, with some distance, Bill's and my problems became clearer. I shook my head. "No."

"We have to trust each other if this is going to work," David said. "We both have history, but that's all it is. History. We're moving forward together."

Suddenly emotionally and physically drained, I yawned. "Okay," I agreed.

He squeezed his arms around me. "And I want you to know—you're the only partner I've ever had without a condom."

I blinked at him and cocked my head. "What?"

"Getting someone pregnant? Fuck no. I wasn't taking that chance." He shook his head. "I couldn't risk it knowing one fuck-up could one day affect my future family."

"Not even Maria?" I asked.

"Especially Maria. She'd drain my bank account before the baby was even born."

"But you did it with me," I said.

He rubbed my back. "You're different," he said and pecked me lightly. "You've always been different."

David's faith in us had never wavered. There'd been a point our first night when we hadn't used a condom. And even though I, too, had been paranoid about getting pregnant at the wrong time, I'd begged him to come in me.

Now that he had, we were relying solely on birth control. He'd come in me three times tonight alone. Would anything stop us from continuing to take that risk? I was still paranoid about pregnancy. Was he?

I was tired. Too tired to go down that path. Instead, I melted into the feeling of his hand on my back.

"You can barely keep your eyes open."

I nodded and yawned again.

"Bed, baby."

"Hmm?" I asked.

I heard him laugh, and he scooted off the mattress to pick me up. I wrapped my arms around his neck, nuzzled my nose into his neck, and drifted.

I can't catch a breath, my chest tight as a fist.

Oh my God.

Hands hold me down. There's blood, so much blood, David's blood, and I'm trying desperately to inhale as everything goes dark . . .

I bolted upright and gasped for air. My hand flew to my bare chest. I tried to scream, but my throat was so dry, I started coughing violently.

A shadow stood over me in the dark. "What's wrong?" David asked. "Olivia. What is it?"

I pressed my hand harder into my throat and gulped in

a breath. "Someone——" I croaked and started coughing again.

His voice raised in alarm. "Someone what?"

"A . . . dream."

"You need water," he said, turning away.

"No!" I exclaimed, grasping his hand. "No, please. Stay."

He crawled into the bed and melded his front to my back. His powerful arms snaked around me, securing me tightly.

"Thank you," I whispered.

"Nightmare?" he asked.

I nodded. "I'm sorry I woke you."

"You didn't. I'd just set you in the bed and was putting out the fireplace."

"Good," I said, gripping his forearms and snuggling closer.

"What was it about?"

I closed my eyes. "I was having trouble breathing. I always do in this one. Someone was holding me down, smothering me. And there was blood. Your blood. You were bleeding."

He made a strangled noise. "I've been too rough with you."

I shook my head emphatically. "I think it's because of the fight with Bill tonight."

"You said 'this one.' Do you have nightmares often?"

"Only since . . ."

"Since what?" he prompted.

"The night in my office."

His head popped up behind me. "With Alvarez? His attack?"

"Yes," I said quietly.

"Oh, baby," he said, burrowing in my neck and rocking me. "It's my fault—I shouldn't have restrained you."

"No." I took a breath. "It's not that."

"I'll never let anyone touch you the way he did." David shook me gently in his arms. "Do you hear me?" he asked fervently in my ear. "I promise. You're safe with me."

"I know," I said. "My superhero."

"Do you need water?"

"Don't leave." I sighed. I rotated in his grasp and wrapped my arms tightly around him. "Don't go."

Chapter Nine

David stirred underneath me. My eyes opened to a light-infused room that felt as warm and happy as I did. His arms pulled me closer, and I lifted my head from his shoulder to look at him. "Did we fall asleep like this?" I whispered.

He nodded.

I sighed. "Sorry."

"Why?"

"I didn't mean to cling to you all night."

His chest shook underneath me with a laugh. "Cling? I believe you ladies call it 'cuddling.'"

"I hate cuddling," I said and frowned. "At least, I think I do."

He laughed harder. "Were you uncomfortable?"

"No. I slept great."

"Then maybe we should do it every night. Until you hate it again, that is."

I smiled and resettled on his chest, relishing the feel of his inviting skin under my cheek. Warmth from a surprisingly peaceful sleep enveloped me. I couldn't help but reach out and run my hand over his suntanned pecs, planes of sprawling hardness with some dark hair. And they were mine to touch, to kiss, to wake up against. He moaned softly . . .

I climbed up swiftly and straddled him, tossing my hair over one shoulder. He raised a perfect black eyebrow at me, and I leaned down to kiss him. He licked my bottom lip and took it gently between his teeth. Propping myself on him, I felt his chest rise and fall faster as the kiss deepened.

He glided his hands over my back and down to my hips, kneading and pulling my ass while my heart rate quickened. He slipped himself inside me easily, as though he belonged there, then pressed his hands against my lower back while he gave me short, deep thrusts.

Our soft moans into each other's mouths contrasted our rapid-fire fucking the night before. I felt every single inch of him moving in and out of me, every ridge and contour. Despite feeling sensitive and sore, his touch alone had me melting like butter on top of him.

He kissed me thoroughly. Eventually, currents of electric bliss began rippling through me. He secured the back of my neck with one hand while the other splayed on my lower back. I could only whimper into his open mouth as my climax crested between my legs and crashed throughout my body. His orgasm started as mine was finishing, and he flexed his hands into my skin, detaining me until he was done. Even after, he didn't let me go, but continued to kiss me sweetly.

"We slept in," I noted, glancing at his bedside clock.

"Yeah. We're supposed to meet my family at the park soon to barbeque."

"Are we still going by the animal shelter?" I asked.

"Yep." He heaved a playful sigh. "We might have to save time by showering together."

I giddily agreed. We got up and moved to the spacious bathroom. Rough stone cooled the soles of my feet, and since glass made up one wall of the shower, my body thrilled at the panoramic views of Lake Michigan. David sat me on the shower's built-in bench and cleaned himself from between my legs with unnecessary focus. When he straightened up, I was faced with a purple mark on his side.

"Oh, God," I said, shooting up. "You're hurt."

"It's fine."

I gently rested my hands on his abs. "Are you okay?"

He grabbed the shampoo bottle. "It's just a bruised rib."

"What? Why didn't you tell me?"

He shrugged. "There's nothing you can do. I've had worse from surfing."

"What if it's something serious?"

He leaned over and kissed my cheek. "Don't worry, sweet girl. If anything, it was last night's activities that aggravated it."

I clamped my hand over my mouth. "It's my fault. I didn't know you were in pain."

"Trust me, I forgot all about it when we stepped through the door," he joked. He handed me different shampoo as he began scrubbing his hair.

I inspected the purple bottle. "What's this?"

"Lady shampoo," he said.

"What's lady shampoo?"

"I asked my sister, she says that's a good brand. I have all sorts of girly shit for you—conditioner, body wash, a pink razor, a fucking pastel loofah."

I laughed. "Don't *you* use a loofah?"

He glared down at me. "I'm a man."

I laughed harder, and his eyebrows furrowed. "Trust me, I'm aware," I said between gasps. "Didn't Jessa ask why?"

"Of course she did," he muttered. "She's nosy as hell when it comes to my love life."

I started washing my hair when he didn't continue. "So . . . what'd you tell her?"

"Just that I'm seeing someone new," he said after a moment.

"Seeing someone new" was a far cry from the loving things he'd professed the night before. I nodded. "Oh."

He looked down at me. "I want nothing more than to tell my family. I'm just worried about how Jessa'll react to our situation. Her husband cheated on her a few months after Alex was born, and it was the final straw for her. Their marriage ended because of infidelity."

David's family knew I was married. I'd told them when I'd met them. Even if I hadn't, it wasn't something I could've really hidden. I chewed the inside of my bottom lip and switched places with David so I could rinse. How would we handle telling David's family? Would they judge me? The idea of admitting the truth made my cheeks burn red.

My heart dropped. Would they be angry with David? And exactly how angry? Enough to try to come between us?

"Hey," David said, lifting my chin. "We don't have to go today if you're not comfortable. We can see them another time."

I shook my head. "No. No more hiding."

He seemed to like that because he grinned.

I turned around to grab the loofah from a hook, and

his hand shot out to catch the back of my neck. "Shit. Did I *bite* you last night?"

"Yes." I squealed. Despite my tenderness from so much sex, arousal bloomed in me at the memory. But when I looked over my shoulder, anxiety was written on his face. "It was seriously *hot*," I said.

He ran a gentle thumb over my skin. "It didn't hurt?"

"Are you kidding?" I asked. "It drove me through the roof."

"All right," he said, and after a brief hesitation, released me.

Following an embarrassing mix-up at the animal shelter where the manager called David "Bill," George from the shelter handed us over two dogs, delighted nonetheless at the extra hands. I braced myself for the fact that there'd be many confusing and uncomfortable situations still to come while David and I transitioned. Before us was an especially difficult one.

We'd gotten lucky with a beautiful November day in the high sixties, and the sun shone against a clear, blue sky. When David's shelter dog proved to be much more energetic than mine, I tried desperately to get him to switch with me. "You're hurt," I pleaded. "Let me handle her. I'm a pro."

"I'm fine," he said with exasperation. "Like I said, I've had bruised ribs before."

"Right. The big, bad surfer," I teased. "I'm not sure I believe you, though. I didn't see any surfboards in your apartment."

"Our apartment," he corrected. "And it wouldn't make

sense to keep them here. They're in New York and San Sebastián."

"Spain?" I choked out.

He looked at me sidelong, a sly smile crossing his face. "Didn't I tell you I have a place there?"

I shook my head slowly, even though I remembered reading it in his 'Most Eligible' bachelor interview.

"Have you been?" he asked.

I continued to shake my head.

"I'll take you."

I nodded.

He chuckled. "Something the matter?"

"I've always wanted to go to Spain," I said.

"Is that why you've weaseled your way into my heart? Trying to get a free trip out of it?"

My eyes widened. "Busted."

He laughed and put an arm around me, but it didn't last. His dog strained against the leash anytime he sensed that David was getting lazy.

As we entered the park, David asked, "Ready for this?"

I followed his gaze to the picnic area. His dad and nephew were stationed by the barbeque as his mom and sister chatted nearby.

Knowing how close David was to his family only made this more intimidating. I had to prepare myself for the fact that they might not like us together. That they might not like *me*, despite how welcoming they'd been a couple months earlier.

I glanced between him and them and nodded slightly. David let his dog pull him ahead, and I approached moments later with a racing heart.

His sister shielded her eyes from the sun but still squinted at me. "Olivia?" she asked and surprised me with a hug. "David didn't say you were coming. Nice to see you again."

I hugged her back. "You, too, Jessa."

"At least it's not freezing," she said. "It's a little weird to barbeque in November, but as you probably know, Notre Dame won last night so that's typically how Dad celebrates."

I grimaced. "I don't really follow football. Even if it is my own college."

"Just smile and nod along if it comes up." She laughed and glanced in David's direction as he beckoned me over. "Thanks for getting my brother out of the house. As you can see, he could really use the exercise."

Even in a jacket, David couldn't hide his muscular physique. Worried my thoughts would wander to our sordid night—and sexy morning—I hurried toward him.

To my embarrassment, David's mom, Judy, gushed about how excited she was to see me again. When his dad hugged me tightly, my arm smarted where Bill had grabbed me, but I controlled my wince. The family seemed oddly happy to see me, even though David and I made no moves to suggest that we were dating.

"I just love that you volunteer, sweetie," his mom said, bending to pet the dog I'd brought.

I smiled. There was something nice about the way her eyes lit up when she called me "sweetie."

The dogs fell into the grass next to the Dylans' German shepherd, Canyon, and dozed in the sun. David took his nephew to a nearby basketball court to shoot hoops as Jessa invited me to sit on an outstretched blanket. As we talked, I couldn't help admiring David's easy nature with his nephew. He lifted Alex up in the air for a slam dunk, and Alex's infectious laughter made me smile. I had to look away to keep from swooning.

And I realized Jessa had been watching *me*. Now, her eyes danced the same way they had the first and last time I'd been alone with her. When she'd looked at me that way before, I'd been tempted to tell her everything about my feelings for her brother. That ability to draw out my secrets seemed to run in the family.

Yes, her eyes danced, but they also held warmth and invitation, as though we'd been longtime friends. I didn't know if David had wanted to talk to her about our situation first, but it was the right moment. Despite the cold, a combination of the direct sun and my nerves had me sweating.

I removed my ivory, cable-knit cardigan, stripping down to my t-shirt. "Jessa, I really like you."

She smiled and grasped my hand. I didn't flinch or pull back like I normally might've. She had a gift of putting others at ease. "I like you, too. A little too much, I'm afraid."

"I'm sorry?"

She turned her head in the direction of David and Alex and sighed. "I just . . . I haven't seen David this easy and relaxed since we were children. Don't get me wrong, he's always playful with Alex, but he just seems different around you. Less edgy. *Calm.* Like he's actually found what he's been . . ." She turned back to me. "I can't help but wish for the impossible here."

I nodded, searching for the words to fill her in. Silence drew out between us and understanding appeared in her eyes. For the first time, she looked at my left hand, her eyes lingering on the empty space.

"I'm leaving my husband," I said, and then added, "for David."

After a moment, Jessa's eyes flicked up to mine. "That must be very hard."

"It is." I glanced over at David, who took my breath away now as he did time and time again. "But it almost feels like I don't have a choice. I couldn't move forward with Bill after knowing David."

I looked back and tried to read Jessa's passive expression. It was hard to gauge her reaction, but there was no judgment, and that was the best thing I could hope for. "All this is just happening as of a few days ago," I continued. "Things have been hectic. Complicated. My parents are divorced, and I swore I'd never go down that path."

She nodded. "It was a difficult time for me."

"What was?" David asked, walking up with the basketball. He dropped it and steadied it with his foot, before whipping off his jacket and tossing it on the blanket.

"Divorce," Jessa and I said in unison.

He froze, his eyes finding mine, then crouched beside us. A sheen of sweat glistened on his biceps, and he wiped his upper lip on his sleeve. "Fuck," he said. "Is it always this warm in November?"

"You just can't keep up with the kid like you used to," Jessa said. "Plus, you look nervous as hell right now."

He glanced between us. "So . . .?" he asked her. "You going to tell me I fucked up?"

"A divorce is a lot to take on, David," Jessa warned him. "It's a *huge* commitment. And if Olivia's in it, so are you—you can't let her do this alone."

"I know," David said without hesitation and smiled at me. "Olivia's worth it."

Happiness swelled in me, but Jessa didn't give me a chance to respond.

"Oh my God," she said and fell back onto the blanket dramatically before yelling up at the sky. "Finally! The pickiest man alive settles down."

"What's going on?" Judy called from across the grass.

"Shut up, Jess," David hissed. "You act like I've never had a girlfriend."

Jessa sat up and ignored him to address me directly. "Olivia, it may be too soon to say this, but I don't care because the energy is good here. Welcome to the family. I can see my brother here is quite taken with you."

I blushed wildly, unable to contain the huge grin spreading across my face. "It's complicated, Jessa," I said, hating to ruin the moment. "There have been . . ." I glanced up at David. "Transgressions. We haven't been as ethical as we'd like."

She arched an eyebrow at me. "Do you think I'm blind?" she asked. "I could tell there was something going on the moment I saw you two together."

"Does that bother you?" David asked.

"Of course it bothers me, David," she said, nodding over at Alex. "He and I went through this, and it sucked. But . . . if that's how it had to go down, then I guess you two have to live with that. I can't condone it, but Alex's dad cheated on me because he was a horny fucking idiot, not because the universe offered him the gift it's giving you guys." She picked a blade of grass, twirling it between her fingers. "It was really just a symptom of a dying marriage."

"So you think it would have happened eventually?" I asked, genuinely curious. "Your divorce?"

"I do. I loved him, and his cheating destroyed me, but after many years I've realized that we weren't a match. He brought me down. I mean, Libra and Virgo—what was I thinking?" She laughed as if I should understand that.

I found comfort in her words, though. The more time I spent with David, the more I realized how out-of-sync Bill and I had been. The recent deterioration of sex had indicated as much. At the same time, David and I had connected on a level that couldn't be ignored.

"We're good, right?" David asked Jessa and grabbed his basketball. "Can I go play?"

She laughed. "Get out of here so I can tell embarrassing stories about you."

He halted suddenly and looked toward his parents. "What am I going to tell Mom and Dad?"

"I suggest you tell them the truth," she said. "Today."

He broke out into a smile and, with a glance to make sure they weren't watching, leaned over to give me a swift kiss.

After he jogged off, Jessa shook her head in awe. "Jesus, I've never even seen him hold hands with a girl in public."

Speaking of girlfriends . . .

"Has David, um, brought many girls home?" I asked, fingering a lock of my hair.

"Here and there over the years," she said, turning back to me.

"Maria?" I blurted.

"Oh, yes," Jessa said, rolling her eyes. "I've met Maria at a couple events. She's a first-rate snob."

I pulled my knees to my chest. "She's not happy about this."

"About what—you and David?" Jessa asked. "She told you that?"

"She came by David's place last night to say she deserves a real chance with him. She even brought up wanting an engagement ring, and I—"

Jessa burst out laughing.

"What?" I frowned. "I worry he might still have feelings for her."

"Don't," she said and waved a hand. "David called me Friday to say he'd met someone. I could hear in his voice how happy he was. Maria never even came up—whatever they had, it's totally inconsequential. It has never crossed his mind to propose, trust me."

I curbed a triumphant smile. That was enough to put my mind at ease for now. "How about you?" I asked. "Are you seeing anyone?"

"I have a few prospects," she said, smiling. "No one I'm ready to introduce around, though."

"Right. Is it hard dating with a kid?"

"Yes," she mused. "But I make it work. Anyway, Alex is more fun than any guy I've ever gone out with."

We watched Alex steal the ball from his uncle. "Seems like it," I said.

"Little boys," she said, shaking her head at them. "They get along so well that sometimes I forget they aren't the same age."

She asked me about my family. I told her about my parents and was surprised to hear that she'd read one of my mom's novels. As she talked about what she was currently reading, I glanced over at David because I couldn't resist. Squatting down, he wiped something from Alex's face with the same care he used when he handled anything he loved, then ruffled Alex's hair. It was a sweet scene. But it didn't inspire the maternal instinct in me that I knew it should, and a tiny knot of warning formed in my stomach.

David's dad, Gerard, called the family to the picnic table. David served me a hamburger exactly how I liked it, and I thanked him with a soft smile. As I took my first bite, I noticed Gerard staring at my left hand. I wiped it on a napkin quickly and put it in my lap. His gaze shifted to my arm.

"What on earth happened to your elbow?" he asked.

David's body stiffened in the same moment that his head turned. Having lived a life with the bruising abilities of a peach, I already knew what I'd find, so I didn't bother to look.

"How did I miss these?" David mumbled, taking my elbow gently and lifting my arm. He inspected the marks as I felt myself reddening. "Jesus, baby."

My color only deepened at the endearment that would give us away, and my eyes dropped to the table. Still, I felt everyone watching as he tenderly stroked my back and examined the bruises.

I grasped for an explanation, but he cut in. "Mom, Dad. You know that for a long time, I've been looking for . . . something more. I've been unwilling to settle for a woman who wasn't 'the one.'"

"Honey," his mom said softly.

"I've found her in Olivia," he said.

A blanket of silence fell over the table as his parents stared at us. My nerves buzzed as my heart thumped with David's doting words. I grasped his thigh under the table as we waited.

"Honey," Judy said again, "I'm confused. I thought Olivia was married."

"I am. I'm sorry. I know this is uncomfortable," I said. "My husband and I have decided to separate." David's leg tensed under my hand at my word choice. I closed my eyes, afraid of what I'd see in theirs as I told the truth. "Divorce, I mean. We're getting a divorce."

When I peeked at the table again, Judy looked between the two of us with round eyes. "Because of David?"

"I've come to realize that things weren't right with my husband," I said, "but I wouldn't have come to that conclusion without David's help. David is . . ." I let the sentence trail as I turned to him. He looked back at me, and I didn't finish because I knew he could see all the things he was to me.

Gerard's voice cut angrily into our moment. "What does that have to do with the bruises, Olivia?" He fixed a stern, dark stare on me. It was a look I'd experienced before—from his son, the time Mark Alvarez had been the one to leave marks on my arm. I tried not to cower down in my seat, unsure of what had caused Gerard's shift in mood. Was he concerned, too? Or angry with me?

David went to speak, but I squeezed his leg and shook my head. I wanted them to know the entire truth, and for them to hear it from me. David's hand moved to my lower back as I began to quake slightly.

"I'm sorry, this is embarrassing," I said, swiping the back of my hand over my forehead. "David and I . . . I mean, I—I was unfaithful. I told my husband about the affair, and we tried to move on from it. I couldn't. Not while I felt this way about David. More details came out last night, and my husband got upset and interrupted our evening—"

Gerard banged his fist on the table, and everyone jumped. His eyes flicked a mile a minute between my face and my arm.

I had my answer. I'd definitely pissed him off. I rose immediately. "I'm so sorry," I said, backing away and holding in tears. "I know that this—all of this—is awful. I'll give you guys a minute."

David called after me, but I ignored him as I walked out to the grass to regain my composure. He followed right behind me, and when I stopped, he hugged me to him. "What'd I tell you?" he asked. "Don't do this alone. Don't run away from me. Let me be your shield."

"They think I'm not good enough for you," I said. "I don't blame them. I had an *affair*."

"*We* had an affair," he said. "I was there, too."

"No. I did this. I have to face the consequences. You

can't protect me from it." I sniffled back tears and rested my head on his chest. My chin trembled. "I just wish it was anyone but your parents."

"Baby, hang on," he said, his brow furrowing. "They're not upset with *you*. My dad's pissed that—"

"David," a voice rumbled behind me. Gerard stepped up next to us. "Go back to the table. Let me talk to Olivia."

I nodded when David hesitated. "It's okay."

After an encouraging look, David walked away.

Gerard's tall frame loomed over me, and he rested a hand on my shoulder. One on one, I noticed how attractive he was up close. He was sturdy, like David, and his hand weighed heavy on me. "I'm sorry if I startled you," he said. "David's right. I'm not angry with you."

I sniffed and wiped my face with the back of my hand. "Please don't be upset with David. This isn't his fault. He's been nothing but amazing to me."

Gerard surprised me by laughing. "I think I have you to thank for his good mood lately. My dear," he continued softly, "I'm upset that anyone put his hands on you in anger. I don't care about the 'details' of your relationship with my son, because I've never seen him this happy with anyone. And if your husband hurt you like this," he said, motioning to my arm, "even once, then I'm even happier that David saved you than that you saved him."

I gawked up at him. "Saved *him*?"

He peered over at his family and then back at me. "David's waited a long time for you to come along. I can't say I've ever been happy with David's choices when it comes to women, so we're thrilled that you're finally here."

"But you barely know me," I blurted.

"We know our son. And to see him with you, we know enough."

My throat thickened. I'd been so worried about how upset they'd get, I hadn't considered they might actually be okay with this. "You . . . I—I don't know what to say, Mr. Dylan."

"This has been hard, hasn't it?" he asked.

I nodded. "I've hurt people, including David, very much."

"Do you love him?"

I looked at David's back as his elbows rested on the table, his forehead in his hands. His fingers swept through his hair. "Yes," I answered. "But if we could keep that between us for now? I haven't . . . it's hard for me to express."

"He knows, I can tell. Life is nothing without love," Gerard said. "My wife taught me that. I could not breathe if not for Judy. If your gut tells you you're doing the right thing, then you are. And you have our support."

"Thank you," I whispered with tears still lingering in my eyes. "You and David are so much alike."

"Lucky for him," he said with a playful smile, and I nodded. "Come on back to the table," he coaxed with an arm around my shoulder. "Tell us everything. And call me Gerard. That 'Mr. Dylan' shit is making me feel ancient."

I followed him back, avoiding everyone's gaze as I sat. David took my chin in his hand, raised my face, and gave me a determined kiss. His mother gasped, and I tried to pull away, but he held me steady. "Are you okay?" he asked, glancing at my arm.

I looked into his eyes and nodded ardently. He released me, and we turned to face the table.

"My baby," Judy said to David, her eyes glossy. "In love."

"Yes, Mom," he said grumpily, and I finally smiled.

When I heard a sniffle next to me, I turned to see that Jessa was crying.

"Oh, come on," David moaned. "Are you guys for real?"

"I'm sorry," she said, blowing her nose into a napkin. "I was worried you'd never meet the girl."

"And she's a Leprechaun to boot," Gerard put in, puffing up in his Notre Dame jacket. "Good game last night, huh?"

As Jessa had instructed, I smiled and nodded—then laughed because my mood had gone from stressed and upset to absolutely giddy.

"*Mom*," Alex said with a groan. "Why're you crying?"

"Don't worry, sweetie." She hugged him sideways on the bench, pulling him close. "They're happy tears."

"Women," he said, rolling his eyes and returning to his video game.

We laughed, and Judy asked us for more details. Given that David and I had only had a weekend together, there wasn't much to tell when we removed sex from the equation. His family was excited nonetheless.

Chapter Ten

As David and I walked hand in hand from the train to his apartment, our warm November day at the park turned into a typical November evening. I burrowed my nose into a scarf David had bought earlier and wrapped carefully around my neck.

"You're quiet," he said, squeezing my hand in his.

Since leaving Bill days earlier—a stressful event in itself—so much had happened. Shopping for and attending a large event. Witnessing a fistfight between my husband and my boyfriend. Facing fears as I'd confronted David's past during the hottest sex of my life. Meeting my new boyfriend's family. I tugged down the scarf. "It's been a long weekend. I'm tired. And sore."

"Sore, huh?" he asked, bumping me with his shoulder.

"*Sore*," I said with the most serious face I could muster. "Like, I might have to start yoga to keep up with you."

"Yes," he said immediately. "The more ways I can bend you, the better."

I grinned. "You're such a hornball."

"You have no idea what you've gotten yourself into."

He stopped and drove my back up against a brick wall. "Think I'm kidding?" he asked, clasping our linked hands together behind his back. "I had the best time today," he said quietly, kissing his way along my jaw until he found my lips.

I'd had a great day, too—getting to know his family, helping out the shelter, spending time with someone who, frankly, I never wanted to be away from. But as our blissful weekend came to an end, thoughts I'd been suppressing began to demand my attention.

It was clear how much David enjoyed being with family, specifically Alex. Did David envision a family of his own? Like Bill, did he just expect I'd get on board? Was it too soon to ask? Was it too *late*?

And tomorrow, we'd be back to reality. My things were at David's place, and he'd asked me to move in. If I was honest with myself, I wanted that, too. I wanted to spend as much time as possible with David. But we were moving at lightning speed, and that scared me. I hadn't thought of Bill much all day, at least not to wonder how he was doing, and that made me feel like an asshole.

"Earth to Olivia," David said.

"Sorry," I murmured against his lips.

"Where'd you go just now?"

"Nowhere," I said. "I'm here."

"Are you sure?"

I'd promised to try not to hide anything from him, and I didn't want to. But as the sun disappeared behind the buildings around us, and David's body warmed mine, there was no sense in ruining a perfect moment. I smiled and touched his cheek. "I had the best time, too. I'm good."

He pulled me from the wall, and we continued to the apartment. When we'd arrived at the hotel, he cursed to himself as we boarded the elevator.

"What's wrong?" I asked.

"I just realized something that does *not* make me happy," he said as he swiped his card to the penthouse.

My heart dropped. I wrung my fingers together, bracing myself for the bad news I'd been expecting—as if I'd just been *waiting* for the bomb to drop that would blow up our perfect weekend, and it *was* Sunday night now, so . . .

"What is it?" I asked.

He jutted his chin at me. "Why are you looking at me like that?"

"I have no idea what you're going to say," I said. "It could be anything."

He laughed and kissed me between the brows. "Honeybee," he said softly, "I'm not going anywhere. Quit bracing yourself for bad news."

My shoulders eased as the elevator slowed. We exited, and he unlocked the door to the apartment. I hung up my scarf and jacket with his in the foyer, then tailed him to the bedroom. "*Well?*" I asked.

"Oh. I'm mad that I've never taken you out on a proper date," he said. "You know—picked you up, driven you to dinner, dropped you off. Kissed you on the doorstep."

I laughed on an exhale, relieved to hear quite the opposite of bad news.

He stripped off his shirt and tossed it into the closet hamper. "Due to the nature of our relationship," he continued, "I've skipped over the entire courting process. So we'll have to make up for that." He turned to me. "Olivia Germaine, would you let me take you out tomorrow night? Anywhere you like."

"Surprise me," I said, scrunching my nose at him before peeking at his six-pack. "Also, is walking around shirtless something you do often? It makes it hard to concentrate."

"I'm thinking 'no shirts allowed' would make for a good rule."

I went to him and wrapped my arms around his warm skin, careful not to touch his injured ribs.

He ghosted a hand over my bruised biceps. "I hate that he got to you before I did." Without making contact, his palm moved to hover over my shoulder blade, to the bite mark. "Did I hurt you last night?"

"No." He'd handled me perfectly the whole night. I tilted my head back to look up at him. "Your dad was pretty upset, though."

"Where do you think I got my temper?" he asked. "He sits on a few boards, one of which focuses on domestic violence."

"He's scary," I said. "Like you."

David laughed just as my cell phone rang. I rolled my eyes and tried to pull away.

"Ignore it," he said, kissing my forehead.

I wanted to, but I couldn't with all the things going on in my life. I detangled myself from his arms.

"Who even has your new number?" he asked.

"Just Gretchen, my dad, and Bill."

"Bill?" David asked as I rummaged through my bag.

"I e-mailed it to him."

"Why?" he asked irritably.

"Like it or not, we're going to have to be in touch." I put the phone to my ear. "Hello?"

"Olivia?" My mother's panicked voice came through the line, and I paled instantly.

"Mom?" I felt behind me to sit at the edge of the bed. "What's wrong?"

"What's going on?" she cried.

My heart sank when I realized from her hysterical voice that she'd probably been drinking. "I don't know. *You* called *me*," I said. "Calm down and tell me what's wrong."

"Don't tell me to calm down, young lady," she said. "I just spoke to Bill, and I just—I just *don't* believe what he told me. Tell me he's mistaken."

Shit. I couldn't believe Bill had gone behind my back and told my mother anything before I could gather my thoughts. How much did she know? After all the accusations she'd levied against my father over the years, I knew what was coming. I curled my toes against the bedroom's wood floors. "Mom, things are very complicated—"

She gasped. "So it's true? You cheated on him?"

David crouched at my feet, and my eyes slid to his. I held on to the encouragement in them as I prepared to break my mom's already damaged heart. He placed a hand on my knee, and I covered it.

"Yes," I said, holding David's gaze. "It's true."

"How could you?" she screeched, and I jerked the phone away from my cheek. "I raised you to be a lady, not a *slut*."

David flinched, and his hand twitched on my leg, no doubt tempted to take the phone from me.

"It's not like that," I said, clenching and unclenching my jaw. "I didn't end things for a fling. My relationship with David is serious."

"Don't be ridiculous. You *love* Bill, and he doesn't deserve this. What has he ever done to hurt you?"

I wasn't playing this game with her. As long as Bill stayed in the role of the good husband, she'd never be able to understand my reasons for leaving. David wiped away my tear before I realized it was there. "I'm sorry, Mom," I said. "I know this must be hard for you to hear."

"It's just nonsense. You stop this immediately, and go take care of your poor husband. That poor, poor man."

"I can't," I said. "I can't be the wife he needs, because I don't love him the way I should. I made my choice."

"A womanizer who can't keep his hands off a married woman?" she asked.

Womanizer. That was Bill's word. "David's not like that," I said.

"Oh, Bill told me everything. Bill deserves better than this. He deserves better than you."

She'd always thought she'd deserved better, too—than my dad. Than her daughter. In her eyes, I'd been an enemy who'd taken my dad's attention away, and then taken *him* away after their divorce. I choked back a sob. "How can you say that to me? You're my mother."

"Because I know what it feels like to be betrayed. How could you *cheat* after you saw what I went through?"

"Dad didn't even cheat on you," I cried in exasperation. "It's in your head—it always has been."

"This is all his fault. Your father did this, always pampering you. He spoiled you, and now you only know how to be selfish. After everything I went through, how could you turn around and destroy a husband who's always been there for you? You're selfish," she slurred, "and you're a fool to ruin the best thing that's ever happened to you."

"Mom, you haven't even heard my—" With a few *beeps*, I pulled the phone away and stared down at the blank screen. "She hung up on me . . ."

Selfish, undeserving, foolish. She'd called me names before, but they'd never felt so true. I couldn't deny that I'd sacrificed Bill's happiness for my own.

I didn't cry over my mother—it was just something I didn't do anymore. So I was confused when I set the phone down, put my face in my hands, and burst into tears. The bed dipped with David's weight, and he lifted me onto his lap, where he rocked me back and forth, whispering comforting words in my hair.

"My mom . . . doesn't . . . love . . . me," I sobbed.

"Oh, baby," he said, clutching me to him.

I looked up at him suddenly and searched his eyes. "This will get better, won't it?" I asked. "Easier?"

"Yes." He paused, stroking my hair. "But until it does, you have me. Let me have some of the hurt."

I nuzzled into his chest again, taking a deep whiff through a runny nose. Then, I imagined Bill calling and telling her everything—how I'd lied to him for months, had used Davena's death as an excuse, had confessed everything over pancakes, had given back the ring and asked for a divorce on a cold, bleary, and otherwise unremarkable night. I cried harder.

"Hey," David said softly, moving me back by my shoulders to look at me. "We'll not only make it through this, but we'll come out better for it. We have something strong. Stronger than all the bullshit."

Do we? I wondered. *Can love alone overcome everyone and everything—even ourselves?*

"I hope so," I murmured, wiping my wet tears from his bare chest. The words *slut* and *womanizer* rang through my ears, a perfect pair. But the man who held me softened the blows. Though I wanted nothing more than to stay there, he set me on the bed and disappeared into the bathroom.

Oh, what a mess I've made. Bill is heartbroken and blindsided. I've lost friends, and now maybe even family. And what will my dad say when I see him next weekend? Why have I done this? What have I done? Is it worth it?

I looked up at a noise. David leaned in the doorway, concern etching his features as he watched me in only his underwear.

He's worth it. For him, I would give up everything.

My body tensed at the unbidden thought. I had this strange feeling that he meant more to me than anything ever had, even though we'd known each other for such a short time. If I hadn't known before, I knew now—I was desperately in love. It was a kind of love I didn't recognize, one that changed a person. A kind of love I'd fended off my whole life. As I stared at him, this man who filled the doorway . . .

Cold, stark fear struck me in the gut.

He walked over, pulled me to my feet, and kneeled in front of me. I gripped his shoulders as, one at a time, he lifted my feet to remove my booties and socks. Next, he pulled down my pants, taking my underwear with them. He rose and removed my sweater. I lifted my arms so he could pull my t-shirt over my head and unfasten my bra.

"Step," he said, and I did, leaving the pile behind. With a hand on my lower back, he guided me into the bathroom where he'd drawn a luminous bath with overflowing bubbles and soft candlelight. The thought of David owning, dusting off, and lighting candles for me made me smile.

"Get in and try to relax," he instructed. "I'll be right back."

Happy to be told what to do so I didn't have to use my mushy brain, I eased in one limb at a time. I couldn't remember the last time I'd taken a bath, and I'd forgotten how healing it could be. I sank down slowly and let the bubbles swallow me, so deep that I heard, rather than saw, David return.

I waved bubbles away to see him holding a bottle of red wine. "Last thing," he said. "It's Merlot. But if you need chardonnay in this moment, I'd understand."

I half-smiled. He didn't want me resorting back to my

old self, but he was willing to allow it if I needed that. I didn't. Not when kind, comforting, beautiful David offered me a different future. "Merlot sounds good," I said.

He poured a glass, handed it to me, and turned. "If you need anything—"

"You're not getting in?" I asked, sniffling back a rogue tear.

He looked back, chewing the inside of his cheek a moment. "I . . . I haven't kept my hands off you since the moment you got here," he said. "You need some time alone."

"I need *you*."

"I want you to feel comfortable here," he said. "To have your own space without me all up in your business."

"Please get in my business?" I asked, biting my lip.

He shifted on his feet. I was beginning to notice that he was prone to do so when he was fighting himself.

I gave him my best, most exaggerated pout, preying on the indecision in his eyes. "I don't *want* to be alone," I said.

"How can I say no to that?" He pulled down his underwear. Presented with his glorious, naked form, which had given me so much pleasure the past few days, my pout vanished, replaced with a smile.

"Like what you see?" he teased.

I splashed him, laughing as he, in one quick movement, submerged himself in the water across from me. His long legs hit the back of the tub behind me, and he broke down the bubbles between us. He found my ankles, circling them in his fists before running his palms along my calves.

"I don't even know your mom's name," he said.

"Leanore."

"She still drinks, I gather."

I nodded. "I don't know how often. We don't talk much. Last time I brought up her drinking, she got angry and said she wasn't an alcoholic because she only drinks when she's stressed."

David sat forward and placed his hands on the outsides of my thighs. His gaze narrowed, and I knew what was coming. I'd heard it before, mostly from Bill. Lectures on how I needed to be there for my mom, to help her through hard times. How she deserved more from me because she was my mother, and family always came first.

"Olivia," he started sternly. "I'm sorry that she called you a slut."

"Heard that, did you?" I asked.

"It's not true."

I shifted against the back of the tub and looked down into the bubbles. "I know."

"Look at me."

I met his gaze, and his grip tightened on my legs. "What you did—what *we* did—does not make you a slut." He took a tentative breath. "Does she call you names often?"

"Only when drinking. She's more of the passive aggressive, cold-shoulder type when she's sober."

"I see," he said. "That's not necessarily better."

I shrugged. "I'm tougher for it."

"You keep people out. Because of her."

I looked away, my mind blanking. *I keep people out?* It wasn't anything revolutionary, but this conversation was beginning to echo one I'd had with Bill six months earlier. "You think I'm cold."

"Cold? Baby, no. Why would you say that?" He scooted closer and flattened his hand on my chest. "You're warm. So warm that you make me warm. I can see you're hurting from all the things you carry inside."

I put my hand over his and squeezed. "Bill thinks I'm cold."

"He doesn't know you, haven't I said that over and over? But it doesn't matter anymore what he thinks. What *I* think is that you take everything in, and you keep it there. You have to let it out at some point. You can't shut down with me like you did with him."

My heart skipped. Most of me wanted that—it was why I was here. But the part of me that feared opening up and letting someone in so deep would always exist. "I won't hide."

"Don't tell me what I want to hear. You will hide, and I will continue to find you. But you have to promise to try. You trust what we're doing here, don't you?"

I bit my lip. "It won't happen overnight, but I'm taking small steps every day. And yes, I'm terrified of this, but there's no one else I would take those steps for. No one at all."

He answered with a goofy, almost proud smile. All because I said I'd *try* to open up—and with his evident joy as my reward, it made me want to.

I inhaled a steady breath and closed my eyes. "I didn't really understand how bad things were between my parents until the last year they were together. Dad told me it got harder to hide their fights from me."

David sat back. "You told me she'd been drinking that night."

I leaned my head against the tub and kept my eyes shut. "Yes. Dad was really late, and he hadn't called. I guess she had some secret stash of alcohol in the house because before long, she was drunk." David took my ankles again and massaged. I gave in to the feeling of his strong hands, of being deliciously shackled by him. "Before I went to bed, she told me that my dad wasn't home because he was 'fucking another woman' and that she was going to leave him in the morning and take me with her."

"Jesus. Or, should I say, *Gina.*"

"Gina. Yes. The woman he ended up leaving my mom for." How had David remembered our conversation that now felt so long ago? I lifted my head and looked at him. "I loved my mom, David, but *she* was cold. To me and to my dad. I never felt like she really wanted me around. I heard her say once that he loved me too much and that I was spoiled because of it."

"She called you spoiled earlier."

I nodded. "Bill thinks I am, too. Because my dad—he's a tough guy, but he constantly reminded me that I was his little girl, and he'd take care of me no matter what. That I was safe with him."

"As he should've," David said with a frown. "You're not spoiled. Not yet, anyway. I plan to remedy that."

I playfully rolled my eyes, knowing he meant it.

David sat forward and stretched for a kiss. "Keep going," he said.

As he started to pull back, I grasped his arm. "Don't leave," I whispered.

He opened his arms, so I turned around and settled my weight against his chest. "I was terrified by what my mom had told me and couldn't sleep," I said. "I didn't want to leave my dad. I mean, it was the alcohol talking—she never would've gone through with ending their marriage."

David sifted my hair through his fingers. "But you didn't know that at the time."

I shook my head. "I told you already I was spying that night. I was so scared. I hid in the next room and watched. My mom was yelling about perfume and sex and lying, and things got very surreal. I can't remember much more than that. She pulled the knife. My instincts kicked in, and I ran in the middle. She lunged. She stabbed me in the side by accident. There was screaming, the sound of the knife hitting the floor . . . I had this long hair, down to my waist —it was tangled and almost black with blood. That's the last thing I remember thinking before I passed out, that I needed to wash the blood out of my hair. I woke up in the hospital. My dad cried and apologized—that was the most painful part, watching him blame himself. He promised I'd never see the inside of that house again because he was divorcing her."

David's fingers paused in my hair, but then continued threading after a moment. "He sounds like a smart man."

"I had just started middle school," I said. "Before that, *divorce* was just a word I'd heard because of Gretchen's parents. Still, I didn't really grasp the concept. I asked the nurse for a dictionary, and when I was alone, I looked it up to make sure I understood it correctly. In the definition, the word I could never get out of my head was *dissolve*. Nothing had dissolved. It'd broken in half, suddenly and without warning."

"And after?" David asked.

I shifted against his body. "Everything changed. I didn't want to be with my mom, but she was still my mom. I didn't want to be away from her, either. He had to stay in Dallas for work, so we moved into a new house across town. I got to stay close to Gretchen, and when she trans-ferred to my school, she threatened to beat up anyone who spread rumors about why I'd gone to the hospital. Gretchen told me that I needed to cry and that she knew how I felt, she'd been through it . . . but I couldn't. I just couldn't. I knew I was supposed to cry, but nothing came. So it built inside of me. And built and built and built. The tears, the shame, the pain."

David continued playing with my hair, soothing and comforting me as he listened. "When did you finally talk about it?" he asked.

I twisted around and steadied myself with a hand against his pec. "I didn't."

His eyebrows lowered. "How's that possible?"

"Gretchen's caught me in a vulnerable moment a few times over the years. My dad took me to a therapist, but she had no patience for me. After our third session she gave up, and I told my dad I never wanted to go to another one." I curled my hand against David's chest. "It's difficult for me to talk about because I don't think I ever really got over how suddenly things changed. This is the most I've ever said about it."

David's eyes grew darker, it seemed, not their normal, beautiful chestnut-brown. "Bill?" he asked gruffly. "Surely you talked about it with him."

"He knew the divorce was hard and that I hated talking about it. I gave him the bones of the story, and he's close with my mom—she told him the details of that night, which I only recently found out. But I drilled into him that I hated having it brought up, specifically that night. He respected that."

"Unlike some people," David said with a half-smile.

Unlike you.

David pushed me in ways others didn't, and for some reason, I gave in. "Going through this separation from Bill has taught me some things about our relationship," I said. "I think I didn't want him to know more because it would mean showing him my pain and letting him in. And on some level, *he* didn't want to know. It was easier for him to ignore."

David leaned his forehead in and cupped my jaw. "That will never be me," he said. "I want you to give me everything, because I can take it. Because I want to take it." He looked at me earnestly, truth in his eyes. He was strong enough to take it all, to shoulder what I couldn't.

"I lied to you," I whispered. "I lied when I said Bill and I had talked about my scar. He never asked, and I never brought it up."

"Never?" he asked.

"A few weeks ago, I finally brought it up to him," I said. "But it was too late."

"Your mom had it the wrong way. *He* didn't deserve *you*," David said. "He was lucky as fuck that he ever got you, but he didn't know what to do with you."

"It was my fault, too," I said. "I kept him at a distance."

"It's not your fault, Olivia. He wasn't worthy, and somewhere inside, you knew that."

I wasn't sure if that was true, but somewhere inside, *something* had kept me from confiding in Bill. I hoped that something was right to share my burden with David. I turned and rested my back against his chest again.

"Things are starting to make more sense," David said as he hugged my shoulders.

"What things?" I asked.

"When you told me you'd never experienced an orgasm with anyone, I almost didn't believe you. But I get it now. You knew it wasn't right. You need to feel safe and loved in order to open up, even physically."

"Bill loved me, though," I said. "I chose him *because* he was safe."

"But you didn't trust him enough to let him have all of you. And you were right not to." He put his mouth to my temple. "You held back for a reason. In the end, no, you didn't feel safe with him, couldn't trust him, and your body knew."

I took a deep breath and let David's words sink in. Bill loved me, but he didn't know me. Not like David did. And

David had waited a while for me to figure that out. "That would mean . . ." I let the sentence trail.

"That would mean that you feel it with me. You know you're safe with me, you can open underneath me, and you do. You open for me like a fucking flower, baby. It's beautiful."

I couldn't imagine anyone else in the world describing me that way. "It's nice to talk to you about this," I confessed. "It's the first time I've ever wanted to."

"You asked me once why it's so nice walking together," he said softly in my ear. "This is why. You and I are supposed to be."

"Do you really feel that way?" I asked, tilting my head to look up at him. "After everything I just told you, and after last night with Bill and Maria, and then my mom—and maybe my dad will have doubts, too. And we might lose Andrew and Lucy. Do you still think this is supposed to be?"

"No question," he said, smiling.

I rubbed his forearm and eased deeper into his body, letting my head fall back on his chest. In a warm bath, with David wrapped around me, nothing could touch me. Not even my past. Safe and protected, I relaxed.

"So sweet to have you fall asleep in my arms," he said.

I blinked my eyes open to a hazy bathroom. "Did I fall asleep?"

"Just for a couple minutes," he replied.

I smiled and sat forward so he could climb out. He stepped over the side while I watched, holding my knees to my breasts as the water drained around me. He dried himself off and wrapped a towel around his waist.

I stood and let him wrap me in a towel, too. He disappeared for a moment and returned with a simple white satin nightie, the partner to his favorite robe. He slipped it over my head when I raised my hands. The fabric cooled and soothed my skin, sensitive from the hot bath.

We didn't bother with anything else except to wind ourselves around each other and bury our bodies under a heavy comforter to block out a chilly night.

I was certain I'd never been so happy.

Chapter Eleven

A weekend of feverish, frantic sex turned out to be the best sleep aide. I woke up to an empty bed and gave my aching body a hard stretch. I couldn't remember sleeping so well two nights in a row. David had worn me out.

And then, he'd helped me relax. After our sweet and sensual bath the night before, something in me had broken free. Finally, I'd told my story, emptying myself of a past I'd locked away and tried to forget. And he'd listened through all of it—and he'd heard me. For once, my emptiness wasn't a bad thing, but a well to be filled by David and our new life.

"Good morning, beautiful," David said from the bathroom doorway.

I blinked from the memory and looked at my gorgeous man. All mine, standing there in nothing but his low-slung gray sweatpants and a toothbrush working in his mouth.

It is *a good morning. Who knew a Monday morning could be* so *good?*

"Morning," I replied, licking my lips. Those gray sweatpants, drooping on his hips, reminded me of our first night together. Chaste as it was, they stirred all sorts of fantasies in me. His long and tan torso, pecs of steel, and arms and shoulders personified strength and power. I thought I'd die there on the spot if I knew I'd never get to feel the crush of those biceps again. Or see that tousled hair, unruly from sleep.

And *fuck* . . . those gray sweatpants. So hot.

He raised an eyebrow at me and stopped brushing. "Love that your office is right by mine," he said. "I'll drop you off at work today. Cool?"

I nodded and took a deep breath. My thoughts jumbled with the fact that he was half-naked and full-sexy in front of me. His six-pack became more defined as he brushed, and it reminded me of the way his abs would flex when he was on top of me, thrusting away.

As soon as he disappeared into the bathroom, I scrambled out of bed. He was bent over to spit when I walked in. As he glanced up, I caught his eye in the reflection, stripped off my white satin nightie in one motion, and flung it at him. He snatched it midair with his free hand as I continued to the shower. He was hot on my tail, and as soon as I'd stepped into the stream of water, he was there, shielding it with his massive shoulders.

He took my face in his hands for a rough kiss before sliding one hand down my back to grip my ass. He pulled me against his hardness, but there was only one thing I wanted desperately in that moment. I dropped to my knees. Bracing my back against the shower bench, I wrapped my mouth around him.

"Jesus," he said.

I took him to the back of my throat and then drew back slowly, sucking as I did. I relished the feel of him growing bigger and harder in the softness of my mouth, the brackish pre-cum that made my jaw tingle.

My tongue greedily paid respect to every ridge and vein of him. I licked anywhere I could, swirling the tip of my tongue over and under his crown until his groans echoed through the bathroom and the glass rattled as he made a fist against it. My eyes flicked up to his as I held the base of his cock in my hand and opened my throat to take all of him.

I was feeling powerful, watching the effect I had on him, until one deep, rolling grunt easily muted my soft moans. He leaned himself on the wall behind me. "Hands," he clipped. I immediately clasped them behind my back. Propping himself against the stone with one arm, he tangled his other hand in my hair as he took over. He thrust as deep as he could and only pulled back when my eyes watered and my throat constricted around him.

"Oh, fuck. Yes, yes, yes," he grunted with each flex of his hips, tilting my head up and demanding my eyes meet his. I grabbed his ass and urged him deeper, excited by the way he unraveled for me. Right as I vibrated a moan against him, he flooded my mouth with thick semen. I swallowed it, thick and gummy as it shot down my throat and dribbled over my chin.

"Christ," he said, resting his forearms against the wall. I coughed into my fist to quell the burning in my throat. When he spoke again, his words were ragged but curt. "Get up."

I hurried up between him and the bench, weak in the knees for what he was planning.

"Turn around, grab the edge."

I faced the wall and bent over to steady myself against the bench. He ran a hand up my right thigh, and it disappeared for only a second. As he brought it down against my ass, the bathroom resounded with a *slap*. I tightened my grip on the edge with the delicious sting.

"Stay," he ordered.

My breathing grew jagged, and the muscles between my legs quivered as I steeled myself to receive him. I bit my lip when I thought of how he'd just come hot and out of control in my mouth. I wanted to feel him inside me *now*, taking what he needed. I almost bit my lip off when I let my head fall between my arms and saw his naked size fourteen-and-a-half feet.

I felt a soapy hand between my legs. "David," I whined. "Please."

"Please what?" he asked huskily.

"Please—I'm so ready."

He skated one hand up my back and grasped the ends of my hair, pulling softly. He set his other palm on my backside and rubbed it gently. As it landed against my skin with more force this time, I cried out.

"Ready for what?" he asked.

"To get fucked," I begged.

"How do you want it, baby?"

"Hard," I rasped. "I need it."

His hand returned between my legs, opening me up. I trembled as he played with me, alternating between rubbing my clit, inserting a finger, and spreading my wetness over me. When I felt the pressure of his cock against my opening, I shuddered.

His other hand pulled my hair at the same moment he shoved into me, propelling me forward. I gasped, my knuckles whitening on the edge. He slid out and then inched back in so I felt myself stretching and then closing around him.

"You're made for me," he said on a growl.

"Because I'm yours."

He gave me another hard thrust, bouncing me forward. "You know I fucking love when you say that."

His body closed over mine, and his breath heated my shoulder. He rocked into me, picking up his pace as he tugged on my hair.

"Pull it," I pleaded through gritted teeth. His fist tightened and yanked. He kissed the skin at the nape of my neck and then between my shoulder blades, all the while driving steadily into me. He wrapped both hands over my shoulders, straightened up, and began hammering me as he pulled me back onto him.

I squeezed my eyes shut and whimpered as I took him to the base. "Oh, God," I yelled into the bite of pain. I braced myself against the bench and pushed back harder.

"Christ, Olivia. Give it back to me," he uttered. I faintly registered the sound of slapping skin echoing throughout the shower. As one hand knotted into my hair, he spanked me again.

Then he was pulling on my biceps, demanding my hands behind my back. His fingers wrapped around my wrists, putting me in his complete control. His grip tightened and my arms twisted as he took me fast, his chest rumbling as he got closer to the edge.

This was his finale; this was how he wanted me to come. My breath caught as my insides coiled for him, lost in the sensation of submission. My toes curled into the stone floor. I held on and clenched around him, squeezing his dick and eliciting incoherent words of praise from him.

As I tipped into oblivion, I had the urge to grab something and hold on, but he still had me tightly in his grip. I could only focus on the heat rippling through my body in rays of molten bliss, and somewhere in my consciousness I heard his roar, felt his warmth begin to flow, pouring himself into me . . .

Only me. I'm *doing this to him.*

I fell to my knees, and once I was down, he released my wrists.

"Jesus," he said, staring at me, his breathing labored. "You're on fire in the morning."

I only looked back at him, blinking and trying to catch my own breath. "It's your fault," I said as he bent down and hauled me to my feet. "Those sweatpants . . ."

His eyebrows shot up. "Sweatpants?"

"You, shirtless, sweatpants," I managed. "Super sexy, honey."

He grinned. "You blow me first thing in the morning. Then you let me fuck you to your knees. Now you're telling me I'm sexy?"

"Not sexy. Super sexy," I corrected.

His eyes darkened, and he seized my waist, jerking me to him. "Mmm," he moaned against my mouth, squeezing me. "I love your pussy that wet, your wrists in my hands, letting me give it to you hard as I can. You're so tight, but you take every inch."

I nodded against his mouth. "I can take it," I whispered.

He drew back slightly, and his eyes changed—softer, but still intense. "I lose myself in you," he said. "I could fuck you again right now, just as hard. I'm like a damn teenager."

I ran my hands along biceps I would never tire of touching. "I lose myself, too."

"Is it too much?" he asked.

I thought about the rolling, destructive orgasm that had just brought me to my knees. It was his utter and complete control that had taken me there. "Oh, God, yes, too much," I said, "and it's perfect."

He kissed me deeply before trailing hard kisses over my temple to the top of my head. I let him hold me for a minute before pulling back. "I'm going to be late," I reminded him.

"I'd better start setting my alarm earlier," he said.

I laughed, even though he hadn't meant it to be funny.

"Holy fuck," he said to himself, shaking his head.

As David dressed, I stood dumbstruck in my robe and wiped drool—real or imaginary, I wasn't sure—from the corner of my mouth. Watching him get ready for work was as beautiful a way to start the day as anything I could think of. It was hard to believe that we'd only really been doing this a few days. He'd shaken me from my waking sleep and introduced me to a life of color, hope, love, and sex. Rip-roaring, amazing, out-of-this-world sex.

He flipped his collar and did up his tie in the mirror while I gaped like an audience member at *Cirque du Soleil*.

"It doesn't normally take me this long to put on a tie, but you're distracting me," he said, his eyes fastened on the mirror.

"Sorry." My cheeks heated, and I looked around the massive closet, taking in the absurd amount of suits, ties, dress shirts, and shoes. My insides stirred when I thought of what I might like to do to businessman David in one of his fancy suits.

Snap out of it! I'd fantasized about David countless times since we'd met, but now I had him—and I'd just *had* him in the shower. Why was I still fantasizing?

I refocused my attention on picking out an outfit for work, eyeing the pieces we'd purchased over the weekend. I smiled when I spotted the simple black dress he'd zipped me into right after he'd made me quietly come with his fingers. Our conversation from that moment filtered through my mind. Something he'd said had nagged at me that day, but in my post-orgasmic stupor, I hadn't been able to grasp it. I replayed the memory.

"You have one like this, don't you? With the thingie?" he asked, motioning to the shoulder of the dress.

I smiled, amused that he was at all familiar with my wardrobe, although I couldn't remember wearing that particular dress around him. "I have one with a rosette, yes. Different designer but similar."

"What's wrong?" David asked, jarring me from the memory.

I looked up. "I've never worn that dress around you," I said.

"Pardon?" he asked, righting his collar and glancing over at me.

"The black dress with the 'thingie' on the shoulder—the rosette. You said I already owned something like it,"—I pulled out the hanger with the new dress—"but how did you know? I never wore the other dress around you."

"Are you sure?" He walked over to peck me sweetly on the lips. His fingers pushed hair from my face. "I've seen you in your work clothes lots of times." He cleared his throat and looked away.

I was sure, because I'd only worn that dress once—to Davena's funeral. Instantly, heavy tears welled in my eyes, and one dropped down my cheek. "You were there, weren't you?"

David took a deep breath, ran his thumb along my cheekbone, and looked directly at me. "Yes. I attended the funeral."

My chin quivered, and I wiped my face, careful not to smear my makeup. "Why?"

His mouth twitched as he looked at me, and finally, he shrugged. "Why do you think? You had her death to deal with, plus Mark Alvarez, plus running out on me days earlier after our night together. I was worried."

"But I never saw you," I said.

"I stayed in the back so you wouldn't."

"You were there, and you didn't say anything?" I asked. "How'd you know when . . . where?"

"It wasn't hard to find out," he said sadly. "I was concerned Bill wouldn't show up because of some bullshit work excuse. But he did. I saw you two together, and that was tough, but it was nothing compared to how heartbroken you were. I could see it in your face . . . and he didn't do shit . . . I wish it had been me by your side."

I stared at him in mild shock. It hadn't occurred to me David might show. That he might watch me go through the motions, ignore Bill's grief and his attempts to comfort me, however lame they were. That he'd be there in case I'd needed him.

After a beat, he asked, "Are you mad?"

"Mad?" I exclaimed. "I can't believe you did that for me."

"I told you I was looking out." He ran his thumb under one of my eyes and then the other. "Don't cry."

"I'm so lucky," I said. Before he could respond, I put back the dress and rose onto the balls of my feet to kiss him, steadying myself on his forearms. Even then he had to lean down to meet me.

"Thank you," I said.

"It was my pleasure." He smiled. "What do you want for breakfast?"

It was such a regular, everyday inquiry, but I couldn't

help smiling wider. We were a couple now, and those were the things couples asked each other. "I've been too preoccupied to think about it."

"Mmm, preoccupied you say?" he asked, reaching under my robe and tightening his hand over my ass. "What do you want?"

I could only focus on the way his hand possessively pulled me against him. "Hmm?"

"For breakfast."

I didn't want to eat. I just wanted to stay there with David all day. "Did I ever tell you how sexy you look in a suit?" I breathed in a rush of air.

"Don't distract me. Breakfast?"

I sighed. "I don't have time. You go eat while I finish getting ready."

His eyebrows dipped together. "Olivia—"

"I don't have time to argue about my eating habits, either," I said, turning away from him. "I promise I'll have a big lunch instead."

He grunted but left me so I could get dressed. I sneaked a peek at his behind as he left the closet and vowed to get myself some businessman David very soon.

Chapter Twelve

The simple act of being driven to work, something that millions of people participated in every day, felt like a gift. Still, though I'd loved spending guilt-free time with David, my anxiety returned as we neared my office.

I could anticipate some reactions, but not my co-workers'. They all knew David as one of Chicago's top bachelors featured in our "Most Eligible" issue months before. And most of them also knew Bill—as my husband, of course. I sighed when I thought of all the explaining I'd have to do in the near future and decided to put it off for as long as possible.

"This weekend was crazy and hectic and a whirlwind," I told David as he drove, "but in the best way possible."

He reached over to rub my knee. "Don't forget, we have a date tonight."

I grinned. "Can't wait."

"Have lunch with me, too. Something big and greasy to make up for missing breakfast."

I laughed. "I have a date tonight. Don't want to look fat."

"Fat?" he grumbled. "Is that supposed to be a joke?"

"Yep," I said. "I know I'm skinnier than normal, David."

"It's not funny."

"*All right.* Yes, handsome, I'll have lunch with you." I waited a moment before peeking over to see if he'd settled. "God, you are handsome, though."

He rolled his eyes. "Take a picture, it'll last longer."

And that's exactly what I planned to do. I pulled out my new phone and found a missed call from the night before. *Bill.* A missed call from the husband I'd devastated a few days earlier was not surprising but definitely unsettling.

I ignored it and snapped a picture of David's perfect profile. The profile that, in this same position, I'd fallen for months ago when I'd agonized over not being able to touch him. For that, I reached over and felt the muscles of his arm under his shirt. When I raised my hand to his cheek, he leaned into my palm. I returned my eyes out the windshield but played with the ends of his hair—so as not to mess it up—until we arrived at my office building.

I reached for my seatbelt, but he stopped me. "I'll get that," he said with a mischievous smile.

My face heated as his fingers grazed the houndstooth wool fabric of my new skirt, and I wished suddenly there wasn't so much of it. He hit the release, but his hand lingered, sliding up my thigh until his fingers brushed between my legs. I involuntarily sucked in a breath.

He leaned over awkwardly in the small space of the car and kissed me on the cheek. "Let's ditch," he said against the corner of my mouth, and I sighed. "I'll take you home, throw you on the bed, watch you ride me till you come on my dick. Then I'll flip you on your back, make you come again underneath me."

I whimpered as his hand compressed my thigh. He turned my face to his so we were inches apart. "You know, when you're about to come, your body trembles like a leaf. It makes me rock hard just thinking about it." He kissed me hard and much too deeply for the start of a workday. His tongue invaded my mouth, thorough and probing like it was searching for something. When he pulled away abruptly, I might have been swaying, and I definitely saw stars. "You're now *officially* late," he noted.

I was somehow both breathless and breathing heavy, and it took me a moment before I said, "Shit."

"Want me to write you a note?" he asked, slipping on his sunglasses as I gathered my purse.

"Beman would be thrilled, actually," I muttered. "He has a crush on you."

David's grin faded. "I don't like your boss, Olivia."

"Yeah, well, I don't like Arnaud," I retorted and clamped my hand over my mouth. "Oops. Sorry."

"Wait, what?" David raised his sunglasses. "Why not?"

"I'm sorry, baby," I said, pecking him on the lips. "I didn't mean it. Have to run." I shut the door and took a few steps before turning and waving quickly.

It wasn't that I worried David would tell his colleague what I thought. I just didn't want David to feel weird bringing me around the office. He'd worked with Arnaud Mallory for most of his professional career, and that included their house-flipping business on the side. I had enough conflict in my life without making enemies of David's friends. And I vaguely remembered David referring to Arnaud as a brilliant architect, which meant he wasn't exactly expendable.

I decided to worry about my careless comment later as I sneaked into the office relatively unnoticed. Oddly, my day continued normally. It seemed, with the uprooting of my life, as if the world should feel differently, as if everyone should look and act differently, but they didn't. Jenny, the office receptionist, remained cheerful. Serena, my assistant, stopped by my office to chat twice before ten in the morning. Lisa, the toxic co-worker, dutifully ignored me when I passed her in the hallway and a curt nod from Beman, my boss, meant he'd acknowledged my existence and nothing more.

A text from David around lunchtime was a very welcome distraction.

David: *Swamped over here. I need an assistant.*

Me: *Want me to come fill in for the day?*

David: *I'd get nothing done.*

Me: *But I think I'd be a good fit for the job, Mr. Dylan.*

David: *Qualifications?*

I smiled. I was no architect, but I could work with what little I knew. Attempting to keep a straight face, I tapped out a response.

Me: *I've been told I have unequaled skills in steel erection… In fact, I was cantilevered just this weekend and can be for hours on end.*

David: *That's all good, Ms. Germaine, but being an architect's assistant is very physical work. It involves a lot of hammering, mounting & screwing.*

Me: *As it happens, I'm a pro at nailing studs. When do I start?*

David: *Right away. We'll begin with any and all cracks that need caulking.*

I clasped my hand over my mouth and giggled.

"Something funny?" I heard.

I jumped in my chair as my head snapped up to find Bill in the doorway. "Jesus," I said, adjusting my mood from giddy to somber. "What are you doing here? How'd you get in?"

"I'm your husband." He frowned. "How do you think?"

"Right. Sorry." I exhaled, trying to get my heart rate to slow. "You startled me."

Purple bruises rimmed his eyes and swollen nose. My heart squeezed at the sight of him. He looked tired, defeated, and though he was dressed for work, I wondered if he'd slept in his rumpled suit.

"You can't ignore my calls, Olivia," he said. "We have things to figure out."

"I wasn't." I refrained from pointing out that *he'd* cut off my cell service. I ignored him and said, "Your nose."

"Broken." He held up his bandaged right hand. "Sprained."

"I'm so sorry." Out of instinct, I stood to go to him but stopped myself. Instead, I gestured at a chair. "Come in. Sit. Are you in pain?"

He furrowed his brows at me and finally stepped in the office, closing the door behind him. "We need to talk."

I nodded and sat back down, scooting my chair under my desk. "Saturday night was awful. I'd really like if we could keep this divorce civil."

Anger crossed his face but disappeared in a flash. He slumped into the chair across from me and sighed while scrubbing a hand over his hair. "God. Please, just . . . think about what you're doing."

I fidgeted with a pen on my desk. "I wouldn't have let things get this far if I hadn't thought long and hard already."

"Babe, take a step back and look at the facts here," he said, growing animated. "This guy is using you. He'll get bored and dump you like the others. You were a challenge, and it won't take long for that to wear off. For him, it's just a conquest. It's just sex."

I shook my head. I'd beat back those same fears too many times to have Bill come in here and revive them. "You don't know him."

"I asked around, Livs. I don't trust him and neither does Andrew. He screws models, never been married, wealthy, charming, all-around player. I don't know why he bought the house we wanted, maybe to show off, maybe because he gets off on it."

"Hang on." I picked up my phone to shoot David a quick text.

Me: *Can't make lunch. Something came up. Explain later.*

"Look, this is hard for all of us," I said, switching my phone to silent. "Don't make it worse. What you're saying about David is conjecture. Gossip. You don't know him," I repeated.

"I obviously care about you, and I don't want to see you get hurt," Bill said. "But what happens when, six months down the line, he leaves and you're all alone? I'm not going to be there, babe. I won't wait for you."

I looked down at my hands. For the first time since all this began, Bill seemed calm and rational. Not only that, but his words made sense. David had a track record. He wasn't hiding it, but I suspected I hadn't even scratched the surface of his past. He'd explained his relationship with Maria. But it occurred to me that David had admitted to me he'd never been in love.

"I didn't love her or any of them," he'd said on Saturday night.

Who'd come before Maria? Had he thought he was in love with them at some point and then changed his mind?

I looked back up at Bill. In spite of everything I'd put him through that weekend alone, he met my eyes with warmth—for maybe the first time in months, actually. Even though Bill hadn't always been there in the ways I'd needed him to be, he'd always wanted me to be happy. He loved me as much as I'd let him.

David was rarely challenged when it came to women. For me, he'd had to work, probably harder than he ever had. If he were to pick up and leave, as Bill was convinced he would, it would cripple me. But what would it be like for David? And had he done that to others before?

Bill lived in a world of facts and order—he was logical. Wasn't that who I was, too? There *was* a chance David only wanted what he couldn't have. Even I had accused him of that. He could easily grow bored with the day-to-day of a relationship.

"Look at what you're giving up for him." Bill's quiet voice cut into my thoughts. "Our love. Our future. Our home. Our past. And what has he given up for you?" he asked, suddenly astute, suddenly paying attention in a way he'd never really been.

"I can't explain what I have with David," I told Bill, "and I don't want to try. What you need is someone who wants what you want, and who can love you in a way I'm not capable of. I never let you in, you told me so yourself."

"It takes work." He sat back. "Maybe this marriage would benefit from both of us working harder."

"I never let you in," I repeated, "and you liked it that way. You didn't want to deal with my shit."

"That's not true, babe," he insisted. "But if that's what you need, I will change. I will be better. I will ask questions like you said you wanted me to. We'll get there, Livs, I know we will."

I was *already* there with David. I couldn't tell Bill that without cutting him deeper, so I took a breath and looked him in the eyes. "I don't think I'll ever get there," I admitted, and in my head, I added, *with you*.

"You don't know that. Look how far we've come since we met. We're different people, better people."

I cocked my head at him. Were we better people? Didn't he ever feel me pulling away? Hadn't I treated him awfully these past months as I recessed into my own depths? Did he mean it, or was he grasping at straws now?

And there was something that had never changed between us, and I didn't think ever would. "Children," I said.

He looked surprised. "Children?"

"Yes. You want them, I don't. Could you be happy if we never had them?"

He ran a hand through his hair. "Look, I know you *think* you don't want—"

"It's not that," I said for the millionth time. "I—"

"Wait. I know you think you don't want them, but you will," he said. "Some women don't get the urge for a few more years. I've always trusted in what we're doing here. All I ask is, if I agree to put it off, that you'll admit there's some part of you that wants it, too."

"Stop telling me what I want," I muttered, resting my forehead in my hands.

I don't want children. With you. I don't want children with you . . . but do I want them with David? Do I want them at all?

The rashness of my decision to uproot my life began to weigh on me. David and I had not discussed children ever, because what other couple would a weekend into their relationship?

It was far too heavy of an idea to lay into, so for now, I pushed it aside. I needed to get my point across to Bill. I raised my head again. "I don't think I want children at all, Bill. With anyone."

He scoffed. "How can you say that? You're a woman."

"Not all women want children."

"David doesn't want them?" he asked skeptically.

I looked at the desk.

He emitted something between a laugh and a grunt. "You don't even know. Liv, honey, what are you *doing*?" he implored. "You left me for another man, and you haven't even discussed the future? Does he say he wants to marry you?"

My eyes jumped to his. "It's too soon for that."

"Too soon? You walked out on me *for him*." He leaned on his elbows and clasped his hands between his knees. "Let's say he's actually serious about you. What happens when he decides he's ready for a family? You going to run away from him, too? Or will you give *him* what he wants?"

My chest tightened. I didn't want to think about that. "Forget him," I said. "This is about you and me. I know you want to believe things were fine, but they weren't. Our problems ran deeper than David, and . . ."

"And?"

I thought back to what Jessa had said about her marriage at the park. That it wouldn't have lasted, even without her husband cheating on her. "You and I probably would've divorced eventually," I told him. "Isn't sooner better than later?"

He gaped at me. "You know, I'm actually beginning to feel bad for David. Maybe *you're* the one who's going to string *him* along and then dump his ass when he wants more from you." Bill shook his head. "I wonder if he realizes just how cold and heartless you really are. Over the years, I've seen glimpses of how deep it runs. You can't even find empathy for your own mom, your *family*. And you tell me you want a divorce without shedding even one tear. I thought it was just a part of you, but this moment I see—that's you to the core."

I flinched. The words stung. If it made him feel better to say so, though, I would take it. Still, I clung to David's words in the bathtub the night before and disagreed quietly. "He doesn't think those things about me."

"How could he?" Bill rolled his eyes. "He's known you all of two seconds."

I realized I was pulling on my earlobe, a sure sign of my discomfort. It reminded me of how David always noticed when I did that—the only person who'd ever wondered about it. "He knows me better than anyone."

Bill started to chuckle, then stopped, blinking at me. With a low whistle, he said, "Wow. Brainwashed after a weekend. I might be impressed actually."

I folded my arms on my desk. "I know it sounds ridiculous, and I don't expect you to understand."

"Try me," he said. "What makes you think he knows you better?"

"I can be myself with him. He anticipates my feelings, and when he doesn't know, he asks. He asks me about myself."

"*I said* I'd ask questions. What do you want me to ask? Better yet, why don't you just *tell me* so I don't have to ask?

You're the one who clams up, and I'm being punished for it."

"Yes," I agreed. "You're right. I admit that I should have done things differently from the start."

"It's not too late. We can start with the scar." He glanced at my desk as if trying to see through it. "You can tell me everything."

"The scar," I said. He already knew the details because he'd discussed it with my mother behind my back. "That reminds me—you told my mom about David before I could. You called her," I accused.

"Because I'm at a loss for what to do, and I'm worried about you." He stood to pace in front of my desk. "I don't know how to get through and show you that you're making a mistake. Your mom knows about this stuff. She has experience."

"She *doesn't* have experience," I shot back. "She's lying. Dad never cheated on her. It was all in her head."

He pursed his lips. "Me and your mom, we're on your side. You're the one who abandoned us. You ran out on her, and now you're running out on me. But . . ." Bill rounded the desk and shocked me by dropping to his knees in front of my chair. He took my hands in his one good hand. "Please, Olivia. Don't do this. I love you, and we can work this out. We'll do counseling if you want, I don't care. I love you," he repeated. "I can change. I'll ask questions. We can put off having a baby. We can get to know each other all over again."

My mind went blank just trying to comprehend what was happening. When had Bill ever begged me for anything? I had no idea how to respond. But finally, he got what he wanted—tears flooded my eyes and fell onto our hands as I cried for us, in his presence, for the first time in a while.

"Listen," he said softly. "Are you listening?"

I nodded because I was. This was a side of Bill I had never seen, and he had my attention.

He looked into me, his familiar brown eyes suddenly intense and lucid. "I don't want you to get hurt. What is he giving up for you? He's never been married because he doesn't want to be. What makes you different? How do you know he doesn't say the same things to the other girls? That's what womanizers *do*, Liv. He gets off on using women and tossing them aside, and you were the ultimate conquest."

Stop. The words made too much sense, and I couldn't blame Bill for saying them. I'd thought them many times myself, beating them back—but with what? Truths or excuses so I have more time with David?

My breath caught in my chest, stuttering to get out. "Bill," I pleaded. "Stop."

"No. You wanted me to break through—that's what I'm doing. He's not good for you. Even Dani says David has no regard for women, and he treats them like trash."

My mouth popped open at the mention of Danielle, Lucy's sister. David's ex. Had he treated her like trash? Hadn't she called him a gentleman? "She's making that up because he didn't choose her," I said, but I heard the wavering in my own voice. I'd never known Dani to be a liar.

Bill shook his head slowly. "I didn't want to tell you, but she said . . ." He hesitated and looked away for a moment. When his gaze returned, his expression softened. "She said after he finally screwed her, she never heard from him again."

My heart dropped. David had sworn to me that there'd been nothing more between them than a one-sided kiss at the masquerade ball. My mind flashed to that night.

According to him, it was the last time they'd seen each other. And that night, he and I had fucked hard and fought harder. He'd cast me aside angrily, maybe thinking he'd never see me again. Perhaps finding comfort in Danielle.

And there was her pink hoodie in his car, physical evidence of their relationship. "That's not . . . true," I said, trying to hide my internal struggle.

Would Dani lie about that? Would Bill?

"Whether or not it's true, it could've happened," he said. "Think about how devastated you'll be if you throw everything away for nothing." He ran his hand over mine. "I'll never leave you, babe," he said as a tear ran down his cheek. "I've been by your side through all of this."

I sniffled, and he winced as he straightened up and took my face. He leaned in, holding me still, until his lips touched mine.

And he kissed me.

Chapter Thirteen

In the middle of the workday, at my office, the husband I'd asked for a divorce kissed me.

It was a different kiss than I was used to from Bill—humble and affectionate until he deepened it. He moaned, opening my mouth with his tongue.

"Stop," I said, pulling back suddenly and wiping my face. "No, I can't."

His eyes, pained either by my words or by his broken nose, darted over my face. "Think about what you're doing," he said seriously. "You're throwing everything down the drain for a fling. He doesn't love you. I do. He doesn't want you as his wife. I do." I watched as more tears fell from Bill's pleading eyes. "Liv."

David *did* want me. He loved me. I couldn't lose sight of that. When he kissed me, fireworks lit up the world. But fireworks fizzled and faded, leaving nothing but smoky imprints in the sky that cleared before dawn. What would be left when David's and my passion waned?

Would *I* be the one on my knees, asking Bill for a

second chance? *No.* I couldn't wrap my head around that. I wouldn't let that happen, and neither would David. I shook my head and looked away.

After a moment, Bill dropped my hands and stood up. "You're making a huge mistake," he warned, wiping the corner of his eye. He backed away and left as abruptly as he'd appeared.

I got up, closed the door, and dropped my forehead against it.

"You're making a huge mistake."

Had David slept with Dani after the masquerade ball? And if so, could I blame him? I wasn't sure that I had any right to—after all, I'd gone home with my husband. But David had definitely denied it, and that was not something I could forgive.

Before my mind could conjure up the image of David and Dani together as it had many times before, I inhaled a soothing breath, returned to my desk chair, and closed my eyes.

This wasn't me—it was the bullshit jealousy I'd learned from my mother.

My gut told me David wouldn't lie to me. I was mildly comforted until I began thinking about the other things Bill had said.

They were logical. They made sense. And I couldn't ignore them.

The truth was, I'd acted rashly. Whenever it came to David, my decisions were made based on emotion. And there were reasons, long ago, that I'd decided I would never allow that. It always led to pain.

Now that David had caught me, how long would he hold me? What rule was there because I'd left my husband for him, he had to love me forever? I knew, I'd always known, there are no guarantees in love. More often than not, irrational love ended in pain. I felt suddenly ill . . . I'd let myself fall so deep in so little time.

My parents had been in love at one point, and they hadn't lasted. Greg and Gretchen had had that out of control, burning love in college, and then he'd walked away without looking back for years. And up until recently, I'd assumed Bill and I would be together forever. I didn't remember feeling one way or another about it, but I never imagined things would end.

Doubts began to tug at me. My father and his ex-wife, Gina. Gretchen's parents. David's sister and her husband. Now, Bill and me. Was there no such thing as forever?

Was Bill justified to say I was throwing everything away?

I believed David—that *he* believed he loved me and wanted to be with me. But he was a man who'd been living the life of a bachelor for a long time. And that meant acting alone. It meant that he might cut and run if things didn't go the way he wanted.

The thought of David leaving me *now,* after only a few days, had me mentally curling up into a ball—how bad would it get if he changed his mind about me in six months, a year, two years?

Lucy had called me strong in the restaurant when I'd told her about David, but she'd been wrong. I'd only pretended to be. My stomach lurched with the harsh realization that I'd held Bill at arm's length because I was *weak.* The truth was, I wasn't strong enough to withstand the pain of losing someone I loved. Or to handle my parents' divorce. After all this time, I still couldn't let it go. Because I was the weak one.

My instinct told me to flee. After a lifetime of hiding

from these feelings, I knew *this* was the moment to get them under control—before they took me down. But for once, my emotions were unmanageable. If I tried to rein them in now, I'd fail.

I started when my office door opened, and David strode in. "What happened?" he asked.

"*David*," I said, my mouth falling open as I stood. "Someone might see you here."

"So what? Everyone's at lunch, like you should be." He took off his suit jacket and tossed it over the back of the chair where Bill had just been sitting. "What happened?" he repeated.

I groaned, dropping back into my seat as I put my head in my hands. "You saw him?"

"Saw who?"

I peeked up at him. "Bill . . . he was just here."

"No, I didn't fucking see him." David took a step forward. "That's why you canceled?"

"He needed to talk," I explained. "And I'm sorry, but that's going to keep happening, and you can't get mad about it. He's still technically my husband."

David took a deep breath. "Get over here."

I blinked, cautiously rounding the desk until I stood in front of him.

"I'm not happy," he said.

"I can tell."

"I don't like you canceling on me and then turning off your phone."

I didn't think I'd appreciate being unable to get ahold of him, either, especially feeling as insecure as I did in that moment. I bit my bottom lip. "Okay."

"And I told you, if he's near you, I want to be there."

"I didn't know he was—"

"But," he added, "for all the excruciating times I stood

in this office and couldn't touch you, I'm going to kiss you right now."

With a small smile, I took a step closer and placed my hands on his chest. His arms came around the middle of my back, and he held me as his lips touched mine.

I felt his love in that kiss. But a small part of me wondered if he knew the difference between lust and love, between now and someday. Bill had asked what made me different from the others. It was true—I had no idea if David had said these same things to other women. He hadn't known Maria had expected more of him—that she one day thought he'd come around. What had he given her that she'd clung to for so long?

"Hey."

I opened my eyes. "Hey," I repeated.

"You're not with me."

I searched his eyes for a moment, wondering how he could tell the moment my mind began to wander.

"Now," he said, "I want to know what he said to you."

I sighed and dropped my eyes to his chest. "He kissed me."

David's jaw squared, his pecs going taut under my palms. "You're shitting me."

"It didn't mean anything. If anything, it reminded me how much—"

"Was it against your will?" he asked.

If I said yes, who knew what David would do to Bill? But the alternative would be worse for me. It was the truth, though. "No," I admitted. "It happened fast, but when I pulled away, he stopped."

"I see."

I heard his disappointment in those two words. "I'm sorry," I said. "Honestly, I felt nothing."

"I have no doubt about that," he said. "I'm not worried about your chemistry."

"No?" I asked.

He shook his head. "If you go back to him, it won't be because he fucks you better, will it?"

A flush worked its way up my neck. I was tempted to shut the office door and ask him to back up that claim with evidence. "No."

David raised an eyebrow. "The correct answer was that you're *not* going back to him."

I bit my bottom lip. "I'm not," I said. "But he said some things I'm still . . . processing."

"*That*," David said, frowning. "That's what worries me. You're letting him get in your head, honeybee."

I smiled barely, a reflex to the endearment. "Whether you like it or not, I've always been cautious. I have to be able to think these things through."

He sighed. "And here, I let myself think I had you."

My smile fell, and I looked up at him. "You *do*."

"When Bill called me a womanizer and tried to make you doubt what you and I have—because I'm certain that was his plan—did you defend me? Defend *us*? Or did you give him reason to think you and I were unstable enough that he could kiss you?"

I dropped my gaze to David's tie. "I told him he doesn't know you or us, and that I'm different with you."

"I called Maria before I came over here to explain Saturday night," he said. "And you know what I told her? That you changed my life. That I'll marry you one day, and that she shouldn't waste her time giving me another thought, because nothing and no one would come between you and me—at least not anyone from *my* past."

My heart skipped hearing him speak with such confidence. He'd never doubted us, and still, now, he put it all on the line. I, on the other hand, had denied him that reassurance over and over. I believed in us enough to dispel any concerns Bill might raise—didn't I? So why hadn't I stood up for David?

He'd marry me.

But I was *already* married. And unraveling a life was a lot more complex than David asking for his keys back.

"You can't expect me to change overnight," I said. "You knew things were complicated. I just need time to adjust. Things are moving so fast with us."

"I know you didn't have that openness with him, so I get that it's scary. But this weekend, Olivia, you *gave*. I saw it, and it was everything I hoped for. But I can feel you taking it away. If you shut me out, this won't work."

"I'm not taking anything away, and I'm not shutting you out. Yes, we had a perfect weekend, but it can't always be that way, David."

He looked away and shook his head. "He has you so fucked, you don't even realize that this,"—he gestured between us—"is how it's supposed to be."

"*You* don't realize that love isn't always enough," I said, my voice rising. "You're talking about moving in and marriage, while I'm still trying to decide if I should stay over at your place another night or go to Gretchen's to give us each some space. I mean, if you and I keep going with the pedal to the metal, we'll crash and burn at the first pothole."

"I never used the word *perfect*. *You* did. That's not what I expect." He shoved a hand through his hair, messing it up. "What I'm saying is that Bill, or maybe your mom, I don't know—they have you believing that you're supposed to do this on your own. That if you let me in, I'll take that trust and turn it on you. You've got to let me help, but instead you want space to think on your own. Without me."

Everything he said held weight, but I thought I *had* been letting him help. Couldn't he see how difficult it'd been for me to open up to him this weekend, even if it'd been equally as rewarding?

David stared at me, eyebrows raised, as if expecting me to respond. But words weren't enough. Only actions would show him I was trying, and by letting Bill get under my skin, I'd already fucked up.

David picked up his blazer from the back of the chair.

"Where are you going?" I asked.

"Go stay at Gretchen's tonight," he said.

I blanched. It was the last thing I expected him to say. David had been pushing for us for so long, his defeat caught me off guard. "What?"

He turned to me as he shrugged on his suit jacket and fixed his cuffs. "I can't be in a relationship with someone who won't talk to me. I can't always be the one doing all the work." He fixed his gaze on me. "So you go to Gretchen's like you wanted and figure out if that's the life you want. A life without me. Maybe it's being single, maybe it's with Bill. But it's without me."

My chin quivered. Suddenly, I didn't want to go to Gretchen's. I'd fucked up by trying to spare David from seeing my weaknesses the way I'd done to Bill—to spare us both from the heartache that could be. I should've just forced myself to share that burden with him. "I'm sorry," I said. "You're right. Tonight, we can talk—"

"No," he said. "I already gave you the chance to talk, but instead you want to keep it all inside so you can make decisions without me and believe *him* over me. You're supposed to be on *my* side, Olivia. Not his. So go and decide if you want what we had this weekend, or if you prefer the type of life where nobody gets in, and it's just you, and you have no pain, but you don't have real love either. Not the kind I'm fucking *handing you* on a silver platter."

My mouth fell open while he spoke. His firm tone faltered with a sadness he didn't try to hide. It burrowed into my heart and made me sad, too. I never would've left Bill if I hadn't believed David's love was real. Of course I wanted that.

David started for the door.

"I'm not doing this to hurt you," I pleaded. "I *am* on your side—"

"Spare me, babe," he said as he turned back to me. "Take the time you need, and let me know what you decide. This isn't an ultimatum. I just need to know that we're on the same page, because by protecting yourself, you're fucking me over. And I put it all out there for you. I don't hold anything back. Now I'm the one who's fucked."

His words landed with a stabbing pain in my chest. Hurting David was the last thing I wanted to do, and I'd committed that crime too many times.

I must've looked as shocked as I felt, because David sighed heavily and walked back over. Gently, he took my chin in his hand. "Did you eat?" he demanded softly.

I blinked. "What?"

"You promised, when I tried to make you breakfast, that you'd have a big lunch."

I sighed. *This* was his concern? "I'll eat now."

"Thank you." He placed a kiss on my lips and then pulled back. "I love you. Okay?"

Somehow I understood there was nothing I could say to change David's mind in that moment. I'd risked everything to be with him, but he'd risked even more. He'd put his entire heart on the line, while I'd kept part of mine shut off. But I couldn't change that in one weekend, and so, we'd slow down. I was the one who'd asked for that.

And now that he'd given me that space, I only wished to take it back and keep him close.

But he was already out the door, leaving me there to wonder if letting old fears push David away had just cost me the greatest love I'd ever know.

Chapter Fourteen

For a Monday night, Gretchen's apartment buzzed with activity. Since nobody had heard me knock, I walked in to find one of Gretchen's roommates cooking cashew chicken, the other pouring wine as she manned a playlist on her phone.

Ava raised a wooden spoon in my direction. "Hi," she called over the blare of Rihanna.

Bethany looked up from her phone and lowered the volume. "Hey, Liv. I didn't know you were coming over."

Gretchen waltzed into the kitchen in jeans and a colorful kimono that billowed after her. "She's spending the night," she said and picked up a glass of wine Bethany had poured.

Bethany took a new wineglass from a cupboard. "Want some Pinot Noir?" she asked me. "Where's your stuff?"

Gretchen hadn't even asked for an explanation when I'd said I'd needed a place to stay tonight—and that I might need to borrow some things. She'd told me to come over, so I'd taken a cab straight from my office.

Before I could answer Bethany, Gretchen grabbed a

leather duffel from one of their kitchen chairs. "Here," she said, handing it to me. "This came for you via a delivery service a half hour ago."

"For me?" I set my handbag on their counter and took the bag. "What is it?"

Gretchen smiled a little. "Well, I didn't go through it, but I have a guess."

I unzipped the bag to find a few work dresses, some undergarments, travel-size toiletries, and an unsigned note in David's handwriting.

To get you through the next few days

Appreciation warred with my disappointment. He was still thinking of me, but I hated the thought of him gathering and packing my things—especially a few *days'* worth. I didn't even want to spend tonight without him.

"He's really thoughtful," Gretchen said, peering over my shoulder to read the note.

"Bill sent that?" Ava asked from where she stood at the stove. "How come you're staying here on a Monday?"

I glanced at Gretchen. "They don't know about . . ."

Gretchen shook her head. "Nope. I wasn't sure if we were telling people."

"Telling people what?" Bethany asked, lowering the volume even more.

The doorbell rang. Gretchen's brows furrowed before easing as she nodded. "I have a feeling that's Greg," she said and called for him to come in.

Greg sauntered into the kitchen seconds later and gave Gretchen a quick kiss before grinning at us. "Ladies," he greeted.

Gretchen hugged his waist as she scolded, "What are you doing here?"

"You said you were having a girls' night." He grinned. "I'm here to crash it, just like old times."

A memory of the four of us playing the Clue board game in our old apartment flashed over me. "Old times, but without Lucy," I said, frowning.

"Lucy'll come around. You know her, loyal to a fault," Greg said. "So what's tonight's topic? Taking a break from all the sex, Livvy?"

Ava's and Bethany's eyebrows shoot up in unison. "What?"

"Can I tell them?" Gretchen asked. "Please. I'm dying to see their reaction."

I zipped up the duffel bag. "It's not really a secret anymore," I said.

"Get this," Gretchen said, facing her roommate with her arms extended as if to brace them. "Olivia spent her entire weekend shacked up with David Dylan. Remember—"

"The guy from Jeff the Chef's restaurant opening?" Ava asked, her eyes widening.

"Get *out!*" Bethany exclaimed in disbelief, fumbling her phone and nearly dropping it. "You slept with that fine-ass hunk of man?"

"Wait, wait, wait," Ava nearly screamed, waving her wooden spoon in the air. "Shut up, Bethany!" Ava's eyes cut to me, and I braced myself for the next words out of her mouth. "But you're married."

I glanced down at my empty ring finger out of habit. "We're separating."

"Separating?" Gretchen asked with a frown.

"You know what I mean," I said, shifting feet, then stooping to take off my heels. "We're getting a divorce."

"Words matter," Gretchen said, almost in warning. "Use the right ones."

"You're leaving your husband for him?" Bethany asked, leaning a hip against the counter. "I have to say, I don't blame you. He's one of the best looking men I've ever seen."

I smiled to myself. There'd never been any question of David's attractiveness. But he was also attentive, patient, kind, and thoughtful—as evidenced by the duffel he'd sent, even when he was upset with me. It was the only thing I'd heard from him since he'd left my office earlier, and my heart sank with his uncharacteristic silence.

"Hello?" Gretchen said. "Liv?"

"Hmm?" I blinked up to find all eyes on me. "Sorry, I zoned out. What'd you say?"

Bethany laughed and glanced back at Ava. "She's obviously picturing him naked right now. And now I am, too." Bethany's eyes twinkled, even as Ava scolded her with a look. "Is he hung?"

"*Gross*," Greg said.

I laughed. "Yes. Seriously *hung*. Can you fucking believe it?"

"Do you even have to ask?" Gretchen said. "You can tell by the way he walks, like he *knows* he's God's gift to women. Not to mention he's like six-foot-three—"

"Four," I cut in. "And Gretch is right. I have absolutely no complaints in that department."

"No guy is that confident if he ain't packing," Bethany said, shaking her head in awe.

"It *must* be good, right?" Ava asked. "The sex?"

How could I put into words the command David had over his body and mine? He worked me good and thorough, pushing me to the edge and then further, fucking me to climax like it was his job. I rolled back my head until my eyes hit the ceiling. "Ava," I said seriously. "You have *no* idea."

The three of them broke into a mixture of giggles, squeals, and I even heard an "Amen." Greg, on the other hand, chugged Gretchen's wine as if reaching the bottom of the glass would transport him anywhere but here.

"That's so unfair," Ava said. "You get two men, and I've got nobody."

Bethany brought me a glass of wine, and I thanked her. "It must be crazy to be back in the dating pool after being married so long," she said.

"I'm not really . . ." Back in the dating pool? I definitely wasn't, but could I blame Bethany for thinking David and I were doing more than just fucking? I took a sip of wine. "Things with David are complicated."

"You're *not* dating around. I've seen them together, and David's way too serious about her for that." Gretchen made a face and turned to the girls. "David asked her to move in."

"If you won't, I will," Ava said with a friendly smile. "Seriously, though. What's stopping you?"

Just my own stupid shit. I opened my mouth to try to put into words what I'd miserably failed to convey to David earlier, but Gretchen interjected. "Nothing's stopping her. Right?" she asked me. "When a girl meets a man like David, she never lets him go. And she certainly doesn't drive him away. Does she?"

Gretchen didn't have to be a mind reader to put two and two together. Especially since David had sent my things. I bit my bottom lip. "She'd be a fool to."

"Are you guys, like, in love?" Ava asked.

"I . . ." I scratched the tip of my nose. "I haven't . . ."

"Olivia," Gretchen said. "You love him. I know you do."

I glanced around at the four pairs of eyes on me. "I do. I just . . ."

"You're scared," Greg said. "I get it. I've been there."

As Greg and Gretchen seemed to share a moment, my heart dropped. I'd known all along Greg had been scared of their connection, and I'd spent years maligning him for it. I didn't want to be Greg, crawling back to Gretchen now, having missed out on her for almost a decade.

"If David breaks your heart, it'll suck. But you're tough, Liv. You'll get over it," Gretchen said and glanced at Greg. "I did."

He leaned in and pecked her on the cheek.

"Get a room," Bethany teased.

"We will," Greg said, "when Gretchen's ready."

"*Still?*" I mouthed at Gretchen, and she nodded. I held my wine up to her and took a sip, shocked that she of all people had refrained from sleeping with him for so long.

What was she waiting for? My gut told me something was off. If she really were over her heartbreak, would she still be waiting? It'd been months.

I didn't understand it, but I of all people knew that sometimes, matters of the heart just couldn't be explained.

"So, hold up," Bethany said. "Not that I care because I like you a lot more, but wasn't Lucy's sister dating David?"

I nearly choked on my wine and started coughing. Evidently, Dani was an issue that wasn't going away, like a fly that wouldn't stop buzzing around me. Everyone stared at me again. "They went on a few dates," I said. "But David says it didn't mean anything."

"It didn't," Gretchen said. "You told me he didn't even do anything with her."

I wavered, not exactly thrilled at the idea of sharing all this with a roomful of people. "Bill came to see me this afternoon."

"Ah." Gretchen walked over to the counter to refill her wine. "No wonder you're here. What'd he say to fuck you up?"

"Well, he kissed me."

Gretchen spun around as her roommates gasped. "*And*?" Ava asked.

"It was . . . different. Not terrible. But nothing like kissing David."

"*Obviously*," Gretchen said. "Please don't tell me you told David."

"I did, and to his credit, he didn't feel threatened like I thought he might. Instead, we fought about how I let Bill get in my head. Including what he said about Dani."

"What'd he say?" Greg blurted. When we all looked at him, he blushed, then shrugged. "What? I'm invested now."

I sighed. "Dani told Bill that she and David slept together. David insists that they only kissed."

"You think he lied to you?" Gretchen asked.

David's eyes had always held truth. He'd done nothing to deserve the skepticism I'd thrown his way earlier. "No," I said. "But I also don't know why she'd lie."

"I don't think anything serious happened," Gretchen said, taking her phone from the pocket of her kimono. "Lucy would've mentioned it."

"Why don't you just ask Dani?" Bethany suggested.

Gretchen cocked her head. "Good idea. I'll text her now. Unless you want to, Liv?"

"What?" I asked, blanching. "No. Don't text her."

"Aren't you the teensy bit curious?" Ava asked.

I thought of David alone at his apartment. He'd made it clear I wasn't welcome there tonight. If he wanted, he could invite over anyone he wanted—I doubted it would take more than a phone call to the right woman.

I glanced at my own phone, glaringly devoid of any messages or calls from him. But I was the one who'd put us in that situation, not him. And I knew deep down, he was upset. I'd been so worried about the women in his past, and part of me couldn't let go of the fact that he might leave one day. But he'd told me over and over that he didn't want anyone else. And I chose to believe him.

"No, I'm not curious about David and Dani. He said they didn't sleep together, and he wouldn't lie," I told Ava, turning to Gretchen. "Nothing happened. You don't need to text her."

"Already did." Gretchen lifted herself to sit on the kitchen counter, and her fingers flew over the screen. "Just a sec. We're talking. Things are heating up."

"Heating up?" I asked through a dry throat. "Why? What's she saying?"

"This is really strange behavior," Greg said. "I feel like I'm in some kind of alternate universe."

Ava threw a wine cork at him. "That's what you get for crashing girls' night."

Gretchen slammed her phone on the counter. "Fucking asshole."

"Who?" I asked, my heart suddenly pounding in my ears. She didn't mean David. She *couldn't*. "Who's an asshole?"

She picked up her phone again, and after a moment of navigating, held it up. On speakerphone, ringing filled the kitchen.

She was calling Dani? I didn't have a chance to tell her to hang up before Dani answered. "What do you want, Gretchen?" she asked.

"Olivia's here," she said. "Tell her what you just told me."

"David and I never slept together. We kissed once," she

said. A modicum of relief passed over me. I'd been right to trust David. Until she added, "Only because *you* ruined any chance I had with him, Olivia."

Irritation quickly flooded out my relief. She didn't know shit about my relationship with David. "*I'm* the reason you and David aren't together?" I asked. "If you think David lets anyone get in the way of what he wants, you don't know him at all."

Gretchen snorted. "A guy who's interested doesn't go on four dates without making a single move."

"Like you've ever made it to four dates, Gretchen?" Dani asked. "Everyone knows you're a slut—'"

I gasped. "Hey! That's totally uncalled for."

"I feel sorry for you, Olivia," Dani continued. "You blew up a perfectly good marriage for a guy who'll throw you out like yesterday's trash when he's done with you."

My face flamed. Who the fuck did she think she was? "I'd rather be trash *and* a slut than a judgmental bitch. You're clearly jealous that David's *mine*, and guess what? He's not going anywhere. That man loves me in a way Bill never could."

Everyone in the kitchen turned wide eyes on me.

"Yeah, so go to hell," Gretchen said into the phone and hung up.

"Holy shit," Bethany said, looking between the two of us. "That was intense."

"Whatever," I said with a shrug, but my heart pounded. I didn't remember ever speaking to someone with such vitriol, but *God*, it felt good to finally stand up for my relationship. "She's been getting on my nerves for a while."

"Mine, too." Gretchen grinned. "I like this side of you. That's the Liv you need to show David. The one who's going to fight for him."

I swallowed down a gulp of wine. Gretchen wasn't wrong. But how did I show him when there was a sudden gulf between us?

"So who'd you call an asshole earlier?" Bethany asked, her brows furrowed.

"Bill," Gretchen said. "Someone lied here, and it wasn't David or Dani."

That was true. If Dani hadn't told Bill she'd slept with David, then he'd made it up. I looked into my wineglass. "He's desperate."

"That's not an excuse," Gretchen said.

"I know." My stomach churned at the idea of confronting him, too, but with the adrenaline rush of what I'd just done, I knew I had to—for myself and for David. "I'll talk to him."

"God, I'm all amped up now," Gretchen said, hopping down from the counter and pacing the kitchen. She nodded at Ava. "Is dinner ready? Let's eat and then go out."

My heart raced, too. I didn't want to stay in. I'd rather have gone to David's, but that wasn't happening, so I took out my cell. "Brian Ayers e-mailed me an invitation to some art opening tonight," I said. "It was meant for David and me, but I don't think Brian'll mind if I bring you guys."

Gretchen rolled her eyes. "I'm not going to stand around some pretentious gallery with Brian the poser. I want to take shots."

"It's not like that," I said, my eyes scanning Brian's e-mail. "It's at a dive bar in Wicker Park. Very low-key, hipster spot."

Ava took a stack of dishes from a cupboard. "Dinner's ready. Let's scarf it down and go see us some art."

Like the gentleman he was, Brian wasn't only happy to

have us, but he even met us out front when our cab arrived. "Well, I'll certainly be the hero of the evening with all these beautiful women on my arm," he said, helping each of us out of the car. He leaned into the backseat to offer Gretchen his hand, then paused when he saw her sitting on Greg's lap. "Make that four women and— Gregor, was it?"

Gretchen scowled, ignoring Brian's help. "Just Greg. My *boyfriend*."

"How could I forget?" Brian straightened up and offered me his elbow. "Shall we?"

Inside, I could barely see the paintings in the dimly lit bar with overhead lights that alternated between yellow and red. At the bar, Brian and I ordered a couple tequila shots.

"She doesn't waste any time, does she?" Brian asked.

I followed his gaze to Gretchen, deep in conversation with Bethany and two men in suits. Greg was nowhere to be seen. "What is it about her that bugs you?" I asked.

"Nothing, honey." He tilted his head in her direction. "Just not my type."

"Why not?" I asked. "You said at the Meet and Greet that you want a 'clever' girl with 'edge,' and she's both of those things. And there's no denying she's gorgeous."

"What you say is true, Liv." Brian tucked some of his blond locks behind his ear. "But she's also high-mainte-nance and snobby."

I thought it was funny how they'd each called the other some form of pretentious—when, at the heart of it, neither she nor Brian was. "Let me get this straight," I said. "Pretty girl tries to kiss you—you turn her down."

"Yes."

"Because she's high-maintenance and snobby?" I asked.

He sighed, still watching her. "Look at her. She's beautiful. Why does she wear all that makeup and dress like that?"

As if she could hear us, Gretchen tugged down her short, skin-tight blue dress. Admittedly, with four-inch heels and fake lashes, she was overdressed for a dive bar. But that was just Gretchen. "I think she looks great."

"Absolutely," he agreed. "But she doesn't need all that. I want a girl who's comfortable in her own skin."

I didn't respond but peered at him. Why was he so concerned with what she wore if he didn't care about her?

"She's pissed off that I didn't fall for her charms," he continued. "She's very smooth, I'll admit. But it doesn't work on me. I don't find it genuine."

I turned back to look at Gretchen. It made sense as to why she'd called Brian names. Not many men had turned her down since Greg had broken her heart in college. Brian had wounded her pride. "She *is* genuine," I promised him. "She dresses up because she's confident and flaunts it. She's a catch. So . . . I guess you both lose."

"You know very well that she has a new boyfriend,"— he looked at me sidelong—"so what does it matter?"

"True. And it's an old boyfriend anyway," I said. "They dated in college."

"Oh?" Brian's eyebrow lifted. "And they're back together?"

"Yes. Back then, he broke up with her suddenly and left for a work opportunity in Japan practically the next day. She was a mess, but I guess now he's back to work things out with her."

I glanced at Brian, who quickly wiped the shock from his face—but not before I'd caught it. "Well, good on them," he said, turning to look over his shoulder. "Where's David anyway?" he asked. "I thought he'd join you."

"Girls' night," I explained. "Plus Greg, and now you, too . . ."

Fuck. I wished David were here. Maybe I should've just invited him, even knowing he'd probably decline.

"Figure out if that's the life you want. A life without me. Maybe it's being single, maybe it's with Bill. But it's without me."

I didn't need to figure out what I wanted. David was everything a girl could ask for. I just had to take the leap with both feet. That was the hard part, not trying to hang on to the ledge of the cliff with one hand, just in case I had to pull myself back up. Just in case David decided one day to walk away. I'd seen him make plenty of decisions over the time I'd known him, and he did them without waffling or backtracking. Without mercy. So far, that had been to my advantage. But I shuddered to imagine being on the wrong side of what David decided he wanted.

"I was most shocked when I found out about you two," Brian said, holding out a shot of tequila.

I blinked several times, returning to the conversation. "You and everyone else."

We each downed our shot, then sucked on a lime slice.

Brian tossed his rind into the empty shot glass and looked me over. "Isn't it going well? It's weird that David isn't out with you. He strikes me as the type to keep one eye on the woman he loves at all times."

I shifted between feet as a tequila-induced wave of warmth passed over me. Brian already thought David loved me? How could he when he'd only been around us once as a couple?

"David and I . . ." I started. "It's hard to explain. We care for each other very much, but divorce is tough on everyone involved. There's a lot of gray area."

Brian nodded pensively. "You know, I like to tease

Dylan. But truth is, I instantly noticed the way he is with you. Different, but in a good way."

My shoulders eased. "Really?"

He smiled down at me. "Really. You bring out something in him. The circumstances suck, but you are a terrific match."

My next question tumbled out of my mouth. "Why aren't I just another one of his girls?"

"Olivia," Brian said, drawing back with surprise. "Any man with sense about him can see that you're not that type. And David has a great deal of sense. He doesn't always use it when it comes to women, I'll admit. But maybe that's because he was doing everything in his power to stay sane until you came along."

I realized I was smiling. Putting it that way bothered me less than thinking he'd slept his way through Chicago. At our barbeque in the park, David had said he'd been looking for "the one" for a while, and his family had seemed to know exactly what he meant. I could definitely envision David—a man used to getting what he wanted—driving himself crazy on his quest.

"And really," Brian added, "your husband is abominable."

I smiled. "You just saw the worst side of him." I rose onto the balls of my feet and thanked Brian with a kiss on the cheek. When I came down, I was met with Gretchen's grimace.

"Have you seen Greg?" she asked.

"Perhaps," Brian cut in, nodding to where Bethany still stood with the suits, "he saw you flirting with those gentlemen over there, and rightly high-tailed it out of here."

Gretchen gave him a blatant scowl.

"That's attractive," he said.

"Oh, fuck off, Brian," she said.

"I will not," Brian said. "I'm not sorry that I prefer your smile over your scowl."

She reddened. Her eyebrows furrowed as she seemed unable to decide if he'd complimented or insulted her. I wasn't really sure myself. After a moment, she scowled harder.

Brian only laughed before sauntering away.

"He is *so* infuriating," Gretchen said.

"Don't let him get to you."

"He doesn't *get to me*," she said, flipping some of her hair over her shoulder. "I couldn't care less what—oh, there's Greg." She ran off.

Brian had moved to the end of the bar, but his eyes stayed narrowed in Gretchen and Greg's direction.

They really don't like each other, I thought.

So Brian had suspected David's feelings for me. And Gretchen had been convinced after spending a little time with us, too. It was clear to everyone that we belonged together. So why wasn't he here with me now?

I pulled out my cell and looked at the picture I'd taken of David's profile. Somewhere between buzzed and drunk, I missed him acutely. I'd spent months trying to stay away from him. Now, I didn't have to. I shouldn't have to miss him ever—it wasn't fair. I missed our weekend. I missed his smile. I wanted it back. David had come after me so many times, even knowing I'd keep pushing him away—it was the reason we'd gotten this far. I had to take that risk for him now. Maybe I'd show up on his doorstep, and he'd turn me away. It would hurt, but he knew that more than anyone. He'd never stopped coming to my doorstep. As Gretchen had said, I had to show him I could fight for us, too.

I told Gretchen I wasn't coming back with her. She

hailed me a cab, put me in, and shut the door before I even had a chance to say goodnight. She either didn't want me thrashing next to her in bed or she believed I was making the right choice.

I only calmed once the driver pulled up to the place that was, for all intents and purposes, my new home. It was late—past one o'clock in the morning—so thankfully, my elevator ride went uninterrupted. My need for David grew quickly, and all I wanted was to feel him any way I could have him.

Using the keys he'd given me, I unlocked the door and eased it shut behind me. I took a step and removed my left shoe, then did the same with the right. I went directly to the bedroom, dropped both heels, and climbed over David as he slept on his side. I pulled down the comforter and touched his hot skin.

"David," I whispered, running my hand over his chest and down his stomach. He sighed and jerked beneath me. My hand continued down, gliding under the elastic of his boxer briefs.

He groaned, and his eyes opened. "Hey," he grated out. I wrapped my hand around him and quieted him with a kiss. Without disconnecting our mouths, I shifted to straddle him, and he flipped onto his back.

"You're supposed to be at Gretchen's," he said. "I'm giving you your space. I need mine, too."

I ran my palm along his shaft. "No."

"No?"

All the turmoil of the last few days gathered in my chest, threatening to cave it in. "I don't want to do this alone. Please, David. I need you to fuck it all out of me," I whispered and deepened the kiss.

He didn't ask what I meant. His big hands just went straight to my hips to squeeze me against him. I moaned at his hardness. I didn't think I'd last two seconds. He hiked up my dress, pulled it over my head, and removed my bra. I straightened up, and his hands went straight to my breasts. I reached between us, shifted my thong, and sank onto him.

I was prepared to ride him in his half-asleep state, but suddenly he was wide awake, fucking all the hurt, guilt, and regret out of me like I'd asked, giving me the gift of temporary oblivion. I bounced forward with his furious upward thrusts, and his hands jumped to my waist, pushing me down to meet him faster. I came quicker than I ever had. He kept his pace until he was gushing into me, growling from his chest. His hold remained strong as his head dropped back to the pillow, and his hips slowed to a gradual stop.

When he finally let go, I collapsed next to him on the bed. He pulled my back close against his front.

"David—" I whispered.

"Sleep," he grunted in my ear, and his breathing evened, so I did as he said, shut my eyes, and drifted, safe back in his embrace.

Chapter Fifteen

The perfect antidote to a mild hangover? A Chicago-style hot dog loaded with toppings. Serena and I each scarfed one during our lunch break, and mine tasted even more delicious because of my late night workout.

That morning, I'd woken up to an empty bed and a note on David's pillow. He'd left early for a full day at work, but tonight, he was taking me out for dinner to talk. I was to be ready by seven so he could "pick me up" for our date at his apartment later, just like he'd promised.

As Serena and I walked off the elevator and into *Chicago Metropolitan Magazine*'s lobby, the receptionist brightened. "Someone got a delivery," Jenny sang, holding out a long, rectangular, glossy-white box with a red ribbon fastened to the top.

Serena scurried over to investigate. "It's for you, Olivia."

Who'd sent it? A remorseful husband or a new lover? Both pairs of eyes watched me until Serena asked, "*Well?* It's not going to open itself!"

I walked to Jenny's desk, tugged one end of the ribbon, and lifted the lid to reveal twelve perfectly formed, long-stemmed roses. The *best* roses, I was sure, in the whole city of Chicago, because their sender wouldn't accept otherwise.

"What's the card say?" Jenny asked.

I picked up an envelope addressed me and read it aloud. "Looking forward to our date tonight."

Love, David

"Wow." Serena nudged me with her elbow. "I didn't realize Bill was so romantic."

I didn't want to lie anymore. It was exhausting, and David had made it clear early on how much he hated *pretending*. In that moment, my chest swelled with love for him, and I wanted the world to know it.

I shrugged and picked up the box. "They're not from Bill," I said, leaving the girls open-mouthed behind me.

In my office, I buried my nose in the bouquet, smiling as its perfume filled my nostrils.

Within seconds of putting down the box, Serena entered the room. "Thought you might need this," she said, placing a vase full of water on my desk.

"Thanks," I said and set to work filling it.

"They're beautiful . . ."

I looked her up and down as I arranged the stems in the vase and waited for the question I knew was coming.

"Who are they from?" she asked.

I laughed. "You are *so* not subtle."

"We're, like, *dying* to know. What's going on?" She lowered her voice and leaned over the desk. "Are you having an affair?"

"Do you think I'd tell you guys if I was?" I rolled my eyes. "Blabbermouths."

"Come on," she pleaded.

"I'm not ready to talk about the state of my love life, but when I am, Serena, you'll be the first to know." I changed the topic to something I'd been avoiding thinking about. David and I had booked flights for tomorrow to spend some time with my dad. I had no idea where David and I stood, or if he'd still want to come, but I was planning on going regardless. "I told you I'm working remotely the rest of the week, right?"

"Yep," she said. "From Dallas."

"You know what would be even more helpful than a vase and idle gossip?"

Her dimples deepened with a smile. "I'll put together everything you'll need for the rest of the week."

I smiled at her. "Thank you."

I stayed a little late at work to make sure everything would be in order while I was away, then headed to David's apartment to get ready for our date.

I chose a tight, black dress with a sweetheart neckline that David had liked on the hanger. He hadn't seen it on me since he'd taken a business call while I'd been in the dressing room. In the mirror, I turned. Three thick, vertical straps ran from the nape of my neck to my mid-back. Sexy enough for a first date. Even though we were far beyond that, my nerves buzzed. And as always when I thought of David, a quiver started between my legs.

I wasn't sure what was in store for David and me tonight. After our last talk in my office, surely he had concerns and would lead the conversation. But tonight, I had to lay it all on the line. To show David my confidence in us, even if I had to *slightly* fake it until my head could catch up with my heart. He needed to know I was willing to fight for us. That I wasn't going to back out. And that I loved him.

I fixed my hair into a soft chignon, leaving some pieces

free to frame my face, and smoothed on red lipstick. I had a feeling asking David's forgiveness would go down a little easier when the request came from a crimson mouth.

When the front door opened, I grabbed my clutch, draped a black cashmere coat with leather trim over my arm, and walked out of the bedroom.

From where I stood at the mouth of the hallway, I could see through the living room, past a marble countertop that doubled as a breakfast bar, and into the kitchen. David leaned a hip on the counter, staring off into space, a sweating beer bottle in one hand.

He remained as imposing as ever, even when confined by walls, and looked distinguished and sexy in a black suit. He scrubbed the beginnings of his five o'clock shadow, then ran a hand through disheveled hair that begged for my fingers to play in it.

He took a pull from his beer, looking deep in thought. His grim expression only amplified his dark, severe features. It made him even more devastatingly handsome. I wouldn't expect anything less, though. I'd been a fool to believe that getting space from him might give me any clarity when just looking at him made me breathless. I was suddenly nervous, and it took me a moment to build up the courage to step into the room.

His head snapped in my direction, and he took a deep breath, staring as I advanced. "Olivia," he said, letting my name roll off his tongue the way I loved. Only, it was different now that I'd tasted that tongue and inhaled my own name from his mouth. Or maybe it was something on his end that made it sound different, an acknowledgement of our time together. It was sweeter.

Though my instinct was to touch him, his unreadable mood dissuaded me, so I stopped some feet away. His eyes never left me for a moment.

"Thank you for the beautiful roses," I said.

"I bet that got the girls talking."

"It did," I said with a shy smile. "I loved them."

"Good."

"Are you ready, or—"

"I'm ready."

"Okay." I tucked some hair behind my ear and waited for him to make a move.

He turned his body to me and stepped forward, reaching out to run his thumb over my cheek. "You're absolutely stunning," he said. "But you'll freeze."

"You'll keep me warm," I said. "Won't you?"

He nodded and left the bottle on the counter to take my coat from me. I let him wrap me in it, and I tied it closed as we made our way out of the apartment.

In the car, I wasn't sure what to make of his mood. Last night, he'd objected to me climbing into his bed, but it hadn't taken him seconds to give in. Fucking me didn't mean he'd forgotten, though.

"I can't be in a relationship with someone who won't talk to me," he'd said. *"I can't always be the one doing all the work."*

Desperate to cut through the silence, I asked, "Did you have a good day?"

"Not particularly."

I didn't want to stare at him as he drove in the dark, so I focused my gaze ahead of us. "Gretchen's was interesting last night."

"How so?"

"We gossiped, mostly about you." I smiled. "We had dinner and drinks, then went out. But Gretchen had Greg there, and it was weird to have our roles reversed. Usually I'm the one with someone by my side."

"Someone meaning a man."

I nodded and glanced at my hands. "I missed you."

He slid his hand along the curve of the steering wheel. "Can't say that doesn't make me a little happy to hear."

"I saw Brian, too," I added. "Just so you know."

"Brian?" he repeated. "Ayers?"

"He'd invited you and me to this art thing at a bar, so I took the girls instead. He and I talked for a while."

"I see." David looked out his window. "How're Greg and Gretchen getting on?"

"Really well."

"Do you think they're a good match?" he asked.

I frowned. *Yes. Does he not think so?* They definitely had been in college. "I think so," I said.

"And what about us?" he asked. "Are we a good match?"

I was thankful he couldn't see my face. The tension in the car thickened as the question hung in the air. "Of course we are," I said softly. I continued to look at anything but him while he stared out the windshield. He hadn't looked at me once since the apartment.

Thankfully, we arrived at the restaurant within minutes.

Inside, at the hostess stand, he said, "Reservation for Dylan, two."

As the hostess led us to our table, David's hand covered mine, warm and protective.

The dim corner where she sat David and me was almost as dark as the night outside with only a couple sconces on the wall and a flickering candle in the middle of the table.

As I untied my coat, David's hands rested on my shoulders from behind. His fingers brushed the back of my neck. I paused, waiting as he seemed to hesitate. He removed the coat, handed it to the hostess, and pulled out my chair for me.

He surveyed our surroundings as he rounded the table to his seat. "Everyone here is looking at you," he remarked with a frown, scanning the room behind me as he scooted his chair under the table.

I followed his gaze. I didn't see anyone looking at me, but I *did* catch a pair of big, bright female eyes focused on him. I pursed my lips and stared at the woman until she noticed and sheepishly glanced away.

David ordered a bottle of something before I even noticed the waiter. I didn't catch the order because he'd made it in French.

I folded my hands in my lap. David's unreadable eyes fixed on me.

If his intent was to make me uncomfortable, it was working. I knew I needed to tell him I'd gotten his point. The moment he'd left my office the day before, I'd wanted to call him back and promise him I'd try harder. But his stoicism tonight made me self-conscious and a little flustered. "Are you having second thoughts?" I asked finally.

"*Me?*"

I nodded hesitantly, put off by his clipped tone.

He dropped his forehead in his hands and sighed irritably. "You're the one hitting the brakes, Olivia. Not me."

"You just seem . . . distant."

He glanced up at me. "Can you blame me?"

The waiter appeared, and David gestured at me. The man poured me a taste from the wine bottle. Without removing my eyes from David, I swirled, sniffed, and took an uninspired sip of red wine. When I nodded, the waiter filled our glasses without a word and walked away.

"I spoke to Andrew," David said. "Apparently, you and Dani had a confrontation? He wouldn't tell me any more. Care to explain?"

Heat crept up my neck. "Bill's concerned about your

past. He thinks you're using me. He said you slept with Dani and then never called her again."

David suddenly looked as red as I felt, but it wasn't because he was embarrassed like me. It was an anger that hit me hard, like the night of the masquerade ball, when he'd seen me dancing with Bill. Now that he was feet away, though, it was more palpable.

"I told you exactly what happened between Dani and me. A kiss that I stopped," David said. "But you believed Bill instead?"

"At first, I questioned whether it could be true," I said, hoping honesty would be the fastest way to fix this. "You had her hoodie in your car, and plenty of opportunities to sleep with her. And you would've been within your right to." I set my elbows on the table. "But I always knew in my gut that it wasn't true, David. Bill lied. Dani confirmed the truth."

"You should have come to *me*," he said, fuming. "No one else. Haven't I told you repeatedly that I won't lie to you? Under any circumstances? If I said I didn't touch her, I didn't. I don't like having to fucking repeat myself."

Oddly, his anger comforted me, an improvement from his indifferent silent treatment. "I'm sorry I doubted you," I said, nodding. "It's partly why I pulled away yesterday."

"Why can't you trust me?"

"I do."

"You don't. It took all this investigative work before you could finally come to me? That's bullshit, Olivia. I should be the first person you come to. This is a bullshit relationship."

My heart dropped. That stung. I'd had a setback, yes, but I'd made a lot of progress with him over so little time. "It was Gretchen's idea to call Dani, not mine," I said. "I told her I didn't need that because I believed you."

"Next time, you come to me. Understand?" Finally, his expression softened. "You got your answer from Dani. So why are you still holding back? What happened on the call?"

"Dani called Gretchen a slut, and she blames me for you and her not working out. She said you're going to throw me out like trash."

He stared at me a moment. When the waiter approached, David clipped, "We're not ready," and the man quickly rerouted away from the table.

David's narrowed eyes never left me. "And?"

"I called her a judgmental bitch and told her you loved me in a way Bill never could."

After a beat, David asked, "Do you believe that? Or were you just saying it to hurt her?"

I picked up my water glass, thankful for how it cooled my suddenly sweaty palm. David had proved enough times that he was in this for good. He'd been chipping away at the walls around my heart before I'd even known it was happening, and it was working. But that brought on new fears and complications. He could spend the time breaking down those walls, but what would it cost me to pick up a hammer and help him? If I fell, he'd catch me, but was I even *capable* of giving complete, all-in, head-over-heels unconditional love? The kind I'd seen as an affliction of my mother's? It wouldn't be easy after a lifetime of trying to limit myself.

It started with telling him I loved him. He knew, of course, but he deserved to hear it. Then what would come next? David said he'd marry me. And I knew better than anyone—with marriage came certain expectations. Ones I wasn't sure I could deliver.

As I tried to come up with the words, a dull, angry

buzzing filled my ears. "Yes, I believe what I said to Dani. I believe that you love me, and I believe in us."

"You can't just tell me. You have to show me," he said. "Months ago, I promised I'd leave you alone if you said it and meant it—if you *truly* wanted that. Now, I need the opposite. I need more than promises. You're not all in with me yet, and I don't know how to get you there. But the deeper I get in this, and the more I risk my heart getting broken."

As the vibrating started again, I rubbed my temples and looked around. "I'm trying," I said. "I came to your bed last night because I couldn't spend a night away from you—"

"*After* you told me you needed space."

"*What* is that noise?" I asked as the buzzing continued. "Is it your phone?"

He took his cell from his jacket, cleared a call, and set it on the table. "Olivia, do you know how it felt to spend those two days with you and then have you withdraw again? I can't make this better if you won't tell me what's on your mind. Even—*especially*—the ugly shit you don't want anyone to see. Remember the bath? You and me? Remember how nice you felt after opening up? Remember—"

"I told you," I snapped, clasping my hand over my heart. "I'm empty inside! I'm trying, but I warned you, David. What if I just can't give you what you need? I don't know what you want from me."

"Everything," he shot back, and his fist hit the table. "I want it all. Don't say you're empty. That's an excuse, and you know it. I've seen the way you can love me. I feel it in your touch, in the way you give yourself over. Just admit that you're fucking afraid and that I'm not worth taking the risk for."

"God*damn* it," I hissed to myself, pressing my palms against my forehead. "Answer your phone. It's driving me crazy."

"We're not finished."

"Someone obviously needs to get ahold of you."

David looked at me for a long moment before answering the call and holding his phone to his ear. "Now is not a good—whoa, Jessa. Slow down. What's wrong?" At his sister's name, I stilled. "The ER?" he asked. "Why?" David's face fell as he listened. "All right, I'm coming now."

He hung up and motioned to the waiter.

"David, what's wrong?" I asked.

"That was my sister." He slipped his phone into his suit jacket. "Alex is in the hospital—emergency appendectomy."

"Surgery?" Before I could stop it, my stomach roiled with visions of scalpels, blood, and doctors in latex gloves. "Oh, God. Is he all right?"

"I have no idea. I could barely understand her through her crying." He stood. "I have to get over there."

"You go ahead," I said. "I can finish up here."

He handed a credit card to the waiter for the wine and demanded my coat. No doubt because of David's tone, the waiter jogged off with the card.

I was about to offer to go with him when he cut me off. "I'll get you a cab home."

"I—home?" Our argument seemed unimportant right then, but would he feel that way, too? "You mean . . . should I go—back to your apartment?"

"Where else?" he asked with a funny look. He took my coat and the bill from the waiter, signed it, and strode to the exit, pausing only long enough to hold the door for me.

He handed the valet his ticket and moved to the curb to search for a cab.

"I can get my own cab," I said. "Alex needs you."

"Right," he mumbled, turning to me. He took my coat and drew it around my shoulders. "Hopefully I'll get back tonight, but I might have to stay with them. We'll finish this discussion tomorrow."

"We—I leave for Dallas in the morning," I said.

He froze, holding my lapels closed. "Without me?"

The whole point of the trip had been to introduce David to my dad, but since then, it'd become just as much about returning home after an arduous few months. Instead of being a cheating wife or a girlfriend who couldn't measure up to David's expectations, I just wanted to be my dad's daughter for a bit.

I stammered for a response. "I-I don't know where you and I stand right now. Do you?"

He tilted his head. "Not exactly."

"And Alex needs you. Go be with him. I'll go to my dad's. When I get back, we can talk."

His brown eyes roamed over me, lingering on my red lips until his car pulled up. "I . . ."

I love you. I waited for him to reassure me it was still true, but instead, he swallowed. "Text me when you get to the apartment," he said and released me to get the car.

We were just going to leave things like that? I couldn't just let him go while he possibly thought I was having second thoughts about us. I only doubted myself. Not him. Not us.

I ran after him, grabbed his forearm, rose onto the tips of my toes, and kissed his cheek. He caught me before I pulled back and quickly pressed his lips to mine. I wiped away the red lipstick I'd left behind. "Let me know when you find out about Alex," I said softly.

I retreated to the curb and watched him drive away. Then, I hailed a passing cab, slid inside, and with a deep breath, gave the driver the address to Bill's apartment.

Chapter Sixteen

The slide of a deadbolt raked across my nerves. The door to my old apartment opened a fraction, and Bill leaned out, shirtless. The sounds of a popular sitcom floated out from the apartment. Bill's eyes scanned my figure and then flicked back up to my face. "What do you want?"

"Can I come in?"

He leaned back and held the door open for me to enter.

"Thanks." The apartment looked eerily similar to when I'd left. It was clean, except for a few empty beer bottles and the lingering scent of cigarette smoke. My scarf still hung on the coatrack. The linens I'd slept on during my last month here sat folded at one end of the couch. It didn't feel the same, however. I was out of place and back home all at once.

"I'm going to my dad's tomorrow, and I need some things," I explained as I undid my coat and draped it over a kitchen chair.

He snorted. "I bet your dad's happy about this. He never liked me."

I wished I could tell Bill that was true, but I didn't know for sure what my dad thought. Only that he'd never taken to Bill like I'd hoped. I glanced toward the hallway. "Do you mind if I . . .?"

He shrugged. "Go ahead. You remember where the bedroom is, don't you?"

I ignored the passive-aggressive jab and asked, "How's your nose?"

"Peachy."

I opened the hallway closet and reached up to pull down a suitcase.

"That one's mine," he said. I paused with my hands wrapped around the handle until he said, "Never mind. Just take it."

I struggled to pull it from the shelf and caught it just as it was about to fall. I wheeled it into the bedroom and started packing for the weekend, adding in some of my favorite things I'd left behind.

"Where'd you get this?" I heard close at my back.

I jumped, twisting to find Bill right behind me. He ran a finger down the side of my dress.

I stepped away. "It's Gretchen's," I lied, remembering how he'd called me a whore to David.

Bill cocked his head, seemingly amused. "You look nervous. What's wrong?"

"Nothing," I said, but my heart rate escalated. I was worried that he might try to kiss me again. He was so close that I smelled the mingling of alcohol and cigarettes on his breath.

"I like it," he said. "You coming from a date, or did you dress up to see me?"

Fuck. He wasn't going to make this easy on me. Maybe it wasn't fair to show up late at night in a dress like this, asking for my things. But taking the nice route with Bill hadn't worked, either. He'd lied to me, taken advantage of my vulnerability, and had prompted a fight—and now a rift—between David and me.

Maybe that had always been his plan. "Don't touch me," I said.

"Relax," he said, withdrawing with a chuckle. "I'm not interested in sloppy seconds. Or would that make you sloppy thirds?"

He turned and walked away. I glanced around the room. He'd made the bed. Tidied up. He'd put our wedding picture facedown, though.

I packed a few more things in the suitcase and rolled it through the living room. Bill watched as I crossed in front of the television and set the luggage by the door.

Bill may have kept things in order as our life together fell apart, but I worried about whether he was taking care of himself. I walked back to the couch, sat, and faced him.

"What?" he asked.

I gestured to a full ashtray on the coffee table. "You're smoking again."

"It makes me feel better," he said with an almost child-like look of innocence.

I appreciated his honesty. "I thought about everything you said yesterday," I told him.

His face turned uneasy. "Yeah?"

"Yeah. You're right about some things. David's got a past. I'm the one giving up everything. And there's no way I can possibly know how things will turn out with him. Honestly, I'm not sure of much anymore."

Bill rested his elbows on his knees as he rubbed his chin. "Then come back, Olivia. I know I said some things, but I didn't . . . what I said just now about sloppy thirds, I didn't mean that. I'm just angry. We can go to counseling. We can make this work."

I inhaled back tears and looked at my hands. I wished I wouldn't think of David in that moment, because I wanted a clear head. I wanted to know that my decisions were free of the spell he held over me. "You lied to me about Dani and David."

He nodded and looked at the floor. "I didn't know how else to get you to see the truth about him."

"But that's not the truth," I pointed out. "It was a lie."

"It could have been the truth. Easily."

I leaned in and kissed him on the cheek. I lingered there with my lips pressed against his face, squeezing my eyes closed. A tear escaped and slid between us. "I'm sorry, Bill," I whispered. I pulled back to look at his profile. "I love you, and I know you love me, but I shouldn't have said yes. We're not right for each other, and I'm not sure we ever were."

He stared at the TV, unresponsive. Finally, he said, "You regret marrying me?"

"No. But you deserve someone who has zero doubts about you. She's out there."

Hi jaw worked back and forth. "Don't give me that patronizing bullshit."

I inhaled a breath. That was fair. If he didn't want me to be gentle, then I'd be direct. "It's over, Bill. I don't know what will happen with David, but regardless—you and I are over. For good. I'm sorry."

"You *cheated* on me, Liv," he said, still looking forward. "I can't just let that slide. I care about you, but I won't let you take me for a fool twice."

I saw his threat for what it was. I'd caused this divorce. He'd make it even uglier. "Fine," I said, looking at my hands. "We'll settle it in court if it comes to that."

"It'll come to that. You better find a good lawyer." He stood and looked down at me. "I think you should leave."

Back at David's, I pulled my hair down immediately and wiped off my lipstick. I texted him that I was home, hoping he'd be too preoccupied to notice how long it'd taken me. I asked about Alex, but by the time I'd changed and finished my nightly routine, I still hadn't heard back.

In his bed, alone, I played the night back in my head.

"Just admit that you're fucking afraid and that I'm not worth taking the risk for."

It gutted me that he thought that. That he'd gone so far to get me, and that I might lose him because I'd conditioned myself not to give anyone what he demanded from me. *Everything*. He wanted *all* of me. And he wanted it *now*, even though I was still learning what a real relationship looked like. How could anyone not find that terrifying?

I knew better than anyone that David's detached demeanor and his short words were a defense mechanism, but one word had been noticeably absent during our goodbye tonight. Didn't he love me still? Why didn't he say it? Why didn't I finally say it? I loved him, and I wanted to tell him, but he'd told me tonight I had to show him my love, and I had to mean it. Whatever fears I had about not being enough for him, about him one day leaving, about how he'd react to my doubts about starting a family—I had to find a way to let go of all of that or I'd lose him before I'd even really had him.

I wrapped the comforter around myself and shivered. It was cold. He was cold, and I was cold. As my lids fell, I wondered what it would take to get warm again.

I still hadn't heard from David by the time I'd left for my flight the next morning. At the Dallas/Fort Worth airport, my father greeted me at the curb with a big, comforting hug. Seeing him again, I realized how much I needed to talk to someone who could help me see everything clearly. My dad's businessman sensibilities, plus his soft spot for me and my wellbeing, made him the perfect person for that.

He held me at arm's length as I looked him over, too. His hair had almost turned completely charcoal now. "You look skinny," he said.

"I know, but I'm starting to put weight back on," I promised.

He grunted and took my luggage. As he loaded it in his trunk, I double-checked that my phone had resumed cellular service since deplaning. Still no word from David. I wished I had Jessa's number so I could check in.

I texted him one more time.

Me: *I know you're upset with me, but please just let me know if Alex is okay.*

My dad drove me straight to the clubhouse at his golf course and ordered enough food to cover the table.

With concern etched in his face, he listened to an abbreviated version of the last month. I told him that the night before, I'd gone to Bill's and had ended it once and for all.

Sitting rigidly straight after we'd eaten, he sipped his signature whiskey on the rocks. "I can't say I ever thought Bill was good enough for you."

"I sort of guessed that," I said. "You weren't great at hiding it."

"I didn't want to interfere, but I'm glad you figured it out."

The waitress brought my dad a second whiskey on the rocks he hadn't even ordered and refilled my iced tea. "Can I get you anything else?"

"No, thanks, sugar," Dad said.

"No problem, Mr. Germaine," she said and cleared our plates before walking away.

Dad shook out his napkin and tossed it on the table-cloth. "So I thought the point of this trip was to introduce me to the new guy. I don't see him here." He smiled a little. "He afraid of your old man?"

Afraid? When I'd brought up the idea of introducing them, David had nearly jumped at the chance. "He had a family emergency, and . . ." I played with the lemon slice that had come in my iced tea. "Well, honestly, we're still figuring things out."

"You don't seem too thrilled, kid. Concerns me." My father sighed. "Frankly, I don't want you jumping from one unhappy relationship to another."

"It's not that David doesn't make me happy," I said. "It's that he makes me *sublimely* happy."

He looked me up and down. "Not sure what that means."

"He's wonderful," I said, but I couldn't exactly explain why to my dad. Somehow, I doubted waxing poetic over David's gorgeousness combined with his limitless patience, borderline obsessiveness, and sheer tenacity to steal me from my husband would go over well. So I spoke to my dad in a language he understood. "David's very successful —one of Chicago's best architects, in fact."

"That so?" He perked up. "Then he has to be smart, and I like that. Regardless, it all feels very fast, Olivia. I wouldn't expect you to leave your husband unless you were in love, but since I've never even heard of this guy until now, I don't see how that can be."

That was because he hadn't met David. It could be. It could *definitely* be. It would be harder for a woman *not* to fall in love with him.

I didn't really have an answer, so I said, "I think you'd really like him."

"I'd say he has the advantage after Bill."

I half-rolled my eyes. "Bill's not that bad."

"As a person, no, but he doesn't make you 'sublimely' happy. You settled with him."

Apparently, I was the last to admit that. I changed the subject, though I wasn't sure why, since this topic would be worse. "Mom has temporarily disowned me," I informed him.

He laughed lightly. "Of that I have no doubt. I'm sure she said you were your father's daughter."

"In so many words. But I'm not you, Dad. I *cheated* on Bill. There's no way around it. David and I started things months ago. And it's hard for me to admit that to you," I said, swallowing, "because I know you're disappointed. But I'm the bad guy here. Not Bill."

"I'm not disappointed," he said simply, picking up his whiskey.

"Yes, you are," I said, sitting back in my seat. "And you should be."

"Olivia, you *are* my daughter. How can I be disappointed when I'm guilty of the same sins?" The one large ice cube in his glass *clinked* against the sides. "I guess now's as good a time as any to tell you this. Your mom wasn't completely wrong. Gina and I were together while I was still married to your mother."

Time seemed to slow as my mind filtered through his words. "But Gina was your client," I said.

"At first, yes. Then, she was more than that. She became a solace from Leanore, a confidante, and one day . . ."

I stopped listening. The restaurant suddenly became very loud with the *ting* of silverware and people talking at unnaturally high volumes. Light poured through the windows, unbearably bright. I stared at my dad, the man I'd not only looked up to my whole life, but whom I'd idolized. And I'd chosen to believe him over my mother. All these years, she'd tried to tell me, but I'd shut her out.

"Now, don't give me that look. You look like a damn frightened owl," Dad said. "I have no regrets about what I did."

No regrets? None? Bill had asked me the night before whether I'd regretted marrying him, and I hadn't needed to think too hard about it. Maybe *he* regretted marrying me, but I appreciated the life we'd had, even knowing it was over. "How is it possible. . ." I exhaled. "Why didn't you tell me?"

"You were so broken up about the divorce. I didn't want to make things worse for you." Dad pulled on his chin. "Frankly, I was afraid you'd get so upset that you'd ask to live with her instead of me."

"Don't you think I should've been able to decide that for myself?" I asked, my temper rising.

He shook his head but didn't speak.

"No?" I asked. "You withheld important information, Dad. Did Mom see something the day she found Gina at your office? That was when she started to *really* change."

"Nah," he said. "Leanore just had that sixth sense you women seem to possess about these things."

I put my elbows on the table and rubbed the inside corners of my eyes. "Why are you telling me this now?"

"Because sometimes we make mistakes, and we learn from them. I want you to learn from my mistakes. Then again, Liv, it can turn out they weren't mistakes at all."

"Cheating on Mom wasn't a mistake?" I asked.

"I'm not proud of it. I wish I could say I'd go back and undo it, but that'd be a lie."

I drew back at his unapologetic frankness. "But . . . Mom told me she wanted me to live with her. Why'd she give up fighting for custody if you'd been unfaithful? Wouldn't she have had a real chance at winning?"

"She put her own daughter in the hospital. And who do you think paid her lawyer's fees?" He frowned. "I didn't want to leave her destitute, but I wasn't going to let her anywhere near you before you turned eighteen. As a guarantee, we settled on a *much* higher alimony if she didn't pursue it."

Blood drained from my face. "You paid her not to fight for custody?"

"She *accepted* more money to stop fighting for you. Without hesitation. Think about that. Like I said, I don't regret it." He rested his ankle over one knee. "Your mother couldn't care for you the way I could, sugar—financially or otherwise. I hate to think how you would've turned out if she'd had her way."

My mother didn't *actually* want me very much. Not more than money. I'd suspected all along, but it'd been just another feeling I'd tried to ignore. Now, I knew it was true. She didn't have it in her to care for me the way a mother should. Her only daughter. Many times growing up, before Dad and I had left, I'd had the vague sense that she loved him more than me and that I'd taken a piece of him away from her.

She was cold, like me, but hot and fiery only when it suited her. Dad had done his best to protect me, but it seemed I'd turned out like her anyway, just like Bill had said. But she hadn't been completely crazy as I'd accused. And my dad? He'd *cheated*. Worse, he'd lied—to me of all people. My rock. My idol.

"Olivia?" Dad asked, peering at me.

I met his concerned stare. "Did you love her?"

"Your mother? Very much, but her anger and jealousy became so difficult toward the end. Gina came along, and she was so easy—well, at first. But that night . . . the night in the hospital? I almost died of regret for not getting you out of Leanore's grips earlier. And for putting you through that. From that moment on, I was done with Leanore. For good. Gina was there with me the whole way."

I gaped at him as something occurred to me. "But I didn't meet Gina until years later."

"I wasn't taking any chances. I had to be sure you were ready for a new person in your life. And I had to know I could bring *her* around my girl."

I searched his face. "You didn't marry her until I left for college. She waited all that time for you?"

"Yes."

"You kept a lot from me," I stated, not exactly sure if I was angry or not.

"It was to protect you."

I nodded as the information filtered in. It was clear by his tone that he believed he'd done the right thing, but he looked hurt. It struck me deep inside, cutting through everything I'd just heard. Nothing was worse than seeing my dad in pain . . . something, I was realizing, that was also true of David.

"Your divorce from Gina must be finalized by now," I said. "But you still love her, don't you?"

"Sure. And I miss her. But that's not always enough. Gina was a lot to handle, too." He blew out a sigh and looked into his whiskey. "I always seem to choose the most difficult women."

And I had been anything but difficult for Bill. Not up until now, when I'd chosen David over him. Was it a coincidence? Or had some part of me been actively trying not to complicate my parents'—or anyone's—lives any further?

"Do you regret it?" I rushed out.

"Regret what?" he asked.

"All of it. Any of it. Mom, me, Gina. If you knew back then that you'd be sitting here now in this moment, would you do it again?"

"What the hell kind of question is that?"

I blanched. It seemed like a perfectly *valid* question. Why would anyone look back over two painful loves, tumultuous marriages and subsequent divorces—and want to do it all over again?

"Why would I regret my life?" he asked. "What's going on with you?"

"I just . . ." I paused, glancing up at the ceiling to blink back tears. "I'm afraid of getting hurt. I've never felt anything like this before. What if one day David realizes I'm not enough—or that I can't give him what he needs—and he has no choice but to leave, even if he loves me? Like you still love Gina?"

My father slid his chair over to mine and put his arm around me. "Don't be so hard on yourself, huh? I don't regret a goddamn single thing. I would love and lose Gina again in a heartbeat, because we're both better people for it. She gave me something so beautiful, I could never regret it." He hugged me to his side. "And your mother gave me you, among many other things. Every decision I made was right at the time, and I can't say that any of them turned out badly."

I looked up at him through tear-blurry eyes and let him hold me. I'd made many regretful decisions, but they'd led me to David. So would I change any of them? And if David and I didn't make it, but we'd still spent this time loving each other . . . how could that be bad? Wasn't it better than never experiencing the bliss of loving him at all?

When we got to the house, I went directly upstairs to my childhood bedroom. The early flight plus the news of my dad's affair had me wrecked, so I lay down and tried to wrap my head around everything I'd just learned as shock still reverberated in me. He'd survived what I was going through. And he'd do it all again.

I'd always thought that keeping others out was the same thing as strength. It made me pragmatic, unemotional. But I was quickly learning that it meant the opposite—strength meant opening myself to another person without a guaranteed outcome.

Later, I woke groggily from a deep nap. As I headed downstairs to find my dad, I took my phone off silent to find two voicemails from David, one from Gretchen, and a missed text from her asking why I wasn't picking up her calls.

I yawned and fell into a kitchen chair to listen to David's messages. My heart skipped knowing that I would get to hear his voice, but before I could, a knock came on the front door.

"Dad," I called to no response. I groaned and padded to the door. When I pulled it open, my heart went from a skip to a leap.

Chapter Seventeen

At the comforting sight of David on my dad's doorstep, relief, love, and happiness flooded through me. I almost didn't recognize the high pitch of my voice as I said his name. "What are you doing here?" I asked.

David nodded at my phone clutched in my hand. "I'm beginning to wonder why I even got you that thing."

I released an awed laugh. "I'm sorry. I was taking a nap. I can't believe you came. I thought . . ."

"What, that I could wait to finish our conversation until you got back?" he asked.

"You're kind of persistent, aren't you?" I teased.

His eyebrows lowered. "When you didn't pick up your phone, I called Gretchen. If not for her, I'd be wandering around the streets of Dallas by myself."

I gaped at him a moment before giving in to a big smile and moving aside. "Come in."

He took a tentative step through the door. "Where's your dad?"

"He's here. Where's your stuff?"

"A hotel."

"Oh." I clutched my heart, hating the thought that David might not think he was welcome. "You shouldn't have done that. You can stay here."

"I don't want to impose."

"You won't." I closed the door and leaned my back against it. "How's Alex?"

David's face lit up in a way that tugged at my heart, and he finally smiled. "He's a trouper. In recovery and doing great."

"Good. I was worried. I should probably be asking how *Jessa* is."

"Stressed," he said, sighing. "But relieved that the surgery went well. We all are."

I wanted to reach for him, to seek comfort in his arms, but after our last tense conversation, I wasn't sure that he'd be open to that. "Can I, um, get you anything?" I asked.

He crossed his arms, and his smile faded. "Talk first, okay? I hate how we left things."

"Me, too," I said just as I heard footsteps on the floor above us.

My dad started down the stairs. "Who's at the door?" he asked.

Before I could answer, David walked to the bottom of the staircase with his hand extended. "David Dylan. Olivia's, er, boyfriend."

"I see." They exchanged a firm handshake. "Nice to meet you, David."

"You, too, sir."

My father glanced at me and back to David. "I understood you weren't going to make it this time around."

"Fortunately, my family emergency got sorted out." David reached back to take my hand, and I stepped up beside him. Looking down at me, he added, "And I have some unfinished business with this one that couldn't wait."

"I think you might be right about that," Dad said, turning for the kitchen. "Come on in, David."

I looked down at the pink-and-white plaid pajamas I'd worn in high school and had found in a drawer. "I should change," I whispered as my dad left the room.

David arched an eyebrow. "I think you look cute."

I blushed a little. "Will you be all right alone with him while I run upstairs?"

"Of course. I'm very popular with parents," he said with a smirk. "Go on."

I bolted up the steps and changed into a t-shirt and jeans, a small but necessary step up from my embarrassing outfit. When I came downstairs again, I was surprised to hear the bellow of two deep laughs emanating from the patio.

My dad was a tough nut to crack, and David had already done it? He wasn't kidding about being popular.

That, or it was thanks to the whiskey bottle on the table and the tumblers in their hands. "I see you two found common ground," I noted, stepping outside.

"I like him already," my dad said, raising his glass to David. "Never understood a man who doesn't appreciate a good whiskey." They clinked glasses of amber liquid and each took a sip. "So, Olivia tells me you're an architect."

"Yes, Mr. Germaine." David smoothed his hand over his hair. "I'm partner at a firm in Chicago, but I've done work all over the country."

I paused and looked at him. "Wait. You're a *partner* at Pierson/Greer? Why isn't your name on the building?"

"I wanted to remain a silent," David explained. "I love what I do for a living, but I hate the bullshit politics of it. I focus on planning and design." He smiled. "And give input when necessary to make sure they don't drive the business into the ground."

"I hear you," my dad said. "That's why I went into consulting. I make my own hours, set my own fee. I love business but not bullshit." He nodded slowly, impressed. "Partner for a top firm, though—that's very good."

"He's one of Chicago's most in-demand architects," I bragged.

"So you've already mentioned," my dad reminded me as David eyed me playfully.

"And he has a Porsche," I added to seal the deal. The fastest way to my dad's heart was in a sports car.

My dad's posture straightened. "That so? What kind?"

"911 Classic," David said, nodding toward the garage. "Was that your C7 in the driveway?"

He nodded once. "And a '68 Shelby in the garage."

"You have other cars, too, right?" I asked David.

"The Mercedes is an SL 65 AMG. Black Series." David's eyes turned wistful as he raised his drink toward the sky. "And in New York, I've got a *beautiful*, copper Aston Martin Vantage."

"Engine?" Dad asked.

"V12."

My dad let out a low whistle. "Shame to keep a car like that pent up in the city."

"Tell me about it." David sipped his drink. "Barely get to take her above eighty, but that baby can fly."

I watched David as he spoke, picturing how he'd handle a fast car on the open road. If it were anything like the way he handled everything else, it would be casually but in complete control.

When I realized the conversation had stopped, I looked from David to my dad, who was staring at me. He chuckled. "Why don't I give you two a chance to catch up?" He headed for the slider. "I'm going to run to the market. Will you be staying for dinner, David?"

"Yes," I answered for him.

Once my dad had disappeared into the house, I sat on the cushion of the nearest chaise lounge. I looked at the seat and then up at David. He swirled his drink thoughtfully, took my cue, and sat beside me.

"I can't believe you're here," I said quietly, placing my hand on his thigh.

"It drives me insane when I don't know what you're thinking," he said right away and picked up where we'd left off. "You tell me you're still empty inside after our weekend? Do you know how it tears me apart to hear that?"

I swallowed. "I didn't mean it that way," I whispered.

"Well, how am I supposed to take it?" he asked. "It's my job to fill you with love and hope and joy. Now, you tell me I've failed."

"No. God, no." I grasped his hand. "I was scared. In that moment, I felt . . . I don't know. Inadequate. Cornered."

"Why?" he demanded. "What reason have I ever given you to feel afraid or inadequate?"

"You asked for everything, and that's what you deserve," I said to him and took a breath. "But I'm scared I can't give you that. Or that my *everything* won't be enough."

He leaned his elbows on his knees and kept his eyes forward. "I'm worried that you're thinking about going back to Bill, and nothing would be worse than that. If you don't want to be with me," he paused, swallowed, and shook his head, "if it meant you were *truly* happy, I would respect it. But talk about being worthy . . ." David turned his head and finally looked at me from under heavy eyebrows. "He *isn't*. I couldn't live with knowing I'd had you—and in the end, you still chose him. I couldn't, Olivia."

"It's over with Bill." I bit my lip. "I went to see him last night, and it's so done."

His muscles tightened along with his jaw. "You went alone?"

I placed my hand on his arm and squeezed. "It's over. Completely. I promise you."

He exhaled but kept his eyes on me. "And us?"

I searched his face. In his eyes I saw everything I wanted. His love. Why couldn't I accept it? What kind of walls had I built around my heart that he couldn't break through? I imagined, all those years ago, it had calcified into something inhuman, something hard because I'd buried it, ignored it, starved it. Davena had warned me my neglected wants and needs could rot my insides, but maybe she'd been too late. And for the first time, I wanted to let someone in. But was there any chance of penetrating my heart's hardened exterior?

David's eyes flashed as I sat looking at him. "Baby," he whispered, his voice turning grave. "Let go, please. I'm here, begging you to let me in. Let me love you the way you deserve. I know you're afraid, but I'm not going anywhere. Ever."

"How do you know?" The happiness I'd felt just from seeing him and the fear his words inspired found their way up my chest. "How do I know you won't grow tired of me like you did the others?"

"Others?" he asked. "Olivia, there are no others. There only is, and only ever has been, you. Finding you finally . . . I've been looking for you for so fucking long. Let me in so I can take care of you in all the ways you've been neglected."

I shook my head as my chin wobbled. "I want that, too. I'm here telling you I want this. I'm ready. I'll do whatever it takes so I don't lose you." My throat thickened with the tears I fought back. "But I don't know how to do this without trying to protect a small part of myself."

"When you protect that part, I can't get to it. And *that* scares *me*. You get to have some kind of back-up plan if you have to cut and run, while I have *nothing* but my faith in us?" He dropped his head in his palms and ran his hands through his hair. "I don't know what to do. I don't know how else to get you to see." He swung his head in my direction. "Is it a ring you need?"

"What?" I gasped, shaking my head. "No. I mean, not that I don't want—but I . . . I don't *need* anything more from you. You've given me so much."

"What then? Tell me. I can't . . ." He put his head back in his hands. Pain radiated from him, and it cut me deeply. I wanted to take it away however I could, no matter what it took.

I dropped onto the concrete and sat back on my calves between his legs. With a hand on each of his knees, I looked up at him through tear-blurry eyes and took a deep breath. "You're right that I've never felt like this about anyone," I said. "Not even Bill, and not even close. You're also right that I'm afraid. I'm scared to death that one day you'll realize you were wrong about me. I'll relinquish control, let you in, and I won't be everything you thought I was."

"You already *are* everything I—"

"Let me finish," I said. "I *know* you love me. I see it in the way you look at me. I feel it when you make love to me. You can tell me it a million times, but it won't change the fact that after only a few days with you, I'm on the verge of a breakdown just thinking about a life without you." Insanity from love—it ran in my family. It wasn't so far-fetched that it couldn't happen to me. "If you ever left me, I'd fall, David. And I'd never get back up."

His beautiful brown eyes darted between mine. I wanted to drown in them. I *could* drown in them, let them swallow me without a fight. That was what scared me most of all.

"You're so afraid," he whispered finally. "I can see it in your eyes."

"I'd lose myself. That madness runs in my blood. If true love doesn't send me there, jealousy could."

"Olivia, that's completely within our control. It's *not* in your blood. We'll fight with each other. We'll struggle." Lines formed between his eyebrows as he frowned. "But we'll also fight *for* each other. This is still new. In time, we'll become so secure in our love, jealousy will be a distant memory. We have a love others can only dream of at our fingertips—but you have got to *let go*. You're killing something beautiful here." I inhaled sharply and tried to look away, but he caught my chin. "Trust me like I trust you. If you leave me now, I'm the one who'll break. Is that what you want? You're it for me. It's you. I love you, and no matter how much shit you put me through, nothing will change that."

My chest stuttered with short breaths as he tore away at my exterior, forcing me to confront my fears or lose him.

"I won't let anything hurt you, my love," he said. "And if it does, you're strong enough to handle it. You've been so strong for seventeen years."

My eyes widened with the unexpected way he cut right to my core. I'd promised that young girl I'd never let her get hurt that deeply again, but in doing so, I'd also taken some of life's most beautiful things away from her. Unconditional love, trust, joy. I burst into tears and tried to look away, but his hand held my chin firmly. "I'm *not* strong, David. That's why I can't handle a love like yours."

"Are you kidding me?" he asked. "You're a fucking

warrior. Since the divorce, you've carried this fear with you. You've grown and adapted and taken care of others. You're strong. You've proved that. Now, let *me* take over. Give it all to me, and let me be strong for you. Please, let go so I can take care of you."

I pulled away finally and bawled into my hands. After a few moments, he tugged on my wrists. "Don't hide from me."

"David," I said through uncontrollable sobs. "When my parents divorced, I realized that there was no such thing as forever. That things could be taken away in an instant. And it scares me to death how strong our connection is because," I paused, whimpering, "because the thought of you taking it away is too much to bear."

He set my hands back on his knees and tucked my hair behind my ear before cupping my face. "You're there, Olivia," he said, his eyes boring into mine. "Keep going."

"But since the moment I saw you," I continued, "I've felt something that I didn't think existed. Real and true love. I didn't recognize it at first because I didn't know what it was."

"Give me all the shit," he said. "Everything you've been through. I will take it. Let it go."

I nodded. "I want to let it go."

"So do it," he said gently. "You're there, just do it."

My face contorted as his words ran through my mind. *Do it. Let go.* He said I'd been strong. He knew the load I carried, and he wanted to take it. I wanted to give it to him. I had to love him fully, without a single reservation, or I would lose him now—and I refused to let that happen.

I surprised him and myself by throwing my arms around his neck. "I trust you. For you, only you, I can do it," I whispered and cried into his shoulder. I cried because the little girl in me, my thirteen-and-a-half-year-old self, could let go. She could finally trust someone enough for me to love—and to let him love me without condition. I cried because I thought I'd never know what it meant to open myself and be at the mercy of another person—pleasure, pain, and all.

His arms tightened around me as he stroked my hair. "That's it," he said. "At your most vulnerable, you're strongest. You can handle anything. But you don't have to do it alone anymore. Not as long as I'm here."

"All I ever wanted was to let go," I said into his neck. I pulled back and looked into his sweet, chestnut-brown eyes. With tears streaking my cheeks and my nose running, I said, "I love you."

"I know," he replied, running his thumbs under my eyes and wiping away the wetness. "I've always known."

From over the rim of my wineglass, I watched David poke at a steak on the grill as he and my dad talked very masculine things I didn't care about.

I had done it.

I'd taken the plunge, and though the fears that came with this kind of love would never fully leave me, for the first time since I could remember, they were soothed by a new inner peace. And blissful happiness.

David had broken through something in me with his words, his eyes, his unrelenting love. How had he known there was a girl in me who couldn't let go? Who'd been hanging on to something for so long, she couldn't remember a life before it? David was the only thing I wanted, and if it didn't last between us, at least I would have these moments with him.

He looked over at me and winked, and I wondered if I'd ever seen a more beautiful sight than that.

It was a perfect night in Dallas, and the sun set over us as we sat at the patio table and cut into our steaks.

"So," my dad said, "what happens next with Bill?"

I sighed as my bliss bubble popped. Peace was always fleeting. "Well, he's been clear about the fact that he's not going down without a fight. I guess that means we'll be going to court."

"That doesn't surprise me," my father said. "I always knew he had a little weasel in him."

"Dad," I admonished. "I'm in the wrong here. Because I was unfaithful, he wants me to pay."

"It's an empty threat," David said. "Illinois is a 'no fault' state, meaning that infidelity will have hardly any impact on the division of assets. I talked to my lawyer."

"You did?" I asked.

"Of course."

David was in the driver's seat now, and I wondered if Bill had any idea what he'd be going up against. I twisted my lips. "Do you think Bill knows that 'no-fault' thing?"

"Olivia, *of course* he does," David said. "He's a lawyer, for Christ's sake. He was just trying to scare you. What sorts of assets do you two have?"

"Not much, I guess." I shifted in the cushioned, rattan chair. "I mean, he's been making more since he started his new job, so there's a little money there. But we rent the apartment. We own a car, furniture, and share a bank account. The car's in his name."

"Do you have any debt?" David asked.

I shook my head. "Dad paid for all my school, and Bill's student loans are minimal. He was—is very frugal. We were pre-approved for a loan to make an offer on the Oak Park house, but that's it."

"I didn't know you'd made an offer," Dad said. "Thank God they didn't accept it."

My fork stopped midway to my mouth.

David also froze, then turned to look at my dad.

"What?" Dad asked.

"They didn't accept Bill's offer because I bought the house," David told him.

My dad's face scrunched. "I'm sorry—*what*? Why?"

"I bought the house out from under Bill," David said. "For Olivia."

Dad drew back. "That's a little extreme, isn't it?"

"Yes, sir. But I always trust my gut, in business and otherwise." David squeezed my leg under the table. "And my gut told me Olivia would eventually come around."

No amount of struggling could suppress the smile that broke out over my face. I really hadn't allowed myself to think too much about the Oak Park house. At first, it'd been upsetting that he'd bought it behind my back. Then, it'd represented a life I wanted but might not let myself have. Now, I knew. David and I belonged there, just like I'd envisioned.

"Well, well. There's that smile," my dad said. "I haven't seen that in too long."

"*Dad*," I said, embarrassed.

"Bill never made you smile like that. Not that I ever saw. Honestly, it . . ." To my horror, my dad stopped and sniffled. "It brings a tear to my eye."

My chin quivered, an automatic response to seeing my dad cry for only the second time in my life. The first had been the night I'd spent in the hospital.

"No, no," he said, wiping his face with his napkin. "No more tears. Let David finish his thought."

David hesitated, clearly at a loss for how to proceed. I

couldn't help but laugh through the lump in my throat. "I'm sorry, honey," I said to him. "What were you saying?"

"Um, well . . . how attached are you to the car and the furniture?"

"God, I hate that piece of shit car," I said.

"I offered Bill the Shelby for your thirtieth birthday this year," Dad said. "He wouldn't accept it. Said it was impractical and too expensive to park and maintain."

I rolled my eyes. "Are you kidding? Bill knows I would've loved that, but he's stingy. And proud."

"So then your share of the bank account is the only real problem," David continued. "Right?"

"I taught you to always have your stash of savings," my dad said. "Right, Olivia?"

I cleared my throat. "Well, yes. But my personal savings is . . . not much, really. Most of my money is in our joint account, which I don't have access to right now. Bill canceled my cards."

David's face changed instantly. "You didn't tell me that."

"It happened a few days ago," I said. "Anyway, my savings aren't enough for a divorce lawyer."

"Mr. Germaine—" David started.

"Harvey," my dad interrupted.

"Harvey," David said with a nod, "I know you've been through a divorce."

"Two," I interjected.

"I want Olivia out of this marriage as quickly as possible," David said. "If it were up to me, it would already be over. I'd like to just wipe the slate clean."

"David," I started, "what—"

"I don't know if she told you," he interrupted me, "but Bill was unnecessarily rough with her."

"Pardon?" Dad said, leaning forward in his seat. "Is this true, Olivia?"

"He just grabbed my arm," I stammered.

"And left marks," David added.

"His pride was hurt," I said. "He'd just learned that David was the one who bought the house."

My dad ran his hands over his face. "Christ."

"David broke his nose, though," I said quickly.

David rolled his eyes. "Trying to make a good impression here," he said under his breath.

My dad laughed darkly. "Fine. What are you asking me for, David? Money?"

"No, sir, just some backup if Olivia plans to fight me on this. I'll get her out, no matter the cost. I'll pay to have everything taken care of as quickly as possible. Unfortunately, it looks like six months is the soonest the divorce would become official, and that's if Bill is compliant."

"David, I can't ask you to do that," I said, my eyes wide.

"You didn't. I'm saying," he continued, turning back to my dad, "I want to do it. I want to spare her the pain of a long-drawn-out process. Let Bill keep everything—the money, the car, the furniture, whatever. No alimony. I have more than enough for the two of us plus a family." David looked at me. "And just so you feel secure, Olivia, you'll keep your salary at the magazine like we discussed. Put it in savings. I'll take care of the rest."

"You'd do that?" my dad asked.

"In a heartbeat. But I need your help." David glanced at me. "Because Olivia will tell me no."

"You're right," I said adamantly. "My answer is no."

"I tell you, sugar, divorce is a bitch," Dad said. "I'd hate to see Bill drag you through the mud when there's another option."

I looked between the two of them, speechless. David worked hard for his money. Even if he didn't, this wasn't his mess to clean up. "This is *my* problem, David. You shouldn't have to—"

"It's our problem, Olivia. Remember what we just talked about?" he said slowly. "You've dealt with a lot from Bill. I know he's been hard on you. Let go, and let me take over from here."

Let go. It was what he'd asked of me not an hour ago, and I'd agreed. This was David's way of telling me I didn't have to do this on my own. "So we're just going to let him have everything?" I asked.

"Do you care?" David asked.

Not if it meant getting out unscathed. I didn't feel any particular attachment to the items in our apartment. "No," I said carefully. "I hate to put you in that position, though."

"Don't look at it that way. This is what we talked about," he said, staring me down. "Giving up control. Letting me help. It's nothing for me."

I shook my head. "I don't know what to say."

"This is no longer just about you. It involves me, too, and this is how I'm going to handle it."

I closed my mouth and stopped my gaping. That was it, then. "Okay," I agreed.

David nodded once. "Okay."

My dad reached over to shake David's hand. "You're a good man, David. I think I might be happy that you're looking after my girl."

———

After the sun had set, our bellies had been filled, and the dishwasher ran in the kitchen, I stood by the front door with David. "I wish you'd just stay here instead of the hotel," I said, running my hands over the fabric of his sweater. The soft cashmere, as always, was the perfect complement to the muscles underneath.

"Believe me, I want to," he said. "I'm feeling . . . restless."

I tugged on the waistband of his pants. "Stay then. We broke through some huge stuff earlier. Now, we should get to celebrate."

David shifted feet, definitely fighting himself. "It's not appropriate," he said, "and I don't want to make your dad uncomfortable."

"You're such a gentleman," I teased.

"Would a gentleman do this?" he asked, squeezing my ass to pull me against him.

I responded with a lustful groan as his length pressed against me in all its glory. A carnal need blossomed in me. "I can't wait," I said with finality. "Sex. Now."

He laughed and brushed a piece of my hair from my face. "If I can, you can. This time while in Dallas is about me getting to know your dad."

"Wait, *what?*" I exclaimed, trying unsuccessfully to push him away. "Don't tell me you plan on abstaining the whole time you're here."

"Sorry, baby, but we're not goddamn teenagers," he said. "We can handle a few days of self-restraint."

I grumbled to myself as he took my hand and led me outside and to a car parked at the curb. "How do you like my rental?"

"I hate it," I said with a pout, and he roared with laughter.

"Don't take your sexual frustration out on the car." He leaned in to give me a sweet kiss. "Thank you."

I cocked my head. "For what?"

"Tonight."

I smiled reluctantly and squeezed his hand in mine. "I'll see you in the morning?"

"Try to stop me."

I turned away, but he pulled me back by my hand for another series of pecks. He let go finally and smacked me on the ass. "Bye, gorgeous." He hit the key fob as he walked away, and the car beeped.

"David?"

He looked at me over the roof. "Yeah, baby?"

"I love you," I said.

He stared at me a moment before responding. "I love you, too."

I curled into my sweater and headed back into the house. I'd finally told him how I felt, but it wasn't nearly the truth. I didn't just love him. That wasn't a strong enough word. Whatever it was, it'd taken root a long time ago, and tonight, it'd finally bloomed. But now, it wasn't just something that lived in me. It was part of my being.

Chapter Eighteen

The distinct aroma of brewing coffee lured me from my sleep the next morning. My dad sat at the kitchen table and barely acknowledged me as he browsed *The Dallas Morning News*.

I poured myself some coffee and tried to seem casual. "So, what do you think?"

"About what, kiddo?" he asked, eyes on the newspaper.

"David."

He paused, folded down a corner of the paper, and looked at me over it.

"Please be honest," I said. "With Bill, you kept your feelings to yourself. The best way to protect me now is to tell me the truth."

He considered this a moment. "I've dealt with a lot of people over the years, and I'm a good judge of character. I like David. Thing I like best is that he adores you. That, and I can see he's strong enough and smart enough to make tough decisions. You don't get as far in business as he has by pussy-footing around."

I twisted my lips. "Do you like him because he's a good businessman or because of the person he is?" I asked.

My dad chuckled. "He's a good guy. And Bill was, too. The difference is that Bill didn't quite know what to do with you."

I blushed at the first thing that came to mind—the biggest change to my life since meeting David. Mind-blowing sex. He knew *exactly* how to handle me in the bedroom.

"You up for a run?" Dad asked.

I wrinkled my nose. "A run? Like exercise?"

"Yes, Olivia, like exercise. Call up David and invite him."

"You want to go for a run with my boyfriend?"

He bristled. "I don't see any reason why not."

The reason why not was that he'd never done such a thing with Bill. "I think he runs," I said, tilting my head. I was pretty sure he'd mentioned jogging the lakefront with Brian. "But I doubt he brought anything with him."

"I have shoes he can borrow."

I shook my head before I fell into a fit of giggles. My dad only stared at me with confusion. When I could speak again, I gasped, "He's . . . a size . . . fourteen and a half."

"Oh. Big feet."

"Yeah." *Enormous.* I smiled as I shook my head again, picked up my phone, and dialed David's number. "My dad wants to go for a run with you," I said when he answered.

"Are you coming, too?" he asked.

"Me? I'm going for a breakfast burrito."

He laughed. "I'll be right over."

The smartest thing I'd done in my old apartment was grab a bikini. It'd been too long since I'd been poolside, and I was happy to park myself in the Texan sun while David and my dad sweat it out on their jog.

I was sufficiently relaxed and reclined on a latticed lounge chair when they returned. I waved from across the backyard. My dad excused himself to shower, and David followed the perimeter of the pool until he was standing over me.

He bent at the hip and crooked a finger under the string between my breasts, pulling up slightly. "Nice biki-ni," he remarked before straightening up again.

I lowered my sunglasses and checked him out. He wore only red and white basketball shorts, having already peeled off his shirt, and the planes of his chest glistened with a sheen of sweat. I wrapped my hand around the back of his knee and ran it up the opening of his shorts. "Hi."

"How long have you been out here?" he asked.

I shrugged, and slid my hand back down his thigh. "As long as you've been gone."

His eyes scanned my body. "Won't you burn?"

"I'm wearing sunscreen."

He picked up the sunblock from the side table and examined it. When he seemed to deem it suitable, he held it out to me. "Put more on."

I pouted. "But I'm trying to get a tan."

"You're beautiful the way you are. This shit," he waved in the general direction of the sun, "causes skin cancer."

"But—"

"More," he cut me off.

I sighed and took it from him. I squirted some onto my stomach and chest and began to rub it in, careful not to miss anywhere that might give me funny tan lines. I lifted the band of my bottoms and smoothed it under. When I looked up, David watched from under heavy lids.

"Perv!" I cried. "You just want to ogle me as I slather it on."

He grinned. "A perk."

A *perk* if he got to act on what he saw. But since he'd imposed abstinence on us, and was trying to be good . . . that meant I got to have a little fun.

I took my time massaging a handful of lotion over my thighs. "Gosh, it's going to be a long few days, isn't it?" I lifted my left leg, rubbed down my shin, and made my way back up.

With a small growl, he adjusted his shorts. "Give me that," he demanded impatiently.

"I'm not finished."

"Now, Olivia."

Without looking up, I passed him the bottle.

"Sit up."

I obeyed, leaning forward and wrapping my arms around my knees.

He threw a long leg over the width of the chair and sat behind me. I dropped my forehead on my knees and sighed while he massaged sunscreen onto my back. He tugged on the tie and let the strings drop. With my breasts pressed against my thighs, I held my bikini top in place.

Even after he'd run out of sunscreen, he continued to knead my skin. His muscular hands pushed into me hard, but I suspected he wasn't even using half his strength. I groaned into the ache as he worked my shoulders and then up my neck. He inched forward, closing any space between us, his erection digging into my lower back.

I bit into my knee, already wet in my bikini bottoms. He swept my hair over one shoulder and pressed his lips to the top of my spine. His hands slipped between my chest and thighs to cup my breasts while he kissed the length of my neck.

"Are you feeling me up in my dad's house?" I whispered.

"Mhm." My nipples tightened under the gentle force

of his fingers. "I'd give anything to be inside you right now," he said into my ear. I sucked in a sharp breath just as his hands fell away to retie my bikini.

"Wait, no." I groaned into my knees. "Don't stop."

"Sorry," he said, tightening the bow. "I don't trust myself one second longer."

In one motion he was standing beside me again.

Despite my frustration, I grinned when I glanced at his tented shorts. "Honey," I said, "can't you do something about that? My dad could be back any second."

"Shit."

"Pool?" I suggested.

"After you."

"Oh, no, I'm—"

He scooped me up, and I squealed as he tossed me into the deep end.

"David!" I swiped hair out of my eyes just as he landed a few feet away.

He resurfaced, whipping his hair away from his face. "We needed to hit the reset button," he said.

"It's cold," I whined but made no move to get out.

"You'll survive."

I laughed. "Thanks for going running with my dad, by the way."

"I wanted to," he said, swimming backward. "He's in great shape."

"What'd you guys talk about?"

"Not much. We mostly ran."

I smiled to myself.

He jutted his chin at me. "What?"

"I was just trying to picture Bill running with my dad. That would never happen."

"Your dad said the same thing."

"He likes you," I said.

David grinned wide, showing off all his teeth.

"I see that makes you happy," I observed with a giggle.

"His approval is the only one that means anything to me," he said.

I cocked my head. "Only his? Not my friends'? My mom's?"

He swam closer to me, his agile limbs cutting through the water like knives through butter. "Only his."

I wished it were as simple as that. Not everyone approved of us, and it wasn't easy to just forget that or move on. "The other night, at dinner, you said you spoke to Andrew."

David nodded. "Yeah."

When he didn't continue, I had a feeling there was a reason. I glanced away. "What else did he say? Anything about Lucy?"

David followed my gaze across the backyard. "In a nutshell, Andrew's loyalty lies with Bill. I can respect that. He'll talk to Lucy, but she's pissed. At both of us."

"I thought I would've heard from her by now," I said. "It's been a week since I told her."

"I'm sorry, baby. I really am." He pushed a hand through his inky wet hair. "Maybe you should try calling her."

I nodded. "Maybe."

"Andrew also said that Lucy and Gretchen are on the outs, but he didn't elaborate."

I gave him a knowing smile. "It's probably because Gretchen told Dani to go to hell on the phone the other night."

His gaze fixed intently on me. "Did you really call Dani a—what was it? Judgmental bitch?"

I swallowed and tried to look contrite as my cheeks heated. "I mean, she was talking shit about you and me."

He shook his head. "Scrappy, honey. I'm just glad you and Gretchen are on *my* side."

"Gretchen's been rooting for you since she found out the truth about us. Especially since she called you while Bill was out of town and told you to come to my apartment. I don't know what you said to her, but she bought it."

"I wasn't trying to sell her anything. I didn't even have to tell her I was miserable. I just told her the truth . . . that I love you. That I'd purchased the house so I could curl up in front of the fire with you. Throw a ball in the front yard with Alex or with . . ."

My stomach flipped with what he didn't say. It was unlike David to hesitate or beat around the bush. I fidgeted with the strap of my bikini. "Were you going to say with your own son?"

"Yeah," he said with a gentle smile.

Kids. The topic had spurred the worst fights between Bill and me, and the sting was still fresh. My perspective on life had drastically changed since David. Had this part changed, too?

I took a moment to picture David with a young, teenaged version of himself, tossing a football in fall with the turning leaves as a backdrop as I watched from our porch. My heart melted. It was sweet. But was it enough to make me want to be a mom?

What if the answer was no?

My stomach churned at the thought of getting back on that rollercoaster of trying to figure out what I wanted, what I owed David, and what my desires—or lack thereof —could do to a new relationship.

Thankfully, David kept talking. "So, if I'm to understand correctly, you've spent the week hearing from Bill and Dani that I'm a player who will soon grow tired of monogamy."

"More or less," I said. "But I have Gretchen and my dad to thank for setting me straight."

"I owe them then."

"My dad said that even though he loves and misses Gina, his second wife, he wouldn't change a thing about their relationship. He said he doesn't regret loving her."

"Why would he regret loving her?"

"I asked if he did," I said.

David inched toward me. "You asked that because . . .?"

"He's been through a lot with her, and I can tell he's hurting over their breakup."

"But why would anyone regret loving someone?" David asked.

"When you love that hard, it's almost inevitable that someone will end up hurt," I said. "Why do so many people risk it? My dad explained that even though he still loves Gina but can't be with her, he wouldn't change their history." I reached out for David's hand and drew him closer, until we were face to face. "I get it now. After last night, after whatever it was you broke through, I get it. If all this, *us*, went away tomorrow, at least I'd have these moments right now."

David put his arms around my shoulders. After a quick peck, he drew back and looked into my eyes. "When you actually talk to me, it helps me see why you've made certain decisions."

"I knew it was fucked up," I whispered. "But I didn't know how to change it. I didn't know letting go could be so right. But seeing you in pain was far worse than my own pain."

"Fuck, but I was afraid I'd never get through."

I touched his face. "I'm sorry."

"Olivia," he said, tucking my wet strands behind my

ear, "promise me you won't hide from me. I not only *want* to hear what you're thinking, I have to. In order for us to be a team and move forward, you have to be forthcoming with me." He smiled mischievously. "I'm fascinated with your every move, and it scares me because I've never felt that way before."

"You get scared?"

"Of course. The moment we made eye contact, I became vulnerable in a new way, too. I was scared the first time I kissed you at Lucy's office—I thought I'd pushed you away. It scared me that you wanted to stay with Gretchen this week instead of me." He frowned. "I get scared, too. Who says *you* won't be the one to wake up one morning and leave?"

"I won't," I promised.

"Trust, baby. It's all we've got."

"When did you get so smart?" I teased.

"One more thing."

I swallowed nervously at the suddenly serious tone of his voice. "Yes?"

"I meant what I said about being alone with Bill." He cut me off when I started to protest. "I *know* he's not a bad guy, and I don't feel good about breaking his nose. But I won't budge on this. I'm not happy that you went to see him by yourself. *Especially* in that dress. That was supposed to be for me, and I never want you out of my sight when you're looking that fucking good."

"You liked the dress?" I asked, feigning ignorance.

"Don't change the subject."

I stuck out my bottom lip. "You *didn't* like it?"

Surrender crossed his face. "Of course I did. You were stunning. And those red lips . . . I kept imagining them wrapped around my—"

"Room for one more?" I heard.

I jerked away from David as my dad slid the back door closed and walked in our direction. With my hand over my mouth, I raised my eyebrows at David and laughed. "Come on in, Dad," I called before ducking under the cold water.

Later, in the kitchen, showered and cleaned up, Dad searched for his car keys as I leaned my hip against the counter. "So, Dad . . . are you dating anyone?" I asked.

"Sort of," he muttered.

Standing in the doorway, David raised an eyebrow at me.

"Well, you either are or you aren't," I responded.

"Yes, I am, do you mind?" my dad said.

I suppressed a giggle and winked at David. "How old is she?" I asked.

"Old enough."

Finally, I laughed, partly at David's confused expression. "Gina was in her twenties when they got married," I explained. When David nodded as though he found that impressive, I rolled my eyes.

"All right," Dad said, dangling his keys. "Last chance for grocery requests. I'm making leftovers from last night, but I have a few other things to grab."

I shrugged. "I think we're good."

"I'll be back soon," my dad said, dropping a kiss on the top of my head on his way out.

Once I heard the garage door shut, I looked at David, who was already staring at me. The space between us thickened with tension. I bit my lip, slunk toward him, and placed my hands on his pecs. "Alone at last," I purred. "Should we head upstairs—"

He backed away quickly. "No."

"What?" I gaped at him. "You're kidding. I thought after the pool, you'd surely break."

"I want to, trust me," he said, his eyes darting around as if we were being watched, "but it doesn't feel right. Not in your dad's house."

I groaned. "Take me to your hotel then."

"My God, woman," he exclaimed. "Control yourself. Surely we can think of something else to do for an hour."

I frowned. "What do you suggest?"

"Show me your bedroom."

"But you just said—"

"I just want to *see* it. That's all. Don't get any ideas."

"Okay, but it's boring," I said. "We moved into this house when I was thirteen so it's all teenage girl crap." I motioned for him to follow me up the stairs. "Dad hasn't done much with it since I left."

"That's fine," David said, and I could tell he was grinning. Maybe he thought he could use my adolescence as an opportunity to tease me. I opened the bedroom door, and he strolled inside with his hands in his jean pockets. He took a moment to assess the room before he said, "Looks pretty normal."

"Were you worried it wouldn't be?"

He chuckled. "No, not really." He made a beeline for my bookshelf, picking up a framed photo of Gretchen and me in our high school cafeteria. We had huge, red-stained smiles plastered on our faces as we both held heart-shaped lollipops. He looked between the photo and me before shaking his head and setting it back down. "You are so fucking cute. I would have died over you in high school."

"Doubtful," I said.

"Are you kidding me?" He held up my prom photo, me

in a champagne-colored polyester-spandex dress that grazed the floor. "You were a knockout."

I cringed. "I hate that one."

"Why?"

"I look young and awkward."

"Hmm," he mused. "That's not what I see at all. Who's the lucky guy?"

"That's Gretchen's older brother. You met him at Lucy's wedding."

David pressed his lips together. "I didn't realize . . . did you guys date?"

I shook my head. "Jonathan was home from college, and he was one of my best friends."

"So you never . . ."

"No, never," I said. "He's just a friend, but a really good one."

"Does he want more than that?"

"I've never seen him that way," I said.

"That's not a 'no.' But I like him," David decided. "He has good taste, and he looks out for you. As long as it's from a distance."

He put down the photo, drew my yearbook off a shelf, and flipped through it slowly. Watching him do anything was entertaining, I was discovering.

"Just as I suspected," he muttered, pointing to something on the page. "You were voted *Best Eyes*."

"It's stupid," I said, waving him off.

"Is it?" He stared at me and I stared back, as mesmerized now as I'd been that first night I'd seen him. What magic did his gaze have over me?

As it occurred to me, I cocked my head. "You, too?" I asked. *"Best Eyes?"*

He smiled slowly. "Yeah."

I told myself it was a silly coincidence, but something

sweet passed between us. He broke the stare and flipped through a few more pages before replacing the yearbook on the shelf. I sat on the edge of my bed and observed as he looked through everything, stopping now and then to read the title of a book or DVD.

After a few minutes, he came to sit next to me. "It's nice being here," he said. "I get to see a different part of you."

"And do you like what you see?" I asked, arching an eyebrow at him.

His eyes moved to my lips, and a grunt was his non-response.

"I'm not supposed to have boys in my bed," I whispered. Before he could stop me, I threw a leg over him and settled astride his lap. "My dad would flip out."

David took two handfuls of my ass and squeezed, pulling me against his crotch.

"You're hard," I murmured, my mind buzzing, my insides thrilling. He skated one hand up my back and stilled me by the nape of my neck. He held me in place as he latched his lips to mine in a sensual kiss that quickly turned hard and greedy. His tongue reached for me hungrily as his hand secured me to him. I gyrated in his lap, and he flexed his other hand against my ass.

"Lose your virginity here?" he rasped.

"College," I breathed and then kissed him again. "You?" I asked into his mouth.

"Sixteen."

"Head cheerleader?" I pushed my hips into him, creating a slow but purposeful rhythm.

"Something like that," he said from behind gritted teeth. "You?"

"Jordan Banks, my," my breath hitched when he pulled me against him harder, "my first true boyfriend."

"I'll kill him," David said, and the playfulness in his threat made me laugh.

He flipped me over onto my back and grasped my hips in his hands. My legs surrounded him as he continued his deliberate movements, his crown grinding against my clit.

"You're . . . making me . . . come," I breathed, gasping with each acute sensation.

With one hand, he popped open the button of my jeans and pushed my pants over my ass. He propped himself above me with an outstretched arm. "Touch yourself in this bed?" he asked. He bypassed my pants to continue his sinuous teasing against my panties.

"Yes," I whimpered.

"Show me."

I hesitated, lost in the sensations singing through my body. He grasped my hand, lowered it between my legs, and clamped it over my mound, circling my fingers over my clit.

"Oh, God," I moaned, bowing my back. "Right there."

"Don't stop," he said gruffly as he removed his hand to undo his fly. I massaged myself and watched his cock fall heavy into his hand. His lids lowered as he stroked himself, never taking his eyes off my hand.

He groaned loudly. "I could come just watching you."

I urged him forward by pushing my heels into his ass. "I want you, David."

He glanced over his shoulder. "We can't."

I kneaded faster over my underwear, squirming beneath him and breathing heavily. "Please," I panted. I reached out to touch him, and his other hand fisted the sheets next to my head. Suddenly, he tore my jeans off the rest of the way, yanked my panties aside, and fed himself into me.

He made a noise from the back of his throat, and his

eyes remained locked on my hand. "Don't stop touching yourself," he rasped, sliding in and out of me. He grasped my hip in one hand and continued bracing himself against the bed with the other. I applied more pressure and circled faster, bringing myself to the edge as he thrust into me. Within a few plunges he was coming with his jaw clenched, clawing at the sheets, jerking as his heat coursed into me. I grabbed onto his t-shirt as my own pleasure crested, seizing and releasing me repeatedly, arching my back and bucking my hips. When I finished, I released my back onto the mattress and let go of his shirt.

"Fuck," he breathed.

I pulled him down by his neck and kissed him. "Thank you, baby. That was just what I—"

When the door slammed downstairs, David jumped back.

"Shit," I hissed, fumbling to button up my jeans. I flew to my feet as David zipped up his own pants.

My dad's voice rang through the house. "Liv?"

After a moment to catch my breath, I responded. "Up here, Dad."

I heard him climbing the steps as David whirled to the bookshelf to pick up my prom photo.

"That was quick," I squeaked as Dad leaned in the doorway.

"Didn't need much," he said with a shrug.

"I was just asking Olivia about her high school prom," David blurted, sweat dotting his upper lip.

Oh, come on. This was the *one* moment where he couldn't be cool? I shifted on my feet when an uncomfortable feeling came over me.

As I cursed under my breath, David caught my eye and mouthed, "What?"

"Ah, yes, the Harper boy," my dad remarked, nodding

at the prom photo. "Gretchen's brother still causing trouble?"

Fuck. I fought the urge to adjust my panties as they dampened with David's semen.

"Olivia?" David asked.

"Um, I don't—not sure."

I grimaced as David furrowed his brows at me. Suddenly, I understood why he'd tried to fend me off—almost getting caught was *not* sexy. When my dad turned to David, I quickly pulled at my crotch.

As it dawned on David as to why I was so uncomfortable, a lewd smile crossed his face. "Should we get started on those leftovers?" David asked, putting down the photo and crossing the room to my dad. "Come on. I'll help."

I silently thanked him for rescuing me and ran to the bathroom to clean myself up.

Once I'd changed, I rejoined them in the kitchen. They were already each a beer deep, so I grabbed a Heineken and sat back as my dad showed David how to make steak enchiladas. David gave my dad his undivided attention, seemingly eager to acquire this new skill. I sighed. If he learned to cook, then he really *would* be perfect, and where would that leave me?

Tired from my day in the sun, I let them talk about work and other things as I ate. David glanced at my empty plate when I sat back in my chair and smiled at me. When I offered to do the dishes, my dad shooed me away, so I flopped onto the couch, completely sated. I wondered, as they cleared the table together, if I should be worried that my dad was treating David more like a peer than his daughter's boyfriend.

I flipped through the channels until they'd finished and put on ESPN at their request. David sat on the couch with his long legs spilling in front of us. I lay my head on his lap and tuned out the sounds of football replays while he played with my hair.

At some point, I heard David's distant voice. "You awake?" he asked.

I opened my eyes. It was dark except for the TV screen, and *SportsCenter* had been muted.

"Did I fall asleep?" I asked.

"Yeah. Your dad just went to bed."

"Mmm, sorry."

He stroked my hair, and I closed my eyes again.

"I'll take you upstairs," he said.

"Not yet," I said softly.

David lifted me to pull his legs up lengthwise on the couch. Because it was a tight fit, I climbed atop him to rest my cheek on his broad chest. He slid his hand under my hair, freeing it from my neck.

"Are you having fun?" I asked.

"Yeah," he said. "It's nice to take some time off work for something important."

I smiled to myself. Most people just wanted an expensive, indulgent vacation, and here, David thought making a good impression on my dad was important. "When's your flight?" I asked.

"I don't have one."

I sighed with gratitude. That meant more time with him. "Why not?"

"I'll buy it when we get to the airport."

"Oh." I shifted on him, my smile growing when I realized he wanted us to fly together. "Good."

His fingers moved to my earlobe and tugged gently. "I'm sorry if we ruined your underwear."

I giggled softly. "It was worth it."

"Yes, but it's not going to happen again. I want to be respectful."

"Sure. Okay," I said, yawning and smacking my lips. I was too tired to get frisky anyway. I twisted to prop my chin on his sternum and look up at him. With his eyes closed, the television glare flashed over his face.

So handsome.

"What was that?" he asked.

"I didn't say anything."

He chuckled. "You sure?"

"Mhm."

"So handsome?" he asked.

"Oh." I bit my lip. "That could get to be a bad habit, thinking out loud."

"I think I'd like it if you did." He inhaled deeply. "It'd save me a hell of a lot of grief."

I rolled my eyes up to the ceiling. "You're exaggerating."

He just smiled and closed his eyes again, humming his satisfaction as he took a deep breath.

David was solid underneath me. Sturdy. Reliable. My father had always been that for me, too—or so I'd thought. I hadn't really thought more about the conversation at the clubhouse since David had surprised me, but it was a weird thing to know I'd gotten wrong such a huge part of the puzzle of my past. "He cheated on my mom," I whispered.

David stilled. "Your dad?"

I nodded into his chest. "He told me yesterday. I always thought it was all in her head, and I've accused her of it many times."

"If I'm honest, Olivia . . ." He opened his eyes and blew out a breath. "I had a feeling. You were always so adamant he was innocent, but I didn't buy it."

"Really?" I asked. "You never said so."

"It was an instinct. Usually in these situations, where there's smoke, there's fire." He ran a hand over my hair.

"But I suspected your dad kept it from you to protect you, so I kept my mouth shut."

I glanced down at his chest, comforted by the way it rose and fell with his breath. "He didn't want me to go live with my mom," I said.

"That's playing a little dirty," David said, "but I would've done the same thing. Sounds like your mom wasn't that stable. But how do *you* feel about that?"

I crossed an arm over David's chest and replaced my chin so our eyes were level. "I'm not happy that he lied to me, but I guess I get why he did it. Strangely, it doesn't make me feel any more sympathetic toward my mom."

He was quiet for a moment. "Probably because your issues with her aren't just about that night."

"Should I start calling you Dr. David?" I teased.

"It has a nice ring to it."

"She agreed to more alimony to stop fighting my dad for custody," I explained. "She'd always told me she'd given up because of the stabbing—that my dad's lawyer was vicious, and he'd make her look like the bad guy. She said she couldn't afford to keep spending money just to lose."

"Do you think you would've gone to live with her if you'd known the truth?" he asked.

I traced a circle on his t-shirt, thinking. "I didn't want to live with her because I blamed her for the divorce. She was jealous, she drank, and I was a little bit scared of her. But if I'd known it wasn't entirely her fault . . . I'm not sure."

"I think most girls would choose their mother in a divorce, regardless of circumstances," David said. "That's why this probably goes deeper than that. The night at the apartment, when she called and made you cry—you said that your mom doesn't love you."

"I did?" I tried to recall the time between the phone call and our bath, but it was hazy.

"Yes. A parent is supposed to love their child uncondi-tionally. If you don't feel that from her . . . well, it'd explain a lot." He paused, seeming to think. "That, in addition to her behavior, could be a large part of why it's difficult for you to open up. If your own mother doesn't love you for who you are, why would anyone else?"

"That sounds so sad," I said.

"It's *devastating*, Olivia. It makes me hurt for you. And it's completely fucked up. But . . ." He lifted my chin to get me to look at him. "You're an accomplished, smart, and kind woman in spite of it. You should be proud."

"I don't know about that considering my actions lately, but I am grateful. I never knew it could be like this. I was happy and content before I met you. I loved, and I was loved." I swallowed, looking into David's clear eyes. "But I never experienced this . . . this desire to give myself over to another person, wholly and completely without holding anything back. It's all new to me. I wouldn't know that if you hadn't fought for me."

He resumed stroking my hair. "You say that like I had a choice."

"I love you."

He smiled. "I look forward to hearing that more often."

"I'm sorry it took so long to say it in the first place."

"I don't care," he said simply. "Because I never had any doubt."

"*Never?*" I asked, fighting my own smile. "Not once?"

I laughed when the corner of his lip twitched. "Well, most of the time anyway."

Chapter Nineteen

With a red pen shoved behind my ear, I hunched over the work I'd spread out on the seat back tray table in front of me. Flying first class certainly meant more space to work, but it was tough to get anything done with David's eyes glued to me.

I looked over at the handsome man in the seat next to me with tousled weekend hair and black-framed reading glasses.

He folded the "Business" section of the *Tribune* in his lap. "Hey."

I shifted so my back was to the window. "I like your glasses," I said.

He studied me a moment. "The better to see you with."

"They're sexy."

It hadn't taken much convincing for the airline to make a space for David on the full flight and—despite my objections—get both our seats upgraded. I implied afterward that the conversation would've gone differently if he'd been talking to a man, but David insisted it was only because he was a good customer.

When he reached over and squeezed my thigh, my stomach dropped in just the right way. I waggled my eyebrows and nodded toward the restrooms at the front of the plane. He shook his head.

"Why not?" I asked.

"I'm not taking you in some disgusting airplane bathroom," he said just above a whisper.

I stuck out my lower lip. "It doesn't bother me. It might be fun."

He eyed me. "I'm starting to worry that you're only interested in me for sex."

I laughed too loudly and shrank down in my seat. "Would that bother you?" He continued to glare at me. "I mean, you're really good at it," I pointed out.

Trying hard to suppress a smile, he shook his head and turned back to his article.

His glasses were definitely sexy, though. And so was the way he'd spent these past few days focused on me and getting to know my dad instead of trying to squeeze in work here and there like I might've expected. David had always known how to back up his love declaration with actions, and I had a lot to learn from him.

"Have you ever been in love?" I asked him.

He blinked at me, his expression going blank as the cabin hummed around us. After removing his glasses, he rubbed his eyes. "I'm not discussing this on an airplane."

"Geez, what do you have against airplanes?" I joked.

"It's just not very . . ." He glanced over his shoulder at the aisle. ". . . private."

"This is something most couples discuss *before* they move in together."

"Does that mean you're moving in?"

I sighed. "That leads me to bullet point number two under *Questions I Need to Ask*—have you ever lived with a woman?"

"I see you're not going to be easily deterred," he said.

"I'm learning from a pro."

"Funny." David stuck the newspaper into the seat back pocket in front him. "Of course I've been in love and, yes, I've lived with a woman."

My eyes drifted over his face as he looked back at me. He'd been in love, and he'd lived with another woman. For thirty-five years old, it wasn't surprising news, but what *was* surprising? Instead of raging jealousy, his past only eased my worries about his ability to commit.

"If you want," he said, "I'll tell you all about them, but it's ancient history in my mind. I've loved two girls aside from you. We separated amicably, but we don't keep in touch. And though I believed I loved them at the time, I now see those relationships differently."

"Differently how?"

"I didn't know the meaning of love until I met you."

I wasn't sure whether to laugh or swoon. "That's nice," I said, "but it also sounds like a line."

"I know, but it's the truth," he said simply. "I loved them differently than I love you. And certainly a great deal less."

There was nothing funny about that. This time, my heart swelled. "That's really sweet, David. Thank you."

"I'm not trying to be sweet," he said. "You asked, and that's my answer."

"Noted," I said, stifling a smile. "So you're not afraid of living with a girl? Hair products, tampons, constant company, sharing your bed . . . you're okay with all of that?"

He narrowed his eyes. "Why are you asking me this?"

"Now that we're on the same page, and we're both a hundred percent in—I mean, I'd understand if you wanted to slow down a little bit. I could get my own place for a while, and we could date until we're ready to take the next step."

He shifted to face me more. "How long is a while?"

"I have no idea—a year, maybe?" I said.

"A year?" he barked, piercing the quietude.

"*Shh*," I said. The passenger across the aisle glanced up, then returned to typing on his laptop. "That's usually how long a lease is."

"No. Absolutely not," David said. The crow's feet around his eyes deepened. "Is that—is that what you want?"

What I wanted was to spend every waking moment with the god in front of me. But more than that . . . "I want this relationship to work," I said.

"It's never going to work with you keeping one foot out the door, Olivia," David said frankly.

"That's not what I'm doing," I reassured him. I'd *been* doing that up until our talk. Now, I just wanted to inject a little sensibility into a mad and passionate love. "I'm not going anywhere. I just don't want to spook you by moving too fast."

"You're projecting," he said. "You think I want something that I don't. It makes me wonder if that's what you want."

It wasn't. And for once, I didn't question that. I smiled and slid my hand over his jeans. "Okay."

"Listen, this isn't my first relationship as you seem to think." David lowered his voice and leaned in. "I know what I want, and it's you—falling asleep next to me every night, waking up with me every morning. I actually don't like having you out of my sight ever."

"Well, it's not exactly possible to keep tabs on me all the time," I said.

"You're telling me." He snorted. "I've tried to think of how I might without scaring you or ending up in prison."

I laughed. "You are so extreme."

"Only when it comes to you."

"And work," I said.

He nodded slowly. "Up until now, it's been my priority. If that's a problem, I'll make some changes to be more available."

"It's not a problem." I rubbed his leg. "I'm just glad you do what you love."

"I do," he said, "but at the end of the day, it's still a job."

"Meaning?"

"Meaning I'd still do it, even if I stopped loving it."

Based on the eloquent way he'd described his hotel project to me, then how effortlessly he'd laid out the Oak Park house's issues, quirks, and imaginary plans, David's work was part of his identity. "But you're a partner," I said. "And I have no doubt you know how to manage your investments. You shouldn't ever have to do something you don't love. Why would you?"

"Wealth, prestige." He sat back and gestured around the first-class cabin. "It allows me this lifestyle."

"This *lifestyle*?" I asked. "Is that important to you?"

"Definitely," he said. "I'll never be the type of man to leave my family wanting."

Aww. Though the sentiment left me warm and fuzzy, my financial comfort was secondary to his happiness. "Baby, knowing you're doing what you love would be a million times more important to me than 'lifestyle.' I know you feel the same about me."

"I do," he said softly. "I'm lucky because I do love it,

but security is important to me. I want you to have everything you want."

"What else could I ask for?" I melted into my seat. "If it all went away tomorrow, but I still had you, I wouldn't be any less happy."

"I'm glad you think so," he said, "but I refuse to find out."

"I'm just saying." I reached out and brushed my fingers over his hairline. "It's not important to me."

He grabbed my hand before I could withdraw and kissed my palm. "So you wouldn't mind if I gave up my place in San Sebastián? And we didn't go to Spain?"

"I know you're teasing me, but no, I wouldn't mind."

"Oh, that's right." A teasing smile tugged at his lips. "You hate vacation."

"Well, I mean, *hate* isn't really the right word," I said, remembering how David had once enticed me with visions of Bali surfing, Montauk oysters, and Swiss Alps hot-tubbing. "If you *want* to take me, I wouldn't—"

"Believe me, gorgeous, you will not hate our vacation. I do want to take you to Spain, and very soon."

"I'd love that," I said. "If I could ever get the time off."

"Don't you have vacation days?"

"Beman doesn't like us to take them."

"I'm pretty sure that's against the law," David said.

"Of course he can't prohibit it, but I don't need additional reasons to piss him off."

He pursed his lips. "Can't say that I love how he treats you."

I shrugged. "He's my boss."

"I can excuse his being demanding, but I can't excuse him being a dick," David said. "Do you like the new position you're in?"

"I like it fine."

"But you don't love it," he stated.

"Like you said, it's a job."

"How about doing some writing? You liked it once. You might find you like it again."

Geez. Memory of an elephant, this guy. "I do write sometimes."

"I know. As I've told you, I've read some stuff on the *Chicago M* website."

"I'm better at editing."

"You can be good at both," he pointed out. "And what I read was excellent."

"You only think that because I'm sleeping with you." I laughed. "And how can you tell from a few stupid articles?"

He gave me a stern, slightly scary look. "Do not downgrade yourself."

My smile fell away. I agreed that was a bad habit, one that David was unlikely to let me keep getting away with. So I nodded. "Okay. I won't."

"What does Beman think of your articles?" he asked.

"Well . . . he's complimentary."

David inclined his head. "And do you think he's just being nice?"

"God, no," I said. "I'm sure he'd relish telling me otherwise."

"Just because your mom's a writer, it wouldn't mean you were following in her footsteps."

"I know . . ." I said, but my voice wavered.

"Know what I think?" he asked. "That you don't want to give it a fair try because you've spent your life vowing not to turn into her."

They were easy dots to connect, though I'd never thought of it in such black-and-white terms—mostly because I hadn't considered writing an option before. "She used to tell me I wasn't any good at it," I admitted. "And it hurt."

Disgust marred his handsome features. "Don't listen to that shit."

"I grew up thinking it was true."

"You say Leanore was jealous of everyone, even you for getting your dad's attention." He stretched his jaw, then rubbed it. "Demeaning you made her feel in control while putting you in your place. I get the feeling whatever your hobby had been, she would've shit on it."

My eyes drifted between us. I'd never had anyone try so hard to figure me out. David wanted to show me the reasons I shut down, discredited myself, retreated, hid behind a mask—why I'd created the mask in the first place. He'd been doing it all week, and it was both unnerving and exhilarating. It was hard for me to admit, but, quietly, I said, "I think you're right."

"I know I'm right, and I want you to prove her wrong."

"But it doesn't change the fact that if I started writing, people would make the connection between her and me. She's Leanore Germaine, which isn't exactly a common surname. I'd be in her shadow."

"Then use Dylan," he said.

At the unexpected suggestion, my breath caught in my throat. *Olivia Dylan.* I tried it out in my head. I liked it. I liked it too much for someone who was still legally married to another man. I *loved* it.

He chuckled, and I blinked up at him. "What's funny?" I asked.

"The expression on your face. I can practically see your mind spinning. And you think *I'm* easily spooked."

I scowled. "I'm not scared of taking your last name," I said. "But anyway."

"Anyway what?" he asked.

"I don't know," I said, grasping for a change of topic.

"*Anyway*, write something," he said. "Do it now. I'll stop bothering you."

"I wouldn't even know where to start," I said, but it wasn't true. I thought back to a short story I'd written for a creative writing course in college. I only had a handful of pages, but it was something . . .

David leaned under the seat in front of me and grabbed my carry-on bag. "Here," he said, excavating my laptop. "Just try it for twenty minutes. If you hate it, we can have sex in the bathroom."

I sat up and widened my eyes. "Really?"

"Really. But I'll be timing you."

I accepted the computer. "Deal."

A few minutes later, my fingers flying over the keyboard, a flight attendant in the aisle waved at me. "Ma'am? Hello? It's time to stow your laptop."

I blinked twice at her. "What?" I asked. "But we're nowhere near Chicago."

David snickered into his fist. "We're about to land."

"But I just started writing." Had I completely lost track of time with my nose stuck in my laptop?

"Please stow the laptop and bring your seat back to the upright position," the flight attendant said.

I shook my head in disbelief but did as she said.

"So, how'd it go?" David asked, grinning as I packed up the computer. "Not well, I presume."

With his ribbing, I frowned, even though I was giddy over the fact that the words had poured out of me. "I didn't want to do it in a disgusting airplane bathroom anyway," I teased.

"Liar."

I snuck my arm between David's back and the seat to

wrap him in a sideways hug and rest my head on his ribcage.

"You realize that you wrote for an hour straight," he said, rubbing my arm.

I'd read over my story, decided I'd liked it, and created an outline. I'd started thinking harder about characters, the ones I already had and the ones I would add. I'd even written another handful of pages. I smiled. He was right, of course. I had enjoyed it. "Thanks for making me do it."

"If it's going to interfere with our sex life, though, I may have to forbid it," he said.

"Impossible," I said through a smile, glancing up to catch his adoring gaze. As the plane began its descent, I reached up to finger a piece of his hair, then touched his lips. He'd done nothing but prove to me over and over that he wanted me by his side. That he wanted me to become the best version of myself. That he cared. "David?" I said.

"Hmm?"

"I want to move in with you."

He squeezed me against him. "Yeah?"

"Yeah." I nodded. "Let's do it. I don't want to wait any longer to start our life together."

"Honeybee," he said, kissing my forehead, "it has already begun."

———

At my new home, I followed David into the apartment and then to the bedroom. I put my suitcase next to his and waited for his next move. Just saying out loud that I wanted to move in didn't make the place feel like *mine*. In my mind, I was sleeping at my boyfriend's place.

He took our suitcases into the walk-in closet. I'd noticed earlier in the week that my shopping bags had been unpacked, and everything neatly hung. Shelves with LED lighting illuminated my new shoes like artwork.

"Did you do this?" I asked, nodding at my side of the closet.

"The housekeeper."

"And she took off the tags?"

"I did that," he said. "To show you that I kept the faith."

"Well, that's just bad business, Mr. Dylan. You would've been out a pretty penny if things hadn't worked out."

He stepped forward and pulled me against his hard body. "I would've been out a lot more than that. Don't do it again."

I nodded.

"Say it."

"I won't leave again," I said.

"Now tell me you're mine . . ."

I smiled. "I'm yours . . ."

"And that you love me."

"I love you."

"I'm hard," he answered.

I laughed as his erection pressed maddeningly against my tummy. "Yes, I can feel that. Is it all right if I shower first, though?"

"Christ," he said, patting my ass and releasing me. "You don't need my permission to take a shower."

I grabbed my robe from a hook. "A new home is going to take some getting used to, David."

"Why?" he asked. "Just do as you please."

I looked at him skeptically. "I'll be in the shower."

"If that's what pleases you."

I rolled my eyes, and he laughed.

"Listen, no bad behavior in the shower," he said. "I've

barely gotten my fill of you this week, so I want your complete attention tonight."

"Yes, sir," I said, squirming.

"That means hands off my shower nozzle."

I raised an eyebrow and gave him my most lascivious smile. Then I left him and his hard-on in the closet. It might be some time before I got used to my new home, but it wouldn't take forever. He made it easy because now, *he* was my home. And like Davena had tried to tell me, it didn't matter where we were as long as we were together.

Like Davena and Mack. Without really grasping it, I'd always envied their love. And now I had it. I held no more doubts that David's and my exceptional love would rival Mack and Davena's. The thought filled my heart with happiness.

I hoped Mack would be able to see how much David meant to me, but I still worried. People's reactions varied greatly, and it wasn't always what I expected.

The heat and steam from the shower loosened my body, but did nothing to diminish my mounting arousal knowing David had plans for me. After I slid into the heavenly fabric of my white silk robe, I found my new roommate focused on the computer screen in his office.

"Get in here, gorgeous," he said without looking up.

"You look busy."

"I am," he said. "Lots of catching up to do. I'm not used to taking days off."

"So I'll let you work," I said with a step backward.

"Wait."

I froze.

"Turn around."

I bit my lip and rotated in a slow circle until I faced him again.

"I maintain—that robe was the best purchase." My

body, out of my control, reacted to the way his eyes drifted over me. My breasts swelled, my tummy tightened, and my hands burned with the thought of touching him. I had urges that I wanted to satisfy by climbing into his lap. He looked like a god, backdropped by the nighttime Chicago skyline. A god in a plain, white t-shirt, and—I hoped—those sexy gray sweatpants.

David pointed to the couch. My gaze followed until it landed on my laptop. "Work with me," he said. "Write."

"I won't distract you?"

"You will most certainly distract me, but this way, I won't worry about what trouble you're getting into."

I smirked. Because I couldn't help myself, I crossed the office and kissed his coarse cheek, then ran my finger over the spot my lips had just been.

"Sorry," he murmured. "I haven't shaved in a couple days." I kissed him again, because I loved the way he felt.

It was easy to get caught up in my new project even though David distracted me as well. When he focused, the angles of his face sharpened so he looked equally menacing and attractive. I sighed longingly even though he was mine for the taking. All mine.

After breaking through barriers and uprooting long-time fears, I was more relaxed than I had been in a long time. But I knew I could've lost him, and so, I was extra grateful to have him. With that in mind, I wanted to make things right with Lucy. Once she saw my happiness, my transformation, she'd understand everything. When I'd finished writing for the evening, I decided to e-mail to her.

From: Olivia Germaine
Sent: Sun, November 18 08:16 PM CST
To: Lucy Greene
Subject: Hi

We need to talk. I miss you dearly, and I want a chance to explain. I'm happy, Luce.

Will you agree to see me for a coffee this week? Or maybe, if I dare, lunch?

-O

I glanced up and caught David looking at me. "Busted," I said.

"What, you're the only one allowed to stare?" he asked.

I blushed, cursing under my breath. "You noticed?"

"I'm acutely aware of when your eyes are on me," he said. "It's actually very frustrating."

I smiled because I knew the feeling well. "It's bedtime," I informed him. I'd had enough staring and was ready to act on the fantasies I'd been having all day.

"It may be your bedtime, but I usually work for another hour."

"Oh, okay." I slammed my laptop shut and stood to stretch. I reached for the ceiling, aware of where that would place the hemline of my short robe.

His gaze dropped to my thighs. He licked his lips. Smiled sinfully. What exactly did he plan to do to me with that sinful mouth?

"But I guess things are different now," he said. "Give me a few minutes to wrap up here."

I smiled giddily and tried not to skip to the bedroom. On my way, I imagined how and where he might fuck me tonight. Against the refrigerator? On the bathroom counter? On the balcony? Standing? Sitting? Right side up? Upside down? An excited thrill made its way through me, but it stopped cold when I grabbed my phone from my purse and saw that I had a text from Bill.

Bill: *If you don't come get your shit tomorrow night, it's going out with the trash.*

Bill had a right to be angry, but his words still stung. I could fight back, or I could give him what he wanted, hopefully putting an end to things quickly. I sent my response.

Me: *I'll do it while you're at work.*

Bill: *I changed the locks. It's already in boxes, I'll be home after 6*

I sighed. This would be tricky. David and Bill had already proven they couldn't be in the same room together. Not that I really wanted to force them on each other anyway. Luckily, the sum total of my things could be moved in one trip, and as much as I admired David's brawn, I didn't need it.

I texted Gretchen to ask if she'd help me in exchange for dinner. Bethany had a truck I knew she'd let us borrow, since David's vehicles wouldn't fit the boxes. I doubted he'd let me drive his fancy car anyway—my dad never had.

I bit the inside of my cheek to the point of discomfort as I sat on the bed and read Bill's texts again. He'd changed the locks already. His patience seemed to be dwindling. I reasoned that my things were constant reminders of my absence, and if I were in his position, I'd want them out, too.

"You're deep in thought," David said behind me.

My head snapped up. I'd been right—David was a god in yummy gray sweatpants. "It's nothing," I said, tossing the phone aside and already envisioning him shirtless.

"Nothing?"

"Bill wants me to clear my stuff out tomorrow night."

David's brow furrowed. "That's fine. We can go after work."

I folded my knee under my bottom and held my palms open in front of me. "Actually," I said warily, "I thought I'd just go with Gretchen. We've already arranged it."

He snorted. "That's not going to happen."

"Hear me out," I said. "Bill's been through enough. Showing up with you to pick up my things would just be pouring salt into the wound."

His eyebrows shot up. "Did you think I was joking when I said you couldn't be alone with him?"

"I wouldn't be alone—"

"Did you?" he barked.

"No," I snapped back at him, "that's why I made plans with Gretchen. I respected your request. Now, you have to respect my decision."

"It's not a request," he said, stepping forward. "Having Gretchen there won't do shit if Bill snaps. My answer is no."

"I wasn't asking," I said immediately.

His face tightened into a steely gaze. "Do not test me, Olivia. I'll take you if you like, but you're not going alone."

"You're forbidding me from seeing my husband?"

"Yes."

"You can't—"

"The hell I can't!" he roared. "You are not to be alone with him. *Ever.*"

My mouth fell open, and we stared at each other for a tense moment. His anger came from a place of concern, but did he really think he could prohibit me from seeing someone?

"It's not safe," David said, softer but still heatedly.

"Is this about my safety? Or something else?" I stood and walked across the room, stopping a couple feet in front of him. "I'm so sorry for how I handled things this week, but I've made up my mind. I choose you. Things are completely done with Bill. He's not a threat."

"That's not my concern," David said, unmoving. "Bill is unstable. I don't want you in a position where you might get hurt."

"He's not unstable, he's in pain. I know him better than anyone—he won't hurt me." I crossed my arms. "All my things are packed. I just have to pick them up."

"How will you transport them?" David asked.

"Gretchen's roommate has a truck. My stuff won't fit in either of your cars anyway."

"I'll find something," he said.

I stared at him. His obstinance could be helpful in some ways, but in this moment, it was uncalled for. Bill had been through enough. I wasn't going to turn the knife by making him watch my new boyfriend essentially remove me from the life we'd built together. "Thank you for the offer, but you can't come," I said. "I'm sorry. It's not fair to him, and it's not necessary."

David's eyes narrowed. "You're with *me* now, not him. Don't take his side."

My anger fizzled slightly. David and I had done a lot of work, and him thinking I'd take Bill's side over his was definitely a move in the wrong direction. If our roles were reversed, I'd be really hurt by that. I took a deep breath and tried a different approach. "I'm on your side. I love you. So much, that I can't contain it around you. It seems unfair to rub Bill's face in how happy I am." I sighed. "Honey, it's just a few boxes."

"Then leave them behind. I'll replace all of it."

That would simply put a Band-Aid over a deeper wound. Bill and I would have to deal with each other in the months ahead, and I couldn't have David trying to control and manage our every interaction. It wasn't healthy for us or him. "They're my things," I said. "I'm going to get them."

David's jaw set. "Your safety isn't a game to me."

Everything in my body tightened as frustration coursed through me. "Well, it's happening," I said and walked over to my bedside table, "so get over it."

"Excuse me?"

I turned to him, unbuckling my watch, and repeated myself. "I said *get over it*."

He folded his arms over his chest, his biceps bulging under his white t-shirt. "Are you trying my patience on purpose?"

"So what if I am?" I asked, tossing my watch aside. "What are you going to do?"

"I'm about to get pissed the fuck off."

"What do you call this?" I asked, waving my hand over him. His frame seemed to grow, but I held my ground. David didn't scare me, but losing myself and my independence *did*. "You can't come," I said. "And now *I'm* pissed the fuck off."

He was almost vibrating. "I told you," he said, each word sharp as it sliced from his mouth, "you're not to be alone with him." He walked toward the bed, bearing down until we were face to face, but still, his voice rose. "He touches you, and that's on *me*. What are you going to do with Gretchen there if Bill tries to hurt you? Huh?" When I just stared at him, he smacked the wall next to us. "Answer me."

My eyes stayed riveted on him as his anger radiated around us. It wasn't anger, though—it was fear. Even though I dealt with my anxieties differently, I still recognized them in him. I was terrified of losing David now that I'd found him, and he felt the same about me. He truly believed Bill could hurt me.

But before I could think of a way to convince David that wasn't true, or even ease his fears, he turned and stormed out, slamming the door behind him.

I didn't want to fight with him. I hated to see him hurt, but I had to set boundaries. David had no right to order me around. In this case, he was wrong. Bill didn't deserve to have his broken nose rubbed in my new relationship.

I climbed back onto the bed, wondering where David had gone. I hoped he hadn't left the apartment. His apartment. His bed. *I* had nowhere to go when I was upset. Would he even want me sleeping beside him? Did *I* want that knowing we'd each be fuming all night?

I grabbed a pillow and silently opened the door. Light spilled out from under the closed door of his office. Relieved that he hadn't left, I skipped the guest room in favor of curling up on the couch by the fireplace.

I sank into the pillow, promising myself that we'd work it out in the morning. That once he'd cooled off, he'd see things from my perspective. He had to. If he couldn't, he'd have to find a way to work through this issue, because I wasn't giving in.

I heaved a sigh and opened my bleary eyes. In the dark, orange light from the fireplace flickered over David's marble features as he looked down at me on the couch. Even through my sleepiness, his handsome face took my breath away. Were his eyes so intense that they could pierce my sleep?

"Why are you out here?" he whispered from above me.

"You're mad at me," I said in a small voice, coiling around my pillow. "And I'm mad at you."

He turned off the fireplace, then crouched down and cleared a piece of hair from my face. "I'll never be so pissed that I don't want you sleeping next to me." He bundled me in his arms and lifted me to his chest.

I closed my eyes and burrowed my nose into his t-shirt, inhaling fresh laundry and David while he carried me. "I'm still angry," I said. "You shouldn't have yelled at me like that."

"I know." He set me in the middle of the bed and wrapped himself around me. "We'll figure this out. Just promise you won't leave my bed again."

I nodded my agreement, already drifting off as I told him I loved him.

Chapter Twenty

I awoke still in my robe, unable to remember how I'd gotten from the couch to the bed. The faucet started in the bathroom, and I quickly ran through David's and my conversation from the night before. My stance hadn't changed, but since my plans for the night had been thwarted, I decided that I'd be up for angry sex if he was.

I wasn't looking forward to our impending conversation, however, so I avoided the bathroom altogether and went to his office instead to grab my laptop from the couch. I stopped at his drafting table to look at a mess of papers that hadn't been there the night before. The blueprint on top was labeled *Home*. I leaned closer, my eyes darting over a drawing of the Oak Park house, and tried to envision what he'd created. Even while upset with me, he'd been thinking of us. My heart filled with love as I took in all the care and detail he'd put into the plans. I ran my fingers over the copious and hasty notes scribbled in his handwriting.

"That's just a rough sketch," he said from behind me.

"Obviously, I'd get your input before we move into the next phase."

I turned around. He was already dressed for work in a crisp, royal blue dress shirt and black slacks. "You're amazing," I said. "And whatever you do will be perfect."

"Perfect?" he asked with an arched black eyebrow.

"Perfect," I repeated because I meant it. With the thought and care he put into things, I couldn't imagine anything less, however it turned out. "Thank you."

He came into the room and stepped around me, pulling the chair out from under his desk. He sat down and rolled closer before gesturing for me to sit on his lap.

I obeyed cautiously while holding my robe closed, unsure of his mood. His fingers grazed against my neck as he swept my hair away, and his chin hovered over my shoulder. "See this here?" he asked into my ear, pointing to the bedroom.

I nodded.

"I'm picturing a bathroom like the one in this apartment but even bigger. We can put in a gigantic shower, and then over here, a clawfoot tub."

"I like those tubs," I said.

"I thought you might. That would mean losing a little space in the bedroom, especially if you want a walk-in closet."

"I do."

"I thought you might."

I smiled to myself as he laid out the rest of the bedroom. Sliding his fingers down the hallway, he explained that he'd need one room for his office, that way he could work from home more often.

But the room across the way had noticeably fewer notes. David's finger lingered there a moment before he spoke. "This is a free room, unless you have any ideas. I suppose maybe a guest room would be a good idea. At first, anyway."

I didn't tense despite my body's impulse to. He would notice, and I couldn't have that. Not after we'd gotten this far and hadn't even had a chance to really enjoy each other yet. Because his implication was clear. In his vision of the future, that room would one day be a nursery. I didn't know how a discussion about children would go, but, it was the only thing left that had the power to destroy us.

"It's not a huge house," he continued, "so as time goes by, we may want to . . . add. In case we need more, you know, space. I've taken this into consideration, and we'll have the ability when the time comes. Unless you want to do it now."

My heart fell. *Add? Exactly how much does he want to "add"? And when what time comes?*

He proceeded through the remainder of the house, describing his ideas and what they'd entail. I was confronted with the immensity of the project, from replacing the plumbing system to reroofing, retiling, repainting . . . I sighed at the fact that he was doing this, essentially, for me.

"What's wrong?" he asked gently, raking his fingers through my hair to tuck it behind my ear.

"Nothing at all," I said. "Except that it's a lot of work, David. And money."

He stayed quiet as he continued to pet me. I closed my eyes, succumbing to the power of his hands on me. "I always knew I wanted to be an architect," he said. "I was lucky, I guess. I never even considered anything else . . . I don't know why. It felt like my calling. It has given me a lot —purpose, gratification, wealth. It's hard work, but it's also my hobby. And you are my passion. I want to do this for you. I need to."

"I love you," I whispered, leaning back against him with my eyes still closed. His now smooth cheek passed against mine. His hands came around the front of my slinky robe, passing over my breasts and hugging me close. He pressed his lips into my cheek, remaining there as my body responded to his touch. Desire, already simmering at the surface, blossomed deep inside of me.

"I have to leave for work," he said without letting go.

I groaned and wrapped my arms over his. "Stay."

"I wish I could, but I have meetings. Canceling one will create a domino effect," he asked. "Do you want to take one of my cars to work?"

"You'd let me?" I asked.

"Yes." He hesitated. "But you hurt it, and there'll be consequences."

Though I didn't think I'd mind the consequences, I only laughed and said, "I'll take the train."

"I have a really full day, but we still need to talk about getting your stuff tonight."

My peacefulness faded. "Yes, we do."

"All right, up you go." He lifted me off his lap and set me on my feet. "Come to my office on your lunch break, and I'll have food delivered."

I nodded, glancing at his dress shirt. "Are we going to fight?" I asked.

"I hope not, baby. I don't like when we do."

"Me neither." I placed my hands on his chest and rose up for a kiss. "Have a good morning."

"I already am," he said. "See you in a few hours."

As the elevator at Pierson/Greer ascended, I tapped my foot and thought about what was to come. Still unsettled over the previous night's fight, I wasn't looking forward to rehashing it. In the office, I met the pretty, young receptionist who'd taken Clare's place, and quickly checked my tinge of jealousy when I noticed how nervous she seemed. She knew who I was and practically knocked over a water bottle while taking my coat.

After informing me David was on his way, she showed me into his empty office. Back in his bubble, I relaxed. I wandered around the room, picked up a photo of him with his family, and got a surge of affection, even though I'd only met them twice. I'd never had those warm feelings toward Bill's stoic family—nothing remotely close, actually.

I heard David send the receptionist to lunch before striding into the office with a plastic bag and shutting the door behind him. Earlier, I'd noticed how his royal blue dress shirt set off his dark features, but now I had the urge to jump into his arms and beg him to take me.

My unsettled feeling returned, however, when I noticed he seemed edgy—a dark, brooding cloud entering my hemisphere. "I don't have much time, so I just grabbed Mexican from downstairs," he said, setting the full bag on his desk.

"I'm not hungry."

The look on his face indicated the scolding to come, but I was saved by the ringing of his desk phone. He whipped off his jacket and threw it over the couch. "One minute," he said. I watched him round the desk and fall into his chair, leaning back as he answered the phone. "Dylan. Yes." His eyebrows knit. "Yes. Go on."

One thing I'd not yet gotten was my businessman David. I'd been thrumming since the night before, and quite often over the past few months, I'd yearned to see what was underneath David's perfectly tailored suits. I strolled over to his chair, and before he even looked up, dropped to my knees between his legs. The leather chair groaned as he sat forward suddenly.

"Yes, that's—that's correct," he stammered into the phone. I looked at him from beneath my lashes. My hands skated up his muscular thighs until one landed on his crotch. He shifted when I touched the hardening length of him through his pants.

His hand dove into my hair, and he pulled my head back so I was forced to look at him. I bit down on my lip, and he smirked at me.

"That will be presented at the afternoon meeting," he continued, staring at me as I blindly undid his fly. "We'll go over—you know what, I have to call you back." The phone was down before he'd even finished the sentence. He grasped my waist with two large hands and hoisted me up onto his desk.

"Wait," I protested, salivating to take him in my mouth.

"Lie back."

"But I wanted to—"

"Lie back," he growled. I complied.

He pulled my hips so I was hanging off the edge, then shoved up my skirt as if we were on a timer. My panties ripped loudly a second before his fingers were in me.

My eyes fluttered closed. "Oh, God," I moaned.

"Mouth shut, eyes open," he whispered, glancing at the door. "Christ, you're wet. You been like this all day?" he asked, his fingers slowing as they leisurely explored me.

I nodded emphatically, pleading with my eyes for him to fuck me, but he shook his head slowly.

"Can you keep quiet?" he asked, and I nodded again.

He crouched down, and I rested my legs on his shoulders as his tongue landed directly on my clit. He was so domineering, telling me what to do, commanding me in his businessman David way that I easily melted into the sensations. My orgasm was already within reach because it'd been nearby all morning. My thighs shook as he lapped at me, hard and then soft until my eyes crossed with my need for release. I strained to keep quiet, suppressing my groans behind airtight lips. My climax churned through me, wave after wave as his tongue prolonged it.

When it ended, I exhaled audibly and dropped my feet, slumping on his desk. I was spent but riveted by the lusty look on his face. Powerful and slightly out of control, he dropped his pants and took my thighs in each of his hands. He squeezed them and licked his lips. "I've missed your pussy. It's far too sweet not to have it every day."

I whimpered as he positioned himself against me and pulled my hips into his first thrust. Even through his shirt, I saw his arms flex as he urged me deeper onto him. Strong fingers spread my legs, so each time he pulled out and slid back in, I had no choice but to feel all of him. I reached behind me to grip the lip of his desk, pushing back against him, clenching around his cock, watching his jaw tighten and release as his drives came faster.

He pinned my thighs to the desk and dropped forward to lock me in a furious kiss. I could taste his desire, and that alone catapulted me into a raw and throbbing orgasm that had me crying his name into his mouth.

He detached from me and ripped open my blouse. His mouth dropped to my chest, sucking and nipping the skin between my breasts so I yelped. His fingers dug into my hips as he came with a gush of hot fluid, groaning against my collarbone as he emptied himself in me, gliding in and out until he was completely finished.

"Jesus," he said into the curve of my neck. He released my hips and fell back into his leather chair. "You'll be the death of me if we keep this up." He paused a moment, looking thoughtful. "Fucking you *would* be the sweetest way to go, though."

I slid off the desk, and he caught me as my legs threatened to give out. I steadied myself against his shoulders and went to pull down my skirt when he stopped me. He groaned from his chest and ran a finger up to catch semen dripping down my thigh. He held it up to my mouth, and our gazes locked as I licked it off.

"There's an image that'll have me walking funny the rest of the day," he said.

I laughed and followed him into his bathroom where he boosted me onto the counter. He ran water over a hand towel, opened my red and raw legs, and wiped me down with quiet determination.

After rinsing the towel, he pulled me close for a series of gentle pecks. His eyes traveled down my neck and stopped.

"My blouse," I said, following his gaze. "It's ruined."

But he wasn't looking at that. He focused on a red mark his mouth had left on my chest, then ran his fingers around it. "Did that hurt?"

"No."

He searched my eyes a moment, then held my buttonless top closed. "What are we going to do about this?" he asked.

"Do you have a sewing kit?" I asked.

"Do I look like an eighty-year-old woman?"

I pursed my lips. "Well, what do you suggest?"

"Mmm." He wrapped his arms around me and kissed his way down my neck. "I keep you in here and make love to you between meetings for the rest of the day."

"I don't know if I'd call what we just did 'making love,'" I teased.

His head jerked back, and his brow furrowed. "It's all

love. Every touch, every kiss. Even when it comes like that. You know that, right?"

I put my hand on his jaw. "Yes."

"We might be fucking like rabbits, but it's always with love."

I broke into a grin. "You really have a way with words."

He laughed until his face fell. "Seriously, though. We need to get you a shirt, and I need food."

I hopped off the counter and grabbed the takeout from his desk to unpack it on his coffee table while he made a call.

After a moment, he said into his desk phone, "This is David Dylan. I have—yes, hello." He paused. "I'm sending my girlfriend over in a few minutes, and I'd like you to put whatever she picks out on my account. That's fine, thanks."

He hung up, immediately came to the couch, and tore into a burrito. "I'm starving," he muttered with another enormous bite.

"Um, who was that?" I asked after I'd swallowed my food.

"There's a shop around the corner. Go get a new blouse." He glanced from his food to my skirt and then back. "Underwear, too."

I stared at him. "You've spent enough money on me. I can just wear my coat at work."

"Do it, don't argue," he said. "We've got enough to fight about. Have you changed your mind about this evening?"

I bristled. "No."

"Then we're at an impasse."

"Not exactly," I said. "I'm going, you're not . . . and that's where we are."

He glared at me as he took another bite, chewing

slowly. He swallowed and sighed. "Look, I'm uncomfortable with you being alone with him. He put his hands on you once, he could do it again."

"I get that," I said, "but it was out of character for Bill. I've been involved with this man for *years*. Don't you think I know him? There's never been a problem."

"*I get that*," he echoed, his frustration visibly mounting, "but things are different now. You can't know where his head's at." David stood up quickly and stalked over to a closed door I hadn't noticed before. After a moment he returned with a folded men's undershirt. "Put this on. It's not a fair fight with your tits in my face."

"Well, in that case—"

"Olivia," he commanded, his eyes narrowing.

I gulped, accepted the shirt, and pulled it over my head. "How come you always call me by my full name?"

He brushed off his hands and sat. "What else would I call you?"

"Uh, Liv," I said.

"Olivia is beautiful, and it suits you perfectly."

I wasn't sure what answer I'd expected, but I was coming to find that when it came to me, David gave thought to every little detail. "Oh."

His eyes scanned my face. "You're cute when you blush, you know that?" he murmured, but he still looked annoyed. "To me, you are always Olivia." He took another mouthful of burrito and chewed quickly. "When I met you in Andrew's kitchen, and I asked you your name, you said, in your sexy, husky voice, 'Olivia.' I'll never forget it."

I sighed like a wilting flower, powerless to the love that coursed through me. I was quickly becoming the kind of girl I'd always despised: one who couldn't stop staring at her boyfriend with starry eyes—even when we were in the middle of a fight.

Fuck. We were definitely still in the middle of a fight. "You *didn't* ask for my name," I reminded him. "You demanded. Like you're doing now."

"This is serious shit," he said. "People have been murdered over situations like this."

I blinked. "*What?*"

"Infidelity."

"Yes, and obviously, having you there would only raise the tension," I said. "If anything would set Bill off, it'd be that."

"Wouldn't matter," he stated. "I'd be there."

I dropped my forehead into my open hand. Bringing David was not an option. It wasn't right. But I hated that he thought I wasn't on his side. Of all the things he'd said the night before, that had struck me the hardest.

I exhaled finally and looked back at him. "What if you drive Gretchen and me but stay downstairs? That way you'll be there if anything goes wrong."

"Fuck," he said to himself. "Why do you have to be so goddamn stubborn? Don't you trust me?"

"Don't you trust *me*?" I said. "Bill's not the monster you think he is. Sweetie, I wouldn't go there if I thought it was an issue. Nor would I take Gretchen there if I thought he was capable of hurting her."

David grumbled his defeat to himself through another bite, and I smiled triumphantly.

"Tell Gretchen not to worry about the car," he said. "I'll get something, and we can pick her up on the way."

"*Thank you*," I said, balling up my trash. "Can you walk me out? I need my coat. And as much as I would love to wear this all day . . ." I peeled off his cologne-scented undershirt and handed it to him. "I'd look a little silly."

He walked to his desk and picked up the phone. "Olivia's coat," was all he said.

As we waited by the door, he leaned in to give me a sweet kiss. "See?" he said. "No fighting."

"No fighting," I repeated with a smile.

He cracked the door a sliver to accept my coat and held it open so I could slip into it. I watched him concentrate on each button as he dressed me. When he finished, he pulled gently on the lapels and kissed me again.

"Thank you for understanding," I told him. "I owe you one."

I turned away and pulled open the door, but he slammed it shut with one hand. "Owe me?" he purred into my ear, molding his hand to my backside.

My insides turned instantly to jelly with his hot breath on my neck. "Yes," I breathed. "Whatever you want, I'm yours."

"If I didn't have so much to do, I'd take you up against this door right now," he said. "I haven't nearly made up for the time we lost last week, so you'd better be ready to spread those long legs for me tonight." He opened the door, tapped me on the ass, and pushed me out into the foyer in a daze. I blinked for a moment until I noticed the receptionist studiously avoiding my gaze. I gave her a quick wave and rushed to the elevator.

On my way to the boutique, I tried not to read into the fact that David had an account there, so I was glad to see they carried men's clothing, too. For some reason, that led to me wondering whether or not he'd had sex on his desk before, and the thought made my lip curl.

After browsing the selection, I interrupted two salesgirls in the middle of a conversation to ask for a fitting room. One turned to me, a pretty blonde, young but with an unfortunate frown. She pointed across the store. "Dressing room's over there." She returned to her co-worker to pick up their conversation.

"I'll need to wear it out of the store," I told her.

"Sure," she said, "but we only take American Express."

"That's fine. My boyfriend called ahead."

She turned back to me slowly. "Oh. You're David's girlfriend?"

"Yes," I said, finding her tone a little too familiar. "Are you a friend of his?"

"Er." She bit her lip. "He usually works with me when he shops."

Awesome, I thought wryly. So he had a regular girl. Why didn't that surprise me? "How about that dressing room?" I asked.

"Right." She shot a look at the other saleswoman as she rounded the counter and led me to the back of the store. "Have you been dating long?" she asked nonchalantly.

"Not very."

She gave me a quick, tight smile, showed me into the room, and shut the door behind me. I stood there a moment with the blouse in my hand, seething. Obviously "working" with David involved more than just shopping. It occurred to me that I might be destined to a lifetime of uncomfortable encounters with David's women. Instead of dwelling on it, I decided to honor the promises I'd made to be more open and ask him directly.

Me: *Curious . . . how many of the women at this boutique have you "worked with"?*

David: *Two, if you count yourself.*

I gave myself a moment to fume. I appreciated his honesty, and the answer wasn't surprising—it had been written all over her face—but that didn't mean I had to like it.

Me: *Why would you send me here then?*

David: *Why else? Good service.*

Me: *You are walking a seriously thin line with that comment.*

David: *Just being honest, my sweet. Don't ask if you don't want to know the answer.*

I could've stopped to consider if he was right or wrong, but I just wanted to be angry. Before I could respond, though, he sent another message.

David: *Look, I wouldn't send you if there was anything to worry about. That shit's so done, it can only be funny.*

Funny—that was an odd way of looking at it. Once a playboy, David could now only find hilarity in the mere thought of wanting another woman. All right. This way of looking at it was getting better.

I inhaled deeply. I had a choice—chastise him for a past that couldn't be changed and was likely to come up often, or accept that it happened, and in the end, he'd chosen me. I twisted my lips in thought right as a knock came on the dressing room door.

"Do you need anything?" the salesgirl asked.

I opened the door and forced a smile. "Yes. Lingerie. Bring the best stuff you have. Anything you think David would like . . . since you've worked with him before."

"Cer-certainly," she stammered, reddening.

I laughed to myself when she'd left. Just because I was

going to take the high road didn't mean I couldn't have a little fun.

As I stood at the register in my new blouse, I studied the girl. All the women I knew of in David's past were beautiful, unsurprisingly. He could have any girl he wanted on her knees in a snap. So I decided I'd take it as a compliment that he'd picked me.

"Mr. Dylan called again," she said as she packaged my purchases. "He wanted me to include this." She showed me a small box with a ribbon around it. "He says you're not to open it until tonight, though."

"Did you pick it out?" I asked.

"No." She shook her head emphatically. "He knew exactly what he wanted, and we had it."

I gave her a once-over and decided that was okay. "All right. Thank you. You've been very helpful."

"Sure," she said. "Maybe we'll see you again."

"Maybe not," I muttered under my breath, but held my smile in place.

In the passenger's seat of David's rental SUV, I bit my thumbnail and stared out the window. I wasn't looking forward to seeing Bill at all. Just the idea had my stomach in knots, and I was beginning to regret my chicken tacos at lunch.

"So, why exactly am I carrying big boxes while David gets to hang by the car?" Gretchen asked from the backseat.

"I don't want to be disrespectful to Bill," I explained to her for the second time.

"Who cares?" she asked.

David snickered. "Gretchen, remind me to buy you a

drink sometime."

"You guys, seriously," I said, exasperated. "I'm still married to the man, for Christ's sake. I don't want to hurt him."

"I'm just teasing," she said, rubbing my shoulder. "It's very mature of you."

"Anyway," I added, nodding at David as I addressed Gretchen, "you've seen these two together. They aren't exactly friendly."

"I promised to behave," David stated, his eyes focused out the windshield.

"My answer is still no—you're staying downstairs."

"Don't worry, David," Gretchen said. "I can handle Bill. I took a kickboxing class in college."

She was trying to be funny, but David's jaw tightened, and I groaned. "Don't needle him, Gretch. We'll be in and out in under twenty minutes, I guarantee."

"I don't want either of you girls in there alone, all right?" David asked. "Just stick together."

"Sir, yes, sir," Gretchen said and saluted. With our answering silence, she added, "Oh, come on, you two. Lighten up."

Since David had been in the car since we'd picked her up, I hadn't gotten to fill her in on how deeply rooted this argument ran. It wasn't her fault we were so tense, so I turned in my seat and smiled at her. "How are things with Greg?"

"I think I'm finally ready to seal the deal," she said. "God knows my vagina is ready."

"Good God," David said, glancing at her in the rearview mirror. "You haven't *slept* together yet?"

"Not since he returned into my life," she said. "I want to make sure he's serious before I give it up."

"You must be going crazy," I said.

She sighed. "Last night he brushed against my boob, and I almost climaxed."

David chuckled to himself.

"This is fun, both of us being in new relationships," I said. "Are you guys doing anything for Thanksgiving?"

Gretchen rolled her eyes. "You know how I feel about holidays. They always sucked at our house."

"Mine, too. High expectations, emotions running wild, plus too much alcohol—a bad combination," I said. "David and I have no plans beyond Thursday."

"Why don't we skip the fanfare and just go somewhere for the extended weekend?" David suggested.

"I *love* that idea," Gretchen said. "Like where? Lake Geneva?"

David tapped his chin. "I was thinking somewhere warm, actually."

She groaned. "That sounds heavenly. I'm already sick of winter, and it's just starting."

"Brian's parents own a beach house near Miami," David said. "I'll bet they'd let us use it."

"Will he be there?" Gretchen asked.

"Probably. He's single, so I doubt he has plans," David said. "Obviously, we'd invite him since it's his house."

Gretchen grumbled under her breath.

"Don't like Miami?" David asked.

"Um, love Miami," she said. "Don't like *Brian*."

"Really?" David frowned into the rearview mirror. "Why not?"

"No reason, really," she said. "Just that he acts like he's God's gift to women. And he wears way too much cologne. Liv, did I tell you he got huffy when I sent my steak back on our only date, even though I was very clear that I wanted it rare? He's a bit arrogant, if you ask me. Thinks he's all that because he's hot, but, really, he needs to get over himself."

"All right," David said slowly, casting me a sidelong, semi-freaked out look. "We can go somewhere else that's Brian-free."

Realizing David was serious about leaving town, I turned to him. "We already told Jessa we'd spend Thanksgiving dinner at her house," I reminded him. "It takes a lot of planning, so I don't want to cancel on her."

"So we'll go to her place for dinner, then leave Friday morning." He grinned at me. "Come on, it'll be fun."

Giddy was not a word I'd typically have used to describe David, but in that moment, that's what he was. "Okay," I agreed, a sucker for anything that made him smile that way. I turned back to Gretchen. "And Miami's a great idea. You can play nice with Brian for a few days."

"*Fine*," she relented. "I've pretty much learned to tune out his flapping anyway."

David laughed in a loud burst. "He does flap. I'll call him up and let you guys know what he says."

"We can work that out later," I said out the window as we pulled up to the curb of the building I'd called home for years. "We're here."

Chapter Twenty-One

David parked his car outside my old apartment. Just before I shut the car door to go upstairs and knock on Bill's door, David stopped me. "Make it quick," he ordered, his giddiness over Miami long gone. "Or I'll come up."

"Don't you dare," I warned him. "We had a deal. Gretchen and I can handle getting my things. You stay here."

He only grunted.

Gretchen and I climbed the stairs of the complex, and I held my breath as I knocked. After an unusually long time, Bill opened the door and peered out. He looked at Gretchen and then back at me. "What's she doing here?"

"Gretchen's here to help," I said. "Don't take this out on her."

"It's fine, Liv," Gretchen said, irritation threading her tone. "Let's just get your stuff."

Bill had stacked large and small boxes in the kitchen. I peeked into one. My razor and a tub of exfoliating sugar scrub had been thrown on a pile of my work attire. "Really, Bill?"

He shrugged and flopped into a dining room chair. "Just trying to help."

Gretchen and I lifted one box together and carried it downstairs, where David took it from us.

"So far so good," Gretchen told him.

The next two were lighter so we each took one. On our next trip, before I could walk out of the kitchen, Bill asked, "Liv, can we talk alone a minute?"

Gretchen returned the glare he directed at her. "No," she answered for me.

"It's okay," I told her. "Go ahead."

"But . . ." She jerked her head in the direction of the front door. "We're not supposed to."

"I won't be long," I said.

She left reluctantly. I set down the box again and walked over to take the chair next to his. "How are you?" I asked.

"All right," he said. "Taking things day by day. You?"

"The same," I lied. I was far better than all right, but he didn't need to know that.

He dropped his gaze to the floor. "Is he treating you well?"

"Yes."

"Good. I should've said this sooner, but I'm sorry he and I got into it." Bill cleared his throat and glanced at my arm, even though clothing covered the fading bruises. "And I'm sorry if I . . . you know, hurt you."

I nodded. "I know you didn't mean it."

"I did. I wanted to hurt you the way you hurt me," he said and scrubbed a hand through his hair. "I can't, though . . . I never could. Hurt you or get to you in any way."

It was my turn to look at the ground. After the Herculean feat it'd taken David to break through to me, I didn't blame Bill. "It's okay," I said about the bruises. "It wasn't too bad."

His shoulders began to quake, and he wiped his eyes. "I still don't get what I should've done differently."

"Bill," I said affectionately. "Don't torture yourself. I'm to blame, too. There's a lot we both could've done differently. I know it hurts to hear it, but believe me, this is for the best."

He nodded and lifted his head. "I wish I'd seen it coming, though."

I resisted from hugging him for comfort, knowing that would only make things worse for all of us. "That's my fault, and I'm sorry."

"I'm really angry with you, Liv, and I can't help it." His voice firmed as his tears vanished. "You know I love you, you know I'm a nice guy, but I feel like I've taken a lot of shit."

"I know," I said softly, touching my earlobe.

"So don't expect me to lie back and let you walk all over me. If you want to proceed with this divorce, I'm going to treat you like I would anyone else in court. Especially if *he's* going to stick his nose in it. And I'm a good lawyer, I think you know that."

Loud banging on the front door startled me. "Shit. Hang on," I told Bill.

"Tell Gretchen to give us a minute," he said.

It wasn't Gretchen, but I kept that to myself as I crossed the apartment. I opened the door a sliver and stepped out, but stuck my foot in the door to keep it from automatically locking. "Everything's good," I said to David. "We're just talking."

He unclenched his jaw. "Fine, but I'm waiting here."

"Thank you," I said and returned to the kitchen. "Go ahead," I told Bill. "What were you saying?"

I stood by the last few boxes, waiting for him to speak. My eyes went to the nearest one, and my jaw dropped when I saw our wedding album. "Bill?" I asked, holding it up.

"I don't want it."

"But . . . you should keep it. I have the originals on my computer." He shook his head, and I frowned. I didn't want to say it, but it would mean more to Bill during this time than it would me. I set it on the counter next to him. "Keep it," I insisted.

"Are you purposely trying to piss me off?" he asked. "First, you give me back your ring, and now this?"

"I made that album especially for you," I said. "And I'm sorry about the ring. You're right—it was insensitive of me, but I know it's a family heirloom."

"So I'm supposed to give it to someone else?" he asked.

"I don't know," I admitted.

He stood, picked up the album, and threw it in the trash. "Happy?" he asked. "Leave."

I glanced over at the remaining boxes. I still had more stuff to take down. But more importantly, I was concerned about Bill. "I really think we should talk," I said. "Whatever's going on in your head, let's get it all out there."

"I can't. Just go." He turned away and pressed his palms into his eyes. "Every time you look at me, it's with pity," he added. "Please."

I walked over and put my hand on his shoulder. "Bill," I said softly.

"I said *go*." He picked up a box, wrenched open the door, and threw it into the hallway.

As he turned for the next one, David caught the door before it closed. "Is that really fucking necessary?" he asked from the doorway.

I hurried over and pushed David out into the hallway. "Don't," I warned.

He crossed his arms over his chest and kept his eyes fixed behind me. "He's going to ruin your stuff."

Bill dropped another box by my feet, then stuck a wedge under the door to keep it open. "Can't go anywhere without your bodyguard?" he asked me, going back for more boxes.

"Say another thing, and I'll shatter your jaw, too," David said.

"Try me." Bill slid a box across the floor, and it tumbled out into the hall. "You're lucky I don't press charges for my nose."

David's arm twitched as he stepped forward, right in front of me. "Do that," he said over my head. "See what happens."

I straightened my shoulders and placed a hand on his forearm. "Don't," I said. "I'm asking you to walk away."

"Yeah, walk away, you noble asshole," Bill said. "Is it noble to swipe another man's wife from under his nose? To buy his future home?"

"I don't expect you to understand," David said. "Unlike you, I'd go to any lengths for her."

Bill scoffed. "How sweet. I'll be sure to remind you of that in three months when you've dumped her on the side of the road."

David lunged forward, almost knocking me out of the way, and gripped Bill by his t-shirt. He slammed him up against the wall and pinned him there. "I warned you once. If I have to shut you the fuck up, I will."

Bill's eyes dropped to David's hands and then jumped back up. I expected to see anger in them, but there was only defeat. I knew David saw it, too, because he released Bill immediately and stepped back.

"Look, man," David said, "fighting won't get us anywhere. Just watch your mouth, and don't *ever* put your hands on her again."

Bill kicked one last box out and disappeared into the apartment, letting the door slam behind him. I stared after him, trying to decide if I should go in and comfort him.

David cursed to himself and rubbed his forehead before looking at me. "Don't," he said. "You'll just make it harder for him."

He was right. Even seeing our wedding pictures was too hard for Bill. My being here wasn't helping.

"Is that everything?" David asked.

"I think there were a couple more boxes," I said, "but let's just leave it."

"You sure?" he asked. "I can go back in and get them."

"I'm sure," I said and picked up a lighter box as David hoisted a heavier one. We walked in silence to where Gretchen leaned against the car, her ankles crossed in front of her. "I don't see any blood on your knuckles," she said to David. "I guess that's a good sign."

"It didn't get that far, thankfully," I said.

"Thankfully for him," David muttered.

Gretchen rolled her eyes. "Bill's a real peach these days."

"I'm sorry he took it out on you," I said, hugging her. "It means so much that you came today."

"It means a lot that you asked," she said softly, smiling. As David jogged up the staircase to grab the last of my things, she added, "But can we go? I'm over this place."

I laughed. "Sure."

I insisted on treating her to dinner, so once the car had been loaded up, David drove us to a restaurant for pizza and drinks. After finishing off my frozen margarita, I slammed my empty glass on the table and Gretchen giggled.

David eyed us suspiciously, but he was in good spirits, despite being the designated driver.

Gretchen started off on something about work, but I could see that David wasn't listening. He watched me instead. Earlier, with the city of Chicago at his back, he'd had his way with me on his desk. I'd gotten myself some businessman David, and all it did was fuel the ache. The more I got, the more I wanted. I eased my foot out of my shoe and ran it along the inside of his leg, glancing over at Gretchen so as not to arouse suspicion.

When she stopped talking to order another drink, I pulled out my phone.

Me: *I have a confession to make…I never bought underwear today*

David shifted to retrieve his phone from his back pocket. His eyes widened as he read, then his fingers darted over the screen.

David: *I don't believe you.*

I arched an eyebrow at him. His gaze turned heated, immediately warming my body. Visions from earlier flashed through my mind. I was feeling just as aroused as I was then, despite having been blessed with two orgasms already. I exhaled audibly.

"Liv?" Gretchen asked. "Are you listening?"

"Yes," I said, my voice creaky.

"*Right*," she said, getting up. "I'm going to the bathroom."

David's hooded eyes scrolled down my body with agonizing slowness, then flicked back up to my face. He scooted his chair closer to mine, wet his lips, and rested his hand on my knee under the red-and-white checked table-cloth. I glanced around the restaurant as his palm rubbed back and forth over my skin. A dull hum overtook my body the instant his hand inched up my skirt. I inhaled a ragged breath, trying to keep it together, while his face gave nothing away. Except his eyes, fiery with need that mirrored my own desire.

Now at the top of my thighs, his fingers slipped between them, finding me slick. "You're soaked," he said, nonchalance threading his tone.

I inhaled deeply as he felt me. "For you."

His jaw tightened as he coated his fingers with my wetness but didn't penetrate. He leaned in and murmured, "If you're still this wet, my job's not done for the day. I'll finish you off tonight with a hard fuck."

My breath caught as my face flushed. "Harder than this afternoon?"

"So hard you can't walk tomorrow." He withdrew before he'd even entered and wiped his fingers down the inside of my thigh. His head tilted, and he kissed me seconds before I heard Gretchen's voice.

"Look at you two," she said. "So cute. Can't keep your hands off each other."

I laughed into his mouth, and he gave me a quick peck before returning to his position across the table.

"Brian e-mailed back," David said. "He says Miami's a go. Have you heard from Greg?"

"Yep." Gretchen nodded. "He's in."

When the waiter dropped off the check, I snatched it immediately. "This is my treat."

"I've got it," David said, holding out his hand.

David and Gretchen were doing me a favor, plus David hadn't let me pay for anything since we'd started dating.

This *was* going to be my treat, even if I had to force it on him.

I grabbed my purse and ran away before David knew what was happening. I paid the waiter in cash and returned slowly to the table, smoothing my hands over my skirt as David sat rigid in his chair.

"Um, thanks?" Gretchen said.

"No problem," I responded, unsuccessfully avoiding David's glare. "But I'm expecting one of you to put out."

Bent at the hip, my hands wrapped around my ankles, I'd assumed the position David wanted me in minutes ago. After enlisting a couple bellhops to carry up my boxes, he'd left to return the rental car. On his way home, he'd texted me how he wanted to find me, and it was like this—my ass in the air, hands at my ankles, and wearing lingerie he hadn't seen me in yet. I nearly dripped with anticipation, and by the time I heard keys in the foyer, I was dangerously close to biting off my bottom lip.

Now, I looked anxiously through my legs at the bedroom door. I was positioned at the foot of the bed, but I doubted we'd even make it there. I heard his dress shoes on the floors as he made his way to the bedroom. He entered but disappeared right into the closet. "You waiting, baby?" he called.

"Yes," I said impatiently.

"I'm coming."

"David." I groaned. "I can't wait any longer."

I heard his chuckle. "So touch yourself."

"No," I said through a squeal. "I want *you* to touch me."

Upside-down, I watched him exit the closet and take

his sweet time while I about burst with desire. He walked over in bare feet, still in his suit pants. "I want to touch you, too," he said, but he said it low and hoarse, and in a way that sounded like he'd been waiting to say it all day.

He removed his watch, set it on the nightstand, and came toward me. "Did you buy this earlier?" he asked of the tea-rose-pink satin bustier trimmed in black lace I'd paired with a matching lace thong.

"Yes."

He came right up behind me so I could feel his heat on the backs of my legs. "You told me you didn't buy underwear today."

"I lied," I said through a smile.

He gasped. "You lied? What did I tell you about that?" As soon as the question left his mouth, his open palm landed on my ass cheek.

I groaned. "Honesty policy."

"If I were a more patient man, I'd tie you to this bed as punishment."

"You would?" I asked hopefully, but also nervous at the prospect of being at another person's complete mercy.

"Instead, you hold on to your ankles like your life depends on it," he said and slid my thong over my ass so it fell to my ankles. When I started to step out of it, he said, "Wait."

He used his foot to nudge my legs apart as far as the underwear would allow. "All day I've been picturing you sprawled out on my desk, letting me have whatever I want."

"I want you to have it all," I said.

"All?" he asked.

"Everything. Take what you want."

He took my ass cheek in one hand and massaged it, spreading me open as I heard his zipper. From between my legs, I watched his pants fall. My breathing sped, my grip tightening, my vision blurring because he wasn't even inside me and I could feel him already.

His fingers skimmed over my wet slit. "You have such a sweet ass," he said. "Have I ever told you that?"

I whimpered softly and froze when I felt pressure on my anus. "David," I breathed, a soft objection.

His finger, wet with my own juices, continued a tenuous circle over me. The pressure subsided, and I felt equally relieved and disappointed.

Tension returned when I heard him spit in his hand. He was back between my cheeks suddenly, teasing me with soft, measured circles. With his finger pressed against my anus, he pushed his cock into me, and I inhaled sharply.

"Made for me, baby," he grated out.

"Do it," I dared him on an exhale.

He folded over my back, sliding so deep that I thought I might rip apart at the seams. "You want it?"

"Yes. Do it." I wanted him to dominate me in every way, but I also knew I had no idea what I was asking for. "One finger."

"I'll get lube."

"No," I bit out, dizzy with need for him. "Just do it now."

He straightened up, and his finger immediately began to ring my asshole, which quivered at the new sensation. His other hand held my hips in place as his cock pulsed into me, gently at first and then faster.

"Hold on to the bed," he instructed, so I let go of my ankles to brace myself against the frame.

His plunges remained deep but steady as he slipped the tip of his finger inside. It was wet, but not slick, so it throbbed slightly. But I wanted to do it for him, so I fisted my hands and said, "More."

He grunted, and his finger went deeper. My face flushed. I exhaled loudly. He held it there for a moment and then pushed all the way in, both painful and sweet. He kept it there as his thrusting increased and suddenly, he was pounding against me inhumanly hard like he'd promised. I pushed off the bed to meet him, his one finger all the way up my ass, and his other hand pulling my hips into each thrust.

Without warning or slowing down, he pushed a second finger in, and I suppressed a cry. My eyes watered as my insides molded around him. I was full, overwhelmingly full, and tempted to push his hand away, but I bit down on my lip instead and let the bite of pain ripple into waves of pleasure.

I closed my eyes and focused on his animal growls and on the feeling of his perfect cock driving in and out. My underwear seared against my ankles, chafing as I tried to spread my legs further to ease the sting.

"Oh, God," I moaned to myself, lost in another world, feeling him as deep as I could get him.

"*Fuck*," he bit out, crushing my hip with his hand as he drove into me. "You're wrapped so goddamn tight around me." I yelped when he twisted his fingers in me, and he stilled instantly.

"Don't stop," I begged and found my bottom lip with my teeth again.

He picked up his pace quickly, shoving me into the bed with each thrust. "That's it, baby. Come hard with two fingers in your ass."

A cry tore from my throat as I exploded with a forceful and sudden orgasm. It was so powerful that my insides cramped and then released and it was over before I knew it. He withdrew from me completely, so I sank down to the floor, still clutching the lip of the bed.

Breaking into a cold sweat, I set my forehead against the frame. My heart pounded everywhere—in my ears, against my ribcage, between my legs. I had no idea if David had even come.

"Hey," he said softly, crouching down next to me. "Are you all right?"

I nodded against the bed but didn't respond. He placed his hand over mine and removed it from the bed. He took my chin so I was forced to look at him. "Are you?" he asked earnestly.

I nodded again, and after a moment, he kissed me.

"Jesus," he said, drawing back and touching his lip. "You're bleeding." He pulled at my lower lip to inspect it. "You broke the skin. Were you in pain?"

I dropped my gaze to the floor. "I don't know. Kind of?" I said. "But it felt amazing, too. I think that's the hardest I've come yet."

"Damn it, Olivia, why didn't you tell me?" he asked as if he hadn't heard the last part.

My chest heaved as I searched his face. Was he mad? Why was he cursing at me?

"I have to know if I'm hurting you, or else how can I trust you when we're having sex?" he asked.

I shrugged my shoulders. "I said it felt good, David. I came really hard."

He sat all the way on the floor, his back against the bedframe. "Shit. Are you in pain now?"

"Not at all." I shook my head, still riding the bliss of my seriously intense orgasm. "Did you finish?"

He just stared at me, so I looked down and found my answer. He was hard, swollen, and glistening with my juices. I turned around, and with my back to him, I climbed astride his lap.

"Olivia," he protested. "You don't have to—" He

stopped as I took him in my hand. My pussy greedily devoured him in one plunge.

I sat motionless, savoring the sensation of his thick, pulsing cock stretching me. I didn't think I could come again, my body was wrecked, but he felt *so fucking good*. His hands parted my hair and pushed it over my shoulders, so it hung around my face. He kissed my spine softly and began to undo each hook of the pink corset. Once it hung open, he slid his hands underneath. "I don't want to hurt you," he said, running his hands over my skin. He reached around and grasped my breasts while moaning against my back. "I love you."

Goose bumps ignited over me as his lips brushed my shoulder. His arms clutched my back to his front, rocking me slowly onto him. I turned my head so he kissed my cheek and the corner of my lips. "I love you, too," I rasped.

He loosened his grip on me, and I lifted to turn around and face him. He held himself as I leisurely sank onto him again.

With my hands in his hair, I said, "That's better."

He put one hand on my face and smoothed the other over my hairline before kissing me slowly. Urgency flowed from him to me, and our hips began their own dance. He touched me, circling his fingers over my clit.

"I can't," I protested. "This time is for you."

"You can," he said, moving his fingers faster.

"David," I whimpered.

"God, I fucking love being inside of you. I own you like this," he said quietly. "When I'm buried in you this way, you have nowhere to go, no way to escape. You're finally mine."

He kissed me heatedly during the slow, rippling orgasm that his fingers and his erotic words sparked. It started between my thighs as if his hand there had ignited the fire now blazing through my veins. I gasped, but he held me still, forcing me to breathe into him as I threatened to float away.

We continued rocking into each other. His hand moved into my hair, and he pulled it when he came. It felt like a promise of forever, him fisting my hair and coming, holding me so close to him with an arm around my back the whole time and for moments after.

His face fell into my neck, and his shoulders swelled with deep breaths. "Are you okay, really?" he asked.

"It was intense," I whispered. "Good intense. But I don't think I want to try anal anytime soon."

His arms relaxed around me, but he remained serious. "You have to tell me if it's too much. Promise?"

I nodded.

In bed, he lay on his back, and I draped one arm across his chest.

"I like you in lingerie," he whispered into my hair.

"Thanks," I murmured, tightening my embrace on him. I ran my foot along his leg, wondering how I'd always despised cuddling. "Did you get everything done at work today?"

"Not really. It's never-ending."

"You work so hard."

"For you, I'm trying to find ways to cut back," he said.

"It's okay. I like that you're passionate."

"I want to see you that way, too," he responded.

I smiled against his chest. "I see you have a new receptionist."

"New receptionist and new problems."

"How come?"

"The old receptionist, Clare, is threatening a wrongful termination lawsuit. She claims Arnaud came on to her several times, and she turned him down, so that's why we fired her."

I lifted my head to look at him. "But that's not why. I was there."

"I know. She called to let me know she's going to hire a lawyer to sue for sexual harassment."

I started to balk when I realized who I was talking to. David's reputation hadn't materialized out of thin air. There was a very real possibility he'd slept with her. "Did you—"

"Never," he said. "I never touched her. I'm not that fucking stupid, and neither is Arnaud."

I believed him, but Arnaud? My creep radar went haywire in his presence. "You don't think there's any chance he tried?"

"Arnaud and I have done business together for a long time," David said. "We would never have gotten this far without being honest with one another. He knows I wouldn't allow that shit in my office. Too risky." His chest rose and fell with a sigh. "I did ask, though, just to be certain. He says he kept things entirely professional."

"Huh."

"What are you thinking?" he asked.

David's work was his life, and Arnaud was a member of his team. But Arnaud was a pig, I could tell. Still, I proceeded cautiously. "Don't disregard her just yet. Maybe she'll drop it if you guys take it seriously and apologize."

"Apologize for what?" he asked. "She's pissed off that I fired her, and she's trying to get back at us. I don't like to indulge that kind of behavior."

I glanced up at him. "If that were true, why wouldn't she accuse *you* of sexual harassment instead of Arnaud?" I asked.

He rubbed his eyebrow. "Good point."

"Do you really want to go through the hassle of a lawsuit?" I asked. "One that would likely end in a huge settlement and a mark on your company's reputation?"

"No."

"So acknowledge that it's possible she's telling the truth. And, honey, I'm sorry, but . . . the way you fired her wasn't very nice."

He grunted and looked up at the ceiling. I ran a finger over each of his eyebrows and then over his lips, still amazed that I was lying in his bed and that I was allowed to just *enjoy* him. He caught my hand in his and kissed my knuckles.

"I don't want to talk about them while I'm in bed with you," he decided.

I resettled my head on his chest. "What do you want to talk about then?"

"I'll probably regret bringing this up, but was it too bad at the clothing store today?"

"No," I said honestly. "I decided I'd better get used to running into women you've slept with."

His chest rose as he laughed. "I'm sorry. If I'd known all along I'd end up here, I would've remained a virgin."

I pinched his arm. "Liar. So long as I'm the one who gets to keep you, we're good."

"Works for me." He sat up, and I rolled back onto a pillow. "Where's the shopping bag?"

"By the closet."

He got out of bed, and I wiggled excitedly under the comforter as I remembered my present. He returned with the box and sat cross-legged on the mattress.

"What is it?"

"I'm not going to tell you," he said, rolling his eyes. "But it's not a ring. Not yet. Just open it."

Too giddy to get even *more* giddy at the thought of him

proposing, I propped myself up against the headboard and unwrapped the box carefully. In my palm sat a small, black velvet box that creaked when I opened it. I gasped at a pair of big, shiny diamond studs. "I can't accept these."

He scooted closer, removed one of the diamond earrings from the box, and tucked a piece of my hair behind my ear to slide it in. "Perfect," he commented.

"David, I—"

"I have an ulterior motive," he interrupted, moving to the other ear. "I thought maybe if I put something pretty in your earlobes, you'd stop nervously pulling on them all the time."

I smiled widely and launched forward, crushing his lips to mine. "Thank you."

"I must say, diamonds suit you. There'll be more where those came from." I opened my mouth to protest, but he cut me off. "Don't argue, just tell me you love them," he whispered.

"Oh." I sighed. "I love them, and I love you."

He rolled me onto the bed and settled on top of me. We remained that way, kissing and whispering softly to each other, until we could no longer keep our eyes open.

Chapter Twenty-Two

Only eleven in the morning, and I already wished the day were over. My co-worker Lisa had just expressed that the layout I'd just finished was "a good start." Instead of plotting out ways to avoid her the rest of my working life, I spent the next twenty minutes fantasizing about how my day would've gone if I'd skipped work to stay in bed with David.

I cursed at my desk phone when it seared through my daydream just as it was getting good. "Yes?" I answered.

"There's a man here in the lobby to see you," Jenny said.

"Who is it?" I asked. "Can you send him back?"

"He won't tell me his name," she said tersely.

I hung up and fixed my hair quickly in the mirror before weaving through the cubicles and out to the front.

A middle-aged man in an ill-fitting suit that reeked of stale cigarettes approached me. "You Olivia Germaine?" he asked.

"Yes."

He jotted something on the clipboard in his hand.

"You're being served with a Petition for the Dissolution of Marriage," he said, holding out an oversized envelope.

There it was. The tragic ending I'd been avoiding since the day I'd looked up the word *divorce* in the dictionary. As Jenny looked on, my face heated. "That was awfully quick," I said.

The man's hard eyes met mine. "I'm here as a favor. Bill's a friend."

"Was it really necessary to come to my workplace?" I asked, snatching the packet.

He shrugged and handed me the clipboard to sign. After he left, I took a deep breath and turned to face Jenny, who'd been joined by a concerned-looking Serena.

"Is everything all right, Liv?" Jenny asked.

My hand began to sweat around the envelope. "It's fine."

"Was that from Bill?" Serena asked. "Were you expecting it?"

I scratched under my nose. "Yes. Just not at work," I said, and crossed the lobby, picking up my pace so I could process this alone.

Seated at my desk, I examined the papers, unsure of what I was looking at. Anything involving the legal system, I would've taken to Bill. Instead of trying to do this on my own or give myself the day to consider my options, I shot David a text.

I didn't have to do this alone, and for once, I was glad to ask for help.

Me: *I just got served.*

My cell phone rang almost immediately with David's call. "What happened?" he asked.

I tucked the phone between my shoulder and ear while

flipping through the paperwork. "Some guy just served me with divorce papers."

"At work?"

"Yes." I groaned. "Talk about embarrassing."

"At least we can get this process started," David said. "I'm actually meeting my lawyer for lunch on Adams. We'll come by afterward to take a look."

I fingered my new earring. Office gossip would spread fast. First, the roses, and now, the divorce papers. People would put two and two together. Did I care anymore?

He sighed when I didn't respond. "You're worried about what people will say?" he asked. "You can come to lunch if you want, but we'll be talking about Clare and some menial items." He paused. "But I want nothing more than to show you off, Olivia You're going to have to tell your co-workers sometime."

This was more than David swinging by my office. Announcing our relationship to the world was an act of faith in us. Up until our time in Dallas, I would've wavered over the decision, but he was right. David wasn't going anywhere, and people would eventually find out.

"No, it's fine," I said and a small smile formed on my face as I realized that I, too, would get to show him off. "Come by when you're finished. I miss you anyway."

"Good call, baby," he said, his voice a little grittier. "See you soon."

I hung up as a grin broke free. I was getting an unexpected visit from my boyfriend. It wasn't the same as ditching work to stay in bed with him, but it would brighten my day considerably.

He texted me on his way over, so I went to meet him in the lobby. Jenny looked about to burst from curiosity, but I ignored her by playing with my phone as I sat in a club chair to wait.

With the *ping* of the elevator, I looked up. David waltzed through toward the glass doors with another smartly dressed man.

"Oh, shit. Is that David Dylan?" Jenny whispered right before they entered.

I stood to greet them. David leaned down, kissed me on the cheek, and introduced me to his lawyer, Jerry.

"Nice to meet you," I said, shaking his hand.

He nodded. "David's told me a lot about you."

I kept my head down as I led both men through the cubicles. I was glad David had come, but there was no need to make a bigger spectacle than I knew his presence would. In my office, I shut the door carefully and handed the documents over to Jerry.

As he looked them over, David put his arm around me and planted an innocent kiss on my lips. "How are you?"

"Better," I said, touching his jaw.

"Me, too. I booked our weekend. Pack your bags, baby, and your teeniest bikini. We're going to Miami." I grinned, and he squeezed me before looking up. "How's it look, Jerry?"

"Standard stuff so far," Jerry said, perching on the edge of my desk. "Bill has filed for divorce."

"Do you know Bill?" I asked.

"Yep." He licked the tip of his index finger and flipped a page. "Nice guy, good at what he does."

I leaned into David. "Will that be an issue?"

"Not at all." Jerry cleared his throat. "Looks like he's filing on the grounds of adultery."

"He warned me he would," I said. "He's pulling this whole 'no more Mr. Nice Guy' act."

"Actually," Jerry started, "it's unusual to file this way because it involves going to trial. That means time and money, evidence and witnesses. And since it doesn't affect the division of assets because of Illinois' laws, he's likely only doing it for one reason."

"To embarrass her," David guessed.

"You got it," Jerry said. "Thing is . . . it *could* work in your favor. If Bill's able to prove adultery, which he will be, they may grant the divorce faster." Jerry looked up, resting the papers against his thigh. "Olivia would deny the charge, but essentially, we'd be throwing the case."

"Isn't that, like, collusion or something?" I asked.

"No, because Bill isn't in on it." Jerry nodded at David. "You said you want fast, this is fastest. Assuming you're willing to spend the money, Dylan." Jerry shrugged. "Otherwise, we can try to convince Bill to agree to a no-fault divorce, which would cost everyone less but could take either six months or two years."

"Two *years*?" I exclaimed.

"The court wants to know that you've had a reasonable separation period," Jerry explained. "That's customarily two years but can be reduced to six months."

That was *ridiculous*. How could a court possibly make that determination? My heart sank knowing how long David had waited to find his future wife, only to have to wait two more years.

"I think you know how I feel, Jerry," David said. "Money's no object if it means moving this along."

Jerry nodded. "Then I'll file the response today. Next thing would be—"

"Wait," I said. "You mentioned a trial. Evidence? Witnesses? Is that necessary?"

"Yes." Jerry sucked in a breath. "That's where the shaming comes in. You should be prepared for it to get personal."

"Let's proceed," David said.

"Hang on," I said, stepping away from David. "What

do you mean by 'personal'?"

"Well . . ." Jerry dropped the stack of papers on my desk and looked around the small office. "Bill will need to submit evidence. This might involve photographs of you two, witness accounts, private detectives—since you're denying the charge so it goes to trial, he'll need whatever he can scrape up to prove that you cheated on him."

"Absolutely not," I said, forming two fists. It was bad enough I'd be branded an adulterer the rest of my life, but ultimately, I was just another divorcée. David had a successful career and reputation to protect. "I'm not putting David through that."

"Baby," David said, "it might get you out faster. It would mean—"

"No," I said resolutely. I didn't need to discuss, consider, or even give it another thought. I turned to face David. "I won't have your name dragged through the mud like that. What about your career, David? The firm? You've worked too hard to get where you are. We can do six months, two years if we have to."

David frowned. "I've waited long enough to call you mine."

I stepped up and took his hand in mine. "I am yours. And you can tell anyone you want, but what's most important is that we know it." Despite being acutely aware of a third person in the room, and slightly uncomfortable with being so vulnerable in front of him, I forced myself to tell David what he deserved to hear. "I'll be married to Bill on paper a while longer, but my heart is completely, irrevocably yours no matter what."

David took my chin and touched his thumb to the corner of my mouth. With gratitude in his eyes, he nodded, then turned to Jerry. "How does it work if Olivia admits to the affair?"

"Like I said, the two-year separation can be reduced to six months if both parties agree to it," Jerry said.

"If he's out for payback, he'll never go for that," David said.

"Unless . . ." I blinked up at him. "Unless I tell him he can keep everything."

"I doubt any amount of money will deter him from seeing us suffer," David said.

I smiled. "Then you don't know Bill. He's pretty frugal."

I'd wanted to shield Bill from getting hurt further, even up until I'd gone to move out my things. But now, my loyalty lay with David. And Bill had gone out of his way to try to embarrass him, so I didn't owe him any more protection. "He doesn't know we were already planning to let him have it. He'll go for it. I just have to convince him."

Jerry pulled at his chin. "Olivia—I'm David's lawyer, but in this matter, you're my client, too." He looked between David and me. "And as your lawyer, I can't advise you to do that. In all my years of practice, I've never had a client hand everything over. If you waive the right to alimony, that's it. No turning back."

David's arm tightened around me. "Jerry. We already discussed this."

"I'm sorry, David." He shook his head. "We go back a long time, but I can't advise a client to enter into that type of agreement no matter how in love she thinks she is."

I wondered if that was true or if Jerry had reservations because of David's history. But it was clear to me, by the way David tensed beside me, and from the time we'd spent together, that my trust in him meant something. It meant a lot. And despite all the times I'd deprived him of it, he'd still fought for me. So I said, "Let the bastard have it all."

Both pairs of eyes cut to me.

"What's the next step?" I asked Jerry. "Getting Bill to agree to six months?"

"Uh." Jerry looked at us with an expression somewhere between confused, delighted, and reluctant. "Yep, that's the next step."

"It's decided then," David said.

"All right." Jerry picked up the paperwork again. "Mind if I take a few more minutes with this?"

"Sure," I said.

As he sat at my desk, David turned to block me from Jerry with his body. He placed his hands on my cheeks. "Thank you," he said.

"I trust you." I held his gaze. "Completely."

His thumb moved over my cheek. "You don't know what that means to me."

I beamed at him.

"What's that smile for?" he asked.

"It feels good to be . . . out in the open."

"It feels *amazing*. I'm sorry I left you in bed this morning, but I wanted to finish up at work in time to drive you home tonight."

I hesitated. "Actually, Davena's husband—"

"Mack."

"Yes . . . Mack. He called earlier and wants to go for dinner. I haven't seen him since before everything happened."

David smiled warmly. "That sounds nice."

I wanted David to meet Mack, but after telling my friends, my office, and most importantly, my dad, the past couple weeks had been a lot. "I understand if you don't want to come."

David studied my face before responding. "I'd like to," he said. "But won't it be uncomfortable showing up with a man who isn't your husband?"

I didn't have the first clue what I'd say to Mack. He'd recently lost the love of his life—would he understand my choice to leave Bill? No playbook existed for this kind of thing. "It definitely will, but I'd like you to be there. I think you understand how important Mack is to me, how important Davena was. They're my godparents."

"Then I'd be honored to meet him," David said. "What time should I pick you up here?"

"Dinner's at seven-thirty, and I want to change first, but it's close to the apartment."

Jerry alerted us that he was finished, so I walked them back to the lobby. I'd hung my head on our way in, so this time, as we zigzagged through the office, I grasped David's hand. He was my boyfriend, and that was what couples did. After a look of surprise from him, I was rewarded with his wonderfully perfect boyish grin—now, one of my favorite sights in the world.

At the elevator bank, Jerry averted his eyes as David swooped in for one last kiss. "See you tonight," he said.

I left them in the elevator bank and returned to the lobby, where Serena and Jenny blockaded me from passing.

"We need details," Jenny demanded.

"Like, *now*," Serena added.

I sighed to hide my amusement. "You two are incurable gossips."

"Is that how the story starts?" Jenny chided. "I didn't think so. *Spill*."

I crossed my arms and leaned a hip against Jenny's desk. "As you may have figured out, Bill and I are getting a divorce." I gestured over my shoulder. "And I'm dating David."

"Get *out*," Jenny said as Serena balked, "Shut up!"

"Well, which is it?" I teased. Finally, I allowed my smile to break through.

Jenny squealed, "How did this happen?"

I scratched my forehead. "It's a long story."

"He's the most beautiful man in Chicago," Serena gushed.

"Who is?" I heard and turned my head. Lisa had appeared in the doorway.

"Liv's boyfriend," Serena said.

"Uh, Bill?" she asked.

"No," Jenny said, rolling her eyes. "She's getting a divorce. We're talking about her *boyfriend*."

Lisa looked at me. "And that would be . . .?"

I raised my chin. "You remember David Dylan?"

Her mouth fell open. "From 'Most Eligible'?"

I nodded.

"Yeah fucking right . . . David Dylan and *you*?" Her back went rod-straight as she looked over my shoulder. "I mean—"

Just for that comment, I decided to brag. "Yep," I said loudly. "David Dylan and *me*. *Me* and, as Serena said, the hottest guy in Chicago. But, believe it or not, he's also incredibly sweet, romantic, thoughtful, and just . . ." I sighed happily. "Just, like, so seriously amazing."

"Go on," came a deep voice behind me, followed by an amused chuckle.

Oh my God. I paled and turned around slowly. David stood at the door, taking in the scene. Jenny and Serena gasped. Lisa snickered. And David grinned—huge. "Jerry took your pen." He held it out. "Asked me to return it."

"Oh. Of course." I smoothed my hand down my front and tried to play it cool as I walked to him and took the pen. It had to be the *absolute* most *ridiculous* reason *ever* to get caught gushing about your boyfriend. I mumbled a "thanks" and turned, but he grabbed my arm and spun me around into his body.

He held me there to plant a sweet kiss on my lips. "*You*, Olivia Germaine, are the one who's seriously amazing," he said loudly enough for everyone to hear, tucking a strand of my hair behind my ear. "And I love you."

The two wilting sighs behind me harmonized with my own. David released me, but not before shooting Lisa an especially chilling glance that made even *my* stomach drop. I watched David return through the doors to where Jerry held the elevator for him. Hands in his pockets, David winked at me as the elevator doors closed.

When I turned back, all three women seemed on the verge of exploding.

"He *loves* you?" Jenny exclaimed. "You are so goddamn lucky."

"I am," I agreed.

"You aren't lucky, Liv. You deserve it," Serena said as if it were obvious. "He's the one who's lucky."

I searched her face and found only sincerity. "Thank you, Serena. That's really sweet."

She smiled, and we giggled conspiratorially when we noticed Lisa had slunk away.

In the foyer of the apartment, as David and I waited for the elevator, his eyes scanned my pink, shimmering, long-sleeved shift dress with lace overlay. "Should I be worried about this Mack?" he joked.

I tightened my ponytail. "Why, is it too sexy?"

"It's the perfect amount of sexy . . ." David bit his lip. "As long as I'm with you at all times."

I laughed as I slipped into my coat. "Then my diabolical plan to keep you close is working."

We opted to walk from the apartment to the restaurant where we were meeting Mack.

As we headed out into the night, David moved to the outside of the sidewalk. "Jerry advised me to lose Arnaud," he said. "He thinks he's full of shit and a liability."

So I wasn't the only one. I glanced at the sidewalk. "What'd you say?"

"I said no. I can't fire a man at the top of his field based on an allegation. Arnaud has given me no reason to doubt him, and he says all his interactions with her were professional." David stared forward. "Anyway, it did remind me that you said you didn't like him a while back."

I linked my elbow with his. "Right."

"Well?" he prompted. "I'm asking what made you say that."

"I really don't want to get in the middle." Did I? Even if I hadn't met Arnaud, I'd be inclined to believe Clare. Maybe she *was* bitter over the way David had fired her, but both things could be true. I'd been hit on by a professor in college, and plenty of my friends had been propositioned by superiors. "He's your friend. It's not my business."

"He's my associate first," David said. "And the people in my life affect you."

That was true. I really didn't like the idea of hanging around Arnaud in any kind of setting. Hiding my feelings to keep the peace was one of the mistakes I'd made with Bill, so I stopped walking and turned to David. "Well, since you asked, I'll be honest. Arnaud makes me *very* uncomfortable. When he looks at me, it's like he's undressing me with his eyes."

David froze, staring at me. "Unfortunately, I'd bet a lot of men look at you that way," he said. "Didn't *I*?"

"Yes, but that was different. It never crossed my mind

that you'd like taking advantage of me," I said. "But Arnaud? I wouldn't want to be alone with him."

David rubbed at the lines between his eyebrows, clearly trying to process something that didn't make sense to him. "Arnaud's intense, and . . . sometimes people don't get his humor because he's not from here. That's why I handle client relations."

I shrugged and resumed walking. "Again, I don't really want to get in the middle, David. But I don't think it's fair to write off those around you who are saying something isn't right."

After a moment, he blew out a sigh. "All right. I hear you. I'll look into it further."

"Thank you." I didn't want to bring down the mood, so I tucked my hair behind my ear and smiled up at him. "Have I mentioned today that I love my new earrings? And that later, I intend to show you how much?"

That got me a grin. "Can't wait."

David stopped me as we approached the restaurant. "I'm going to wait at the bar and give you and Mack a chance to talk first. And if you change your mind about us meeting, come find me when you finish."

"Thank you, honey." I lifted my chin, and he kissed me quickly.

Mack took the news well. He'd suspected something had gone awry with Bill after our last conversation, where I'd broken down in tears in Mack's arms. I explained that in addition to my despair over Davena, I'd spent the months after her funeral trying to convince myself I wasn't in love with another man.

"I can tell you're much lighter, Olivia," Mack said and took my hand over the table for two he'd gotten near a window. "Much, much lighter. The difference is appalling, actually. You're glowing."

"I'm happy, Mack. And in love. *Real* love." I blushed. "I'd like to think maybe even the kind you shared with Davena."

He looked taken aback. "This is a side of you I've never seen. I should like to meet the man who's brought this out in you."

"Actually . . . he's here," I said, pushing some of my hair behind my ear. "He wants to meet you, but we weren't sure how you'd react."

"He's here now?" Mack asked.

I glanced toward the front of the restaurant. "At the bar."

Mack stood immediately and signaled for a waiter. "Bring him over, dear. I'll get us a table with a place for him."

"You're sure?" I asked, getting up, too. When he nodded, I smiled and kissed him on the cheek. "Thank you for being supportive."

I found David on a barstool with his back to me, whiskey in hand. When I touched his shoulder, he turned. I meant to peck him quickly on the lips, but when our mouths met, I lingered there for a moment. "Mmm," I moaned. "Whiskey reminds me of our first night together. You tasted so—"

"Do not say another word," David warned. "Or else I'll meet your godfather with a hard-on."

I exhaled a laugh and held out my hand. "Come on. It's going well."

We made our way over and Mack stood as I introduced them. They shook hands, and David expressed his regret over Davena's death. I remembered then that David had been at the funeral, and I squeezed his hand.

As David slid out my chair for me, Mack said, "Liv's a different woman. Thank you for that."

"She deserves better than what she was getting," David replied and sat.

Mack set his elbows on the table, his eyebrows high. "You don't mince words, do you, David? Bill was all right. A bit of an ass if you ask me, though."

My mouth dropped with shock as my eyes shot to Mack. He was almost always overly polite, although that didn't mean he held back. "You really thought that?"

"Sorry, dear, but I didn't care much for his disposition," Mack said, unfurling his dinner napkin. "I wish Davena were here to see this. She was supportive, but we wondered several times what it was you saw in him."

"Apparently, you're not the only one," I said with a deep inhale. "Surprisingly, others have expressed their support, too. Not everyone, but that's understandable."

"Your mother?" Mack asked astutely.

David put his hand on the back of my chair. "Not supportive," he said.

Mack grimaced at me. "After her history with your father, I can see why this would upset her."

"She's more than upset," I said, and David's hand dropped to massage the back of my neck. "She's practically disowned me."

"If Leanore were a rational woman, I'd say once she sees you two together, her opinion will change," Mack said, and looked to David. "Unfortunately, I think this will be a long battle."

Would my mother ever even give us the opportunity to show her? I had a hard time envisioning it. Enough time had passed that if she wanted, she could have called to apologize for what she'd said. I tried to think of a time in my life when she'd apologized for anything. "I hope she comes around one day, but I'm not holding my breath."

"She sounds like a complicated woman," David said.

Mack laughed. "Yes. She's always been headstrong, but *complicated* and *difficult* are also words frequently used to describe her."

"Difficult, yes," I agreed, and covered Mack's hand. "Thankfully, I had Davena as a stand-in."

As our dinner proceeded, David and Mack discovered some mutual business acquaintances. David listened intently about the foundation Mack had started in Davena's name, offering his services should Mack be able to use them. At some point during the night, I remembered that I'd once asked David if things were ever going to get easier.

It seemed that they were.

———

Burrowing under the comforter to combat a particularly cold night, and feeling loose after the wine I'd had at dinner with Mack, I wondered what was taking David so long to join me. "Are you coming?" I sang, growing impatient.

"Where are you?" he called.

I pulled the comforter down a little so I could see him. All six-feet-four of him—long, lean, and gloriously naked. Even in my flannel pajamas, I shivered. "It's so cold."

I squealed when he jumped on the bed. He climbed under the sheets to cover me with his warmth, tucking my arms under his elbows and my legs between his.

"That's perfect," I exhaled, instantly cured. "Never leave."

"Deal."

I giggled when he bent his head and breathed hot air on my neck. I wanted to reach up and brush my hand through his soft hair, but he kept me securely pinned under his body. Up close, I could see every strand, and when I spotted something new, I grinned. "Are you getting gray hairs?"

"Probably," he grumbled, "considering what you've put me through the last few months."

I gaped at him, holding back a laugh. "You're blaming *me*?"

He kissed the underside of my jaw. "That's a resounding yes."

"Well, that's fine," I said, "because I actually find it quite distinguished and very sexy. Like really, super sexy."

"*Super* sexy, huh?" He moaned against my skin and continued trailing kisses wherever he could reach. Being restrained by his body, all I could do was squirm—and bite my bottom lip, which I instantly released since it was tender. I'd almost forgotten I'd made it bleed during our bedroom adventures the night before. "What's with all the flannel?" he asked, rising onto his hands and knees, tenting the comforter.

"It's winter, and you weren't here to keep me warm," I said defensively.

He began unbuttoning my pajama top, smiling like the scoundrel he was. His eyes grew hungry as he muttered to himself, "It's like opening a present."

I sighed happily and let my lids fall shut as my nipples hardened, anticipating David's mouth on them.

Until David's voice boomed through the room. "*Fuck.*"

My eyes flew open. "What?" I followed his gaze to a dark purple bruise forming on my chest in the spot where he'd bitten me the day before.

He sat back, and the comforter slid off his back. David pushed up my shirt, then yanked down my pants. "What the fuck?" His fingers gently spread my thighs, and I moved up on my elbows to see what he was looking at. He ran his hands over my hip and ushered me onto my side. "You are covered," he paused to inhale, "in *bruises*."

Ah. I hadn't even noticed, but it wasn't all that surprising. David and I had been going at it hard ever since we'd returned from Dallas. "They're no big deal," I said. "I can't even feel them."

"I was too rough with you yesterday," he said, staring at my legs.

"And I *loved* it," I said, looking him in the eye so he wouldn't get weird about this.

He raked a hand through his hair and looked away, clearly distraught.

"Hey," I said, trying to catch his gaze. "Look at me. I'm *fine*."

"Fine?" he asked, and I silently cursed myself for using what had apparently become a trigger word for us.

"Yes, I am," I said. "And I'm not just saying that. Frankly, I've never been happier."

It was an honest and big confession, but David didn't even hear it. His jawline flexed as he muttered something about Bill.

I instantly recoiled. "David, the marks he left behind came from anger. This is completely different. Remember what you said about us? It's all love."

He blinked his eyes to me then. "I'm so sorry. Seeing what Mark and Bill did to you, I lost my mind." He shook his head. "And now this? It won't happen again. You have my word."

Wait, what? That was the exact opposite answer I'd been hoping for. I scrambled to my knees and took his face in my hands. "You didn't hurt me," I said emphatically. "Sometimes we're loving. Sometimes we're rough. I would tell you if it was too much."

"You didn't last night, though." His eyes fell to my mouth. "You bit your lip bloody instead."

"I didn't stop you because I liked it," I said gently. "I trust you."

When he didn't respond, I hoped it was because he understood I meant every word. I fell back onto the bed and playfully nudged his thigh with my foot. "Now, come back here. We—"

"I can't." He pulled my pants back up. "Not tonight."

"David, sweetie," I said, putting my hand over his to stop him. "Don't do this. I want you."

"It's late," he murmured, doing up the buttons of my top. "You should sleep."

"Where are you going?" I asked.

"Office," he said, jumping off the bed and pulling on his sweatpants.

"What?" I asked. "You're going to leave me here, horny and alone? And cold?"

At the word *cold*, he paused, shifted on his bare feet, then took a step back. "The more I get done tonight, the more time I can spend with you tomorrow."

"Yeah, I'm not buying that." I rolled over onto my side and muttered something about blue balls.

The mattress gave when he climbed over me. "Don't pout, honeybee. I really do have work to do, but I'll be in soon." He kissed me on the cheek and then on the shoulder before disappearing.

David turned down *sex*? Couldn't he see that hurt more than a few bruises I hadn't even noticed? I wasn't cold anymore. Just angry. I kicked off my pajama pants and stripped out of the shirt. Maybe he'd find me naked, wake me up, and we could do it then, I reasoned. Despite him telling me not to pout, that's exactly what I did until I dozed off.

Chapter Twenty-Three

I didn't remember David coming to bed the night before, but in the morning, big arms clutched me from behind. I smiled, perfectly content to remain pinned against him while I waited for him to wake up, too, but he stirred soon after and sighed against my hair.

"The first time we woke up together, you jumped out of bed before I even had the chance to kiss you," he said. "It was total bullshit."

I laughed lightly and rubbed his arm. "If it's any consolation, I was dying for that kiss, too."

"It is."

I rolled my head back to take in his sleepy face. "Were you up late?"

He just nodded and shifted to kiss me. As it grew heated, I moaned into his mouth. He pulled back suddenly. When his eyes fell to the bruise on my chest, he released me and climbed out of the bed.

I groaned and moved onto my back, cursing my sex-battered body. This act was going to get old really fast. I decided to try convincing him it was nothing again and headed into the bathroom to find him brushing his teeth.

"I've got an issue," he said before I could speak. He spat into the sink and set down his toothbrush. "I spoke with my engineer yesterday and things are falling behind on my New York project. I've been away too long, and they took my absence as an excuse to fuck off. I need to make a trip."

"Oh." I wasn't thrilled about spending time apart, but I'd gotten almost all of his attention lately. "When?"

"I'm going to see if I can get a ticket this afternoon."

"*Today?*" I exclaimed. "David, Thanksgiving is tomorrow."

"I know, but this is important." He grabbed my robe off a hook and passed it over without looking at me. "Put this on."

"Why can't it wait until next week?" I asked, slipping into the robe, trying not to feel hurt.

"I let some shit slide for too long, and now it's catching up to me."

I knotted the sash at my waist. "Who's even working on Thanksgiving?"

"They will be," he said simply, "because they fucked up my schedule."

I gaped at him. "You can't be serious. You're going to fly in and out in one day?"

He turned his back to me. "Actually, I'll have to stay through the weekend."

What the hell? That made no sense. It was a holiday weekend, and nobody would be working. Not to mention we had plans. "Your sister's expecting us," I pointed out.

"She'll understand. You can still go without me."

"Of course I'm going," I said, bristling. "It would be rude not to."

"All right." He walked over and kissed the top of my head. "Come on, beautiful. Let's fix us something to eat."

As I followed him to the kitchen, it dawned on me. This had nothing to do with a fuck-up in New York. It was about David's perceived mistakes here in our bed. Would he seriously go all the way to New York to ensure he didn't hurt me again? "What about Miami with Gretchen and everyone?"

"I'll have to cancel with Brian," he said. "I'm really sorry. I know you were looking forward to it."

"But you already bought the tickets."

"They're just miles," he said, retrieving a mug from a cupboard.

He couldn't even look me in the eye. Something dark was definitely brewing in that head of his, and for once, he was the one trying to shut *me* out. But I wouldn't let him, just as he'd never let me. "This is about the marks, isn't it?"

He paused and let his hip fall against the counter. "I *am* needed in New York. If not for you, I would've been there almost the entire past two weeks." He scratched the back of his neck. "But the *bruises* do concern me."

"They're nothing to be concerned about," I said as patiently as I could.

"Maybe they don't hurt," he said. "But they're there because I lost control. Sometimes I'm so consumed with you, I . . ." He shoved a hand in his hair and shook his head. "I don't think straight. When I saw the evidence of that on your body, it hit me hard. I could go overboard, Olivia."

I crossed the kitchen and placed my hands on his chest. "I trust you. I'd be more concerned if you didn't lose yourself in me, and frankly, it hurts that you want to be away from me."

He set down his mug. His hands slid under my hair and

clasped around my neck. "You know I don't want that. But the only thing I want more than to be with you is to know you're safe."

"So why do you have to go away?" I asked. "Couldn't I meet you there on Friday?"

His hesitation was all the confirmation I needed. He *was* willing to put distance between us instead of hearing the truth. I slipped out of his grasp and walked out of the kitchen.

"Where are you going?" he called after me.

"Work."

"Olivia," he said, but I ignored him and headed for the shower.

The drive to work was predictably quiet as I agonized over what this could do to us. If David tried to throw cold water onto our sex life, where would that leave us?

When he pulled up to the curb, I kept my eyes down on my hands.

He leaned in and kissed my cheek. When I didn't respond, he said, "Come on. I know you're upset, but I need a better send-off than that. I won't see you for a few days."

"That's not my fault," I said.

After a moment of silence, he said, "Look. I'll think about changing your flight from Miami to New York on Friday, all right? I just need a night to myself to think through this. To get a clear head."

So it was okay for *him* to need space and figure this out without me? Maybe it was childish of me, but I wasn't going to go along with his plan. I tore my gaze from my lap and looked at him. "I'm going to Miami."

He drew back. "What?"

"If you want to throw away your ticket, that's fine. But I don't see why I should have to."

"Why would you want to go without me?" he asked.

"Because I was looking forward to it, and everyone else is going, and . . . and it wouldn't be fair to Gretchen if I ditched her."

And because I know you won't want me to go without you.

"Olivia, be reasonable," he said. "Don't just go because you're upset with me."

"I'm not."

"Yes, you are. You're picking a fight with me. Don't test me."

Don't test me . . .

It was turning out to be his favorite thing to say, and incidentally, in the wrong situation, something that pissed me off. "You can't order me around," I said. "I'm supposed to be your partner, not your plaything."

His eyes widened. "I *know* that. We are partners. And I'll take you to Miami whenever you want, but—"

"That's not the point," I said.

"Precisely. You don't even care about going, you just want to defy me."

"*Defy* you?" I gaped. "Are you my father? My babysitter?"

"The point is, because I need time to think and because I must work, I can't be there this weekend. I don't want you going."

"You always tell me not to run away," I said, unbuckling my seatbelt, "but that's exactly what you're doing. This sex thing is something we need to work out together."

"I agree," he said. "But I get so caught up in you—I don't . . . I don't trust myself right now. Going away means I can sort through this and keep my hands off you."

"Sort through it *alone*. Which is exactly what you told me not to do." I grabbed the door handle.

"Hang on, Olivia."

"No." I got out and slammed the door before he could convince me otherwise.

I flew by Jenny's desk and threw my things on the couch in my office.

How dare he? Does he think he can just order me around?

I sat at my desk and tried to work, but with every passing hour, I gradually admitted to myself that I'd intentionally pushed David's buttons. There was no part of me that wanted to go to Florida without him, but he needed to see that his guilt was baseless.

I sighed at my computer screen.

We were both wrong. He was running away from something he'd convinced himself was a problem, and I hadn't handled it well. Fighting with David was my least favorite pastime, so I broke down and sent him a text.

Me: *Can we talk? Been thinking lots. xo*

I felt instantly better as I went back to work. But once lunchtime had passed, and I still hadn't heard from him, I realized there was a chance he was already New York-bound. I hated the idea that he'd left while we were on bad terms, so I wrote him an e-mail.

David,

I'm sorry about this morning. I shouldn't have stormed off.
I know you're only being protective, but you can't treat me
like a possession. If I want to go to Miami, I will. That
said, I'd rather not be there without you. Gretchen will be
disappointed, and I am, too, but we can go another time.

Olivia Germaine
Senior Editor
Chicago Metropolitan Magazine
ChicagoMMag.com

In the late afternoon, my heart skipped happily when my
phone rang, and David's name flashed across the screen.
"Hi," I answered.

"Hi, beautiful," he said. "Thanks for the e-mail. Sorry
I haven't been able to reach out until now."

"I hate when we fight."

"Me, too. Listen, I had some time to think on the
plane. I was an ass about Miami. And I love to hear you
say you're mine, but in no way do I see you as a possession.
Just the woman I love and want to keep safe."

"I get that," I said, flicking a paperclip against my
thumbnail. "But I have my own life, David. And sometimes
you won't agree with my choices."

It took him a moment, but he said, "Noted." I thought I detected some hesitation, but that didn't surprise me. I'd been married five years and had learned how to compromise—as a long-time bachelor, David was just starting that journey.

"I know you were looking forward to Miami," David continued, "and so was I. I'm going to move some things around, and I'll meet you there—"

"Really?" I exclaimed.

"Yes, but not until Saturday morning. That way I can work late Friday to wrap things up."

"That's a lot of travel," I said before getting too excited. "You won't be too tired?"

"To see you? No. And I'll get to relax once I'm there. It's the best I can do." He said something away from the receiver, then to me, "I have to run. Anything else?"

I hesitated, not wanting to reopen a touchy subject but also worried about how he'd act when I saw him next. "What about the bruises?" I asked.

"We'll figure it out together when I see you."

"Thank you. I love you," I blurted and smiled. "And I miss you already."

"Miss you more, baby. I'll call you before bed."

I hung up feeling much better. We were back on the same page, *and* we'd get our weekend in the sun.

I'd never been alone in David's apartment for an extended period, and it would take some getting used to. I didn't like sleeping without him, and I told him so. His place was big, quiet, and unfamiliar. Without him, my nightmares crept back in. They weren't as jolting as they'd once been, but they still edged my sleep. And I could tell over the phone that it tore him apart to hear that.

I spent Thanksgiving morning writing, which made David ecstatic for some reason. I continued to do it because I enjoyed it and because I especially liked anything that made him that happy.

In the afternoon, I got ready to drive the Mercedes to his sister's place in Joliet for Thanksgiving dinner. I'd gotten a stern lesson from David about handling his baby, during which I'd painted my nails and made an occasional noise to indicate I was listening. So, I drove carefully, and it took me about forty-five minutes to get there, but I found Jessa's house easily—a two-story, traditional-style home with dark green shutters and a matching door.

Jessa came outside to greet me with a hug. Inside, there were obvious signs of a ten-year-old boy strewn around the house—toy trucks, athletic trophies, video games, well-worn tennis shoes.

"Sorry it's a mess," she said, even though things had been mostly put away.

"It's not," I said. "It's a home."

"That, it definitely is," she agreed.

It was just the three of us, as David's parents were on a cruise for the week. Jessa had promised a casual meal for that reason and had charged me with bringing a pumpkin pie.

She motioned that I should sit at the kitchen table as she finished cooking. "Excited for Florida tomorrow?"

"Oh, yes," I said. "I could use the beach time."

"Sounds nice." She took a bottle of red wine from her pantry. "Merlot all right?" she asked. "David said it's your favorite."

I smiled to myself. *David* was my favorite. David and his

bold mouth calling me *"full-bodied . . . with an aftertaste that sticks on my tongue."*

"Merlot's perfect," I told Jessa.

As she uncorked the bottle, Alex scurried into the kitchen looking for food.

"Say hello to Olivia," Jessa said, pouring two glasses.

"Hi," he said. "Where's Uncle David? Are you his girlfriend?"

I laughed, more out of surprise than anything. "You don't miss a thing, do you?"

"He misses *everything*," Jessa said under her breath. "But it's kind of impossible in this case considering David won't shut up about his new girlfriend."

I fought back a shy smile and answered Alex. "David had to work, but he sends his love and pumpkin pie," I said. "How're you feeling since your appendectomy?"

"Huh?"

"Your surgery, sweetie," Jessa said.

He shrugged. "Fine."

"I was more freaked out than he was," Jessa said. "He had these awful cramps, so I took him right to the hospital. Good thing, too, because they said his appendix almost burst."

"That sounds terrifying," I said and took a sip of wine.

She nodded. "Thank God for Uncle David. I was a mess. He told me he ran out on an important date with you, so thanks for letting us steal him for a night."

"Of *course*," I said. "Gosh. I'm just glad Alex is okay."

I did a double take when Alex narrowed his eyes at me. I was getting the feeling he didn't like me, but I always got that impression with kids. I remembered I'd told Lucy that once, and she'd assured me it was my imagination.

When Alex disappeared to play *Halo*, Jessa gave me a sly smile. "So," she said, drawing out the word. "David says he's hoping to start work on your guys' new house in the next couple weeks."

I set down my wineglass. "Wait, really? I didn't know that."

"Oh, shit. I hope he wasn't trying to surprise you." She laughed. "Whatever. You must be excited. Going to get in there and knock down some walls?"

After the way he and I had argued about him buying the house, I doubted he meant to surprise me. I nodded but bit my bottom lip.

Weeks? That soon? But why was I surprised? David moved at lightning speed when it came to me.

Jessa arched an eyebrow as she removed candied yams from the oven. "You seem nervous about that."

I shifted in my seat, wondering when I'd become such an open book. Or maybe reading minds was a Dylan family trait. "Those smell amazing," I said. "Where'd you get the recipe?"

"My mom. I'll give it to you," she said. "And nice try. In case you haven't figured it out, nobody in this family will let you change the subject."

I laughed into my Merlot. "That much is obvious." I sighed. "I'm excited about the house, I just didn't expect it so soon. It's a lot of money and a big commitment."

"Well, David's over the moon about it. I don't think he cares how much he spends." She slipped off her oven mitts and waved one around the kitchen. "He tried to fix up this place for me, but I told him not to bother. Alex would destroy it anyway."

I smiled as Alex yelled something from the other room.

"Ignore him, he's gaming," she explained, rolling her eyes.

"They're close, aren't they?" I asked. "David and Alex."

"Thankfully, yes. Alex's dad has a new family now, so they don't see each other much." She picked up her wine and glanced toward the door Alex had gone through. "Al looks up to David, even though I wish he was around more. He works a lot."

I nodded. "David's very passionate."

She snorted. "He's working on fucking Thanksgiving. But aside from that, he's great with Alex. He's completely devoted when he cares about something."

"I've, um, noticed," I said.

"Don't let his work schedule deter you, though."

"From what?" I asked.

"Once he slows down—and he's already starting to since he met you—he'll be a *great* father," she said and waggled her eyebrows.

"Oh."

Fuck. Shit.

It occurred to me for the first time that this whole children topic wouldn't just affect David and me, but his family, too. Did his parents expect more grandkids? How would they feel if I never came around to the idea? I wasn't sure I could bring myself to disappoint them.

Or David.

What did that mean for our future then? How far would I go to keep him, and, by extension, his wonderful family?

I cleared my throat. "I agree. So for the yams—"

"You've talked about it then?" Jessa asked. "Kids?"

My heart sank. I hadn't even had this conversation with David yet, but it didn't look like Jessa would let me off the hook. "Well, no, not really," I said. "It hasn't come up."

She inclined her head. "It *hasn't?*"

"No," I admitted. "Do you, um, think that's something David wants?"

"You should probably talk to him about that, not me." Jessa came to sit down next to me. "*But* I guess I brought it up, so . . ." She leaned in conspiratorially. "I don't think you need to worry. He hasn't mentioned starting a family with you yet, but I'd be shocked if he wasn't ready soon."

Soon. Oh, God.

Bits and pieces of past conversations with Bill pelted me like little bullets.

"When?" I asked. "What's soon to you?"

"I don't know. Six months?"

I stared at Jessa and made no move that might give me away.

"I need more time," I said.

"I'm ready now."

I whirled from the sink to face Bill. "Now?"

I couldn't believe I was already back in this place and with no clearer answers as to how to handle it.

Jessa laughed softly. "Aw, honey. Don't look so nervous," she said, rubbing my shoulder. "I know my brother can be a little stiff, but you've seen him with Alex. He'll loosen up. I don't think there's anything he wouldn't give you. Really, don't stress."

Panic settled in my chest. "I . . ."

She stopped rubbing my shoulder. "Oh my God," she said in a whisper. "Are you already pregnant?"

"*No*," I exclaimed. "Oh my God. No."

Her eyebrows knit. "Then what . . .?"

It wasn't something I'd really planned to discuss yet, not even with David. But Jessa looked so concerned. And in a way, although I knew it wasn't possible, she felt like a neutral party. With a kid of her own, and a divorce under her belt, she might even have advice in this area.

I waited until I had resumed air intake. "Bill wanted children," I said. "I didn't. It was a very contentious topic."

"Oh. I . . ." She exhaled as realization dawned. "Are you saying you still don't want them? Even with David?"

"I—I don't know, Jessa." I put my head in my hands. "I've barely had time to think about it—everything has been such a whirlwind. It seems too early to even bring it up." I peeked up at her. Her eyes glued to me, but she wore no expression, which I guessed was better than judgment or horror. "Did you have doubts before you had Alex?"

She shook her head. "No, sorry. I always knew I wanted kids, and if I ever marry again, I'll have more."

"Oh."

She chewed the inside of her cheek. "I'm sure it feels super confusing. I feel for you." She sat back. "But you have to have this conversation with him."

"I know I do," I said, looking away. "Things are still so new, though. I mean, in a way, we're still getting to know each other. It seems too soon."

And I don't want to lose him. I can't *lose him.*

"Olivia," she said, "my brother is *crazy* about you. It's definitely not too soon to bring it up." She leaned in to take my hand. "If you're as serious about him as he is about you, then you need to bring it up soon."

"I've never been more serious, not even with Bill," I promised her, and my heart squeezed. Kids? Already? Not weeks ago, I'd been having that same dreadful conversation with Bill. Didn't I get some time to adjust, to just *enjoy* what David and I were doing?

"You know, some women don't feel maternal at your age," she pointed out. "You might feel differently after you and David have been together a while."

I might, yes. Or, I might never feel the desire to have children. And then what?

I nodded and forced a smile because I didn't know what else to say. "You're right. I'm sure it'll be fine."

She opened her mouth and paused before speaking. "Raising a child is not easy, though. Don't . . . don't do it for the wrong reasons."

I swallowed dryly. If it was a dealbreaker for David, I wasn't sure I could make Jessa that promise.

"I won't say anything to him," Jessa continued. "But for your own peace of mind, you should talk to him soon. He's planning his whole life around you. He needs to know if kids aren't in the cards."

My gut ached with the truth in her words. With Bill, I guessed that I would've eventually caved on having children, whether or not that was what I wanted. I'd thought I'd owed it to him, and I knew, in the end, how hard he would've pushed to get his way.

But David would never push me. If I told him the truth about how I felt . . . he'd never ask me to go through with it. So that left only two options: David's sacrifice or mine.

Or the third option, of course. If neither of us was willing to give, then we'd have no choice but to go our separate ways.

Chapter Twenty-Four

I would've never thought spending a couple days without my boyfriend would be so hard. Even though Bill had traveled frequently for work, and at times might be gone for up to two weeks, I'd always managed fine. By Friday, missing David had made me frustrated, restless, and lonely. That was when I realized that not only was he my boyfriend and my exceptional love, but he'd also become my best friend.

Something had been weighing heavily on my mind, though, and I wanted to take care of it before I saw him next. He wouldn't be happy about it, but I wanted to do it for him most of all.

On my way to the airport to catch my flight to Miami, I stopped by Bill's office. Since I hadn't made an appointment, I wasn't sure he'd be there. But last year, he'd worked the day after Thanksgiving, so I took my chances.

I stopped in the doorway of his fancy leathery office. Our photo on the lake had disappeared from his desk, and he'd gelled his brown hair away from his face, a style I'd never seen him wear to work. "Hey."

His head snapped up, but he didn't look surprised.

"Olivia." He stood and straightened his tie. "What can I do for you?"

So formal after the way he'd humiliated me at my office. "A very friendly gentleman delivered divorce papers to me at work earlier this week."

He nodded. "I'm aware."

"You're filing on grounds of adultery?" I asked. "I was hoping we could go about this differently."

"Why?"

"That won't affect how much you get in the divorce, and you might still have to pay alimony."

"You've done your homework," he said, tilting his head. "Or maybe you have a lawyer already?"

I took a couple steps into the office, keeping my handbag at my side. "All I can think is that your intent is to embarrass me with a trial."

"It's not." He stuck his hands into his pockets. "My intent is to embarrass you both. David should be exposed for what he is."

"Bill, look." I went and sat in one of the cushy chairs in front of his big, wooden desk. "I'm not denying that what we did was awful, and that we're in the wrong. But it doesn't make sense for you to waste resources on this." I appealed to his logical side as he'd once done with me when my emotions had taken over. "Trust me, David has no problem shelling out whatever he has to. You're smart about money. Don't burn it just to watch me suffer."

"Well, shouldn't I get something out of all this?" he asked, throwing up his arms. "Chicago has this guy on a goddamn pedestal. If I don't get a trial, then I'm going to the press. He deserves to be outed as the homewrecker he is."

"We *all* wrecked this," I snapped. "You, me, and David. You share some of the blame, too."

His eyes narrowed on me. "If you want something from me, this isn't the way to get it."

"I'm sick of both of you acting like little boys fighting over a toy," I said and pursed my lips. "It was my decision to make—not his, not yours. David has the money to fight back in ways that could devastate you, and if you try to hurt him, I won't stop him from trying."

"Jesus." Bill scoffed. "You have an affair for months, lie about it, call Lucy's sister nasty names, and now you're threatening me? I don't even know you anymore."

The truth was, he never really had—not the whole me. He'd chosen to accept the parts that suited him and ignore what didn't. And David had shown me that was no way for either Bill or me to live. "I want you to drop the adultery charge," I said. "And I want the divorce in six months instead of two years."

"Why would I agree to that?" he asked. "So you can run off and marry him?"

"I'm trying to protect you, Bill," I said. "I don't want to drag this out. It's not healthy emotionally or financially. I want us all to move on."

"Move on?" he asked, rounding the desk with his brows furrowed. "It's only been *weeks*." He stopped a few feet away, looking down at me. "Well, weeks for me. But I guess you've been planning this for a while."

"You know that's not true," I said. "This is all new to me, too."

He blew out a sigh, glancing out his office window. "What's messed up is that even with what you did, *I* could still, somehow, get stuck paying alimony."

That was true, unfair as it was. But I could prevent it. All I had to do was let go of the things that scared me and trust in the decisions I'd made. David's love had done something to me. In the little time we'd spent together, he'd proven his love was real and that I not only had it . . . I deserved it.

There was no victim here, and no villain, either. Bill and I had both made mistakes that caused us suffering. "I've put you through a lot," I said, "and I'm sorry. I really am. But I think one day you'll see that this isn't all my fault."

"I don't think—"

"If you agree to the six months, I'll waive the right to alimony," I said. "Not only that, but you can keep the car and everything you didn't throw in those boxes. All I want is what I contributed to the savings account."

"Are you crazy?" he asked. "Your contributions are measly compared to what you could get in alimony. Why would you do that?"

I picked at my fingernail. "I have my reasons."

Bill's eyebrows rose. "He put you up to this?"

"It's my decision," I said.

"Your share isn't even enough for legal fees—or anything really."

"I know."

His tongue shot into his cheek as he thought. "So I just get . . . everything else?"

"Yes. I'm asking you this final favor. For me," I pleaded. "If you ever loved me . . . let me go."

I read the pity in his eyes clearly. He was thinking that David would leave me with nothing. He knew, as a lawyer, the risk I was taking, and I'd figured he'd try to talk me out of it. But he didn't.

"All right," he said slowly. "If I'm completely exempt from alimony, I'll agree to six months. But I have a condition."

I folded my hands in my lap. "Okay," I prompted.

Hesitation crossed his face, but it was fleeting. "Beyond

the divorce proceedings, you and I no longer have any contact whatsoever."

And just like that, in a matter of weeks, our relationship had come to its abrupt end. It had never occurred to me that Bill would one day be just a memory. Something that had happened but was no longer. And that one day, the years I'd given him would seem like so little time.

Bill's request only came from anger and hurt, but, regardless, he was right. It would be easiest to make as clean a split as possible. I looked at him with sadness and regret—not for losing him but for the pain I'd caused him. I now knew that we were wrong for each other, but it didn't change the fact that we had loved each other. And I didn't want to hurt him anymore. For that, I knew the only way to make things right was to cut him free. So I said, "Agreed."

Gretchen, Greg, Brian, and his new girlfriend had all been in Florida since the day before, so they were already settled into Brian's parents' house by the time I arrived. Just outside Miami, the four-bedroom place on the water comfortably fit the group of us. Brian showed me to a room upstairs. We had plans for a sunset dinner, so I dropped my things and changed into a navy shift dress and knee-high brown boots.

As I curled my hair, Gretchen knocked and poked her head into the bathroom. "Ready yet?" she asked.

"Almost, but can you curl the back of my hair?"

She assumed the position behind me to fix the pieces I'd missed. "So," she started, "I have something to tell you that you're not going to like."

I sighed. That sounded about right. "Already? I just got here."

"Sorry." She twisted her lips, focused on the curling iron. "Apparently, Greg still keeps in touch with your ex, Jordan."

Jordan Banks. My first real boyfriend, to whom I'd also lost my virginity. "I didn't know that, but it makes sense," I said. "Greg introduced us freshman year."

"Well, Jordan lives in Miami now," Gretchen said, and met my eyes in the bathroom mirror.

"Gretchen," I warned. "Please don't tell me Greg invited him tonight."

She cringed. "I told him to undo it, but he's bitching about how rude it would be to disinvite him."

"Ugh," I said, glancing at the ceiling. "David *won't* like me having dinner with my ex-boyfriend."

"I know." She nodded. "I tried to tell Greg he'd have David to answer to, but it's like he's making up for lost time or something. Greg thinks us hanging out will be like 'the good old days,' which, by the way, is his favorite phrase as of late, and I *swear* if I hear it one more time, I'm going to strangle him."

I was beginning to think Greg had less desire to atone for the past and more desire to *recreate* it. Could he be stuck in "the good old days" with a case of Peter Pan syndrome?

"Well, Greg just has to be an adult and cancel," I said resolutely.

"Jordan's already on his way," she informed me. "Sorry, girl. I won't tell David if you won't."

"You're delusional if you think he won't find out," I said to her reflection. "The man knows *everything*."

"Deal with it tomorrow?" she suggested.

"I guess." Seemed as if it was already time for me to back up my speech about letting me make my own choices.

"If I were still with Bill, I wouldn't even think twice about it."

"Seriously. It's been years—it's just a simple reunion, not a set-up," she said. "So did you meet Brian's new girl-friend or whatever she is?"

"No, how is she?"

"Kind of quiet from what I can tell." She set down the curling iron and half-rolled her eyes. "We haven't exactly been chumming it up, the group of us."

"Sorry David and I left you hanging last night," I said.

"No worries." She plucked at my curls and drew back to study her work, then gasped as my earrings caught the light. "Whoa. I've never seen these before."

I smiled slyly. "A gift."

"So let me get this straight—David's gorgeous, sexy, romantic . . . *and* he buys you expensive things?" She sighed wistfully. "You must be a tiger in the sack."

I laughed. "All evidence points to yes."

"There must be something wrong with him," she said.

"Well, he can't really cook," I offered with a shrug. "Although he tries with breakfast food, which is nice. And . . ." I hesitated, fixing my watch on my wrist. "He can be a little possessive."

"So I noticed. And kind of controlling, Liv." She walked around to perch on the counter in front of me. "Is that something I should be worried about?"

"We're working through it," I said. "Ultimately, he means well, and I like that he's so into me. I'll take him being a little overbearing when he makes me this sublimely happy."

"Make sense . . . lucky bitch," she said with a giggle.

"Greg made you that happy once," I pointed out. "Doesn't he still?"

"Sure." She reached out to pick a strand of my hair off

my shoulder. "I think this weekend away will be good for us, though."

"How come?"

"You know how it is in the city," she said, looking to one side. "Work, cramped spaces, stressful commute. It's a lot for a new relationship."

"Is everything all right?" I asked.

"Yeah, of course. I'm getting what I didn't realize I still wanted. All this time I never stopped thinking about Greg. So, yeah, I'm glad he finally came around."

"Okay." I nodded, trying to determine if that was the whole truth. "But it's perfectly fine to change your mind about him, too. You know that, right?"

"I know." She linked her elbow with mine, her blue eyes shining. "Let's chow down."

I grabbed my purse, and we went downstairs. Brian introduced us to his girlfriend, Kat, who had waist-length brown hair and squeaked like a mouse when I shook her hand.

To enjoy the temperate night, we walked the few blocks to the restaurant. The moment we entered, Greg yelled across the restaurant to Jordan, who was seated at the bar. I hadn't given Greg a thorough lashing yet, mainly because I hadn't had a chance. And I knew David would get to it himself.

As soon as Jordan's eyes locked on me, he grinned and stood from his barstool. "Hey, you," he said and wrapped me in a hug. "Long time."

"Hi, Jordan." He and I had dated on-and-off my first two years of college. After he'd dumped me for good, we'd remained distant friends because of Greg. Even though it'd been years, I still got a few butterflies seeing the first boy I'd loved. With dark blond hair and green eyes, he was solid and tall, but nowhere near David's towering frame. He'd always been good-looking, but he'd known it.

I remembered Jordan as a bit more straight-edge, a bit of stability during a fresh start at school, but now, a tattoo peeked out from his sleeve. "That's new."

"Yeah. You like it?" He placed his hand on my shoulder and guided me over to the table where a hostess seated the others. "You look great, Livvy," he whispered as he pulled out my chair and then sat down next to me.

Brian cleared his throat from one end of the table, giving Jordan a once-over. "I don't think we've met," he said.

"Jordan, meet Brian," Greg said. "J's an old friend of ours from college."

"Aha." Brian's eyes darted between Jordan and me, and he scratched the back of his head. "Nobody told me we had a sixth."

"Greg's fault," I said, shooting Greg a daggered look that he ignored.

We promptly ordered a few bottles of wine. As Brian lamented about the day's poor surf conditions, Jordan leaned over to me. "Greg told me about Bill. Sorry to hear it," he said, but he smirked.

"*Are* you?" I asked.

Jordan grabbed a bottle of white wine from the center of the table and poured me a glass. "Not really. You got me."

"Jordan," I admonished.

"No, I'm just messing," he said, raising his glass. "Divorce is rough, babe. Or so I've heard."

"It is, but I have someone to help me through it."

"Gretchen?" he asked with a playful waggle of his eyebrows.

"No," I replied and *clinked* his glass with mine. "My amazing boyfriend. Did Greg mention him?"

"Yeah. I'm glad Greg invited me tonight," he said, ignoring the topic.

I sipped my wine and looked into the glass. Chardonnay. *Great.* That made me miss David's company all the more. "Why's that?" I asked.

"Just because," Jordan said. "Haven't seen you since graduation. We get to catch up."

I nodded but narrowed my eyes at him in warning.

Since David and I were the reason the group had come together, I did my best to keep the conversation flowing. Greg, Gretchen, Jordan, and I reminisced about college, memories that came easier the more we drank. Whereas Gretchen and I got giddier as we drank, Greg and Jordan seemed to get more nostalgic. The way they grasped at a long-gone past only made me more grateful my present was as close to perfect as ever.

When Jordan excused himself to the bathroom, Greg leaned over Gretchen's lap to get my attention. "So?" he asked just above a whisper. "Jordan?"

"Jordan what?" I asked.

"You guys seem to be getting along."

I raised my eyebrows. "Yeah. And?"

"I'm just saying." Greg grinned. "How awesome would it be if you guys got back together now that you're single again? It'd be like the good old d—"

"Don't fucking say 'good old days' one more time," Gretchen interrupted. "And what the hell are you even talking about? Liv isn't single."

"You know what I mean." He jutted his chin at me. "She's no longer hitched."

I glanced at Brian, who was thankfully preoccupied with his date. I didn't need him relaying any of this to

David and getting him riled up from twelve-hundred miles away. "Did you set this up on purpose?" I asked Greg.

He shrugged. "I just think it would be cool."

Gretchen grimaced and beat me to my response. "You're a dick."

He glanced at her. "Why, babe? I thought you'd be into it."

"Because I'm with David," I said.

Gretchen just shook her head and gave me an apologetic look.

Greg leaned back into his seat, but not before he said to me, "Think about it."

The waiter arrived with our meals, and as he distributed them, I studied Greg. We'd been best friends in college. I'd enjoyed getting to know him again, but the bond we'd had before didn't seem to exist anymore. Gretchen was right—he was a dick. Maybe he always had been. Inviting Jordan with the assumption that he could lure me away from David made me mildly sick to my stomach.

I wasn't the only one watching Greg. At first, I assumed Brian's thoughts were also on protecting his friend David as he stared at Greg over his glass of wine—until his eyes shifted to Gretchen. Did I detect a hint of jealousy in them? I forked a bite of salmon and decided to ask her later if she'd ever give Brian another chance.

"So, Jordan," Gretchen said, "seeing anyone special these days?"

"I see some special girls at this table right now," he said, glancing between the two of us.

"Well, hands off, chap, they're all spoken for," Brian said, and his usually jovial tone held an edge of warning.

"I know, dude," Jordan replied. "I'm messing around." But he was giving me his best fuck-me eyes, and he had been all night. Flirtatious by nature, but not afraid to go for what he wanted—it was what'd drawn me to him in the first place. I silently thanked the universe that I had David and wouldn't have to make up an excuse to shake Jordan later.

Jordan lowered his voice. "So, is it serious with this new guy?"

"Yes." I nodded, biting off the tip of an asparagus spear. "*Very*."

"And where, pray tell, is he tonight?" he asked.

"New York for work." I inclined forward as if to tell him a secret. "He gets here in the morning."

"Ah, interesting," Jordan said.

I turned to Brian's new girlfriend, who I'd almost forgotten was here, and asked her what she did for a living. Her voice was so soft that I could barely hear her response. I just nodded and took another bite until she stopped talking.

Gretchen leaned over a moment later and whispered, "What's with her? She's creepy."

"She is *not*, Gretch," I said. "Maybe a little shy."

"She's barely said a word. Which is probably why Brian likes her," Gretchen reasoned. "She won't complain when all he talks about is himself."

"Be nice," I scolded but stifled a laugh.

"Do you think she's cute?" Gretchen asked.

"Yes." I arched an eyebrow. Perhaps the jealousy I thought I'd seen in Brian ran both ways. "Why?"

"She's all right, I guess," she said and then sat back and kissed Greg on the cheek.

I wondered if Brian had heard her, since he made a fist around his fork. His eyes quickly shifted to me, and he smiled. I smiled back. Regardless of Gretchen's opinions, I liked Brian, and I could tell that he was watching out for me in David's absence.

"More wine?" Jordan asked, positioning the mouth of the bottle over my glass.

"I shouldn't."

"Come on."

"No," I said. "I think I'm good."

"Aw, Livvy," he sang, the way he used to when he was trying to convince me of something.

"Jordan," I replied in the same voice, shaking my head.

He put the chardonnay down and his eyes drifted to my neck. "Did I tell you how pretty you look tonight?"

"Why are you looking at me like that?" I asked.

"I was just thinking about us. You know." He shrugged. "We have a long history."

"History, yes," I said. "Future, no."

He laughed a little, then stuck out his bottom lip. "I'm not a kid anymore. I was stupid to let a girl like you get away. I'm happy to hear this Bill guy's out of the picture."

"How can you say that?" I asked at his offhand comment when the last several months had been anything but easy. "That was my marriage."

"Candidly . . . because it gives me a second chance," he said.

"It doesn't, though," I said, folding my napkin in my lap. "I told you. I have a boyfriend."

"Who's in New York," he pointed out. "So, maybe you and I could, you know, get a drink after this. Without the others."

I stared at Jordan a second. The idea was so ridiculous that it fizzled my anger, and I burst out laughing.

His expression fell. "What's the big deal? You cheated on Bill, didn't you?"

My laugh vanished with his proverbial gut punch. So because I'd done it to Bill, I would to David? Jordan's interest had just gone from harmless to insulting. "The big deal is that my boyfriend is ten times the man you ever were."

"Aw, Liv, come on," Jordan said. "You don't even know me anymore."

"I don't need to," I said. "Sorry, *babe*."

Jordan inclined farther toward me, and I realized I'd slid to the opposite edge of my seat. "Think about it," he said. "We make perfect sense. We were college sweethearts."

"There's literally nothing you can say to convince me," I told him. "So you can back off. I'm totally and completely taken. I might as well be—"

"Olivia," I heard behind me.

I whipped around at the endlessly deep voice that made my heart soar. David stood over me, arms crossed, wearing an expensive suit and a hard gaze. Just his tone alone was enough to quiet the table.

I jumped up and threw my arms around his neck. "What are you doing here?"

"Who's this?" Jordan asked behind me.

"Boyfriend," David bit out. "Who the fuck are you?"

Since David was still as a statue, I drew back. "You came early," I said as my shock melted into a big smile.

"Who is this guy?" David responded, nodding over my head.

"It's Jordan Banks, my—"

"Jordan? Ex-boyfriend Jordan?" David clipped. His nostrils flared and his gaze cut across the table. "Brian?"

"Sorry, mate," Brian said. "I didn't know until I got here, and they told me he was just a friend."

"Mate?" Gretchen uttered under her breath. "Is he Australian now?"

David's eyes met mine. "Outside. Now."

"Is there a problem, Liv?" Jordan asked.

"No," David answered for me. "And I'd advise you to keep your mouth shut."

Before leaving the table, I turned back to Jordan. "Ten times," I reminded him. "I mean it."

Outside, I shivered despite a much nicer evening than it would've been in Chicago right now.

"We're apart a couple nights, and you're having dinner with your ex?" David started.

"It's not like that," I said, rubbing my hands over my sleeved arms. "Greg has some twisted idea about recreating the past, and he invited Jordan without telling anyone."

"You didn't know he'd be here?"

"No, baby. I swear. I'm totally uncomfortable with this. Trust me?"

David pressed the bridge of his nose between his thumb and index finger. "Yes. I trust you, and I trust this," he said, motioning between us. "It's everyone else I don't trust. And I don't like the way he was leaning on you."

I didn't love it, either, if I was honest, so I remained quiet.

He cocked his head. "Why aren't you arguing with me?"

"Because you're right."

He frowned. "Excuse me?"

"You're right. I was clear that I have a boyfriend, but Jordan won't back off. He seems to think because I cheated on Bill that I'd . . ."

"Are you *fucking* kidding me?" David asked, shoulders tensing. "He said that?"

"Not outright." I put my hand on David's forearm. "But I'm trusting you not to explode. If you freak out every time I confide in you about something I know you won't like, I'm going to stop." I slid my hand up his biceps until he visibly relaxed. "It doesn't matter to me. I see right through his garbage. He's no threat to you. Nobody is."

David's eyebrows knit. "Since when do you like tattoos?"

I laughed. "I don't."

The look on his face betrayed his skepticism. "What does 'ten times' mean?"

My shoulders eased as David began to thaw. "I told him my boyfriend is ten times the man he is."

David looked me up and down. "Ten times, huh? Did you use a ruler to figure that out?"

I blushed and glanced at the ground. "I didn't have to. You're ten times any man I've ever been with." When I looked back, a silly grin spread across David's face. I arched an eyebrow at him. "Don't act as if you don't know you have a huge cock."

He laughed his surprise and then leaned into me, taking my entire jaw in one big hand. "What a dirty mouth you have, Miss Germaine." Finally, he kissed me. "I might have to spank you for that one."

I wriggled, smiled, and hugged his neck. "I'm so happy you're here."

He let go of my face, and his arms surrounded my waist. "You look beautiful. Too beautiful to be out without me." He ran his hand over my hair. "You're cold."

"I'm getting warmer, sexy."

He laughed. "Feisty tonight?"

"Very. I'm just glad I don't have to spend another night alone." I batted my lashes. "What are you doing here?"

"I wanted to surprise you, so Brian told me where you guys would be. What he failed to mention was that you already had a date."

I laughed. "Poor Brian had no idea, but he was keeping an eye on Jordan. You have a good friend there."

"Speaking of, you say that Greg orchestrated this?" David asked.

I nodded as my smile fell. "I understand if you're pissed. I am."

"Damn right I'm pissed, and I'll tell him next chance I get. I don't like that shit."

"All right." I took his hand. "Come on, and help me finish my dinner."

"I'm not sitting next to that tattooed asshole."

"Don't whine," I said, leading him back inside. The group was already settling the bill so David took my seat, and I perched on his knee.

"Did you eat?" I asked, nodding at my dinner. "Because I'm full."

"I ate on the plane," he said right before making short work of cleaning my plate. With his last bite, he picked up the bottle of chardonnay between Jordan and me to inspect the label. "What is this garbage?"

"Jordan picked it," I said.

Jordan frowned. "I mean, it's just your basic house wine . . ."

"Yeah," David said, setting the bottle aside. He thrust my glass away as if it'd offended him. "Not in my house."

I giggled as David winked at me, and the others just looked confused.

"Well, I'm going to take off," Jordan announced. "Got plans tonight."

I wasn't surprised Jordan didn't want to stay, as David literally used his large body to block him off from the rest of the table.

Even though he'd irritated me, he was harmless, and he was still my friend. Or he had been once. I tried to get up and hug him good-bye, but David's arm tightened around my waist, securing me to his knee.

"Well, bye," I said.

Jordan stood awkwardly for a moment. "Okay, then. Have a good weekend, guys."

"Ready to rip tomorrow, Bri?" David asked Brian, ignoring Jordan as he waited a moment and then left.

"I don't know, man," Brian said. "Waves are looking a little bleak. We'll give it a go, though. Greg?"

"I might just hang back with the girls." Greg looked over at David. "I had a two-hour phone call with planning and zoning officials today. Feeling like a zombie."

David rubbed my knee as he asked Greg, "You invite that guy Jordan?"

Greg cleared his throat. "Ah, yeah. We're old friends."

"Not now, honey," I said near David's ear.

He glanced around the table, then at Greg. "We're going to chat tomorrow."

"Maybe *we girls* want to go surfing," I said to dispel the awkward silence.

"Do you, baby? I'll take you," David decided before I could respond. "Brian and I are going to hit the line-up pretty early, but mid-morning should be good for beginners."

"How about you, little lady?" Brian asked.

"I'm in," Gretchen exclaimed and then reddened when she realized he was talking to his date. Kat only shook her head.

"We'd better get some rest then," David said to me.

I clasped the big, rough hand moving back-and-forth on my leg and whispered back to him, "Don't count on it."

On the way back to the house, we fell into couples. "I know I said it already, but I missed you," I told David as we walked hand in hand.

"Me, too." He passed his thumb over my knuckles. "Baffling how we went all those months away from each other."

I snuck my arm across his lower back. "You must be tired," I murmured, snuggling into him.

"Yes, and I didn't even get everything done."

"I'm sorry," I said, because it sounded like an admonishment.

"I'm not," he said softly and stopped walking. I looked up at him as we stood still. "Everything is better when I can look into your eyes. That's what I realized being away from you." He touched my cheek. "They're the most beautiful shade of green. They're the first reason I fell in love with you."

Warmth spread through my body, and I wrapped my arms more tightly around his waist. David could be so rough with me sometimes. In the beginning, I never would've believed he could also be endlessly romantic. "What did you see that first night at the theater?" I whispered.

"Hmm?"

"At the ballet when our eyes met. What did you see?"

"I just saw you. Clear. Raw. I felt like I was witnessing something I shouldn't be. I've often wondered what you were thinking in that moment that you'd let me see inside you like that. Ironic, because for months after, you tried admirably to shut me out like everyone else."

I closed my eyes and smiled as I remembered the night that changed everything. "I was with Bill, Lucy, Andrew, and Gretchen. The performance was so beautiful, wasn't it? I remember thinking how much I loved it, and how I wished life was that perfect and flawless. I didn't know that it's not supposed to be that way," I said, my voice suddenly hitching. "That a messy life can still be beautiful." David raked a hand through my hair, soothing me. "I was thinking about how, even in a room full of people, I could still feel so alone. That's the last thought I remember before I saw you."

"You let someone in before you could stop yourself. You let *me* in," he murmured. He pressed his lips to mine, and my body reacted instantly, melting into him. "I hate to think what would've happened to you if we hadn't found each other," he said.

"I had a good life, David. I never would've known anything else."

"I can't think of anything worse than nobody loving you as much as I do."

My heart throbbed painfully with his words. I didn't know what I'd done to deserve him, to deserve words like those from his mouth, but I promised to be good every day of my life to keep him.

He took my hand again, and we continued walking. At the house, he grabbed his bag from where he'd left it on the back porch. Though the rest of our group had already cracked open a round of beers in the kitchen, David and I said goodnight and went upstairs.

In the hallway, he dropped his bag with a loud *thud* and embraced me, dipping me slightly for a kiss. My arms automatically went around his neck. I was happy to know, and feel, that despite his fear of hurting me during sex, his desire hadn't waned in the slightest. But I had yet to see if he'd still be able to let go with me.

With a low moan, he deepened the kiss while fumbling with the door to our room. I heard him kick his bag in without slowing the pace of our kiss. He backed me into the nearest wall before slamming the door shut with his foot. "I need you," he growled between breaths. "It's been too many days."

"I tried to warn you," I whispered back.

His lips devoured mine greedily as he pulled me away from the wall and closer to his body. He tugged the hem of my dress up around my waist as my hands plunged into his hair. His fingers hooked into my thong, and it dropped around my boots. I kicked it away, and his hands slid under my ass. He pried my cheeks apart while pulling me against him, inspiring a feverish heat between my legs.

His fingers found me wet, and I shivered against him when they massaged me. He slid two in slowly from behind, pulling out every few seconds to fondle my clit.

I writhed against him as his other hand wrapped around my shoulders and under my hair to hold me still.

"I want to be buried deep inside you where I belong," he said into my mouth.

His fingers continued to leisurely probe into me as I hastily undid his pants. My impatient hands found him impossibly hard, and he sucked in a breath with my touch. I stepped back to tug his pants and underwear down, and when he squeezed me back to him, his erection dug into my stomach.

When his hand withdrew, I hopped up suddenly so he had to catch me. He smiled into my mouth right before I sank onto him, and we effortlessly came together. Frozen, we adjusted to each other, exchanging charged breaths. My arms and legs wrapped tighter around him, and I moaned from the way he completely possessed me. His hand ran up my back and gathered my hair before pulling lightly. I drew back from his mouth to look at him.

He didn't say anything, just looked into my eyes as we stood, immobilized by the overwhelming connection. There were no words so we remained that way, breathing and kissing and feeling each other. We were so lost that once we started to move, it didn't take long for each of us to climax. I held on to him as my orgasm swelled through me like my love for him: steadily, no end, no beginning. He rested my back against the wall right before he came with shuddering intensity, pulling my hair gently and groaning against my neck.

Later, I fell asleep with him hugging me so tightly, he was almost crushing me. I didn't ever want it any other way.

Chapter Twenty-Five

At some ungodly hour of the morning, David shuffled around the room as light began to filter through a window. I threw an elbow over my eyes with a groan. "What time is it?" I asked.

"Surfing time. Sorry, baby." The mattress dipped, and I lifted my arm. He climbed on top of me in only his board shorts and kissed his way up my neck until he reached my mouth. "Smell that ocean breeze?" he asked.

I smiled sleepily with closed eyes. "Mmm."

He laughed. "Go back to sleep. I'll be done in a few hours." And then he was gone, so I rolled over and pulled his pillow between my arms.

I woke up later to a knock at the door. "Who is it?" I asked, slightly disoriented.

"Me." In that one word, I heard Gretchen's voice crack.

I sat up quickly and grabbed David's undershirt from the floor. "Come in," I said, throwing it over my head.

She entered with a red face, lifting her eyeglasses to rub her eyes. "Hey."

"What's wrong?" I exclaimed.

She climbed onto the bed to sit cross-legged in front of me and took a shaky breath as if holding back sobs. "He's gone," she said.

Greg. That fucker. "What happened?" I asked.

She shook her head, and once her shoulders had stopped quaking, she continued, "I don't know. When we went to bed last night, we were fooling around, and he wanted to have sex. I wanted to also—we haven't done it yet, and it's been months. But I couldn't bring myself to, Liv. I don't know why. I said no, and he got pushy."

My teeth ground together. "He got *pushy*?"

"Enough for me to kick him out of the room. This morning, I heard a commotion, so I went downstairs. David and Greg were face to face, arguing about Jordan."

My heart dropped. David wasn't known for controlling his temper. "Oh, no. Please don't tell me they got into a fight."

"They didn't," she said. "But seeing Greg standing there, waiting for me to defend him, I just . . . I don't know. I didn't feel any sympathy or like we were on the same side. So I said, 'David's right. You were out of line.' Greg called me a frigid bitch, and before I even had a chance to respond, *Brian* appeared out of nowhere and grabbed him by the shirt!"

My mouth hung open. "Brian defended you?"

She nodded quickly. "He shoved him into the refrigerator. Greg said, 'Fuck it,' gathered up his stuff from the couch, and left. Just left." She looked like she was about to laugh, but she burst into tears instead.

"Jesus." I scooted close enough to embrace her. "Have you been crying all morning?"

"Yes, but I'm not even sure why."

I pulled back to look her in the eye. "What do you mean?"

"Greg wants everything to go back to the way it was, but . . . it can't." She looked at me. "He acts like you and Lucy are still his best friends."

"Me? I've barely seen him since he moved to Chicago."

"I know," she exclaimed, "and he's only seen Lucy once!" She pulled her glasses away and rubbed her eyes again. "I don't know. The fact that he left without talking to me makes me wonder if he's changed at all."

Thinking back over the past twenty-four hours, I didn't have to wonder long. "He hasn't. I'm so sorry."

She sighed, wiped away another tear, and looked around the room. "Gross. I'm sitting right where you guys had sex last night."

"*Pfft*. No, you're not." I grinned. "We didn't even make it to the bed."

She made a strangled noise, and her face crumpled. "Even fooling around with Greg wasn't that great. I remembered it better."

As the words left her mouth, loud footsteps ran up the stairs.

"Crap," she said and stood. "They're probably back from surfing."

"Don't go," I said.

"I'm a mess." She straightened her shoulders, tugging at her pajama top. "I need to change."

David started through the door, wet and shirtless, then stopped. "Hey," he said.

"How was surfing?" I asked.

"Good, fine." His eyes drifted between us. "Everything all right?"

Gretchen dropped her face in her hands and shuddered with her back to the door.

"Yes," I said, "but can you just give us a minute?"

Brian appeared behind David and peered in. "Gretchen," he said softly.

"Just go away, Brian," Gretchen muffled from her hands.

He ignored her and pushed David aside to enter the room. My mouth fell open when Brian took her arm, pulled her off the bed, and wrapped his arms around her. "He's not worth it."

Gretchen stilled, and I was afraid she'd push him off, but instead, she moved into his chest and unleashed a fresh set of tears.

I glanced at David and mouthed, "*Oh my God.*"

He shrugged.

"You guys ganged up on him," Gretchen said into Brian's chest.

David crossed his arms over his chest, and his expression hardened. "He crossed a line."

"But he was right," she continued. "I was frigid not to sleep with him and a bitch not to defend him."

"*Hey!*" Brian cried as if offended. He lifted her chin with his finger and looked down at her. "That's a load of shit. He was disrespectful to David and Olivia and to you. You were right not to defend him."

"He's a coward," David said, still near the doorway.

"And a chump," Brian added.

Gretchen laughed softly and pulled away from Brian. She removed her glasses and wiped her cheeks with the backs of her hands. "I'm sorry. This is embarrassing."

"I didn't know you wore glasses," Brian commented.

"Contacts," she said, nodding. "Usually."

His eyes darted over her as she cleaned her glasses on her t-shirt. She was red and puffy, but her eyes shone blue. Just like Brian's. It struck me then how similar looking they were. Soft blond hair, tan complexions, and striking, Windex-colored eyes. How had I never noticed before?

"How about a surf lesson?" Brian asked her. "David's taking Olivia. I can take you."

"What about your girlfriend?" she asked with a sniffle.

"She doesn't want to get wet." Brian shrugged. "Go figure, we're at the beach."

"I've taken lessons before, but . . ." She looked at the floor. "Sure. I guess."

"Atta girl," Brian said. "Go put on your bathing suit, and I'll meet you downstairs in ten."

She smiled with her eyes still downcast and nodded before leaving the room.

"Thank you, Brian," I said. "I know you two don't get along, so I really appreciate that."

"No worries," he said, then added to himself, "She's not so bad underneath it all."

I arched an eyebrow. "What was that?" I asked.

He looked up. "Nothing," he called over his shoulder as he left.

David sighed and finally entered the room. "I say good riddance."

I rolled my eyes. "Did you wake Greg up from the couch just to yell at him?"

"Yep."

"Do you feel macho now that you've put him in his place?"

I expected David to defend himself, but his chest just puffed up. "Yep."

I laughed.

"Brian likes her, you know," he said. "I can tell."

"Gretchen?" I crinkled my nose. "I was wondering if he might, but she made a pass at him a while back, and he turned her down."

"Trust me," David said, running a hand through his damp hair. "He's into her."

"They act like they hate each other," I said.

"There's a fine line between love and hate, baby," he said, rifling through his bag. "And she likes him, too."

"Now *that* is definitely not true," I said. "I believe 'pompous prick' is how she once described him."

"You and your dirty mouth again, Miss Germaine." He glanced up from where he squatted. "I never did give you that spanking."

My eyes widened. "Give it to me now, then."

"No, not now." He pulled out a fresh change of clothes. "We still need to talk. You seduced me into forgetting that I was supposed to be restraining myself."

"So, let's talk."

He stood, shut the bedroom door, and came to sit on the edge of the bed. "Here's the thing, though," he said. "I don't have an answer."

"I do." I crawled over and set my hands on his damp swim trunks. "There's nothing to worry about. I meant what I said. I trust you, and I promise to tell you if it's too much. Maybe I should've said something the other night, but I was confused because I liked what you were doing to me . . . even though it hurt a little."

"I don't want to hurt you," he said earnestly.

"Your pleasure turns me on—you taking what you need from me drives me wild." I bit my lip. "I love knowing I can give you that."

"Only you."

I nodded. "You won't go overboard because you know, and always have known, exactly what I need. But I promise, if you ever do, I'll tell you."

"All you have to do is say 'stop,' and I will, no matter

what." His brows furrowed. "I'll never get so far that I can't stop."

I smiled and leaned over to kiss his cheek. "I know. Now, are you going to spank me, or are we going to surf?" My laugh turned into a squeal when he grasped my waist and dragged me facedown across his knees.

"Like this?" he asked. Since I was only wearing his t-shirt, he pushed the fabric up and exposed my backside. His hand ran over it tenderly before giving me a hard slap. I groaned with a quick exhalation, and he began to knead my skin, running his hand over the backs of my thighs. "Okay, up you go," he said suddenly, lifting me onto my feet.

"No," I protested.

"Yes. It's time to surf. Let me see that itty-bitty bikini. Although, no—not with Brian around." He frowned. "Actually, did you bring a one-piece?"

I laughed and shoved his shoulder before dropping to get my suit out of my suitcase.

Downstairs, Brian waited in the kitchen by himself.

"Ready to *shred*?" I asked and glanced at David. "Is that the right word?"

Brian laughed. "Yes, ma'am. Just waiting for your friend."

With a small shuffle of feet, I jerked my head toward the pantry, where Brian's girlfriend stood. Had she been there the whole time? "Oh. Morning, Kat," I said. "Didn't see you there."

"Hi."

"Are you getting a lesson, too?" I asked.

She shook her head, the corners of her mouth drooping. "I burn easily."

"Oh."

David's face brightened as if that reminded him of

something. He grabbed a bottle of sunscreen from the counter and passed it to me. "Slather it," he said. "Don't argue."

The Miami sun had the potential to destroy me, so I did as he said. As I finished rubbing in the suntan lotion, Gretchen appeared, all shiny again with her hair and makeup fixed and her contacts in. "Let's hit the beach," she said cheerily.

David and Brian stuck longboards under their arms as the four of us made the short walk to the ocean. "The waves are small right now," David observed. "We can just practice in the whitewater."

"Whatever." I shrugged. "Let's go."

"Uh, not so fast, little mermaid," he said. "First you have to practice on land."

"Why?" I wrinkled my nose. "Can't we just do it?"

"No." He set his board on the sand next to Brian's. "On your belly."

"Yes, *sir*," I teased.

His expression remained serious. "The ocean is no laughing matter, Olivia. And these have to go," he said, sliding my sunglasses off and tossing them with our stuff. "You need to be alert out there. No messing around. You could get hurt."

I saluted him. Gretchen and I giggled, but his jaw hardened. We stopped laughing immediately and dropped onto the boards. He demonstrated how we should paddle and pop up. We both imitated what he'd done and held our poses as instructed. David squatted next to me, fixing my stance by adjusting my legs, as Brian did the same for Gretchen. I tried in vain to flirt with David as he corrected my back foot.

"What's all this?" I heard Brian ask Gretchen. When I looked over, he was waving his hand near her face.

"What?" she asked.

"All this hair and makeup just to get in the water. It's ridiculous."

"So I want to look good." She shrugged. "Who cares?"

"I do. You don't need all this. You looked prettier this morning. Bed hair, no makeup, and pj's."

"Shut up, Brian." Her lips drew into a line. "Why do you have to be such a sarcastic dick?"

His brows knit. "I'm being serious."

"Well, then," she said, shimmying to straighten her back, "I don't need your pity."

"No need to get defensive," Brian said. "All I asked was what the point is. It's going to get ruined anyway."

"It's waterproof makeup," she pointed out as if it was obvious.

"Oh, is it?" he retorted. "Let's test it, then."

He scooped her up before she knew what was happening, and she screamed as he ran her to the ocean.

I cringed as he tossed her in easily. "He is so dead," I muttered.

But she came up laughing.

"See?" David said. "They like each other."

Gretchen and I splayed out on our towels, wrecked after two hours in the water.

"I think I could be really good at surfing," I said to Gretchen. "I mean, I stood up almost every time. You only got up, like, twice, right? And you've had lessons before. David said I was a natural."

"Whatever," she said, huffing from behind her sunglasses. "It's not a contest."

"So, um . . ." I failed to hide a smile. "You and Brian were sort of chummy out there."

"*We* were chummy?" She balked as she got up onto her elbows. "I'm pretty sure small children had to be removed from the beach because of you and David."

"Oh, please," I said, reddening. "A little making out never hurt anyone. I mean, have you *seen* David without a shirt?"

She lowered her sunglasses to look at me. "Good point."

"So?" I asked. "You and Brian?"

"Ugh, what?" She flopped back onto the towel. "I don't like him. He's been actually tolerable today, but that doesn't mean anything. Right now, I'm just trying not to think about Greg."

I nodded. "You're right, I'm sorry. It's just that David thinks he likes you."

She popped back up on an elbow and lowered her sunglasses again. "He said that?"

"Yup."

Her answering laugh sounded forced. "That's crazy."

"Is it?"

"Look, I never told you this, but after the one date we had . . ." She hesitated. "I kissed Brian."

"I know. He told me."

"Of course he did, the rat." She narrowed her eyes toward the ocean, where David and Brian had gone back out with their boards. "Did he also tell you that he shot me down?"

"Yes," I said. "So what? That was a while ago."

"Guys don't shoot me down, Liv. *Clearly*, he's not into me. Not that I'm into him, but, anyway, he's not into me."

"Okay," I said, offering up my palms. "But either way, maybe you should take a break and be single for a while."

"Or *forever.*"

"Don't say that," I said. "Greg sucks. Not all guys are like him."

She squinted ahead. "Jesus, they're smoking fucking *hot*, though, aren't they? Look at them."

I followed her gaze to where David and Brian sat in the line-up—David dark and sexy, Brian blond and goofy. Both looked drop-dead gorgeous shirtless, though. "Brian's pretty ripped, huh?" I asked.

"Would you stop?" she asked, exasperated.

"Just calling it like it is. But yes. They're *extremely* hot," I said, my eyes drifting to some female gawkers on the shore. "Those girls over there are checking them out."

We laughed and reclined back again. I closed my eyes to soak in the warmth of the sun and was almost asleep when I heard the bass of David's voice.

Gretchen, already up on her elbows, yawned. "Look," she said, jutting her chin at the water. "They're talking to the girls."

I squinted through my sunglasses at the shoreline. Three girls in bikinis, ankle deep in the surf, shaded their eyes with their hands as they looked up at Brian and David. I sat up all the way, and David lifted his hand in a wave. A pleasant warmth washed over me, and I smiled. Despite all my worrying that I'd inherit my mother's madness, I realized there was too much love in my body to leave any room for jealousy. Those girls could flirt their asses off, and it looked as if they were trying to, but they'd never steal even a fraction of David's attention from me.

David broke away, jogged up the sand, and dropped his surfboard next to me. He fell over me gracefully, propping himself on outstretched arms and dripping water onto my warm skin. "Sorry, honey. Hope you don't mind getting a little *wet*," he said.

"Let's see a push-up," Gretchen demanded.

He lowered himself, kissed me on the lips, and pushed himself back up. "One," he said and repeated the motion, this time kissing the curve of my neck.

"Two," I said breathlessly as a tingle made its way up my tummy.

"Okay, that's enough," Gretchen said. "I don't want to know what happens when you get to ten."

He laughed and rolled over onto the sand. "God, I love the beach."

"Word," Gretchen agreed as Brian strolled up and plopped down next to her. "How was the surf?" she asked.

"Shit," Brian said. "But it's okay because we had longboards."

"Dude, did you see that little kid ripping out there?" David asked.

"He was like ten years old," Brian told us, "but he trounced the rest of us."

"I'd start my kid surfing the *second* he could walk," David continued. "Boy or girl, I wouldn't care. Snowboarding, too."

A tremor of dread worked its way through me. From behind my sunglasses, I noticed Gretchen glance at me. I couldn't believe that hearing David talk about children would be one of the most terrifying things in my life. Jessa's warnings from the other night tried to pop into my head, but I pushed them away.

And gave way to my own harrowing thought.

Someone will have to sacrifice.

"Same here," Brian agreed. "Hey, we could move out to Florida and raise a professional surf team."

"I'm in," David said. "I don't know if your lady friend would be up for that, though. She doesn't seem to like the beach."

"Who, Kat?" Brian laughed. "No, definitely not. Sadly, I think our time together is coming to an end."

Gretchen twirled a finger in the sand beside her towel. "She, um, doesn't seem like your type."

"Oh, yeah?" Brian said. "Why not?"

"Well, for one . . ." Gretchen looked up. "She doesn't ride a broom."

Brian's answering laugh was so loud, it seemed to echo around the beach. He fell back on the sand. "*Gretchen.*" He groaned, covering his face with his arm. "Quit busting my balls, would you?"

I looked from Brian to a grinning David. Florida looked good on him. I took a mental picture of his profile, wanting to remember this carefree, in-his-element David forever.

Because deep down, I knew.

It couldn't last.

As long as we hadn't discussed the one thing that could still break us, stormy waters lay ahead.

Chapter Twenty-Six

I awoke completely tangled in David, my hands in his hair, and my arms around his neck while his circled my waist. Our legs entwined like vines attempting to merge. A gray hue darkened the room, and rain lightly drummed the roof. David sighed and pulled me closer. With messy, jet-black hair against a stark white pillow, he looked peaceful but still severe, even in repose. I bit my lip to keep from waking him with a kiss.

I closed my eyes again. It'd been another perfect weekend. After our surf session, David and I had made love in the shower, then napped until dinnertime. Brian and Gretchen had prepared seafood pasta while Brian's girlfriend had watched. By the time we'd gone to bed, only Gretchen and Brian had remained awake.

I was high on everything—David, the change in scenery, the possibility of Gretchen and Brian—but still, I managed to give in to a second round of sleep.

We were still interwoven when I woke again, except I was practically on top of David as he lay on his back. I lifted my head to find him watching me. "We slept late," he said softly.

I nodded and resettled my head against his chest, not ready to separate. The *thud* of heavy raindrops comforted me, and David plus the sheets warmed my skin. I closed my eyes as he stroked my hair.

Suddenly, he flipped me onto my back. "You're going back to sleep?" he cried. "It's almost noon."

I giggled as his face hovered above mine. "I had a stressful week."

"Were you dealing with unruly workers and asshole engineers like I was? I didn't think so."

"I'm sorry, baby, but I have you beat," I informed him. "I was stuck in a debilitating state of sexual arousal for *days*. I could barely function."

"Yeah, right," he said, shifting and pulling me closer.

"Really," I said. "It was exhausting."

"Well, whoever left you that way should be tried and charged with stupidity of the highest degree."

I laughed and pushed his shoulder, but he caught my wrist. His smile fell as his expression sobered, his eyes intense as they darted over my face. "Marry me."

I sucked in a sharp breath at the completely out-of-the-blue question. *Statement*, rather. Apparently, he didn't even need to ask. "What?" I asked.

He blinked, and his eyes continued to scan my face. "Marry me, Olivia," he said just above a whisper.

My heat skipped with joy as my stomach simultaneously churned. I didn't know what to feel. There was still so much we hadn't discussed. And so much to be *done*. "David, I—I haven't even started the divorce process yet."

"These past few weeks have been the best of my life," he said. "Surfing with you yesterday, hanging out on the beach, seeing you light up with laughter . . . you've been in my life for so little time, yet I can't imagine it without you." He slid his hand from my wrist to interlace our fingers. "I want you to be my wife. Maybe it can't be for a while, maybe you even want to wait a couple years. It doesn't matter to me. Just tell me one day, you'll be my wife. Tell me yes."

It was a moment every girl dreamed of. A moment I *desperately* wanted. But my mouth went desert-dry as my heart pounded against my chest. Jessa had told me to talk to David quickly. But I'd thought we'd had more time. Now, it was both too soon and too late. Here he was, asking me to make the same promises Bill had. And I knew that with the one simple discussion we hadn't had, everything could change. *Everything*.

I looked away so I wouldn't have to see his expression. "It's too soon," I said.

"I know. It is too soon." He stroked my cheek with his thumb. "But we don't have to tell anyone."

"I'm sorry," I whispered, my throat painfully thick. "I —I can't. Things are too . . ."

"Hey," he called softly. "Olivia, look at me. It's okay. Don't freak out."

"I'm not freaking out." I turned back to him with a forced smile, but he wasn't buying it.

"I'm happy to be here with you now," he said. "That just came out. I meant it, but I should've waited."

Coward! I screamed at myself. He didn't deserve this. He needed to know that the subject of starting a family had been the beginning of the erosion of my marriage. And that even though so much had changed . . . my feelings about motherhood hadn't. "David," I started.

He looked at me expectantly. He was so open, his eyes clear, and his love pouring over me. For God's sake, he'd just asked me to marry him. How would I survive if he never looked at me that way again? If this one last piece of the puzzle didn't fit for us? I didn't know, but I never wanted to find out.

In that moment, I wanted to deflect, but I forced myself to be honest. "I am freaking out."

His body stiffened, and he moved back to sit on his calves. "All right." He paused, as if searching for the words. "About the proposal? Or about us?"

I don't want kids. The thought stopped my heart, stole my breath, ceased body function of any kind. This one thing could give David every reason to walk away. Now. To leave this bed, taking his warmth and love with him.

But if it was going to be a dealbreaker—wasn't it better to know sooner rather than later?

Yes. That was the only answer. But the potential consequences of that conversation could be devastating. And they could sever a perfectly pure, once-in-a-lifetime love.

Let me have today, David. "I need a little space to sort through this."

"Space? I . . ." He rubbed his chest. "Olivia, we've talked about this. I realize the proposal was sudden, but slowing our relationship down isn't—"

"No, no." I needed perspective. A clear head. I needed to make some decisions and to work up my courage. I took his hand. "Not that kind of space. I just need to, I don't know—go for a walk."

"Alone," he guessed.

I nodded. "I'm not doing this on my own, and I'm not running away. But there will be times when I need to gather my thoughts."

He got off the bed and went to peek out the window. "It's raining."

"I don't mind."

He disappeared into the bathroom and returned in his

board shorts. "If you feel you need space, I can't stop you," he said, doing up the tie. "But promise me you won't make any decisions about us without me."

That was a fair demand—not just because he deserved input, but because I'd shut him out before. I went to him, rose onto the tips of my toes, and gave him a kiss on the cheek. "I won't."

David glanced at me sidelong. "You know that to be a runaway bride, you actually have to be a fiancée first, right? And then make it to the ceremony?"

I half-laughed. "I'm not running anywhere. If anything, I never want to leave this place."

David glanced at the clock. "Our flight is this afternoon with everyone else," he said. "I could see if Brian'll let us spend another night. Just you and me."

"I'd like that," I said. I knew David wouldn't let me off the hook tonight, and having this conversation after traveling all day didn't sound fun. "I'll take a personal day tomorrow."

"Or—" He paused.

"What?"

"Never mind. It might be too much for today."

Never mind? Since when did David not say what was on his mind? I studied him a minute. "I'm not freaking out about us, David," I said. "I promise. I'll be here as long as you'll have me."

"I'll always have you," he said.

It was a promise, but one he was making without all the information. "I know it's unfair to ask when I'm not reciprocating, but please tell me what you were going to say."

"Fine." He nodded once. "You *could* just put in your notice at work."

I blinked at him. "*Quit?*"

"I'd planned to tell you once I got more info, but I have another work opportunity in New York," he said. "This one is full-time, six months. And after that, who knows? It could be anywhere. We could do some traveling."

Six months in New York, a new adventure. And then seeing the world with the man I loved. I wanted it so bad, I could taste it.

"I won't take the assignment if you don't come with me," David added when I didn't respond, "but you could if you weren't tied to Chicago."

"What about the house?" I asked.

"It won't be ready for *at least* a year, probably longer. But no matter where we go, it will always be our home."

A year. If I didn't tell David the truth tonight, couldn't I have that time with him and deal with the topic of kids when we returned?

I couldn't. That wasn't fair to either of us. The fantasy faded before my eyes before it'd fully developed.

"I can't just end my career to travel," I said.

"Well, you could," he said. "I have no problem with that. But I'm not asking you to do that. I know work is important to you. You could write."

"Like what I did on the plane back from Dallas?" I nearly laughed. "That's just a hobby, David. I don't see it going anywhere."

"Freelance for other magazines, start a blog about our travels, write a book. You'd have options. Plus . . . it would make you more available for the shelter. You could volunteer there regularly when we're home. And when we're not, well, Chicago isn't the only place with needy animals."

I stared at him, my heart warming at the thought of spending more time at the shelter. Or was it that he'd known how much it meant to me? I wasn't sure. "You've given this a lot of thought."

"Just consider it. Whatever you decide, I'm behind you a hundred percent." He kissed my forehead. "I'm going to find Brian to squeeze in another surf. But, Olivia? Don't walk too far today."

I glanced at my hands. I couldn't blame him for being worried I'd stray from us, but with my history, I had no way of reassuring him that wouldn't happen.

"And be safe," he added. "You don't know the area."

Once he'd left, I squatted to my suitcase to change. I hadn't brought any sneakers, so I went to find Gretchen. I could always count on her in a fashion pinch.

I found her on a call, pacing her room as she seemed to listen. She motioned for me to come in, rolling her eyes at the phone, so I sat on the edge of the bed to wait.

"Well, you should've thought about that before abandoning me again," she said calmly and paused. "Yes, if you'd stayed and talked to me like a mature adult, we *would* be having a different conversation . . . how am I supposed to trust you now? Frankly, I think you did both of us a favor because now . . . yes, I said *favor*, because now I see that this isn't working."

It had to be Greg. I wasn't all that surprised he'd called to beg her forgiveness. I gave her a thumbs-up as encouragement, grateful she didn't need me to point out it was time to move on.

Gretchen looked at me as she listened. "I'm sorry, Greg, but you only have yourself to blame. We're not in college anymore, and you have to grow up. We can talk more at home, but I have to go now." She hung up abruptly and flopped next to me on the bed. "Oh my God."

"That was Greg, right?" I asked. "What the hell is his deal?"

"He's *so sorry* for bringing Jordan. I'm not really mad,

am I?" she said, mimicking him. "He hadn't *meant* to call me a bitch—David and Brian had just pushed him too far. He didn't even realize that I'm more upset he left instead of talking to me."

"And he's not even taking accountability for himself," I said. "I think he's stuck at the age he was when we last knew him."

"Totally. On some level I'll always love him, but this was definitely a wake-up call." She blew out a sigh. "He's obviously got commitment issues on top of all that, but I don't think I even care anymore. Whatever we had is gone."

I cleared my throat and picked at something on the comforter. "Could, um, Brian also have a little bit to do with your change of heart?"

She laughed. "No . . . I don't know."

"You two were still talking when we went to bed." I poked her arm. "Did you guys . . .?"

"No, of course not," she cried, her eyes huge. "For one, *gross*. And for two, his girlfriend is here, remember?"

"Oh my God. I'm awful," I said, covering my eyes. "I keep forgetting about Kat."

"I think he does, too," Gretchen said. "Brian and I were up late last night, and we just . . . talked. A lot. Like, until dawn."

"Really?" I asked, beaming. "And you still think he's gross?"

She hesitated. "I mean, I guess he's not *gross*. There was this brief moment where I thought he might kiss me, but he didn't. And I was kind of disappointed."

"Wow. Strange how one weekend can change everything," I muttered.

"Yup." She sighed. "I'm hoping this rain burns off so we can hit the beach before we leave."

"David and I are thinking of staying another night," I said. "Actually, I came to ask if I can borrow some sneakers. I'm going for a walk."

"Like a stroll?"

"No," I said. "Like a walk. Maybe even a run."

She raised her eyebrows at me. "You don't run. *Unless* something's really bothering you. I remember from living with you."

"Yeah." I scratched the tip of my nose. "It helps me sort through everything. And before you asked, I don't really want to talk about it."

She got up from the bed and went to the closet. "Is it about David?" she asked.

"Yes."

She held out a pair of sneakers. "Is it bad?"

I accepted them with a sigh. "Yes."

"How bad?"

I shook my head, rolling my lips together. "I don't know yet."

"Look, if there's one thing Greg's idiocy has taught me, it's that communication is key." She opened her suitcase and pushed some things around. "Just talk to David. He loves you so much."

"I don't know if that's enough this time," I said, picking at the bedspread. "This might be the one thing David can't fix."

"Ah." Absentmindedly, she picked out a pair of athletic socks, then glanced over at me. "Is this about what he said on the beach yesterday? About wanting to teach his kid to surf?"

It wasn't hard to put two and two together. Gretchen knew about my struggles with getting Bill to see I wasn't ready and may never be. "Yeah," I said. "David wants it all. He's ready to start on the house. He's already said he

413

wants to marry me. But we haven't talked about what comes after that."

"For once, I don't really know what to tell you. Just that you need to talk to him. He can't help if he doesn't know what you want."

"*I* don't know what I want, Gretchen." Except, that wasn't entirely true. Maybe I already knew the answer, but I was too scared to admit it to myself.

She handed me the socks. "This is going to be one hell of a run."

I headed out into the humidity, tightened my ponytail, and looked up at the gray sky, requesting that it wait until I'd finished to open up again.

My mind instantly replayed the morning.

Quit my job. Travel the world. Marriage. Children.

It was more than a girl could ask for. Was I a fool to question everything David offered me?

I wondered if he'd meant to propose. It'd happened so suddenly. Despite knowing he'd want that one day, it hadn't occurred to me that he was already there. Then again, maybe he hadn't known he was, either. He'd said it had just come out.

Surely, he'd thought about having a family. Had I given him the impression that I wanted children? Was it on me to admit that outright, from the start—when we hadn't even *had* a start? Or was he to blame if he'd just assumed I'd want kids?

Did David know that Bill and I had argued about that over and over? How *could* he know that? Had I never told him?

I picked up my pace as my thoughts came faster and heavier. All my arguments with Bill washed over me. I couldn't ensure the shame again—of not wanting what I was supposed to. Of doubting myself and my role as a woman. Of disappointing a man I'd promised to make a life with.

Could I do it? Could I make the decision to keep my doubts to myself and have a baby if the alternative was losing David?

My heart nearly broke at the thought. Was that any way to bring a child into the world?

I pictured David as a father, teaching his kid to surf or snowboard. I thought of the way he handled the things he loved and how his face somehow conveyed gravity, focus, *and* happiness when he played with Alex.

Fuck. I couldn't take fatherhood away from him.

And I couldn't picture myself as a mother.

I'd never felt particularly warm toward children, but everyone said I'd feel differently about my own. That was a huge and irreversible chance to take when my heart told me otherwise. Not that I wouldn't love and care for my own, but that ultimately, my life wasn't meant to include them.

I jogged by a stroller-pushing woman in athletic wear who'd stopped mid-run to comfort her crying baby. A pit formed in my stomach. She wasn't me. I wasn't her. Maybe I'd change my mind one day, but I hadn't with Bill, and the thought of entering a relationship with that kind of pressure again . . . I wouldn't do it.

Being a mom wasn't in the cards for me.

But David—I'd never find a love like his again. And I never wanted to.

So the question was, could I do it for David? Was there anything I wouldn't do, wouldn't give up for him?

David texted me that Brian would let us stay another night, and I agreed. He was still gone when I returned from my workout, so I treated myself to a long shower. As I washed my sweat away, I let myself think momentarily of traveling the world on his arm. Writing, eating, fucking, sleeping . . . no rude boss to answer to, no judgmental friends or family, no children stealing our attention from each other. Just the two of us living the dream . . .

But is that all it is? A dream?

David had given me so many invaluable things, including his trust. I not only owed him my honesty—I wanted to give it to him. My instinct was still to run, hide, and retreat—that wouldn't change overnight. But I had deeper, stronger reasons to share with him. Once I found the courage to do it.

I changed into a striped sundress and went downstairs to find that the sun had come out and chased the clouds away. Gretchen and I walked into town and had lunch until it was time for her to catch her flight. I called her a taxi, and just as she was loading her luggage, David and Brian jogged up with their surfboards.

"See you guys back in Chi-town," she called, laughing as she waved.

"Gretchen—" Brian started, but paused when Kat appeared on the porch. "Uh. Just have a nice flight."

"Thanks," she said with a large smile. Even with her hair tossed in a ponytail and in less makeup than I'd ever seen, she looked stunning. Brian watched until her taxi turned a corner and disappeared.

David put his hands on my shoulders. "You're a beautiful thing to come back to," he said, and I turned my head for a kiss before he added, "I like this dress."

"Indeed, Liv," Brian said. "It's quite fetching."

David shot him a glare, and I grinned. "Did you guys have a nice surf?"

"Excellent," David said. "Waves were much better this afternoon. Did you eat?"

I nodded. "Gretch and I went to lunch."

"Good. I'm going to rinse off and drive these two to the airport."

As he did that, and Brian and Kat packed, I sat on the porch with a book. After a while, Brian came out, freshly showered and dressed in a t-shirt and shorts. He sat down in the rocking chair next to mine, glanced over his shoulder quickly, and then back at me. "I had a great time this weekend."

"Me, too."

"No. I had a *great* time, Liv. Call me crazy, but . . ." He scrubbed a hand through his damp blond hair. "I think I'm going to take my chances and ask Gretchen on another date."

I closed the book and looked him over and tried to look surprised. "Really? What changed?"

"She puts up this shield, right?" he said, growing animated. "But when it comes down, she's lovely. Kind, smart, and a little bit goofy, too. I never dreamed she was so goofy."

I laughed. "Greg's the reason for the shield. When they met, she changed for him—started wearing her hair differently, tried different diets, dressed up all the time. But when he left? That's when something *inside* her changed. I'm afraid that after this time, she'll have trouble trusting again."

"Then I have my work cut out for me," he said. "But I have a feeling she'll be worth it. I want to see more of the girl in the glasses."

I smiled, but it quickly turned to a frown. "I think you'd better take care of the situation here first," I said, jerking my thumb toward the house.

"I already did," he said. "I ended things with Kat this morning, and she took it well. At least, I think so—she reacted about the same way she does to everything." He shrugged. "But in any case, it's over."

"Then you have my blessing," I said.

"Do you think Gretchen'll agree to a date with me?" he asked. "I would've tested the waters before she left, but I didn't want to be disrespectful to Kat."

I bit the inside corner of my cheek, trying to decide whether to give Gretchen up. Remembering how she'd gone to David when I'd needed him most, I nodded. "I'm pretty confident she'll say yes. But you should know—Greg called her this morning trying to feed her some bullshit."

"Understood. I'll reach out to her tonight." He kissed me on the cheek and then wiped it with his thumb. "Oops. Don't tell your boyfriend. I hear he has a temper."

I smiled. "Wouldn't dream of it."

When Kat opened the screen door, Brian popped up to help her with her bag. David breezed out next, dropped a kiss on my lips, and ushered them into Brian's parents' car.

Unable to concentrate on my book, I walked to the grocery store to purchase some things for dinner. I got the idea that we could picnic on the beach as the sun went down, so I picked up an assortment of snacks and a bottle of red.

This is how life could be. Just us, no bullshit, watching the sunset and drinking wine.

At the house, I prepared the food and found a basket and large blanket in a hallway closet. I left David a note and walked down to the beach where I unfurled the blanket and watched the water while I waited.

When, eventually, I had the distinct feeling that he was behind me, it was because he was. He sat behind me, his front against my back, his long legs bent on each side of me. "This is nice," he said, putting his cheek to mine.

"Finally alone," I responded. I leaned forward and

excavated plastic cups from my bag to pour us each some wine.

I passed him a cup just as he rubbed his eyes with tense fingers.

"Tired?" I asked.

"Stressed."

"How come?" I asked.

He took the wine and opened his arms, so I settled back against him, comforted by the rumble of his chest as he spoke. "I have the New York project falling behind, and I also need to figure out this potential lawsuit with Arnaud and Clare."

Before I could ask him to elaborate, he added, "And then there's you."

I glanced up. "Me?"

"I want to start moving on our house soon. But after everything we talked about this morning . . ." He looked down to meet my eyes. "I'm afraid I pushed you too hard and fucked up somewhere."

"*David*. Honey." I put down my wine. "You didn't fuck up. Everything you're offering me—it's more than a girl could ask for."

"And you want . . . what?" he asked. "*Less?*"

My heart thudded once. I was running out of time—to tell him the truth, to sit here with him, to enjoy us *finally* as a carefree couple. Was I running out of time with him, too?

I heaved a sigh and looked out at the water. "Let's just enjoy the sunset for now."

I gave him my weight and ran my hands over his shins. "That feels nice," he murmured. "I'm sore from surfing."

"I could give you a massage later," I offered.

"I'd be forever in your debt."

I smiled and continued rubbing his legs as we looked out at the water.

"How's my Mercedes, by the way?" he asked. "I tried to get Alex to scope things out when you were there for Thanksgiving, but he's a lousy spy."

"Hmm. There was a pretty significant dent in the hood before you left, right?" I teased.

He groaned. "Don't fuck with me."

"The car's *fine*," I said. "Thanks for letting me take it. It was nice spending time with Jessa."

"I warned her if she told any embarrassing stories about me, she'd be out a babysitter for life."

I squeezed his knee. "Somehow I doubt you've *ever* done a single embarrassing thing."

"Of course I have," he stated. "I proposed to my girlfriend, and she said no."

My cheeks warmed. "Did you mean it? Or was it an in-the-moment thing?"

"I meant it," he said. "I'm sorry it wasn't more romantic."

"It was perfect," I said, because it was. I couldn't think of anything more romantic than blurting it out because he couldn't keep it inside another second. "Everything you do for me, you do with love. I *know* that."

We sat in silence until the sun dropped behind the horizon.

"Canyon passed away this morning," he said.

I gasped. "Your family's dog?"

"My mom called. They had to put him down."

I turned between his legs and sat back on my calves. "Honey. I'm so sorry."

"He was sick, as you knew. It was his time, but I thought we had a little longer." He avoided my eyes, so I waited until they drifted back to mine. I couldn't help tearing up at his crestfallen expression.

He touched the corner of my eye with his thumb. "It's okay," he said, but I could see that he was hurting.

I nodded and leaned in to comfort him with a kiss. His hand moved to my hair to hold me there as he kissed me back, slowly at first, then deepening it. As dusk settled around us, I unfolded my legs and wrapped them around him so we were as close as we could get.

"Good thing I'm wearing a dress," I said.

He laughed softly. "I thought you hated beach sex."

"Apparently, I was doing it wrong."

His voice lowered. "I'm not going to have you here in front of everyone."

"It's almost dark," I replied. "The beach is empty."

"Still."

I could feel his heartbeat, strong and solid against my breasts. I hugged him closer and whispered, "I'm sorry about Canyon."

"I know."

I didn't want David to hurt, but there was no way my confession wouldn't cut him deeply. Either he'd lose me or he'd lose a future he'd envisioned for himself. For us. From the start, he'd known I was the one.

"David?" I asked.

"Hmm?" he answered, brushing his lips over mine.

"Do you believe in soulmates?" I asked, even though I knew what he'd say.

But he paused, and to my surprise, responded with the opposite answer. "No."

I drew back. "Why not?"

"I don't need it. I believe in you. I believe in us."

I swallowed through the lump in my throat his sweet words inspired. "I believe in us, too."

He looked me fully in the face, ran his big hands over my hairline, and held them there. Even in the semi-dark, I could see his eyes burning. "My turn," he said. "Are you still empty inside?"

My words from his mouth were sharp and painful. I inhaled back tears. "No." I wasn't. He'd filled me with goodness and killed any poison in me.

"Good." His hand moved to my jaw, and he pecked me. "Ready to go up?"

I shook my head no, so he stayed and kissed me a little longer until it was completely dark. Eventually, we gathered up the blanket and walked back to the house holding hands.

I unpacked the picnic we hadn't touched and the wine we'd barely drunk, and we ate to the soundtrack of waves crashing against the shore.

After we'd cleaned up, I asked, "How about that massage, surfer boy?"

He scooped me up in one swift movement and carried me up the stairs. "I love having you all to myself," he said and set me down in the bedroom.

"Strip to your underwear," I instructed as I went into the bathroom. I swapped my sundress for the silky white robe I'd brought from home, then grabbed some body oil from under the sink.

When I came out of the bathroom, the look on his face stopped my trek to the bed. "You brought your robe," he said and bit his bottom lip. "I love that fucking thing."

"I know you do. Now, get on your stomach, facedown. And no screwing around," I said, mimicking his surf lesson on land, "or you might get hurt."

He chuckled as he shook his head and got into position. He waited with his arms tucked under his head. I went to turn out the lights but decided against it. I didn't want to miss anything.

I climbed over him, parted my robe to straddle his firm ass, and squirted oil onto his back. I dove my hands into it, spreading it from his broad shoulders down to his narrow hips. I rubbed and kneaded, savoring every inch of him and working myself into a decent state of arousal. I loved the way his skin felt under my fingertips and how his muscles relaxed at my probing touch.

"Turn over," I said after a while. I lifted onto my knees to allow him to flip onto his back. When I settled my bare pussy on his underwear, we both inhaled sharply. He looked up at me from under heavy eyebrows. I filled my hands with oil, took a deep breath, and touched his chest. I felt his pecs, his shoulders, his biceps. I made my way over the contours of his taut stomach. When I looked back at his face, he'd closed his eyes in peace.

I was aware the moment he hardened under me. I was already wet against his underwear, had been for a while, and was further excited when the ridges of his cock twitched against me. I suppressed a moan at the thought of taking all of my man inside of me.

You're unreal, I thought as I looked at him. *What if this has all been a beautiful dream? And when I wake up, it'll be too soon . . .*

My tear fell onto his stomach, but with his eyes shut, he didn't notice. I slid my hands under his lower back and dragged them back up. I let my fingers graze under the waistband of his underwear, and he jerked.

He sighed heavily without looking and ran his hands over the outsides of my thighs. My hand skated up his stomach and then down again, reaching slightly farther under his waistband. He inhaled slowly but loudly and coaxed my hips over him, back and forth.

Finally, he opened hungry eyes and slipped his hand inside my robe. It grazed up over my breast and neck until he cupped my jaw. "You look like an angel." He pulled me down, and I curved my body to meet his lips as he added, "A fantasy."

I cocked my head slightly. *A fantasy*, I repeated in my head. *A dream. A fantasy.*

He kissed me slowly, and I responded, unhurriedly letting my tongue memorize his mouth. My hips moved on their own, finding pleasure against the length of him. Without disconnecting from his mouth, I pulled down his underwear and put him inside me. We moaned at the same moment, exchanging hot breaths.

A dream. A fantasy. A dream. A fantasy.

The words ran through my head like a prayer, an appeal to something higher.

Don't take this away from me. I can do it for you, for you I can do anything. I could never walk away. David . . . my David.

"David," I whispered. "My David."

"Olivia," he responded with his hands tangled in my hair. "Open your eyes."

I let my face fall into the space between his neck and shoulder and gyrated faster.

"Baby." I could hear him gritting his teeth, and I knew he was close, so I kissed his neck the way he liked.

A dream. A fantasy. A dream. A fantasy.

He pulled my hair so I was forced to draw back, but I avoided his eyes. I held on to his shoulders and clenched his cock inside of me to push him over the edge. "Come, baby," I coaxed.

"But you—" he bit out, inhaling through his mouth. "Fuck," he said when I picked up my pace and squeezed again. He was gone. I dug my fingers into his skin as he shuddered and released into me, gripping my hips. I watched his face with fascination as it contorted with carnal bliss. While his muscles relaxed into the mattress, I kissed his jawline reverently, made my way down, and tucked my face into the crook of his neck.

"Olivia," he whispered hotly.

This was it. I'd had my day with him, a beautiful day filled with his love. Now, I owed him the truth. I didn't move, unable to face him.

"Hey," he said, pushing me off of his torso gently. "Whatever it is, you can tell me."

"I know." I nodded. "I love you."

He ran his hands over my body, feeling my back, my arms, my neck, my scar. "Tell me what you're scared of, and I'll fix it. I promise."

"My superhero." I looked down at my hands and body, covered in oil. "Let me just rinse off first."

I crawled off the bed, closed the bathroom door, and steadied myself against the counter. In the mirror, I told myself I could do this. I had to. Afterward, nothing would be the same, but the thing was . . .

I didn't regret any of it. I'd fought so hard to keep from getting hurt, but as the pain filtered in, I also found strange and overwhelming peace in my endless, absolute love for David.

Chapter Twenty-Seven

The shower's hot water soaked me. Under the beating stream, the past few months rushed out through scalding tears—Bill's harsh words, my mother's disappointment, all the fears I still had and the ones I'd already conquered, and of course, the possibility of losing David now.

And my heart leaked through my eyes for everything we'd built, everything we'd *fought* for. Were things meant to end this way, everything swirling down the drain? I heard the door open, but I stayed facing the wall. Moments later, his hand ran over the hair plastered to my back. My sobs redoubled at his touch. Despite the burning of my eyes and the trembling of my body, his touch soothed me.

"I'm sorry," I said.

"For what?" he asked softly.

Finally, I turned to him and stared at him with wonder. He *was* a dream, even in soaking wet boxer briefs. "I should never have let things get this far," I said, exhaling a shaky breath.

He shut off the water before stepping out of the shower. I followed, and he wrapped me in a towel, securing my arms to my body. He guided me onto the edge of the bathtub, squatted on his heels, and looked up at me. "Let what get so far?"

"I thought I'd change my mind," I said. "I thought being with you would change everything, but . . . it hasn't. I still feel the same."

"I don't understand, Olivia," he said, cupping my jaw.

I took a deep breath as a sense of calm fell over me. Thankful that there were no tears left in me, I looked him in the eye. And I said it. "I don't want children."

His hand withdrew immediately, and his expression cleared.

In the ensuing silence, I tried to read his reaction, but he just stared at me with huge brown eyes. It took a lot to shock David, but now, he seemed unable to even process what I'd said.

So, I continued.

"I've seen you with Alex," I said. "I know you'll be an incredible father. You want it. I can see it. I'm sorry for waiting this long to tell you, but . . ." I paused when my voice wavered. "I honestly thought we had more time."

I was wrong. I was not cried out. Tears began to spill again, sliding down my cheeks and dropping into my lap.

And for once, David didn't catch them. He looked away and focused on the tiled wall. At least it gave me a moment to trace the lines of his jaw with my eyes, to memorize the curve of his magnificent lips and the chestnut, golden color of his eyes. He really was the most handsome man I'd ever seen. And he'd almost been mine.

"I'm sorry," he said to the wall. "I don't know what to say. I need . . ."

Space. He didn't have to say it. I'd asked for it often. Sometimes he'd granted my wish. Others, he'd pushed back. This wasn't something either of us could push, though. I knew that. I'd been pushed in the past, and it'd driven me away.

I stood from the edge of the tub, walked to the bed, and slid between the sheets. Covering my face with my hands, I cried. David never came, and eventually, I fell asleep.

I opened my eyes to a dark room, my towel still wrapped under my armpits, my pillow damp from my hair. I sat up slowly, trying to orient myself.

"Olivia." David's figure sharpened in the dark. He leaned forward and turned on the bedside lamp.

"What time is it?" I mumbled.

"Three in the morning."

"Have you slept?" I asked, rubbing my eyes.

"No. I've been downstairs." With a bath towel in his hands, he climbed into bed behind me. He straddled me and ran the towel through my hair, scrubbing lightly. "What have I told you about going to bed with wet hair?" he said in quiet admonishment.

"I didn't mean to," I said with a quivering chin.

He continued to pat my hair, and when it was as dry as possible, he threw the towel and my pillow on the floor. "Turn around. We're going to talk about this," he said. "No more hiding."

I did as he said, my shoulders slumped forward. "Do you want children?" I asked.

He hesitated. "I always imagined I'd have them, yes. I never really questioned it. I assumed it was what you wanted, and so . . . I just figured it would happen."

Each of his words stung like little knives in my heart, not because of what he said, but because of the picture he painted that would never be. I gave him a shallow nod. "I understand. I should have told you."

"I should've asked."

"It doesn't matter," I whispered, looking down. "It's no one's fault." After a brief pause, I said, "I understand if you need space right now."

He sat cross-legged and quiet in his plaid pajama pants. "What do you mean?"

"You need time to process this—away from me, from us, because this," I gestured between us, "clouds your judgment, just like it did mine."

He lifted his chin and said evenly, "Don't tell me what I need."

"But you should take it."

"I don't need time. I don't want to lose you, so we'll find an answer."

"There's no answer, David," I said. My urge to wallow had passed, and now, it was time to put the entire truth out there. "I could never take fatherhood from you. I won't do it."

"I can make my own decisions."

"I know you can."

"Every time we get close, you run. Now you're trying to get me to run. I can't help but feel like you're sabotaging what we have." He shook his head and looked away. "It sounds like you want me to leave you."

"Of course I don't want that," I cried immediately. "But the only thing worse than you leaving would be you resenting me years down the line because I took this away from you."

His jaw set, and he turned back to me. "I've been thinking a lot, and I have some questions."

I dipped my head into a nod. "Ask me anything."

"Why don't you want children?"

Well, that wasn't just any question. It was *the* question. And there was no clear answer. "I've tried to rationalize it. I can't," I said. "It all comes down to my gut. My instinct says motherhood is not the path for me." I rewrapped my towel around myself and tilted my head. "I don't see it in my future, David. And if I can't see it with you, then I never will."

"Can you see me in your future?"

"You're all I see," I said quietly. "That's why this has been so confusing."

His expression remained hard, as if he were trying to push through this instead of—what? Did he want to walk out? Cry? Beg me? Shake me?

"Does this have something to do with your mom?" he asked. "Are you afraid?"

A fair and crucial question that I'd had time to think about considering . . . "Bill asked me the same thing."

"Because you're *not* her, Olivia." David's features finally softened. "You'd make a phenomenal mom. You're so loving. You have so much to give when you let yourself."

I blinked at him. Did I? Was I this warm and loving creature David thought I was, or cold and heartless as Bill had accused? Could I be warm, loving, and selfless and still not want children? "You're right," I said. "I'm not her. I'd never be the type of parent she was."

With his elbows on his knees, he steepled his hands in front of his face, as if interacting with a client. "So this isn't because you're afraid of turning out like her?"

I'd learned a great deal about myself over the past few months. But long ago, I'd learned from my mom's mistakes. I'd thought I was destined to become her, but David had proven to me that I could handle what came my way. My mother was an example of what I didn't want to become. In that respect, at least, she'd been the right kind of bad role model. I wouldn't be the same kind of mother, so I shook my head. "No," I said. "I recognize that fear of becoming her, and I've already overcome it once to keep you. I could do it again. But this is something else. It runs deeper."

He nodded slowly, resting his forehead against his fingers. "Explain something to me if you can," he said and peeked up at me. "Why was it so hard for you to let go with me?"

I'd lived in a quiet, safe cage, and David had rattled it, broken the chains, opened the gate to set me free—only to have me stay inside where I'd been comfortable. Now that I'd finally stepped out, I could never return to that. "I was afraid once I let myself love you, I'd lose you," I said. "And I didn't think I could handle it."

"Are you sure this isn't the same thing?" he asked. "You're not afraid of loving a baby too much?"

"The idea *does* scare me," I admitted. "That I'd be responsible for this being, and there'd be no second chances, no room for mistakes."

"All parents make mistakes." He arched a dark eyebrow. "Jessa does all the time."

I half-smiled. "I know. But it's *not* just that. It's instinct. And I know what you say about your instincts . . ."

"I never ignore my gut," he said, quoting himself. "Even when it gets me in deep shit."

"But, David, if the alternative is losing you . . ." Walking away from him now wasn't an option. I was committed. Everything I had, everything I was, I wanted to share with him. If he wanted to end this, I would respect that, even while it killed me. But I'd spent all day wondering if I'd willingly walk away, and the answer was— I wouldn't.

"I could do it," I whispered, searching eyes that had the

ability to melt away all my fears and doubts. "For you. I could make you a father."

David's response came out strangled. "I would never let you do that for me, Olivia. You know I wouldn't."

Of course I'd known—it was part of what I'd been hiding from. David would let me go before he asked me to do this for him the way Bill had.

"*Fuck.*" David dropped his head in his hands. "I never gave having children much thought, I guess because I just figured it would happen one day."

"It's the *only* reason the proposal scared me." I wrapped my hand around his wrist, and he raised his head to look at me. I took his coarse palm in my hand. "I loved everything you said this morning. I would've accepted on the spot if I could've." I swallowed. "I want you to know that I wouldn't change anything about the decisions I've made. I'd leave my life behind all over again, and I'd let you tear down my walls a second time, even for the short life we've led together. Thank you for showing me—"

"Oh, come on, Olivia," he said almost angrily. "You don't think I'd give up that easily, do you? Give me some fucking credit."

I withdrew my hand, surprised by the tidal wave of anguish that crashed over me. The most heartbreaking part was that we could no longer fight. There was nothing to fix. We'd each given it our all.

"You *have* to give up." Tears spilled from my eyes. "Fighting it will only make it harder. The sooner we end this, the better."

"What the fuck?" he asked. "Is that what you want?"

"Of course that's not what I want!" I nearly screamed and choked on a sob. "I want you all to myself for the rest of my life. I want to quit my job and travel the world with you and eat and drink and fuck and love you forever. I

433

want to go to Spain and lie on the beach and eat oysters and write my book, but this is real life, David. This is not a dream or a fantasy. What choice do we have?"

He blinked at me a few times, as if speechless. "I want those things, too," he said, but his voice wavered.

"You say that now, but you don't know what you'd be giving up. Because I love you, and I want your own happiness more than my own, I can't take this away from you." I couldn't help myself from crawling into his lap and wrapping my arms around his neck.

He sat back against the headboard, squeezing me to him. "But I love you," he said, almost under his breath.

I wanted to claw open my chest and rip out my heart so I could give it to him.

Take it. Take it all, because I will never need it again. I don't want it.

I wasn't sure if he fell asleep, but his hold on me never loosened. This was my dream, my fantasy, my heaven, my nightmare, to be bound and wound with a love as strong as this.

Eventually, when light began to filter through the shades, I sat up.

David sighed, rubbing his eyes. "We have to go if we're going to make our flight."

While he showered, I knotted my tangled and unruly hair back and brushed my teeth. With puffy eyes, a red nose, and an empty gaze, I fleetingly thought . . .

This is exactly how I imagined I would look at the end.

Chapter Twenty-Eight

David and I returned to a snowy Chicago. The stark contrast from Miami wasn't only apparent in the weather. David and I had traveled in relative silence. He'd been attentive as always, making sure I'd been comfortable during the flight, but I could tell he'd been deep in thought. I, on the other hand, finally had nothing left to think about.

Fortunately, I'd taken the day off, but David had booked us an early flight so he could go in to work. After putting me in a cab with our luggage, David had gone straight from the airport to his office.

I spent the day in the den, watching movies in the dark, because the alternative was worrying myself sick. I hated being in limbo, not knowing what David would decide. I couldn't envision anything beyond the end of us. David was right—I *did* see him in my future, and I'd seen him in that house. So didn't that mean something?

My anxiety heightened when the third movie ended, and I realized it was nearing ten o'clock at night. My phone had been quiet. I picked it up from the coffee table and checked my inbox. A subject line jumped out at me.

Re: Hi

Lucy had responded to my last e-mail.

I'd been much more optimistic when I'd written to her. Now, I wasn't in the right state of mind to hear anything but encouragement, and I wasn't sure I'd find that in her response. I put the phone back down.

I'd just started another movie when I heard a noise. I immediately hit *Pause* and looked up from the couch to see David in the doorway. "You're home," I said dumbly.

He nodded, his hands shoved into his trouser pockets.

"It's late," I added, noting his tousled hair, the same foreboding black of his loosened tie.

"I was out looking for something," was all he said.

I understood. He'd been searching for answers all day, and I'd been here, numbing myself with nothingness and not making plans or decisions as I should've been. I hoped David would find his answers soon, because it killed me to see him this way.

"I'm exhausted," he said.

I reached for the remote, shut off the TV, and went to stand. "Let's go to bed."

"No."

I paused at the edge in his tone. Without the TV glare, the only light in the room came from the doorway behind him, turning him into a silhouette. I sank back into the couch. "Okay."

"I fired Arnaud."

"What?" I widened my eyes. "How come?"

"I found him in his office, door closed, with the new receptionist. Normally, I wouldn't have thought anything of it, but after Clare's allegations, I wasn't taking any chances."

I braced myself. As much as I disliked Arnaud, I didn't want the sexual harassment claims to be true. I hated picturing Clare, the new receptionist, and however many others in that position. "Did you walk in on something?"

"Not exactly. They were sitting on the couch. Again— any other day, I wouldn't have noticed. But this time, I looked at her, and she seemed scared. I pulled her out and asked if anything had happened." David paused, and even in the semi-dark, I could sense his jaw clench and unclench. "Arnaud had tried to touch her a few times, and warned if she kept denying him, he'd find another secretary who wouldn't."

"Oh, God," I said, sick to my stomach for them. "I'm so sorry. Did you confront him?"

"Obviously. He denied everything. But after what you said about not wanting to be alone with him, I pushed. It took some, ah . . . *pressure*—but eventually, he admitted to it. Clare, and the girl before her, too."

With a small gasp, tears pricked my eyes. *That piece of shit.* The first time I'd met him, I'd *known* something was off. "I should've said something sooner."

"It's my fault," he said.

"It's *not* your fault, David." I wanted to comfort him, but his stiff bearing kept me where I was. "You didn't know."

"I should've. I let them down. I tried to *defend* him." He swallowed audibly. "And at some point, you could've been alone with him, too."

I resisted going to him, assuring him with my touch that he would've done something if he'd even the smallest inkling. But I didn't think he wanted comfort right then, so I just said, "You did the right thing."

"He not only crossed the line, but he put the business in jeopardy, too—which means he gambled with *my* life.

And *our* future," David continued. "Those girls could sue us."

I crossed my legs under me. "And what about your partnership flipping houses? Will you see that through?"

He gave me an incredulous look. "I'll never work with that piece of shit again. He'll dissolve our contract without a peep if he's smart. I don't care how much money either of us loses."

His vehemence relieved me. I'd be thrilled to never be in Arnaud's presence again. But something he'd said snagged my attention. It was no secret David had a temper. Even now, hours after the fact, fury radiated from him. And the wrong decision in the heat of the moment could change everything for him. "What did you mean when you said you used a little *pressure* on Arnaud?"

"I didn't hit him," David said calmly, "even though I wanted to. If it'd been you in his office, I would've." He took a step. "But I focused on you. On what losing control could mean for me and how it would affect you."

"Thank you," I whispered.

"But I shook him up a little," he said, then amended, "well, a lot."

I could picture it too easily, Arnaud's slight frame pitted against David's massive one. It made me want to smile, but I said, "I'm sorry."

"Don't be," he said. "I should've listened the first time you told me how you felt about him."

"What about Clare?" I asked.

"I apologized, said I had no idea about Arnaud. She's going to reconsider the lawsuit, but I assured her I wouldn't blame her if she proceeded with it."

"I wouldn't, either."

He cocked his head. "She'd be coming after my money, too," he said. "That doesn't worry you?"

"No." I didn't have to consider it. "I told you already. I didn't need any of this. I only wanted you."

"Wanted?" he asked.

Want. Desperately. But showing him that would only make this harder. I clenched my teeth to stem a wave of tears. David had seen me cry enough and not being able to comfort me hurt him. "Can we go to bed now?"

"We're not finished."

My heart thudded once with his clipped tone. What if . . . was it possible he'd already gotten the answer he'd been looking for?

"Did I, or did I not," he said slowly, "tell you *several* times not to go see Bill without me?"

Shit. I'd known David wouldn't like that, and also that he'd find out eventually. My throat was suddenly dry so I nodded. "Yes. You did."

He gave an empty laugh. "But why the fuck would you listen to anything I asked of you, right?"

"I went to Bill's office, where I knew it would be safe," I said defensively. "He'd never jeopardize his job for me, and he didn't. He was perfectly compliant."

"It doesn't matter," David said. "I want to be there. It's not just about whether he gets physical. If he's shitty to you, if he calls you names, I promised I'd be your shield. Why won't you let me?"

Exhaustion rolled through me. I didn't want to fight. "But it was good news," I said. "He'll grant the divorce sooner and without a trial. He agreed to the six months."

"Six months, and your share of the savings. Jerry told me."

"It only makes sense," I said. "It's my money."

David took a step toward me, and my breathing shallowed. "You'll do whatever it takes to keep one foot out the door."

I wasn't doing that, but keeping my savings was proving to be the right call. David still hadn't given me his decision about us. I'd *need* that money if this was over. "I'm just being practical."

"You said, just now, that you *wanted* me. Past tense." His next step gave way to a prowl. "In your mind, this is already over."

I'd let my guard down with David. Completely. The only defense I had now was bracing myself for impact. "I still want you," I breathed as he stopped at the end of the couch. "No matter what happens . . . for me, this will never be over."

Everything about him tensed, including his expression. He grabbed the undersides of my knees and dragged me to the edge. Back in his possession, after keeping my distance all day, my coiled desire sprung free, sending a thrill up my spine.

Positioning my pelvis so it was vertical against the arm, David licked his lips and looked into my eyes as he undid his pants. In his eyes, I saw his need for me, and he needed me bad for whatever he was going through. Not just physically, but emotionally. And I could fill those needs for him. Something told me I'd been the only woman who ever had. With my nightgown bunched around my waist, he removed my panties and flung them aside.

He propped himself over me with one hand next to my head and grabbed his cock in the other. I opened my legs wider as he fed himself into me, grasping at tiny breaths as I took his length slowly. I clutched desperately at each inch, as if it were the last time. He rooted himself as deeply as he could before his thrusts began.

"You want me to leave you?" he asked solemnly.

"No."

"Want me to throw you out with nothing?"

"No," I said, and his drives grew harder, mashing me into the couch.

"Want me to break you, once and for all?"

I gasped as he hit a spot that sent tremors of pleasure through me. "No."

"Then tell me so," he said through his teeth.

Above me, his beautiful face blurred with my tears. His pain, on clear display, hurt worse than my own. "I love you."

"Tell me you want me to stay."

I put my hand to his cheek. "I want you to stay."

"Beg me," he commanded with hardness in his eyes.

"Please stay," I breathed.

"That's not good enough."

Salty tears fell down my cheeks, and I bit my lip. He'd never tell me no, and he'd never let me sacrifice myself for him. Asking him to stay meant asking him to give up a life he wanted and deserved. For me. It was selfish, but he needed me to be selfish now.

He wrapped his large hand at the base of my throat to pull me onto him harder. "Beg, Olivia."

"Don't . . . leave me," I choked through a sob. "Don't ever leave me, David, please. I'm begging you. I couldn't take it. I love you and I need you, God, I fucking need you more than anything in the world—stay, stay forever, David. Don't leave me."

As the pleas tumbled out, he straightened his back and levered my hips up in the air. His hands wrapped around my waist and pulled me into each harsh thrust. His eyes glazed over, but I trusted him, and I let him take me how he needed until I was squirming under him, fisting the couch, arching my back and mewling, sobbing, begging him to stay, and finally, climaxing with shudders that were lost in the aggressive way he fucked me.

"I've asked, I've begged, I've fought to give you everything. I want everything from you now," he growled. "I'm sick of asking for it, and now I'm taking it." He fucked me faster, my body just a receptacle now, each thrust with a louder grunt until—as if he was going in for the kill—his jaw set, his grip tightened, his head jerked up to the ceiling, and he erupted into me. He held me there a while longer as his eyes remained fixed upward, his wet cock sliding in and out of me slowly, leisurely.

He pulled out and dropped me back on the couch. I'd done hardly anything and I was breathing hard, but his chest heaved. Without a word, he turned and left the room.

I stood shakily and pulled my underwear back on. In the bedroom, David had sprawled out on his stomach, over the comforter, in just his boxer briefs. He was already passed out. I climbed in next to him and shut my eyes.

In the darkness of night, the rebelling tide threatens to pull me out to sea with each lap at my ankles. A presence behind me tries to both protect and consume me. It slides itself around my neck, pulling me close until it's so tight that I can no longer get air. I try to pull it away, but it's not the presence anymore that's strangling me—it's a snake with rough scales that slither along my bare skin. I open my mouth to scream, but I'm voiceless. As the presence dissolves, the snake untangles itself and swims away into the night. I dive in after it.

I jerked awake. Despite the cold, sweat trickled down my temples. I'd forgotten to close the blinds and moonlight streamed through the bedroom window, striping the comforter. David slept serenely, his back rising and falling evenly in the position I'd found him earlier.

I took my phone from the nightstand and opened Lucy's e-mail.

From: Lucy Greene
Sent: Mon, November 26 04:16 PM CST
To: Olivia Germaine
Subject: Re: Hi

Dear Liv,

You know how much I've valued your friendship over the years. It's rare to stay so super close after college. But I don't feel like I know you anymore. Since you met David, you're not the same person. Bill tells me that in the months following the funeral, you were so upset because of losing David, not Davena. That's beyond me, especially considering the way you treated Bill during that time and even us, too, when we tried to help. Also, the Liv I know would never treat my sister the way you have.

The way you broke your vows makes me sick to my stomach. What you said at my wedding was beautiful, but knowing that it didn't mean anything is a slap in the face. I've always liked David, but he's a bad influence on you. Even though I disagree with your choices, I don't want to see you get hurt. I know that the divorce is already underway, so I can only pray that you've made the right decision. And I *will* pray for you.

We have so much history, and I don't want to dishonor that. At the same time, Bill and Andrew are closer than ever. I must respect Andrew's friendship, because at the end of the day, my loyalty is to him. I think it's best we don't speak for a while.

Best wishes always,

Lucy

I ran the back of my hand over my wet cheeks. There was nothing left to say. I knew there'd be consequences to my choices. Losing a best friend was one of them.

Even though the love of my life slept right next to me, I missed him keenly in that moment. Like a wilting flower, my petals browned at the edges and dropped one by one without David's nourishment. I needed to be held by him, to be revived by his love. And he was so close, within reach, but he seemed far away.

I eased out of bed and tiptoed over to the window. Soft snow danced in beautiful chaos. As always, Chicago's cityscape stunned me, sleeping but still alive. I let myself get lost in its powerful, raw, dark beauty as I stood at the top of the world.

The first time I'd seen David smile at Lucy's engagement party, it'd nearly knocked me off my feet—how had I not known then I was in love? Then, there was the first time I saw all of him, still mysterious and sinister, even when stripped down to nothing. Or when he'd let me cry into his chest after we'd made love in The Revelin hotel suite. It had been that moment when I'd known I was caught in a storm with no shelter.

I wasn't ready to say good-bye. I wanted him to stay so fucking bad. I'd meant every begging word earlier. At least I'd held nothing back. Finally, I'd not only opened up for him, but I'd asked for what I'd wanted. Even if it made me selfish, I wanted him to stay.

I jumped at David's touch. His arms slid around my shoulders from behind, and he pulled me against him. "Honeybee," he whispered in my ear.

My tears had dried, but I shook in his embrace. "I don't want to lose you," I said to our faint reflection in the window. "Don't walk away from this. Please."

We sat that way for a while. When my trembling subsided, he released me, leaving me bereft. I closed my eyes at the loss, but it wasn't long until he returned. His arms went back around me, and his lips came to my ear. "Were you afraid earlier?"

"No," I whispered. "I trust you."

His grip on me tightened. "Even though I knew my mind wouldn't change, I spent a lot of time thinking today and last night. I thought about life with and without children. About life," he paused, and I felt his tentative breath, "without you."

My hands shook again as I realized what was coming. I pulled away, and he let me.

This was it.

I had to be strong. I'd laid everything on the line, and that was all I could do. I collected myself and turned to look at him.

The bright moon showed everything on his face. His eyes were so clear and determined that I touched my palm to my heart. And I knew that whatever he said next would be the truth. His eyes were his soul. They'd never lied to me, and for that, I would always be grateful. "David," I prompted, not recognizing my own voice.

"There's nothing in this world I want more than you, Olivia."

My heart jumped into my throat. I laced my trembling fingers over my chest. "But?"

"But nothing."

My ears rang as I struggled to process his meaning. He'd stay. He wasn't giving up on us despite all the reasons I'd given him, and no matter how many times I'd pushed him away. My eyes watered, threatening a celebration of tears. "David?"

He placed a hand on the side of my neck and leaned in. "I would kill for you. I would die for you. You are my everything. If you don't want children, then we won't have them. And if you change your mind, that's fine, too. Just know that nothing can keep me away."

I choked back a sob, overwhelmed with love and gratitude. David had seen me when others couldn't or wouldn't. He'd given me what I hadn't known I'd needed. And now, I not only had a great love, but I could keep it.

His brows drew together. "We fought hard for this. If it's you and me for the rest of our lives, how could I ever complain? It's exactly what I wanted."

I threw my arms around his neck. "Oh, David," I whispered. "Do you know how much I love you? More than the moon, the stars, the world. You're everything I never dared to dream."

He shuddered under my body, then pried my hands away and stepped around me to stand in front of the window. Suddenly, he was alert in a way I'd never seen— nervous even. He was big, always dark and brooding in his own way, and so incredibly gorgeous in just his underwear standing with his back to the city.

"What—"

"I want that life with you, too," he interrupted. "Traveling, eating, making love, sleeping with you in my arms, thanking my lucky stars every night, waking up to your beautiful face every morning. That's what I want."

My gaze dropped to his hand, tightly curled around something. In one fluid motion, he dropped to his knee. His fingers unfurled to reveal a black velvet box.

Yes.

The word I should've said the morning before

resounded through my head as my eyes darted between the box and his face.

"Were it anyone else, I would've walked away in the beginning. Were it anyone else, I would've fucking stayed away. But it's not. It's you. It always has been, and always will be, you." David opened the box, showing me an engagement ring. "Marry me, Olivia."

Fresh tears welled, but I inhaled them and laughed. "You said *fuck* in your proposal."

"Damn right I did."

I took a step forward, sat on his bent knee, and wrapped my arms around his neck. I rubbed my face against his bristly cheek, and in his ear, said, "Yes. You are my love, my home. *Fuck* yes."

His shoulders deflated with his exhale, and I pulled back to look at him. It was my favorite thing in the whole world, the boyish, blissful smile on his face. *Pure happiness.*

He caught my lips with his, both of us smiling through a series of small, sweet kisses. We both watched as, slowly, he slid the platinum ring, glinting and magnificent in the moonlight, onto my finger. The band was slight but the cushion-cut diamond was not—large, and blindingly beautiful, simple and clear.

"It's perfect." I shook my head in awe, unable to tear my eyes away. "How did you know?"

"Why wouldn't I?" he asked, confused. "When I said earlier that I was looking for something, it was this. I went to every jewelry store in search of it. It took me all day, but the second I saw it, I knew it was right."

I glanced up as his words echoed in my mind. Finally, it was right. So right.

Everything was *right*.

Epilogue

As David and I waited for the *Walk* signal to flash so we could cross the street, I shifted a bag of groceries into one hand and squinted up at my beautiful husband.

"You're staring," David told me.

"Sorry," I said but didn't look away.

He was so damn distracting, that—

"Oh, *shit*," I said and frowned. "I forgot Manchego cheese. We can't have a Spanish feast without Manchego."

"Certainly not," he said with a half-smile. "I'll run back. Wait here?"

"Where would I go?"

We'd driven into the city for one of David's events the night before and had stayed at the penthouse. Now, we grabbed last-minute groceries before heading home to Oak Park for our impending party.

David dropped his plastic bags right there on the sidewalk. In one swoop, he embraced me, bending me backward over his arm. I squealed just as he locked his lips over mine for a passionate kiss.

"What was that for?" I asked breathlessly when he pulled away.

"Nothing, honeybee. I just couldn't go another second without doing it."

A large, all-consuming smile overtook my face as I blushed.

"Actually, *that's* why. That smile right there," he said quietly, running his thumb over the corner of my mouth. "I'll be right back."

He gently righted my body, steadying me when I swayed slightly. His kiss still had that effect on me.

When he turned away, I was hit by a familiar glare from the patio of a café across the street. Bill, my now ex-husband, sat at a small table with Lucy and Andrew. I froze as his eyes bored into me and sent a chill down my spine.

I wanted to look away, but I couldn't. I hadn't seen Bill —or Lucy—in almost two years. From the outside, he hadn't really changed. But did he feel like a new person the way I did?

Bill finally blinked and turned back to Lucy, who appeared to be mid-story as she gestured in Bill's direction. Andrew rubbed her back as she spoke. She wore her hair even shorter than she used to, whereas I'd let mine grow. They all broke out in laughter simultaneously, and my heart tugged. For a moment, I entertained the thought of going over to say hello, but what would be the point? I had nothing new to say to them, and I doubted they wanted to see me.

I'd reached out to Lucy once more since I'd read the e-mail she'd sent the day David had proposed, but nothing had come of it. It'd taken a while for me to grasp, but I eventually realized that for her, the friendship was over. She and Gretchen had made up and remained close, so I heard bits and pieces of Lucy's life that way. I could see, even from a distance, that she was happy, but I still missed her friendship.

Bill, on the other hand, had made it hard to miss him. The six months David and I had waited for my divorce had been grueling. Though David had assured me he was fine keeping our engagement a secret, I'd wanted him to know how proud I was to wear his ring. Bill didn't hide his disgust at the news. Fortunately, he and David never laid hands on each other again, but there were times I'd thought David would push Bill through the wall for the way he'd spoken to us during the proceedings. A year and a half had passed since we'd seen him, but from the look in his eyes just now, nothing was yet forgiven. It made me all the more sure that I'd made the right decision.

Not that I need any reassuring.

David exited the grocery store with a big smile, his aviators locked on me, his gait leisurely and confident. An attractive woman did a double take as she passed him. She turned and lowered her sunglasses to get a better look. My chest swelled with pride as she checked out my man, but I couldn't help laughing a little when she stumbled over a curb.

"Manchego," David said, holding up the block of cheese. "Crisis averted."

"My superhero," I said.

He leaned over and picked up all the bags, including mine. "Let's get this party underway."

As we walked away, I shot one last glance at the table of friends. They made a good group and seemed happy. I couldn't be upset about that. I stuck my hand into David's back pocket, and we made our own heavenly way back home.

In the car, as we pulled up to the house, I smiled. I always did. David's vision, with some input from me, had blossomed before our eyes. The sylvan paradise had come to life again—or maybe for the first time, I wasn't sure. The newly fixed stone walkway led a natural path to the front door through green grass, and a revived, leafy landscape.

Before David had taken the six-month job in New York, he'd warned me that I might not like his overly "masculine" apartment in the city. I'd teased him that *masculine* was code for bachelor pad. To both our surprise, I'd fallen immediately in love with it. Unlike his bright, white Chicago apartment, New York was dark and woodsy, with exposed brick walls and dim, yellow lighting. The vintage furniture was heavy leather and oak, worn but solid.

I'd suggested we decorate our house somewhere in between the two places. Sliding glass doors lent themselves to good lighting, especially in the mornings, but the wood-heavy home, earthy and sturdy, reminded me of David, which I loved most of all.

It was a perfect Chicago night for a party. David opened up all the doors and windows for the setting sun. I'd almost finished laying out a buffet of food on a table in the backyard when a knock came at the front door. David and I met in the entryway, the same spot I'd told him over two years before that Bill had put in an offer on this very house. We kissed quickly.

"We can see you," David's sister called as she peered through a vertical window that ran alongside the front door.

David opened the door and groaned. Equipped with margarita mix, wine, whiskey, and other assortments of alcohol, stood our friends and family: Jessa, her son Alex, Gretchen, Brian, Mack and Cooper—who'd become friends—and David's parents, Judy and Gerard. Just past them, Serena and her fiancé, Brock, climbed out of his car.

"Well, baby," David said, looking down at me, "I'd say we have extremely punctual friends."

They all piled in at once, and David assumed bartending duties. They were a rowdy bunch, and sometimes they were weird, but I couldn't complain. I loved them.

"In honor of David and me returning from our recent trip to Spain, we're having tapas," I announced in the backyard. I gestured to the expansive spread. "Help yourselves."

"So?" Jessa asked, linking her arm with mine. "How was the honeymoon?"

I smiled wistfully and attempted to think of a word that could possibly do it justice. "*Magical*," I decided, every detail of the memory clear.

I waved back at David—my husband—from a beach towel. He looked sexier than ever, perched on his surfboard, waiting for the water to swell. His stomach flexed into a delicious six-pack. Riveted, I watched as he caught a wave, fluidly hopping onto his shortboard and riding it down the line.

I reclined back onto my towel, inserted my earbuds, and closed my eyes to soak in the hot Spanish sun. Cool drops of water punctured my relaxed state. I opened one eye and squinted up at David.

"I couldn't help noticing you from the water," he said. "Mind if I join you?"

"Actually," I purred, "I was thinking of taking a dip myself."

He set his board down next to me and held out his hand. I took out my earbuds and let him hoist me up with one pull.

He scooped me off my feet. "I was hoping you'd go for a swim."

"Well, actually, I was just planning to get my feet wet . . ."

David cut gracefully through the sand. "I don't think so, honeybee. The water's perfect."

"But—" A squeal tore from my lips when he threw me into the sea. I popped up, gasping for air, and splashed him as I tried to run ashore.

He caught my waist and spun me into him. I breathed hard as he captured my lips in a quick kiss. "You look incredibly sexy, Mrs. Dylan."

Ah, Mrs. Dylan. *I was certain hearing my new name would never get old.* "Thank you for this," I said, motioning in the general direction of San Sebastián. "All of this."

"Thank you for all of this," he replied, running his hands greedily over my body. His fingers teased the straps of my bikini top. One hand skated down to my lower back and pulled me so close that my entire body warmed with his heat, even through the cold salt water.

"David Dylan, you scoundrel," I teased.

"Olivia Dylan, you temptress."

"Do you intend to take me in front of all of Spain?" I asked hopefully.

"Would a gentleman do that?" He smiled and then peered over my shoulder. "Remind me to find us a private beach next time."

"I don't care," I said, kissing his briny neck and then working my way down to nibble on his shoulder.

"I know you don't," he said, shaking his head and pulling me off. "But I do."

"Damn it," I said under my breath, and he laughed. But I wasn't ready to give up. "It's our honeymoon—we're supposed to do this sort of thing."

"Oh, we *will* do this sort of thing, as much as possible, and as long as possible—in a place where I'm the only one who gets to see you naked." He kissed me. "Oh, how I do love that pretty pout, though."

I caught myself fingering the gold disk that hung between my breasts from its chain. I raised it toward him. "Read it to me again," I said suddenly.

We'd spent the first week of our honeymoon in the South of France before making our way to Spain. I'd learned that my new husband spoke French, and he spoke it beautifully. He'd impulsively stopped in a small jewelry shop and unbeknownst to me, ordered a hand-engraved gold necklace that we'd later picked up on our way out of town. I'd never heard the famous quote by French poet Rosemonde Gérard and made David repeat her words often.

"Haven't you memorized it by now?" David asked, bringing me back to the moment.

"No," I lied.

"Car, vois-tu, chaque jour je t'aime davantage, aujour-d'hui plus qu'hier et bien moins que demain."

I smiled and looked at him, waiting.

He covered my hand that held the delicate disk. "For, you see, each day I love you more, today more than yesterday and less than tomorrow."

The honeymoon had been three weeks of espresso, navigating tiny streets, laughing until our faces hurt, and sex in cramped places. We learned even more about each other during the trip, and though we fought at times, the arguments always ended in either fits of laughter or steamy sex.

My heart began to race when Serena approached me in the backyard, her lips quirked into a small smile. During my time away, I'd given her a very special assignment, and I was as worried as I was excited to hear her feedback.

"Well?" I asked.

"I *loved* it," she said. "Genuine, fluid, and actually quite funny. Your first novel is going to be a smash hit."

I exhaled a rush of air. I'd finished my first draft right before we'd left for the honeymoon, and I'd needed someone to look at it and tell me I wasn't crazy to pursue an agent. "Thank you," I said. "It still needs a lot of work, but it's a start. Please tell me you have notes."

"Meet for coffee next week to discuss?" she asked, swirling her margarita. "Tonight, I'm about to get drunk-ity-drunk."

Once I'd begun to make real progress on the book, I'd quit my job at David's urging. Since I was now Olivia Dylan—happily—I'd use that name to distance myself from my mother's work.

In a final attempt to get my mother to accept our upcoming nuptials, David and I had stopped to see her as we'd driven my dad's early wedding gift, the '68 Shelby, from Dallas to Chicago. Despite telling her we were coming, or perhaps because of it, she'd been drinking when we'd arrived. I'd tried to convince her to let me take her to a fancy rehab facility David had found nearby, but she'd refused. She didn't like David because of the affair, and whenever I'd used the word *alcoholic*, she'd become more combative.

After hurling one too many insults at me, David had marched me back to the car. It was with heavy hearts that we'd left, but I'd known we'd run out of options.

David and I hadn't gotten married right away. With his ring on my finger and, finally, my entire heart in his hands, he respected my request that we wait a respectable time after the divorce was finalized. We'd had a small, intimate affair held amongst the peacefulness of the Alfred Caldwell Lily Pool, followed by a bigger party for all our friends and extended family. My mom hadn't attended, but I'd had my dad along with David's family, who'd become mine, too, and who couldn't have been more loving and supportive.

And, of course, Mack Donovan had also been in attendance as he was tonight.

"I haven't had a chance to thank you properly since

you left right after the wedding," Mack said as I made him a margarita. "You and David are both angels," he said warmly. "Just like my Davena."

"Contributing to Davena's foundation was the least I could do for both you and her," I told Mack. I vividly remembered David's and my conversation one evening as we'd sat at our new kitchen table, planning the wedding.

"Is there anything you want that you don't have?" David asked. "Anything in the world, baby."

I smiled at him and moved from my chair to his lap. My arms wound around his neck. "Nothing."

"Think really hard. Anything at all."

"Nope." I shook my head and kissed him on the lips.

"Then, in lieu of wedding gifts, I think we should have our guests donate to the animal shelter," David said.

My eyes watered instantly as chills lit over my body. David always prioritized me, no matter what, and sometimes I thought he knew me better than I knew myself. "I love that idea," I whispered. "But I have a better idea. What if they had the option to donate to the foundation Mack set up in Davena's name, too?"

He touched the tip of his nose to mine. "And I'll match the final donation to both."

"Oh, honey, you don't have—"

"Shh," he said softly. "I want to. My gift to the bride."

I blinked back tears and kissed him again, this time for his generous and loving spirit.

When I saw Gretchen leaning against the bar outside by herself, I made a beeline for her. She'd recently cut her hair shorter and was wearing it straight these days. She looked happier and much less angular, having put on a little weight, which suited her.

"So, how was the trip *really*?" Gretchen asked. "Did you put a dent in Europe from all the fucking?"

"Yes," I confirmed. "It was amazing. You'd love Spain."

"I have no doubt."

"In fact, I brought back a special Spanish wine just for you," I said, walking behind the bar to grab it. "Want to try it now? It's yummy."

"Um, well, no," she said, picking at her fingernail. "I'm not thirsty."

"Not *thirsty*?" I asked, gaping at her. "I don't think I've ever heard you turn down an alcoholic beverage."

She gave me a slight smile that slowly spread across her face as she failed to suppress it. "By the way," she said, "I hope you're free next month. Brian and I are moving up the wedding, and we're doing it here at home."

"Wait, *what*?" I exclaimed. Ever since Brian had proposed, Gretchen had been talking non-stop about her grand plans for a destination wedding. "Why?"

"Well, I don't want to look like a porker in my dress," she explained.

I frowned, confused. A few pounds did not a porker make. Gretchen looked fabulous. Was she planning to put on more weight?

That made no sense. Unless she was . . .

An arm landed around my shoulder, and I looked up as Brian squeezed me to him. They exchanged a look.

I gasped, and my gaze shot back to her. "Are you *pregnant*?"

She nodded and walked into Brian's open arms. "We're having a baby," she said. "A happy accident."

"An *ecstatic* accident," Brian corrected.

I squealed, drawing David immediately to my side. "What?" he asked with an edge of panic.

Brian put a hand on Gretchen's tummy and looked at David. "Thirteen weeks pregnant."

I fanned my face to hold in tears as David gave Gretchen a gentle hug. I turned and announced the news at the top of my lungs, receiving cheers in response.

Once dark had fallen and everyone had gone home, David and I cleaned up the party. "Go to bed," David said when we'd almost finished. He threw an empty beer bottle into an oversized black trash bag. "I'll finish this."

"You're a good husband," I called back to him. I let him clean because I had plans to reward him copiously. In the bedroom, I pulled black stockings up to my thighs and attached them to a matching garter belt. I slipped into one of David's favorite pairs of stilettos and topped everything off with a short black-lace negligée. I snuck into our sprawling master bathroom to fix my hair and then perched on the bed to wait.

Our sex life had become a drug for both of us. Like our connection from the day we'd met eyes, it only intensified the more we gave in to it. The more we pried each other open, the more we spilled into each other—and the results had been mind-blowing.

David had lovingly escorted me to the best gynecologist in town to hear our options concerning sterilization. For now, we'd decided to leave our options open just in case. The fact that he would be willing to get a vasectomy for me, though, was a testament to the love and faith he had in us.

When I got bored of waiting for David to come to bed,

I slid open the door to our built-in balcony and let the cool night wash over me. I hopped onto the ledge. David hated when I sat on it, but to lean over our own backyard and feel the breeze exhilarated me, even if it was only from the second story.

I heard him in the bedroom so I got into position by straightening my shoulders and spreading my thighs. "Out here," I called.

"Holy fucking shit," he drawled when he walked outside. "You look good enough to eat, but if you don't get down right this second, I'm going to be pissed."

"How pissed will you be?" I asked, grasping the wood railing between my legs and leaning back slightly.

"Olivia, I'm not fucking around," he said, approaching cautiously as though I might let go. He leaped and grasped me in his arms. I giggled as he threw me over his shoulder and swatted my lace-covered behind. "You are in so much trouble."

"*Yes*," I whispered excitedly under my breath.

"What was that?"

"I said, 'Please be gentle.'"

He vaulted me backward onto the bed, and I landed in a pile of soft down. "I gather you aren't aiming for gentle in that outfit," he rumbled, standing between my legs and running his hands along my thighs.

I licked my bottom lip, bit it gently, and shook my head. "No, sir."

His lids lowered. "Turn over, ass in the air."

I obeyed and pressed my cheek against the mattress. He spread me open, pushed my panties aside, and slipped in one finger. "Always so wet for me," he murmured.

I agreed with a muffled purr. He bent to kiss me between the legs, then ran his tongue along the length of me and inserted another finger. "Do you want to come like this?" he asked.

"No," I breathed.

"How then?"

"I want you inside me."

He chuckled. "Of course you do." He fingered me slightly harder, causing me to writhe. "Hold still."

I fisted my hands into the sheets and took it, trying not to squirm as he tongued me—but I couldn't help it.

Without removing his mouth, so I still felt his breath between my legs, he asked, "Will you hold still, or do I have to tie you up?"

"I want to be bound," I said. "But only by you."

He climbed onto the bed, and I offered my hands behind me. He grasped both of my wrists easily in one big hand, yanked my underwear to my knees, and pressed the head of his cock against my opening.

"Please," I said with a moan.

His grip tightened around my wrists while he slid his crown up and down my wetness. My body shivered with anticipation. "I will," he said, "when you stop squirming."

I took a deep breath and forced myself to relax.

After a moment, he bent over my back so his mouth was at my ear. "That's a good girl," he said and rammed himself in to the base. His hands moved to my biceps as he straightened up and pulled me onto him as he thrust once.

"Oh, David," I rasped.

"Love when you say my name," he grated out and thrust another time, still keeping me in a stronghold.

"David," I whimpered, and his pace quickened, giving it to me hard as he used my own body as leverage. "Oh, baby, you feel so good," I cried out brokenly. "So fucking good."

My shoulders ached, and my cheek burned from the

463

comforter, but he went faster, harder, and without mercy. In his control, I could only moan my satisfaction into the mattress.

I could tell he was close when his fingers squeezed my arms. "You look sexy as fuck right now," he said. "Come on, Olivia."

"Come with me," I pleaded.

I clenched around him, and he yelled out, jerking my arms back as he gave me a punishing final thrust and began to spurt into me. I quivered as I both came apart and drank him in at the same time.

"Christ," he breathed. He pulled out, and I dropped my hips, flattening out on the bed. I stretched and shook my arms, and he climbed over my ass to straddle me.

I groaned happily as he kneaded out my shoulders and arms. "Orgasm *and* a massage?" I asked. "Best husband ever."

"Best what?"

"Best *husband* ever."

He leaned over my back and growled into my ear. "Say it again."

I knew what he wanted. Since the wedding, he'd grown very attached to his new designation. "*Husband.*"

He flipped me onto my back suddenly and looked me in the face. His hand smoothed over my hairline, and before he could say it, I cut him off. "Love you," I whispered.

He smiled. "Love you, too." And then he pinned me with a passionate kiss. Within seconds, he stiffened, long and hard against my thigh.

"*Mmm.* Again?" I asked hopefully into his mouth.

He nodded. "Again."

I jerked awake to our bright bedroom when David's phone vibrated on his nightstand. His arms disappeared from around me as he reached for his cell.

I groaned at the loss. "Who's calling at this time on a Sunday morning?"

He ignored me and answered the call with a curt, "Dylan." I closed my eyes and listened to his rumbling voice. "Right now?" he asked and paused. "Yes, yes. That's good. I'll be there."

"Honey?" I asked when he hung up. "What's going on?"

"I have to run into the city for a little bit."

"No," I said. "Not now. I'm cold."

He laughed and wrapped me in his big, warm arms. "I hate to leave you cold, honeybee, but this is important. I promise I won't be long." He pulled my earlobe between his teeth. "Nightmares?" he whispered.

I smiled and shook my head. I hadn't had one in more than a year, but that didn't stop David from checking now and then.

"All right," he said. "Go back to sleep. You won't even miss me."

I sighed, and though he pulled the comforter up high around me, I shivered in his absence.

I fell back to sleep and didn't wake again until I heard the familiar rumbling of David's Porsche out front. I hopped out of bed and pushed open the window to see that he'd parked at the curb instead of in the garage.

The memory of the night before stirred in me as I watched him round the car to the passenger's side and squint up at me. I smiled at my weekend-David in his t-shirt, jeans, and aviators. "Get down here, beautiful," he yelled.

Snatching his t-shirt from the floor, I ran down the

stairs two at a time as I pulled it over my head. I burst through the front door, meaning to run and jump into his arms but stopped short. I gasped as my hand flew to my mouth. A black and tan furball bounded through the grass in my direction.

Tears pierced my eyes as I caught the puppy and hoisted him into the air. His tail wagged excitedly, and he licked my face, causing me to squeal with delight.

"Oh, David," I said as he approached. "Is he . . .? Can we . . .?"

"Anything that makes you smile like that, baby, yeah. We can keep him."

"A German shepherd puppy," I cried.

"Yes."

"Like Canyon."

"Yes, just like Canyon. My favorite breed." He grinned. "I told George at the shelter months ago that if a German shepherd puppy ever came in, to call me immediately."

I jumped up and down, and David laughed heartily. "He's perfect," I said. "Just perfect! Do you think we're ready?"

He nodded. "I've already arranged for him to stay with Jessa while we're in Greece next month. Alex is thrilled."

"I'm sure he is." I buried my nose in the puppy's fur, and he licked my nose. "What should we name him?"

David put his arm around my shoulder and kissed my temple. "How about Prince Siegfried?"

I laughed. It was the name of the lead character in *Swan Lake*, the ballet where David and I had met. Where we'd first met eyes across the lobby of the theater.

"Well, hi, darling Prince," I cooed, cuddling the puppy close and looking up at my husband with pure love and gratitude. "Welcome to the Dylan family."

Also by Jessica Hawkins

LEARN MORE AT WWW.JESSICAHAWKINS.NET

White Monarch Trilogy

"Exciting and suspenseful and sexy and breathtaking." (*USA Today* Bestselling Author Lauren Rowe)

An enemies-to-arranged marriage series about a cartel princess caught between two feuding brothers who share only one thing —a desire for her.

Violent Delights

Violent Ends

Violent Triumphs

Right Where I Want You

"An intelligently written, sexy, feel-good romance that packs an emotional punch…" (*USA Today*'s HEA) A witty workplace romance filled with sexual tension and smart, fun enemies-to-lovers banter.

Something in the Way Series

"A tale of forbidden love in epic proportion… Brilliant" (New York Times bestselling author Corinne Michaels) Lake Kaplan falls for a handsome older man — but then her sister sets her sights on him too.

Something in the Way

Somebody Else's Sky

Move the Stars

Lake + Manning

Slip of the Tongue Series

"Addictive. Painful. Captivating…an authentic, raw, and emotionally gripping must-read." (Angie's Dreamy Reads) Her husband doesn't want her anymore. The man next door would give up everything to have her.

Slip of the Tongue

The First Taste

Yours to Bare

Explicitly Yours Series

"Pretty Woman meets Indecent Proposal…a seductive series."— (USA Today Bestselling Author Louise Bay) What if one night isn't enough? A red-hot collection.

Possession

Domination

Provocation

Obsession

The Cityscape Affair Series

Olivia has the perfect life—but something is missing. Handsome playboy David Dylan awakens a passion that she thought she'd lost a long time ago. Can she keep their combustible lust from spilling over into love?

Come Undone

Come Alive

Come Together

About the Author

Jessica Hawkins is a *USA Today* bestselling author known for her "emotionally gripping" and "off-the-charts hot" romance. Dubbed "queen of angst" by both peers and readers for her smart and provocative work, she's garnered a cult-like following of fans who love to be torn apart...and put back together.

She writes romance both at home in New York City and around the world, a coffee shop traveler who bounces from café to café with just a laptop, headphones, and a coffee cup.

Stay updated:
www.jessicahawkins.net/mailing-list
www.jessicahawkins.net

Copyright